Ed Roberts is one of the few footballers to have won promotion from the Fourth Division to the top tier of the Football League with the same club. He represented England and was one of the first British players to sign for a European club, before injury cut short his career. Having played for Northtown United for nine seasons, he later returned as manager.

For Richard, Helen and members and wives of the GL club.

Ed Roberts

Mud and Thunder

Austin Macauley Publishers
LONDON • CAMBRIDGE • NEW YORK • SHARJAH

Copyright © Ed Roberts 2023

The right of Ed Roberts to be identified as author of this work has been asserted by the author in accordance with sections 77 and 78 of the Copyright, Designs and Patents Act 1988.

All rights reserved. No part of this publication may be reproduced, stored in a retrieval system, or transmitted in any form or by any means, electronic, mechanical, photocopying, recording, or otherwise, without the prior permission of the publishers.

Any person who commits any unauthorised act in relation to this publication may be liable to criminal prosecution and civil claims for damages.

This is a work of fiction. Names, characters, businesses, places, events, locales, and incidents are either the products of the author's imagination or used in a fictitious manner. Any resemblance to actual persons, living or dead, or actual events is purely coincidental.

A CIP catalogue record for this title is available from the British Library.

ISBN 9781398469570 (Paperback)
ISBN 9781398469587 (ePub e-book)

www.austinmacauley.com

First Published 2023
Austin Macauley Publishers Ltd®
1 Canada Square
Canary Wharf
London
E14 5AA

Thanks to John Hole for his "sense-checking" and tough tackling.

Table of Contents

Part I: Basement Blues and Promotion Pomp   11

  Chapter One: Not at All Posh at Peterborough   13

  Chapter Two: From Corfu to Skegness   25

  Chapter Three: A Misfiring Start   33

  Chapter Four: The Longest Trek   38

  Chapter Five: A Pointless Christmas and New Year   42

  Chapter Six: Back in the Boss' Office   52

  Chapter Seven: Promotion Push, Relationship Relegation   56

Part II: Into the Promised Land   73

  Chapter One: An Easter Rising   75

  Chapter Two: Stuck in Second and the Road to Goodison Park   84

  Chapter Three: Own Goals   93

  Chapter Four: Captain's Log   100

  Chapter Five: Blotts on the Landscape   110

  Chapter Six: Out of Second   122

Part III: Dining at the Top Table   141

  Chapter One: Failing to Reign in Spain   143

  Chapter Two: A Highbury High   151

  Chapter Three: Cup Fever   156

  Chapter Four: China Crisis   169

Chapter Five: Taking Stock	180
Part IV: Going InterContinental	**185**
Chapter One: Split End Our European Dream	187
Chapter Two: Saunders' Bombshell	206
Chapter Three: Player Power	215
Chapter Four: Going Dutch	228
Chapter Five: Duty Calls and Chopped by Souey	237
Chapter Six: A Brit Abroad	247
Chapter Seven: Back Home	264
Epilogue	**274**

Part I
Basement Blues and Promotion Pomp

Chapter One
Not at All Posh at Peterborough

London Road, Peterborough. Saturday, 23 April 1978. Peterborough United v Northtown United. League Division Four

The last match of the season.

Thank God.

The sun is shining, the pitch is baked hard and rutted. Apparently, there was once grass on it. Hard to believe.

The dressing rooms are cramped and smelly—there is no way the spotty-faced apprentices have been doing their stuff in here.

The showers work but only dispense tepid water.

Our levels of enthusiasm are close to zero; many showing complete disinterest and giving the impression they are here only because they are contractually obliged to be.

It's been a disastrous season and a terrible one for an apparently talented and ambitious nineteen-year-old midfielder who has broken into the side. That apparently talented and ambitious midfielder was me.

In the stadium, a couple of thousand spectators are spread thinly around the terraces. One coach full of our die-hard supporters has made the ninety-minute journey to London Road.

The chairman is also here. None of his fellow directors have accompanied him. Nothing unusual there.

I am in awe of the fans' loyalty, especially given our struggles of the last few seasons. "Sad bastards," is how Tom Border our captain and chief barrack room lawyer describes them. Tom may be playing for a knackered club in the basement of the Football League, but he is a First Division cynic.

"OK, listen up lads." The voice of manager/gaffer Frank Matthews cuts through the stink of Deep Heat and liniment.

"Last game of a fucking dreadful season. Let's set down a marker for the start of the next campaign. Show these Posh bastards we mean business and get your retaliation in first."

No tactics. There have been none during the week so why should I expect any today? Training in the build-up to the game consisted of relentless running, re-rehearsing some (ancient) set piece skills and a few exercises. Footballs had been only occasional visitors to the training ground.

Frank is as washed up as the team; the team is as washed up as Frank.

"And let's put in a good performance for our fans."

"Sad bastards," says Border. "Must have something better to do. Could be starting their Christmas shopping."

My heckles rise. It's not that long since I stood on the terraces and cheered this idiot. I want to say something, but it will count for nothing. The sniggering which accompanies Border's comments confirms this.

The bell rings. There are a few half-hearted "shouts" of encouragement. We file out of the dressing room, down the short and narrow corridor and emerge into the sunlit stadium.

A Peterborough fan, decked out in blue and white bobble hat and scarves, and ordained with a ridiculous number of metal badges, stands at the entrance to the tunnel. He blows a hunting horn but is so fat he can hardly muster enough puff to register a noise.

The smell of fried onions and burgers, which should come with a government health warning, wafts through the air. It's unpleasant but makes a welcome change to the stale dressing room, where the varying and combined odours of Deep Heat, liniment and, inevitably, the odd fart lie heavy in the atmosphere. It's no different to Sunday League football. There have been times this season when the standard hasn't been much higher.

We start brightly enough. We even have the first shot of the match, although the ball ends up closer to the corner flag than the goal. In fact, it doesn't even go out for a goal kick, rolling slowly before coming, apologetically, to a halt still in play. The home fans love it.

That's just about as good as it gets in the first half. We concede twice in the space of a few minutes and Posh can smell blood.

They are solid mid-table and have "nothing to play for," but they are committed and dedicated and motivated. Adjectives not associated with us I'm ashamed to say. They are also fitter despite our relentless running during the week. Maybe we had been subjected to too much of that and have nothing left to give.

I run around to no great effect. Huff here. Puff there. Put in a tackle or two. Concede a free-kick for a trip. The ref takes pity on me as it's the last game of the season and tells me to watch it. But he won't book me this time. A midfielder never booked does little for my reputation as a "goody two shoes" with the die-hard professionals at the club.

We manage to steady the ship until the stroke of half-time when our 'keeper, Mike Williams, drops a cross at the feet of a Posh forward who gleefully crashes the ball home.

Williams will tell anyone who will listen—and although that's not many he does have the ear of Border—that he is an ex-Welsh international. Apparently, he once played for Wales schoolboys in the (very) dim and distant past.

Welsh he undoubtedly is but he's no international.

We slope off to the supposed sanctuary of the dressing room. The fat bloke with the hunting horn is at the entrance to the tunnel again. Sweating profusely. "Great stuff, lads." "Magic, Lenny." "Great goal, Stevie." It's as if he knows them personally. Every club has one. Border may have a point here; this guy is a sad so-and-so.

In the dressing room, both the tea and the milk have been on the table for too long meaning the tea is lukewarm (at least the plastic cups don't collapse as they usually do when hot liquid is poured into them) and the milk is curdled.

"Fucking shithole, I've always hated playing here," explodes Andy Adams (aka AA), our centre forward. With six goals in thirty-plus appearances, this season, he's hardly been in explosive form on the pitch.

The dust bowl of a pitch and, inevitably, the referee are the reasons we are 3-0 down and haven't had a shot on target. Given the pitch is "the same for both sides" and that we have been so passive the ref hasn't had a decision to make, other than to show me some leniency, this is just another case of inept footballers hiding behind their usual pathetic excuses.

The manager/gaffer has little to offer. He was part of the side when we won two promotions in three seasons a few years ago. As manager he has overseen a relegation, a mid-table finish and now the club's worst ever season.

He doesn't know what to say, which way to turn. His half-time performance is as abject as his team's first half showing.

The dressing room door opens and in steps Mr Bushnell, chairman and co-owner. He is accompanied by another suited and booted bloke, who is not introduced to us. The second man is at least thirty years younger than Bushnell and unlike his older companion has had the good grace to wear a suit—expensive—which fits properly and a shirt and tie combination which actually matches. He looks like a freshly-dressed tailor's dummy. Bushnell, in his crumpled suit which could do with a trip to the dry cleaners or maybe even a jumble sale, mirrors his club. Tired and like his manager, washed-up. Decent bloke, apparently. But you wouldn't think he was the club's most senior figure.

"Carry on, Mr Matthews," says Bushnell. "Don't let us get in your way."

Any self-respecting manager would have told them to get out or at least make it obvious the uninvited presence of the chairman and a stranger in the dressing room at half-time isn't welcome. But Frank is stimulated into panicked action.

"Yes, thank you, Mr Chairman. We were just talking about making a change. We need to pep up midfield. Pull a goal back early on and we're back in it."

Who's he kidding? Everyone, including the suits, stare at the floor.

For an awful moment, I think he is going to take me off. Youngest member of the team. Least experienced. Not likely to make a fuss. Just fucking try it, I think.

He doesn't and opts for Dave Flowers, who's as pissed off as I would have been. He flings his shirt at the laundry hamper, kicks off his boots and takes off his shorts and underpants. He bends down directly in front of the manager, so Frank gets a bird's eye view.

There's some stifled laughter. The new suit looks… suitably unimpressed. The bell rings to signal the last forty-five minutes of the season.

At least, we draw that last three-quarters of an hour 1-1. In fact, we do grab a quick goal courtesy of an AA header from our first corner of the game. A not-so-magnificent seven then for AA. Jack Winters, who comes on for Flowers, plays well and he and I dovetail quite nicely in the middle of the park.

Peterborough score a fourth a few minutes from the end. No blame attached to Williams this time as the ball is arrowed into the top corner from the edge of the box. But it's a sod we allow them to score again.

The final whistle sounds. Handshakes all round. Back to the dressing room. The fat bloke with the hunting horn is nowhere to be seen. Perhaps he's expired in the heat.

The atmosphere in the changing room is jollier than it should be. We have lost. Again. A fairly abject performance. Again. Don't these blokes have any pride? I sometimes doubt it but the thought of ten weeks of sun, sand and sex consumes them. They are like schoolchildren breaking up for the long summer holidays. Not a care in the world.

"Great half, lads," extolls Frank. "Play like that next season and we'll be pushing for promotion. Wouldn't you agree, Mr Chairman?"

The suits had sidled, unnoticed, into the room.

"Let's hope so," says Bushnell. His dapper mate says nothing. His face is expressionless.

I wonder what the hell is going on. We have just finished fourth from bottom of the Fourth Division making us the eighty-ninth worst team out of the ninety-two in the Football League and having to apply for re-election. We may not even be members of the Football League next season. Admittedly that's unlikely given our record over the years but here we are thinking of holidays and talking about promotion prospects.

We had won only one of our last ten matches, losing seven. We hadn't even averaged a goal a game in that period and we had shipped thirty-two. Even when applying for re-election became a distinct possibility there was no reaction from the players, no rallying call from the manager and his staff. The directors remained anonymous and aloof.

This is a club which is deep in the mire. Everyone knows it, but no one will—or wants to—take responsibility to turn things round.

From a personal point of view, I feel my game has gone backwards over the last couple of months. Not surprising given the circumstances but if I am to succeed, I need to rise above the inertia which has engulfed us.

I would have to think about that… while I was lying on the beach.

Showered but hardly refreshed given how crap the showers are, we gather in the players' lounge where we are served bottles of lager which hadn't seen the inside of a fridge and sandwiches even British Rail would be embarrassed to dish up. Nevertheless, there are some who will get as much down their necks as possible as long as it's free. I can't wait to get home and leave this lot behind. I will be seeing my mates, well away from these morons. I look at my watch. I should be with them by 9pm.

The coach stops as it is pulling out of the car park and Bushnell and the mystery man, whose presence is beginning to become more annoying than mysterious, climb aboard.

"Who is that bloke then?" It's Border speaking. What's more he's speaking to me. He never *speaks* to me. He only communicates with me when we are on the pitch, shouting encouragement like "Fucking move your arse" and "shit pass."

"No idea, skip," I reply.

"I'm always being told you can read a game. Can't you read what's going on?"

"Not from here, skip."

"I always said you were overrated. Grammar school education as well."

Border returns to his game of cards.

I wasn't exactly a popular member of the squad. I had only joined the club eighteen months previously after being spotted playing in a local Saturday league. I was offered a trial and then terms almost as soon as the final whistle of the trial match sounded.

"You're good, son," I was told. "You could be very good."

My fast upward trajectory hasn't gone down well with the old lags who had served apprenticeships and had to wait, in some cases, a few years before getting a sniff of first team action. The fact I was grammar school educated, even though I hated every moment of school and much to my father's dismay had not put education high on my list of priorities, also counts against me.

The coach pulls into the car park in the shadow of our Wood Lane stadium. Before we get off, Bushnell stands up and reminds us that we need to be back here on Monday morning. "Usual end of season formalities. You will also need to be here on Tuesday morning as well."

There are groans and some quietly dissenting voices. "I'm going on holiday on Tuesday, Mr Chairman," someone shouts.

"Make alternative arrangements then," snaps Bushnell before turning his back on us and disembarking.

I notice that Frank looks surprised. And not because Mr Bushnell has been brusque for the first time in living memory. We all knew we had to check in on

Monday. Frank was as much in the dark about Tuesday as the rest of us. I wonder if Border has picked up on this. I have no intention of telling him.

The Press Room, Northtown United. Monday, 25 April 1978.

Mr Bushnell, wearing the same suit he had sported on Saturday, but thankfully a change of shirt and tie, sat behind a table on the dais. The mystery man, wearing a different but still expensive suit and a smart casual shirt but no tie, sat beside him.

Bushnell rose.

"I would like to thank you for your efforts this season."

A pause for impact.

"But I'm not going to."

"With a couple of exceptions, although hardly notable ones, you've been a fucking disgrace." None of us had ever heard Mr Bushnell use the F-word before.

"You've let yourselves down. You've let your manager down. You've let your club and its supporters down.

"This club is eighty years old and you are the worst team in its history—on and off the pitch.

"Whatever you may go onto achieve, and I use that word advisedly, that will always be on your CV. It should remain on your consciences. But I doubt it will.

"Quite a few of you will not represent this club again."

"Hold on a minute. You may be the Chairman but you've got no right to speak to us like that." Border. Inevitably.

"And seeing as you talk about letting down the manager where is he? And who's your mate?"

Bushnell simply brushed Border's attempted interception aside—just as the vast majority of his opponents had done during the season.

"I have to add that you are not the only ones who have underperformed.

"So have I. So have my fellow directors. We should all have acted more quickly and decisively after we were relegated a couple of seasons ago. We have nothing to be proud of, either.

"The fact we have also under-performed is one of the reasons I am standing down as Chairman and co-owner and have sold all my interests in the club to Mr Roger Palmer." Bushnell indicated the man sitting next to him.

A name at long last.

"My last act as Chairman was to relieve Frank Matthews of his duties as manager and it was one of the most unpleasant and painful acts of my life. Frank Matthews cared far more for this club than the vast majority of people I am addressing."

Cue hubbub as the players started to process and discuss this information.

I was unmoved. Surely this is exactly what we need? A new direction from the top and fresh ideas (any ideas come to that) on the pitch.

Things calmed down.

"Guys," (note guys, not gentlemen) said Palmer. "I just want to introduce myself and give you a broad outline of what I intend to achieve." Intent not merely hope. Even better.

It turns out that Mr Palmer—"please call me Roger"—is a multi-millionaire, who has made his considerable fortune from property development in this country and abroad. He is a football fan but can't pretend to be an expert. He can spot a great business opportunity though and football has become business.

A business which apparently will only become bigger and bigger in the coming years. He knows how to be successful. He would be a failure if we weren't playing First Division football within five years. Five years! The stadium was going to be completely revamped. He had the resources to make all this happen.

"But it doesn't matter how grand my ideas are and how much money I am prepared to invest, there has to be someone who can turn water into wine. So I want to introduce you to our new manager, Tony Saunders."

If you could have heard a pin drop when the new owner was talking, you could now hear a feather hit the floor. Tony Saunders! This is a huge surprise, a real turn-up for the books.

Tony Saunders made a dramatic entrance, like a celebrity about to appear on a TV chat show, from a side room. He had taken completely unfashionable Doncaster Rovers out of the Fourth Division in his first season in charge with a record points haul and the most goals ever scored in the division. He had damn nearly taken them into the Second Division this season.

He is young. A tracksuit manager. A tactician of some repute. One of the "new breed" of manager. And he's here. Manager of Northtown United FC. People have worked wonders to keep this news under wraps.

But why? He should be moving up not dropping down. Is it about money? Something about him says not.

Somebody asked him why he's here. What's the appeal of leaving a club on the up for one which is damn close to rock bottom?

Oh God, it's me!

"Good question, son. I was hoping someone would ask." I can see a lot of the others thinking "fucking grammar school kid." I hoped that anyone thinking along those lines and giving me looks of disgust wouldn't be here next season.

Saunders explains there is far more potential at Northtown than Doncaster, he and "Rog" are old mates and speak the same language. This is just the kind of project he's always wanted to be involved with. We have the potential to become a leading club and not just in the lower leagues.

"What happens if we don't get re-elected?" asked Kevin Marr, one of our defenders.

"I don't think that will happen," said Palmer. "If it does, we have a Plan B." The fact Saunders is here must mean they already know how the other clubs are going to vote and that our Fourth Division status is safe.

Sensing we needed to talk about the morning's events and the fact that a press conference was to follow, Rog calls a halt to proceedings. He warns us not to talk to the press and that all of us were to be back here tomorrow morning at 9am.

Sharp.

"I will see all of you individually for ten minutes," explained the new manager. "I'll be telling you what's required of you over the summer." What! Summers for sitting on our arses, lazing on the beach, sinking a few pints and shagging a few birds. At least, that's how it had always been painted to me by the senior pros. And although I'm dedicated to my profession I was quite looking forward to indulging in those activities in the coming weeks.

"I warn you; no one is to report for pre-season heavier than they are now. Quite a lot of you will need to lose weight while you're doing nothing." There was a slight grin on Saunders' face. He wasn't joking but he was certainly enjoying the moment, putting down an early marker.

A few jaws need rescuing from the floor. Even the likes of Border and Williams were lost for words. As we filed out the press began to make their entrance. We kept our eyes on the floor or on the middle distance. We didn't acknowledge any of them, not even Dave Craig, the Northtown Observer football reporter and a friend of some of the let's say more established members of the squad. This will be the biggest story he has covered to date. He will be fried alive for not breaking it as an exclusive. New owner. Tired "old" manager out. Fresh young manager in. First Division football within five years. He didn't have a sniff. Little wonder he looked so sheepish.

The feeling was we should go for a drink to discuss. Surprisingly, I was invited. For once, I accepted. It was pretty much a waste of time though. Many were sceptical of the plans. "Pissing in the wind," said Dave Flowers. "A pair of smarmy twats" was Mike Williams' telling analysis. Referring to Palmer and Saunders.

Interestingly, Tom Border kept his own counsel. When pushed for his opinion, he tells us the word on the street is that Saunders is a very good manager. "I've also heard he will break balls if he has to. I've a feeling things are about to change."

It was the most insightful thing I had heard Border say. It was also the last thing I heard him say as captain of Northtown United.

A few, including myself, were delighted with developments. I wasn't asked for my opinion. I didn't offer it. I left the meeting an hour later much happier than I had been on Saturday afternoon.

The Manager's office, Northtown United. Tuesday, 26 April 1978.

"I like you, son."

I wasn't overkeen on being called "son," but I was pleased Tony Saunders liked me.

"You played well against us, Doncaster, last season. Actually put in a call to your last boss to see if he would sell but he didn't want to do business."

I was delighted to hear this but didn't disclose there was no chance I would have moved to Doncaster. I get a nose bleed if I go north of Luton.

"I've known for some time I was coming here so I've had people watching the last four or five matches. You may not have pulled up any trees but you were one of the few who gave a shit, showed a bit of fight and passion."

The meeting was going better than I could have hoped for. At this rate, I'll struggle to get my head through the door.

"What's your best position, son?"

"Central midfield. Err… "

"Boss. Call me Boss, son."

"How many goals did you score this season?"

"Three Boss."

"Not enough son. Not nearly enough. Double figures next season, son. I can see you pushing up, playing just off the forwards."

Great. I'd never thought of playing in that sort of position.

Just as I was imagining celebrating yet another winning goal in front of the River End, Saunders breaks the silence.

"That is, of course, if I pick you." I tumbled back to earth.

"Like a drink, don't you, son?" I headed for middle earth.

Where did that come from? True, I like a drink but not to excess. Well, not often. I must have shown my surprise.

Saunders grinned. "My job is to know everything about everyone, son. Nothing wrong with the occasional drink. Just don't make it a regular thing. Anything you want to ask me, son?"

"Yes. Boss. What are your hopes for next season?"

"Promotion. Four teams go up. We should be one of them. And don't forget, Mr Palmer wants us in the First Division in double-quick time. And so do I."

I began to question Saunders' sanity. Great that he's an optimist but we are complete rubbish. How can he possibly transform us from applying for re-election to a promotion side in one season? He performed miracles at Doncaster, but they were mid-table when he took over.

"Got a holiday planned?"

"Corfu, Boss. Two weeks."

"Lovely. By the way, I want you back half a stone lighter. If I were in your trainers, I would do a lot of running. Pre-season will be a bastard."

I left Saunders' office bemused. He likes me, wanted to sign me, expects me to score more goals, may not pick me, knows I like a drink and reckons I need to lose weight.

I made my way to the physio's room which was occupied by Laurie Campbell who joined the club with Saunders. I introduced myself to Campbell who was business-like, stand-offish, dour.

"Scales," he said pointing to a set in the corner of the dank and dingy room.

"You want me to climb aboard?"

"Obviously. Strip down to your undies and get on 'em."

"Do you think I'm overweight, Laurie?"

"The Boss says you are and that's what matters. You're twelve stone. Come back in eight weeks weighing eleven-and-a-half."

"Don't you mean ten weeks?"

"Things are changing around here. It's eight weeks and if I were you, I would be here bang on time and bang on eleven-and-a-half stone."

That afternoon, as I was sitting at home processing what had happened over the previous twenty-four hours, Jack Winters rang.

"He's releasing Border, Williams, Garvey, Howe and Flowers. Told them he doesn't want or need them back for pre-season. AA's been transfer-listed. I reckon more than that will be going."

Border and the other four had clocked up over seven hundred appearances between them but I had no sympathy. To hell with evolution, we needed and were getting a full-blown revolution, let heads roll. Cruel to be kind etc.

"Fancy a drink tonight?" asked Jack.

"I can't mate. I'm already out," I lied.

I went to the kitchen and opened the fridge. I stared down the cans of Carlsberg, the contents of which I was eager to empty into my digestive system and shut the door on them.

I then did something I had never done before of my own volition. I went for a run.

Things were already changing.

The follow morning and the national newspapers liked the story and were grateful of it to help fill some column inches before the international cricket season kicked in.

Multi-millionaire takes over ailing football club and appoints bright young manager to achieve his vision equals decent copy.

The usual pictures of new owner and manager holding club scarf and shirt respectively adorned the back pages. The Northtown Observer, a daily paper which comes out every afternoon and is available where I live, had gone to town, dedicating their front and back pages to the story. Dave Craig had even managed to get an "exclusive" interview with Tony Saunders. No doubt that would have put him in slightly better odour with his editor.

There was even a teaser telling readers that Saunders would be writing an "exclusive" weekly column, which no doubt Craig would ghost write for him. I don't think The Observer had ever shown any interest in the gospel according to Frank Matthews.

Chapter Two
From Corfu to Skegness

It was going to be a strange summer.

I wasn't due to go on holiday for a fortnight, which meant that after I returned there was another month before pre-season training began. And I was worried about pre-season given Saunders had promised it was going to be a "bastard." I was going to have work hard on my fitness if I were to impress the new Boss.

Had Frank Matthews told us we needed to lose weight over the summer break he would have been laughed out of court. Tony Saunders was a very different kettle of fish to Frank Matthews. Here was a man who meant business—even though I didn't know him I listened to what he said. And he backed up his words with action as Border, Williams, Garvey, Howe and Flowers could testify.

I had time to lose some weight—and although I was sure I didn't need to shift it—I ran and ran. And I hated it.

At least, I started off hating it. The boredom. The effort. The time it took to recover. But then I began to dislike it less, probably because it became easier and I wasn't so knackered when I finished. And I did feel fitter.

Before the holiday, I limited myself to a maximum of two cans of lager a day. Not every day I hasten to add. I drank just the occasional glass of wine. Spirits were strictly off limits. Quite often I stuck to tea. I even began to show an interest in water. Previously, I had only ever boiled it for tea and coffee and washed in it and had "rehydrated" on anything but H_2O.

I even stayed at home to avoid temptation I knew I wouldn't be able to resist if I went out with mates.

All of which was a rare demonstration of willpower on my part.

And in another previously unthought-of move, I packed my trainers when we went to Corfu. And I did some early-morning running while we were there. Although I lazed on the beach for fourteen days, my "one-to one" with Saunders meant I ate more sensibly and drank considerably less than I would normally have done.

I was probably slightly withdrawn at times as I pondered my future. I was intrigued by what lay ahead. Would I be in the team? If not, what would I do? Where does a Fourth Division reserve head but downwards? If things didn't work out for me under the new regime, what would I do? I didn't want to do anything other than play football. I put these thoughts to the back of my mind and decided I would deal with them if and when. I had always been adept at "shelving." So the only fly in the ointment on the holiday was the incessant playing of Boney M and their infantile hits. Lying on the beach or eating in a taverna and you were guaranteed to hear Mary's bloody Boy Child played endlessly.

Despite Boney M, it was a great holiday.

When I got home, there was a letter from the club, telling me where and when to report for pre-season training. And what to bring. And that we were going to be away for five days.

Written communication from my employer. A definite first. I wondered what some of the players' wives would say about their old man being away given these trips have a certain reputation. Mind you, the list of what we needed to take with us strongly suggested enjoyment wasn't going to be part of the mix.

Also included was our fixture list. Halifax, Darlington, Stockport. Barrow, Grimsby, Scunthorpe. Mansfield, Crewe. Hardly a roll-call of England's most salubrious tourist spots.

Our opening league fixture on 12 August was against Newport County—away. The short matter of a three-hundred-mile round trip to start the season. Next up, the following Wednesday night, we were at home to Northampton before another away trip to Crewe, a three-hundred-and-ten-mile round trip. But as there was a direct rail route from Northtown to Crewe, who finished rock bottom last season, and we have a new owner who wants to introduce high standards of professionalism, we may just travel by rail instead of coach.

A quick glance at the Christmas fixtures saw us hosting Bradford City on Boxing Day, travelling to Aldershot three days later and away to Darlington on New Year's Day. Bradford had been relegated on the final day of last season and were hot favourites to go back up. The festive fixture Gods had looked relatively favourably on us. Aldershot, being less than fifty miles away, constituted something of a local derby for us, along with Northampton. Unless you include

Leyton Orient, who are closer than both Aldershot and Northampton, but because they are based in London they somehow don't qualify as "local." Darlington away on New Year's Day didn't look like much fun though.

There were some other hideous away journeys for us to endure and quite a few of them were midweek. A real test of our mettle. And of the coach's staying power—the motorised coach, that is.

The morning we were due to report for pre-season training I climbed into my not-quite-clapped-out Datsun Cherry and drove the twenty-five miles to the undoubtedly-clapped-out stadium. But when it came into view it didn't look like a Fourth Division ground anymore.

While we had been away, the decorators had been in. And the builders. And the carpenters, electricians and plumbers.

The ground had been given a complete makeover.

Inside as well as out. Offices had been repurposed. Walls had come down, rooms extended. New furniture bought. The musty smell signalling damp had gone. It was light and airy. Farewell dinginess, hello modern world.

The changing rooms, which had been an embarrassment, were transformed. New flooring. Benches with padded seats (no padded seats for the opposition, though. Quite right!). The introduction of lockers. Showers replaced with equipment worthy of the name. A wall had been knocked down virtually doubling the size of the home room.

The corridor from the changing rooms to the stadium entrance was the same one but wasn't. New flooring. Walls painted in the club colours of black and gold, pictures adorning those walls (although not of glory days because there hadn't really been any) which was a first for the club.

As we entered the stadium, it was obvious a lot of money had been spent here as well. New crush barriers, painted in the club colours, had been installed. Sprinklers soaked the grass which was a resplendent green. Harry, our vintage groundsman, sat happily on some non-vintage equipment for the first time in many years. The grass was cut quickly and patterning the pitch was a cinch. And the ancient Observer advert which had sat on top of the River End, for as long as anyone, including Harry, could remember, had been replaced. There was even a new clock. One which actually worked and which fans could see.

In just over two months, the entire appearance of the stadium had been totally transformed. It must have cost a pretty penny. It was a massive statement of intent. Mr Palmer undoubtedly meant business.

We gathered in the revamped Press Room which bore no resemblance to the one where we first met Palmer and Saunders. Palmer was joined on the dais by two more new faces, both in spanking new club tracksuits and virginal training shoes. No sign of Saunders though. The two new guys were introduced as Rob Riley, assistant manager, who had joined us from Gillingham, and First Team coach, Ronnie O'Reagan, a gruff Irishman, who had made a similarly short journey from Oxford United. Saunders we were told had hand-picked the pair. Like Saunders, both had come from bigger clubs to join us. A further statement of intent. This was their first appearance of any kind. Even the press didn't know about them yet.

Palmer again stated his intention of us becoming a First Division club within five years, and that if we were to think big, we needed to look the part. All of a sudden, we did.

But where was Saunders? And last season we had a first team squad of twenty-four players. Now just fourteen of us were gathered. And we were far from the most experienced and talented group of fourteen players ever assembled. Even by Fourth Division standards.

Somebody should ask about this. No one did. So I took the plunge.

No "fucking grammar school kid" looks this time. What a difference a couple of months had made.

"Call me Roger" told us that we would be seeing Saunders later that day and he would outline his plans for the squad and the new season then. We had lunch. Surprisingly, we were served fish and chips from the Golden Cod, opposite the ground.

"Enjoy that boys, it will be a long time before you eat that sort of crap again." This from our new assistant manager who sat with our new first team coach on a table away from the players. The seating arrangements were noted but not commented on.

We then climbed aboard the club coach. Those of us looking forward to a thoroughly modern vehicle with onboard toilet were disappointed. This was one area where Mr Palmer hadn't splashed any cash. Plenty of time for him to do so before our journey to Newport, though.

And when we got on it, we discovered we couldn't sit where we wanted. Pieces of card, with our names on them, were scattered around the seats. There was no sitting next to each other. There was no sitting in the row immediately in front of or behind each other. No one was going to sit in the back row. With only fourteen of us, that was easy enough to organise. If the morning had been positive, the afternoon was starting on a negative note. I felt I was back at school. Serving a detention.

Riley and O'Reagan sat at the front. Next to each other.

Half an hour into the journey they started to make their way down the coach. One of them spent a few minutes with each player. A proper introduction. They also left us with a pen and a short questionnaire. "Quite simple," we were told. Write down your ambition for the club this season. What you hope to achieve as an individual. What are the strengths of the club and where it can improve. After that, spend the rest of the journey thinking about the coming season."

Four hours later our ancient coach lumbered into the car park of the Durham Miners Club in Skegness. It could be worse, I thought. I have been known to be wrong.

There to greet us were Tony Saunders and Laurie Campbell. I had kept up my attempts at losing those seven pounds and knew damn well I had made it. I was also in no doubt this cold fish of a physio would let me know one way or the other in the near future.

Saunders seemed delighted to see us. He ushered us into a hall where there were boxes of new trainers, club tracksuits and training kit. Again, this was all very new and different for us. Again, sure signs the club was heading in the right direction.

We moved to a dining area, where we all sat at the same table. We were served pasta with a tomato sauce. And the sauce was fresh, as in not out of a tin. Nothing special though. Not a fan of pasta, me. But at least we weren't told where to sit. A glass of red wine wouldn't have gone amiss. Isn't that how the Italians do it? No alcohol in sight. Not that I seriously expected there to be.

Then it was into a meeting room for a presentation by Saunders, Riley and O'Reagan and Campbell. I wasn't one for official presentations especially as the overhead projector usually failed or the acetate sheet had been placed upside down. But this was interesting with quick-fire thoughts on what we should and shouldn't eat, how to look after ourselves after training and between matches and quite a lot more besides.

We were then weighed. It wasn't as big an occasion as I had expected. Everyone hit the scales at the right mark or under. I had lost ten pounds. No real acknowledgement of my considerable achievements which had required a major change of approach to my lifestyle. It was eight weeks since Saunders had spoken to us and everyone had listened. Northtown United players listen to manager shock! Yet another first in my experience.

Saunders stepped in. He told us we would be an offensive side. He wouldn't change formation or personnel from match to match unless form, injury or suspension dictated it. "Why should the away team always play defensively and be on the back foot? We have the ball we go forward; the opposition has the ball, and we all defend. Attacks start from the back, defending starts from the front. Anyone who doesn't buy into that won't be here for long."

He also told us to cherish the ball as we would a lover. Work harder off the ball than on it. No cliques. Only winners required. It's all about the club. Talk to him or any member of his staff if we have problems of any kind.

Talking of lovers, we were told no sex for forty-eight hours before matches. And no alcohol for up to forty-eight hours before a match. We weren't to go out for forty-eight hours before matches.

A quick calculation.

We were playing, more or less, twice every week on Saturdays and Wednesdays. That meant Thursdays, Fridays, Mondays and Tuesdays would be days of total abstinence as far as sex and booze were concerned. Given we would be playing Wednesday nights and would be home late that would probably be another day of non-indulgence. That meant weekends, especially Sundays when we could presumably fill our boots all day long, should be fun. Somehow I didn't see this working. I didn't think my girlfriend, who I was about to co-habit with, would be delighted either.

I felt this all had to be open to interpretation.

We discussed our opening fixtures and discovered our pre-season friendlies. Between late July and mid-August we would play three games against local non-league opposition and one against Second Division Charlton Athletic, who Saunders once played for. "Call me Roger" wasn't splashing the cash here either. Skegness was the best we were going to get before the season started. Finally, we looked at the answers to the questionnaires which didn't throw up anything radical, other than a few asking when there would be discussions about new contracts. "When you show me, you're worth it," was Saunders' succinct comment.

I hadn't considered this, but it made me think. My contract ran out just after the end of the coming season. I would need to give this some thought.

Having told us we should cherish the ball as we would a lover, Saunders ended the session by telling us we wouldn't see a football all week. "You're going to become the fittest team in the division. It's going to be hard work. That's something else you will have to buy into." I got the distinct feeling that if you didn't invest in Saunders' way of doing things you would soon be toast.

Everyone, including the manager and the backroom staff, slept in the same dormitory. Lights out 10pm.

"As the days go by, you'll be wanting to turn them out a lot earlier than that," smirked Saunders. Never a truer word.

As we bedded down, I noted there were two spare beds.

It may still have been summer in England. And Skegness may be in England. But it wasn't summer in Skegness. Not by most people's standards. Skegness may appeal to the hardy Durham miners and presumably their families, but it was freezing and downright unpleasant for us Southern Softies.

We were put through our paces by Riley and O'Reagan. Saunders and Campbell watched and discussed. Saunders occasionally joined in. He was as fit as a butcher's dog. All we did was run. Run on the beach. Run up sand dunes. Run around an athletics track. Whenever we ran there was a biting wind to contend with. And that wind, inevitably, was always a head wind.

We also did loads of sprints on the sand and on the track. And exercises which tugged muscles and tendons we had no idea existed. It was, as Saunders had promised, a bastard. I was very glad I had put in all that work of my own. If I hadn't, I would have been in big trouble. Even though everyone had hit the scales at the right weight, a few really struggled. A couple threw up and failed to finish sessions.

On the journey home, we could sit where we wanted and with whom we wanted. But we all wanted a double seat to ourselves so we could stretch out and sleep.

The two spare beds were for two new signings, who we met on the first full afternoon. Iain Moy had netted twenty-four goals for Cowdenbeath the previous season and was Scottish through and through. The training camp came as a huge shock to him, but if he wasn't exactly lean, he certainly came across as mean and at £12,500 looked to represent very good business. Steve Mower had been a reserve forward at Millwall and had only played a handful of games in three seasons, scoring just a couple of goals. He was a free transfer, and the jury was out on him. More signings, Saunders told us, were in the pipeline.

We needed them as well. We went to "Skeggie" with fourteen players and returned with sixteen, which included the transfer-listed AA. I reckoned we needed four, maybe as many as six, new players. We had no obvious captain, and we didn't have a single goalkeeper on the books. Saunders faced as much hard work away from the training ground as his players did on it.

Chapter Three
A Misfiring Start

Over the next few weeks, a number of new signings arrived. Goalkeeper Steve Bamford came in from Second Division Cardiff City. He was to be backed-up by Rob Keen, previously Fulham's third choice custodian. Rod "Steamy" Windows, a rugged centre half, and Mark Bailey, a no-nonsense midfielder, both joined from Second Division Luton Town who were having a before-the-start-of-season clear-out. Neither had been first-team regulars. Defender Tommy Butler came in from First Division Burnley, where he had been a regular reserve for a couple of seasons. Don Tyler, a midfielder who also played on the right flank signed from Blackpool, while Terry Green joined from Nottingham Forest, both clubs being in the Second Division.

Seven new faces, mostly younger than those Saunders had let go, but none of them particularly well-known. Bamford arrived with a good reputation and Windows was known not to take prisoners while the others, although they had experience of the higher divisions, didn't quite set the pulse racing. No marquee signings as such. They all trained well, though, and showed considerably more enthusiasm and professionalism than those who had been shown the door. Saunders, in his new weekly column for The Observer, told everyone the new arrivals were ideal for our pattern of play. These days he would no doubt have talked about how they suited his "philosophy."

The training sessions were excellent. Long, hard and intense but never boring. Plenty of ball work, one- and two-touch exercises, lots of set piece practise, offensive and defensive. There were sessions when we weren't allowed to use our stronger foot. If we did (and it was spotted), we conceded a free-kick. We worked slavishly on our shape, with and without the ball, wherever it was on the pitch. Everyone knew exactly what was expected of them. We were beginning to resemble a football team.

Saunders told us he wanted to play with four at the back and four in midfield with the wider two pushing up when we attacked, operating almost as wingers. When we did that, the full-backs moved up, so we didn't get outnumbered in midfield. That meant full-backs, Butler and Green, needed to be fit and quick. It looked as if Bailey and I would operate in the middle of midfield with Bailey holding back slightly. There had been no further mention of my playing closer to the forward line and at this stage I wasn't completely convinced I would be starting. If I did play, I would be one of only three players from last season along with central defender Kevin Marr and Ronnie Jackson, who played on the left of midfield.

Whether we were home or away, we would have two up front, Moy and Mower, with the latter playing just behind Moy already the undoubted leader of our pack. Strong, good in the air as well as on the ground and happy to make his presence felt, Moy looked like a bargain. At this stage, Mower looked a little pedestrian to be acting as a link man between midfield and attack. Apart from that everything was looking positive and the bookies had us one of the favourites for promotion, along with Bradford, Swindon, Mansfield and Notts County, who had missed out on promotion last season only by goal difference.

There are advantages and disadvantages to pre-season friendlies. It's obviously good to get away from training day-in day-out and into some action—get some miles under your belt—but the team is chopped and changed as the manager and his staff experiment with different formations and players, the weather tends to be hot and the pitches hard. And sometimes when you play non-league opposition you come up against individuals who are more interested in making a name for themselves by kicking lumps *out* of you rather than trying to impose their skills *on* you.

No problem at Athenian League Chesham United, whose ground was only a couple of miles from where I lived. However, the new approach meant that instead of making my own way there, I had to drive in the opposite direction and report to the club ground making what would have been a four-mile return journey into one of over fifty miles. But this is what Saunders wanted so fair enough. I wasn't going to be the first one to upset the applecart. We had no problems with Chesham, sweeping them aside 8-0.

Wealdstone, of the Isthmian League, gave us a tougher game and it was easy to see why they were highly fancied in their league. We twice fell behind but managed to win 3-2. Walthamstow, also of the Isthmian League, were somewhere between Chesham and Wealdstone in terms of skill and we won relatively easily, 4-1, but got a tongue-lashing from Ronnie O'Reagan for conceding a late goal. There weren't many players without bumps and bruises after the last two games. Let's just say they were both tough opponents.

We had enjoyed a few training sessions on the lush turf of Wood Lane, while our first match there under Tony Saunders was on Saturday 5 August against Second Division Charlton Athletic. Although the cricket season was in full swing, a decent crowd turned up to watch us come down to earth, losing 3-1. I had played in some of the other friendlies but there had been too much chopping and changing for me to get into my stride. Against Chesham, I even started, came off and went back on. That certainly doesn't marry with modern-day thinking, while the longest continual period I had played for was half-an-hour, so I didn't feel very well prepared for the first league match of the season.

The five days before the Newport match didn't see much change from previous weeks in terms of training. In fact, we had been doing it for so long the initial enthusiasm had begun to wane. We just wanted the season to get underway.

We travelled to Newport on Friday, after training, instead of a ridiculously early start on Saturday and stayed in a hotel which would now struggle to be described as "budget." In those days, it was known as a "dive." Still, better a dive than a dawn departure and arriving stiff-legged an hour or so before kick-off. There was a fair amount of hanging around to cope with on Saturday morning before a squad meeting at 11am in what the hotel described as an "Executive Meeting Room." They could—maybe should—have been prosecuted under the Trade Descriptions Act. Saunders named his team: Bamford; Butler, Windows, Marr, Green; Tyler, Bailey, Roberts, Jackson; Mower, Moy. Winters was sub. We went over how we would play, our strengths, Newport's weaknesses. We had never been so well prepared and were eager to prove ourselves.

Somerton Park, Newport. Saturday, 12 August 1978. Newport County v Northtown United. League Division Four.

We never got going. Neither really did Newport. It must have been dreadful to watch. It was bad enough to play in. It was more like a meaningless end-of-season mid-table clash.

Newport's winner, a header from a corner, came midway through the second half. Why we were so poor was beyond us—Newport were no great shakes and we had expected to win but certainly weren't over-confident or complacent. I was as unimpressive as everyone else and was awarded a five (bang average) in The Observer's match report. Everyone, apart from Bamford and Tyler, who reached the heady heights of six, were rated fives.

Although Saunders had rightly been deeply unimpressed with our showing in Wales, he kept the faith for our first home match, four days later against Northampton, and named the same side. We were better but still nowhere as impressive as we would have liked in a 1-0 win to register our first two points of the season. Iain Moy hammered home a loose ball after about half-an-hour. As at Newport Don Tyler, wide on the right, was our most dangerous outlet and he created good chances which Moy and Mower missed—but 3-0 would have flattered us.

Next up, Crewe away. Another long journey. We didn't travel by train as we had hoped but followed the pattern of the previous week and travelled after training on Friday and stayed at a hotel, which was a step up from the dump which had accommodated us in Newport. It was still a dump though.

We started well and took an early lead through Mark Bailey's long shot. That spurred Crewe into action, and they were level by half-time before running out convincing 3-1 winners. It was hard to believe they were the worst team in the Football League the previous season. Surprisingly, Saunders was relatively upbeat. "Early days, lads. Don't worry, it will all come together." Nevertheless, it was a quiet coach journey home. I had had an indifferent match (bang average again) and although we went out after I got home my heart wasn't really in it.

Not much was made of the League Cup in those days so losing 2-0 on aggregate over two legs to Third Division Bournemouth hardly registered and certainly wasn't viewed as a disaster even if we were racking up more defeats than wins.

Our second home League match, against Leyton Orient, was beginning to take on some significance. If we lost, we would have just two points from four games and would be hanging out with the division's bottom-dwellers; win and four points would see us in reasonable shape. Such is the fickle nature of football.

I've never understood why this isn't considered a local derby but given today was our first Saturday competitive home fixture under the "new regime," the sun was still shining, and it was the last weekend of the school holidays, a decent crowd of almost thirteen-thousand turned up (last season's average home attendance had been less than seven thousand). We were keen to do well for the supporters—no cynical Tom Borders among us now—and to kick-start our season which had got off to a damp squib of a start. The same could be said of Orient, who had been stuck in the basement division without ever threatening to go up or down for years.

We made a tentative start—not surprising given our form to date—but took heart from Orient's negative approach. Tyler was again our major threat, while Iain Moy bullied Orient's centre-half pairing. Tyler and Moy scored in the first half, while Steamy Windows and Steve Mower both bagged their first goals for the club in the second. The only blot on the copybook was conceding just before the end. But we would all have taken a 4-1 win before kick-off. Everyone played well and for the first time this season I was happy with my game and felt Bailey and I had "bossed" midfield.

Windows, who was our self-appointed social secretary and who had an opinion on everyone and everything, wanted us all to go out and celebrate but too many of us already had arrangements. Windows, unattached, was disappointed but no doubt found something or someone, or both, to entertain him.

Chapter Four
The Longest Trek

Barrow-in-Furness, Cumbria, North West England. Wednesday, 8 November 1978. Barrow v Northtown United. League Division Four.

We moaned about Skegness. We didn't know we were born. The longest journey from the comfort of Wood Lane. Two-hundred-and-seventy miles and at least a four-and-a-half-hour coach journey. Each way.

And we are playing Barrow on a mid-week night at the start of winter. Who dreams up these fixture lists?

The only good news is that the manager has persuaded the directors that we need to travel the day before the match and stay at another "budget hotel." We hear whispers that some of the directors, none of whom will make the journey, are not happy with all the expenditure. Maybe staying at a mega-cheap hotel still blows a hole in the club's travel budget.

We train, have some lunch and climb aboard the coach. A card school starts with Windows, Bamford, Moy and Jackson the eager participants. Others, like Tyler and Bailey, resemble cats and can sleep anywhere for long stretches of time, and close their eyes as soon as they sit down.

I can never sleep on a journey. Trains, planes or automobiles—or an omnibus—it doesn't matter. I can't sleep. So I read. To Kill a Mockingbird, a gift from my father. I've read it before but it more than merits a revisit. Last season many of my teammates would have had something to say about the grammar school kid with his nose buried in a book. On one trip, I stupidly left a book on the seat when we stopped for a toilet break. The book's ending didn't make sense because, I later learned, someone—my money has always been on Border—neatly cut out the final chapter. I'm more than happy to sit and chat as well but today I want to finish my book.

Our journey begins in the early afternoon which means the further we travel the slower the progress as the roads become clogged by parents collecting their children from school and people leaving work. The coach is hardly going to break any land-speed records, and it dawdles north behind a wagon train of lorries. When the driver does overtake one, it takes at least one mile to implement and complete the manoeuvre, much to the annoyance of car drivers stuck behind us who are quick to vent their frustrations. Other motorists hoot and signal their derision when they spot the club emblem in the back window. There are no encouraging "toots" from passing cars occupied by supporters. Surely there can't be any making this ridiculous midweek journey.

We stop for a break at a service station of sorts after a couple of hours. We are dressed in our club tracksuits, which I hate. I've always disliked "sports leisure wear" and I think the bright white socks are what I hate most about this get-up. We receive some good-natured abuse from a few members of the public. Nothing wrong with that as it helps break the tedium and is a talking point for some when we get back on the coach.

I finish the book, which I enjoyed as much this time as when I first read it and talk with Tom Butler and Terry Green. Full backs on the pitch they seem inseparable off it. Rob Riley meanders down the coach and stops to see how the card school is progressing. The players, frowns of concentration etched on their foreheads, just about acknowledge his presence, and he returns to the front of the coach with Saunders, Ronnie O'Reagan and Laurie Campbell.

Time is not fast disappearing and it's gone 7pm by the time the coach pulls into the hotel car park. Just as we go to check-in so do a number of people attending a conference the next day, although surely not at this dive. Another company doing things on the cheap. They get to the desk moments before we do so it's almost 8pm by the time we enter our rooms. Why has it always taken so long to check in and out of hotels? Things aren't much better today.

It's then straight to the dining room where the choice for dinner is roast beef paired with rock-hard roast potatoes and leathery Yorkshire puddings, cod and chips or chicken curry and rice. I opt for the latter which, as expected, doesn't taste of curry but the rice is palatable. Just. Everyone is tired, bored, stiff, fed up. We go back to our rooms. At least, the management team doesn't impose a "lights out by 10pm" curfew on us. We may be tired, but sleep is elusive. I'm rooming with Tyler and we watch crap TV until the national anthem signals the end of transmission at midnight.

Wednesday morning is grey and dull, and rain is forecast. We breakfast on toast which could have doubled as frisbees and bacon with more fat than pig, go through some light training at a local park (dog shit included free of charge) and return to the hotel for a tasteless lunch. We talk about Barrow, who are struggling near the bottom of the table and look destined to apply for re-election for the fourth time in five years. At the end of the season, they did have to apply for re-election and were voted out of the League and replaced by Wimbledon.

We are then told to go to our rooms and rest. That's not for me. I'm no good at going to bed to rest before a match. I don't sleep. It's not nerves, I just want to "get at 'em." I should have brought another book. I wander aimlessly around the hotel and bump into Laurie Campbell who, for once, is approachable possibly because he's also bored. We have a coffee together and talk about his career and aspirations. He still thinks we could go up this season.

By the time we get on the coach at 5.30 pm, it's blowing a gale and the rain is coming down like stair rods. We crawl through a couple of miles of slow-moving traffic to what is loosely described as a stadium. If I thought we were a club in crisis at the end of last season, I dread to think what Barrow is. The facilities, it is agreed by all and sundry, are the worst anyone has come across in their professional careers. Not surprisingly, the crowd is sparse. Probably the smallest any of us have played in front of in our professional careers.

One end of the ground is totally open to the elements and of course this is the end through which the gale is blowing straight off the Irish Sea. It's not quite at the level where the ball goes back over your head when you kick it into the wind but it's not far off. The match ends in a 1-1 draw. Barrow may be struggling but they are not short of effort and maybe they thought us Southern Softies would capitulate in the face of the conditions. We fall behind in the first half and equalise in the second through Butler's long-distance punt. Both goals were wind-assisted. Given all the circumstances we were happy with a point.

It's 10pm by the time we leave the ground. We stop almost immediately for fish and chips. The food is lukewarm, the chips floppy and the batter as soggy as the pitch we had just played on. A crate of tepid light ale has made its way on to the coach to help wash down the "food." At this stage, you take what you can get. The smell of stale fish and chips lingers on the coach for the remainder of the journey. This has hardly been a standard bearer of a trip in terms of dietary excellence for professional sportsmen. For once, I drift in and out of sleep as we crawl home. It's 4.30 on Thursday morning by the time we get to the ground, just gone 5am when I creep through my front door.

To avoid disturbing Hannah, I bed down on the sofa, get up when she does at 7am, go to bed when she leaves for work and get up again at noon. There is no need to go to the club unless you picked up an injury at Barrow. It being a Thursday no one is around, and I quickly become bored. I toy with the idea of preparing a meal but decide we will have a takeaway, promising myself I will get back into the swing of a proper diet tomorrow. I start another book but can't concentrate on it. I then have a brainwave and go out and buy a cassette tape recorder so I can listen to music on the other long trips we have this season. None as bad as Barrow but a couple which will require Shackleton-like endurance.

Hannah gets home at 6.30pm. We are both tetchy. I am tired and restless, she's peeved that despite my best efforts to keep quiet earlier this morning I had, in fact, woken her. Neither is she pleased that I've "wasted" money on something as frivolous as a tape recorder. She doesn't want a Chinese and opts for an early night, stropping off to bed at eightish. I sit on my own watching more crap TV, trying to convince myself that the chicken Chow Mein I am eating does have some taste to it and isn't overcooked.

Tasteless chicken curry, soggy fish and chips and a partly-incinerated Chinese takeaway plus a row with my girlfriend in twenty-four hours and people think that being a footballer, even a Fourth Division footballer, is glamorous and that our bodies are temples.

This was not what I had signed up for.

Chapter Five
A Pointless Christmas and New Year

I had made my first team debut on Boxing Day two seasons ago, against Plymouth, having played only a handful of matches for the reserves. I had been in the first team match squad a couple of times before but hadn't made it even as far as the sub's bench.

My first Christmas as a pro saw me train on Christmas Day, which was a shock to the system. At the end of the session, Frank Matthews called me over. "You're in son. You're playing tomorrow. Now go home, don't eat too much and don't fucking drink."

Frank always had a way with words.

The next day I was a bag of nerves, but they disappeared when we went out for the pre-match warm-up. Back in the dressing room Frank gave one of his motivational speeches which was memorable for all the wrong reasons—he seemed to think we were playing Portsmouth and he got a couple of other names wrong as well.

Plymouth, who had set off at dawn for the two-hundred-and-fifty-mile journey, showed little appetite for the match and we won 3-0. I was pleased with how I played, and the two points were very welcome for the team after a recent poor run. I only played another dozen matches that season which was frustrating. Every time I thought I had a foothold in the team I was left out. Frank would justify his actions by telling me it was all about getting the right levels of experience. I was tempted to point out that I couldn't get the required experience if I wasn't playing but decided antagonising the manager would mean a very quick return to the reserves.

We finished that season twelfth, slap-bang in the middle of the table, having been relegated the previous season. Supporters had hoped we would go straight back up, but we were a pretty poor team in a pretty poor division. We won as many games as we lost. We were never in the hunt for promotion, we were never in danger of finishing in the bottom four and having to apply for re-election. We were consistently inconsistent.

Despite being in and out of the team and the malaise which hung over the club (players past their best with negative attitudes, dwindling attendances, an archaic stadium), I enjoyed the life and worked hard to improve my game. I was beginning to establish myself around, if not in, the team I had supported all my life. There wasn't anything to complain about. The highlight had obviously been my debut on Boxing Day. All this was going through my mind as I drove my still-not-yet-clapped-out-Datsun Cherry to Wood Lane one year after making my debut.

Wood Lane Stadium, Northtown. Tuesday, 26 December 1978. Northtown United v Bradford City. League Division Four.

Bradford City, relegated last season but riding high this, look odds-on to go back up. We are currently eighth and haven't yet been in the top four, which is both a surprise and a frustration. It being Boxing Day and given the opposition, a bumper crowd is expected—The Observer has even predicted a sell-out. I make my way through the players' entrance and drop off my bag in the dressing room before heading for the players' lounge for a light lunch and the pre-match team meeting.

We are going into today's game on the back of a bad run, having not won in five and struggling to score goals. Swindon away (0-2), Peterborough home (1-1), Mansfield away (0-2), Newport home (0-0) and Colchester away (1-3) meant our confidence was hardly sky-high. We had been booed off after the Newport game and there were a few fans' letters in The Observer questioning whether Saunders was, in fact, the right man for the job.

Water off a duck's back for the thick-skinned Saunders who, despite being disappointed we are not doing better, is aware he's undertaken a massive job and things won't be rectified overnight. But he also knows he needs to do something to turn round our recent form.

After the obligatory lunch of poached eggs and baked beans, Saunders announces today's team. He has left out Iain Moy, our signing from Cowdenbeath and top scorer. Moy is not happy. "Why are you dropping me for fuck's sake? I can't score goals when no one's creating chances for me." Moy continues to rant, and his mood is far from improved when he hears he's being replaced by Steve Mower, the free signing from Millwall. Mower made only a handful of appearances for the Lions without pulling up any trees. He's only made a handful of appearances for us and netted just once.

I'm also dropped.

I'm not even named as sub. That honour goes to Moy although if he continues to rant and rave he may just shout himself off the bench.

Unlike Moy, I'm speechless. I hadn't seen this coming. I can't pretend I have been playing particularly well but my form has certainly been no worse than others.

I want to say something but it would only be a stream of invective so I keep quiet. But I am pissed off big time.

Rob Riley takes me aside. "How do you feel?" A stupid question. "Stunned. Pissed off. I don't understand the decision."

"Well, the Boss has to do something. We've been lacking all over the pitch recently. And you've not been at the races. You've had a good run in the team. Best thing you can do is go away and think about how you've played over the last month or so and how you're going to improve."

I sit in the stand and watch. My loyalty is split. I want us to win. I think. If we win without me it could be a while before I get back in. Jack Winters has taken my place. He's a mate and deserves a chance—albeit not at my expense—but I'm afraid I wish him a poor game. Maybe a draw with Jack having a stinker is the best option. I'm thinking about what Riley had said.

And I also think Saunders should have had a private word with myself and Moy before announcing the team. I'm sitting just a few rows from four mates who I've organised tickets for. When they see me and learn I've been dropped, they suggest a few drinks tonight. I'm sorely tempted.

The ground is rocking. It is a complete sell-out and Bradford have brought several coachloads of fans with them and they contribute enormously to what is easily the best atmosphere of the season. My mood darkens further. I want to be on the pitch lapping this up.

Bradford start brightly. They play the ball around at real pace with crisp, incisive passes and force several corners in the first twenty minutes. We struggle not to concede. It's easy to see why they are top of the table.

They are playing without fear and a neutral would think they were the home side. This is how we are meant to be playing!

Inevitably, they score. A pinpoint pass from midfield to the right winger who skips past a couple of challenges and puts in a cross which their centre forward buries with an emphatic header from ten yards out. Bamford no chance.

Half-time 0-1. Lucky it's not worse.

I may not be playing but I still have to go to the changing rooms during half-time. Saunders is his usual calm self, but I get the impression he's not sure which way to turn. He doesn't have many options at his disposal. Doncaster must have been a piece of cake compared to this.

The second half starts as the first ended. I reckon if Bradford get a second they could win by four or five. They hit the post. Then the bar. We hang on. After an hour, Saunders makes his change. Why so many substitutions are made after an hour has always baffled me. If things aren't working, change it at half-time. Or earlier.

Winters comes off. He's been ineffective. So has everyone else other than Bamford in goal. You can almost see the steam coming out of Moy's ears. Here's a man with a very large point to prove. He puts himself about and chases everything. Our tactic seems to be to just lump the ball to Moy and let him do the rest. He puts in a couple of meaty challenges and is booked for the second one which is high and late. The Bradford fans want this Jock, who according to them has no father, sent off.

He stays on. He's lucky.

To rub salt into Bradford's wound, Moy then goes on a twisting run and is upended. Penalty. A few Bradford players surround the referee more out of duty than actually disputing the decision. They know full well it's a penalty. Moy picks up the ball and puts it on the penalty spot. Tyler is our regular penalty taker but he's not having this one. Don isn't brave, or stupid, enough to try and take the ball off Moy. I strain to see Saunders' reaction to this turn of events. Impassive. Moy blasts the ball home. The ground erupts. From being all but overrun we're suddenly level. Funny game, as they say.

Bradford, to their credit, don't sit back and settle for a draw. And in the dying minutes their enterprise is rewarded. A long cross beyond the far post. The centre forward heads it back into the danger area and the ball is forced home.

Cruel game as well as a funny one.

The dressing room is quiet, but Saunders is animated compared to how he was at half-time. The second half was the best we've played for weeks, he tells us. Even if the tactic was simply to hump the ball forward to a pissed off and fired up Jock.

I reckoned I would be back in the side at Aldershot. Another case of misguided thinking. Moy was back in. No surprises there. At least I was "promoted" to the subs' bench.

I came on for the last fifteen minutes after we went 3-0 down, eventually losing 4-0 in our worst performance since… Peterborough at the end of the previous season. It may even have been worse. Hard to understand or explain after our second half performance against Bradford. Saunders, O'Reagan and Riley are at a loss.

Next up, on New Year's Day, it's Darlington away. I had spent New Year's Eve holed up in my flat wondering if I would be recalled to the team. I really didn't fancy the idea of a very long and uncomfortable journey followed by getting splinters in my backside as I sat on an equally uncomfortable bench in the freezing cold. No thermal insulation for substitutes in those days! A tracksuit and you could just about get away with wearing a bobble hat without your sexual preferences being called into question. Especially in the frozen wastelands of the north. Staying in on New Year's Eve had been very hard and was made worse by Hannah going out and coming back obviously having had a great time. Our relationship wasn't what either of us had anticipated.

Another early start. Another stint on the subs' bench. Another defeat. Another late return. Darlington were no great shakes, hovering just a couple of places above the re-election zone while we were sliding down the table. At this rate, they would climb above us. We had no steel, no backbone, no fight, no confidence. The pitches now resembled mud baths so trying to play good football was just about impossible. I came on when we went 2-0 down and scored a rare goal but we couldn't claw it back and get a point. We didn't deserve one anyway.

If we were a ship, we'd be taking on water.

I cornered Rob Riley as he was a go-between for the players and Saunders. I told him I wanted a chat with the Boss. Nothing heavy. Just a "why did you drop me and how do I get back into a side which is playing crap and continually losing" sort of chat.

"Leave it for the moment, son," I'm advised. "I'll let you know when the time's right to talk to him."

A complete kop out as far as I am concerned.

Saunders had told us just four months earlier to speak up if we had a beef. I wondered if I should ignore Riley and go direct to the Boss but decided to think about it on the journey home. At Doncaster, supposedly, Saunders was completely hands-on. At the moment, he is distant. Aloof. A lost soul?

We had now passed the halfway stage of the season with a record of played twenty-six, won eight, drawn six, lost twelve, goals for thirty-one, goals against forty, points twenty-two, position twelfth. If we didn't improve in the second half of the season, we would finish with forty-odd points—over the last few seasons at least fifty-eight points were needed to finish fourth, the last promotion spot. But the "P" word, which may have been used occasionally at the start of the season, hasn't been part of our lexicon for months.

There had certainly been no public declaration of promotion this season, despite Roger Palmer talking to us of First Division football within five years. If we didn't go up this season, we would have to win promotion in each of the next four seasons. Northampton had once achieved that and come back down just as quickly. It was one hell of an ask.

And if we were to go up, we would need (probably) at least thirty-six points from our remaining twenty-three games, or one-and-a-half points per match compared to the less than one per game we had so far achieved. To put this into perspective, last season's Fourth Division champions, Barnsley, had won at a canter averaging… just under one-and-a-half points per game over the course of the entire season. And we also needed a couple of the current top four—Bradford City, Grimsby Town, York City and Stockport County to have bad runs.

The cliques which Saunders was so against had been forming for a while and were in full view on the coach back. "If he wasn't on a long contract and loads of money, he'd be history," said Steamy. "Fucking should be as well."

There were no dissenters.

No one could understand the lack of reaction or urgency. Why weren't we buying new players? The longer our poor form went on the harder it will be to attract decent players. Our recent record read played eight, won none, drawn two, lost six, goals for four, goals against sixteen. Two points out of a possible sixteen. Saunders was an improvement on Frank Matthews but at the moment you wouldn't know it. The improved stadium, facilities and kit, all planned and implemented by Palmer, were tangible and positive. Although training and our general approach was a lot more organised and professional, our performances and results were not much better than last term.

Had no one ever told Palmer that beauty is but skin deep?

I had never been much of a fan of Dave Craig, the football man from The Northtown Observer, who followed our fortunes up and down and across the country. He was too close to some of the old brigade. I even heard he babysat for Tom Border and his wife on a couple of occasions. As a result, he was unable to be objective and never criticised the team or individuals for fear of reprisal when he next saw them. He also used to occasionally travel to away matches on the coach. Saunders had quite rightly put an immediate stop to that.

So it came as a surprise when the first Observer of 1979, circulated on Friday 5 January, laid into the owner, the manager, the club and the team. I doubt it was Craig's initiative, but his by-line was liberally sprinkled over the front, back and a couple of inside pages. And it all made for interesting reading.

What's going on at Northtown United? Why hasn't Saunders turned things round? Why isn't there a clear and obvious way of playing? Why aren't we attracting new players? Why is the owner hardly seen?

Craig had been out and about asking supporters whether they thought Saunders was the right man for the job. A lot of them wanted change; a roughly equal number felt it was too early to make a change but were definitely underwhelmed. Craig also wrote a "half-term report" on the players. Interestingly, from my point of view, he felt I should be in the side and that dropping me was the wrong call. Maybe he did know his stuff after all.

There were no quotes, anywhere, from Palmer or Saunders. Palmer had been abroad working on a major property development scheme, but Saunders should have been contacted for his view. There were, however, quotes from "someone close to the team" and these weren't invented, non-attributable quotes in an attempt to give the content more substance. Steamy's quote on the coach back from Darlington about Saunders' length of contract and level of pay appeared. As did a couple of other things he'd said in recent weeks such as Saunders being too distant from his players and failing to explain his team selections.

Supporting all this was an Editorial which called into question Saunders' transfer policy, criticising the lack of signings and their quality. It noted the first choice 'keeper, Steve Bamford, signed from Cardiff City, was an undoubted success as was Don Tyler although his form had dipped recently. Iain Moy was a relative success but would be more effective if he had some heavyweight support around him; Steve Mower was a complete failure, and the jury was out on the others who had arrived since the end of last season. Put in these terms the wheeling and dealing in the transfer market could not be described as a success.

The piece also hinted, very strongly, that the funds promised for the "type of player who would win us promotion" had not been made available to Saunders and the money spent on the stadium had possibly bled Palmer dry. The writer asked what had happened to the extra income generated by increased season ticket sales and improved attendances.

To cap it all there was an interview with ex-skipper and "club legend" Tom Border, who was deeply scathing about the way he and his teammates had been "thrown out," the "unfair dismissal" of Frank Matthews and Tony Saunders' recruitment and tactics.

Border claimed he still had friends in high places in and around the club and had an "inside track" into exactly what was going on. The players, he said, were close to revolt. It was, he argued, threatening to be the worst season in the club's history. Pretty rich coming from a man who less than one year before had skippered the club to the indignation of applying for re-election. Total rubbish but the sort of stuff readers would lap up and enjoy debating over a couple of pints. And many of them would believe this rubbish.

Other than not giving Palmer and Saunders the opportunity to respond—as well as the quotes from the washed-up legend with an axe to grind—it was hard to argue with much of what appeared.

How would Palmer and Saunders react? That was the million-dollar question. Very differently to how we had expected was the answer.

We were sat like kids in a classroom in the Press Room, a copy of the previous day's Observer for each of us. Now placing footballers in a classroom doesn't work very well. We are an impatient lot with a very short attention span. Most of us say we hate training but give us bench presses and endless sprints any day over this environment. And although, by and large, we act like children we don't appreciate being treated like them. And we had sat here just a few months before and things hadn't gone nearly as well on the pitch as we had expected after that session.

Most of us would point the finger at the manager—and when the manager loses the confidence of the players…

At the same time, we were intrigued. We wanted to know how our bosses were going to react to what The Observer described as a "crisis." Did they consider we were in crisis?

Palmer, our head master, was looking relaxed and tanned having hot-footed it back from Spain. "Guys" (yuk!) "I'm sure you've all seen The Observer. I'm not going to stand here and rant and rave at who I presume and hope are the converted, although I think the quotes from Tom Border are those of a bitter man. I want to try and put things in perspective."

Already a few of the "guys" were restless and wanted the head master to cut to the chase. Palmer told us any rumours of Saunders being sacked were without foundation. This is a long-term project. Last season we were bottom four; this season we are currently mid-table which means there are definite signs of progress. Our stadium is at least Second Division standard. Seven players had been signed and the manager and his staff were working tirelessly to improve the standard of our reserves and the club's younger players to ready them for future first team action. Had The Observer sought comment from anyone within the club this would have been explained. There would be a full response from Palmer in the programme for our next home match. The fans needed a balanced and considered overview.

Palmer added that he and Saunders had been working hard to bring in other new players, but his wealth was a hinderance. "Because I have money clubs ask ridiculous fees. The couple of players we have had dialogue with wanted unrealistic wages and add-ons which you simply don't get in the Fourth Division." However, there was some positive news regarding transfers, and he handed over to Saunders.

Saunders had a reputation for having the gift of the gab and although he had rarely shown it in recent weeks he went into overdrive. The message was that the club had signed two new players, who would add extra quality and depth to the squad. John Halliday had been brought in from Blackburn Rovers. A tall (well over six feet) gangly forward, Halliday had scored goals for fun in the lower divisions with Bury and Rotherham before his transfer to Blackburn where he didn't quite cut it. A long-term injury hadn't helped but on the face of it he seemed like a useful acquisition. Our second new face was Dave Walters, who had spent most of his career in the higher divisions before a transfer at the start of last season to Doncaster. He was obviously a favourite of Saunders.

Walters was another midfielder, which of course is where I had been playing. And I was currently out of the team. Did this mean I was on my way out of the club? Maybe I should look to engineer a loan move?

Walters' signing wasn't the sort of news I wanted to hear given my confidence was already fragile after being dropped.

We had no match on the coming Saturday as it was FA Cup Third Round Day and we had fallen at the first hurdle, back in August, losing 1-0 to Crewe. If nothing else happened in my career, at least I had played in the world's greatest club knockout tournament. We didn't have to train after the meeting with Palmer and Saunders—class dismissed, home early for good behaviour—but to report for training at 9am the following morning (an hour earlier than usual) when we would meet Walters and Halliday.

Chapter Six
Back in the Boss' Office

The new signings were keen and fit. The midfielders and the forwards worked together, separately from the defence. Interesting. This hadn't happened before.

At different times, Saunders paired Walters with Bailey, me, Winters and Jackson. The presence of Walters had put an extra zip into the rest of us midfielders as it seemed clear he would go straight into the side leaving Mark, myself, Jack and Ronnie fighting for one place. We all wanted a piece of the action. Don Tyler's place on the right seemed assured.

As we finished training Saunders called me aside. "Ed, once you've showered come and see me." Again, interesting. I was worried I was going to be told I was out of the first team picture.

Saunders' door was open (some irony there), and I shut it after entering. He looked up from his desk and said: "I'm told you want a word." For a moment, I'm flummoxed. Then I remembered my conversation with Rob Riley after the Darlington match seven days ago. Quite a lot had happened in the intervening time.

Riley had obviously tipped Saunders the wink that I wanted a word.

"Yes Boss. Thanks. It's just that I wanted to ask why I've been dropped recently and what I have to do to get back in the side."

Saunders gave me a long look. "Why do you think you've been left out?"

"I don't know. I haven't been playing brilliantly but then again I don't think anyone has. I don't think I've been worse than anyone else in midfield."

Another long look. "Bailey's been playing better than you. Tyler has been our best player. If I had wanted to leave Jackson out, you couldn't take his place, you haven't got a left foot."

I couldn't argue with his comment about my left foot. I didn't think Bailey had been playing better than me but something told me Saunders wouldn't appreciate my telling him that.

"After Bradford and Darlington, I thought I would have been back in against Aldershot. Boss."

"What are your thoughts on the new signings?" If nothing else, Saunders knew how to wrong-foot you during a conversation.

"I think they are good signings, Boss. We needed more depth." I wanted to ask if the signing of Walters put me further down the pecking order. It seemed pretty obvious it would.

To hell with it. This meeting is about me.

"I'm worried that my being out of the team and Walters coming in makes me about sixth choice for midfield. Boss."

"Listen, son. I've been disappointed with your performances for some time. Perhaps I should have called you in and told you. But from my point of view players have to take a responsibility; I can't hold your hand when you're on the pitch and I don't think you've done nearly enough. You're young so you've got time on your side but you're not showing yourself to be as good as I thought you were. That's a worry. You're going to have think more about how you manage your game."

What the hell does that mean? Saunders saw my puzzled expression.

"You run around like a headless chicken, so you're knackered after an hour, you take too many touches, your passing hasn't been up to snuff. You've got a way to go before you get back in the team."

This was all news to me. Neither manager, assistant manager nor coach had mentioned any of this although I could now work out for myself, I was going to have a struggle to get back in the side. Had I been resting on my laurels? That wasn't in my nature.

I sat there, mute.

"Keep your head up son. You're not on the scrapheap yet." Said with a smile on his face. Presumably meant to make me feel better. I got up to leave. "One other thing son. The comment in The Observer about me not communicating well with the players and not explaining my selections. Was that you?"

I had not been expecting this. "No, Boss! I may not agree with everything you've done but it's not my style to talk about people behind their backs. I think someone should have told me why I was dropped but I haven't said anything to anyone. In fact, I don't think I've ever spoken to the anyone at The Observer."

"Ok, son. I'll take your word for it. Now go away and have a good think."

Although I was worried about regaining my place, there was no doubt we needed new players. Moy needed someone playing alongside him as Mower, hard as he tried, was severely limited. He was to stay with us until the end of the season but then fell into non-league obscurity. I knew Walters was a good addition, he was experienced, busy, tough and scored goals from midfield. Although I was critical of Saunders and some of his methods, I also had some sympathy for him. He didn't have a lot of options at his disposal and had we suffered any injuries or suspensions he would have had to call on completely untried players. Given our poor form he must have wanted to shuffle his pack but it was a pack seemingly devoid of any aces. I felt we could still do with more defensive cover and maybe another forward given Mower's obvious limitations.

Not having a match for almost two weeks gave me plenty of time to reflect on what Saunders had said and to act on any of the points I agreed with. I went out for a meal with a couple of friends, who were semi-regular visitors to Wood Lane. I told them about my chat with Saunders and what he had said. I wasn't looking for sympathy; I wanted their opinions.

I also sought out Mark Bailey. After all, he and I were meant to be partners on the pitch. Although we didn't speak much off, it he was very approachable. "I don't agree that you run out of steam, but you don't impose yourself on games as much as I thought you would, even those we have won.

"When I was at Luton, I heard about you. The word was you were very promising. I don't think you're living up to that reputation. There are some good parts to your game, and you read things well to get the ball, but you also get caught in possession.

"If I were to give you one piece of advice, it would be to pass the ball quicker. I know the Boss talks about cherishing it as if it were a lover and he's right, but what he really means is don't lose the fucking thing. You do. Work on improving your passing as well. Don't worry, you'll be back in soon."

I enjoyed the conversation. It was one I should probably have had a while ago.

"Don't worry." Both Saunders and Bailey had said it. The manager and the senior pro.

I wasn't and never have been an inveterate worrier. I don't lie awake at night because my mind is in turmoil or because I'm nervous about an upcoming match. It's simply not in my nature. As Hannah had told me on more than a few occasions it was both an advantage and a disadvantage.

I put everything Saunders, Bailey, Hannah and my mates had said, plus some thoughts of my own, into the melting pot…

I probably had been cruising without realising it. Not through arrogance but purely because I hadn't been thinking enough about my game. If individuals like Saunders and Bailey, who had been in the game a hell of a lot longer than me and know far more about it, pinpoint the same weaknesses there was obviously something to it. I wasn't living up to my potential (I hadn't realised I had a reputation as being "one to watch" as Bailey had indicated).

I didn't want to be a lower league footballer for much longer. I wanted to play at the very top. I hoped this would be with Northtown United but if not then I'd move on. I was beginning to think I might have to take a sideways step, or even a backward one, to help me move forward. Surely, there would be some takers? My contract was up for renewal at the end of the season. I wanted the club to be desperate for me to sign a new contract. It was down to me to make sure that was the case.

My thought process had given me some goals to aim for; some ambitions. I was determined to improve and develop my game. I now had an understanding of what focused, driven and determined meant.

I started arriving early for training, giving me time to work on one- and two-touch ball skills. After training, I put out cones around the pitch and passed balls to them. I moved the cones, so I was hitting short, medium and long passes, aiming for the ball to land about a foot in front of them and then to knock them over. In the evenings, I did some running, even though I was happy with my fitness levels. I practised dead-ball kicks. I set myself the target of becoming our dead-ball specialist. Corners, free-kicks, penalties. I wanted to take them all.

In short, I worked my nuts off. And I determined to keep all this up (if and) when I got my place back.

Chapter Seven
Promotion Push, Relationship Relegation

Our Christmas record was hardly full of good tidings and joy. Played three lost three. Goals for two, goals against eight. Points none. We had one good half against Bradford City, were rank at Aldershot, not much better at Darlington. It was obvious to everyone Saunders would ring the changes, especially with two new signings to play with.

Training in the week after the Darlington match was intense and focused and we were champing at the bit to get out on the pitch again, even if the weather had turned and the pitches had gone from grass to seas of mud, seemingly overnight.

Not surprising John Halliday and Dave Walters started in our next game against Chesterfield.

So did I.

Was it because of my new approach? Was it because my presence had been missed? Perhaps I had made enough of a difference when I came on as a sub against Darlington and Aldershot? None of the above. When we got to the ground, the team meeting was held before the lunch. Saunders explained Halliday and Moy would play together up front. Mower was out of the picture. Ronnie Jackson, who had been no more than steadyish on the left of midfield, was playing in the centre of the back four. Bailey was on the left of midfield leaving Walters and myself in the middle. Tyler, obviously, was on the right.

This meant Steamy Windows was dropped. In fact, he was nowhere to be seen.

Saunders had somehow discovered Windows was responsible for some of the comments which had appeared in The Observer. I hoped Windows didn't think I had told Saunders—he knew I had been in the Boss' office just a few days before—as Steamy had a habit of seeing red mist and throwing the occasional punch if he thought he had been wronged. I didn't want to be the recipient of one of them.

Saunders told us to get the ball to Bailey and Tyler on the flanks as quickly as possible and they should get it into the box asap. Halliday would win most of the aerial duals and Moy would pick up the pieces. Walters and I were to push further forward but shouldn't get caught upfield. Given the muddy pitches this tactic seemed sensible.

"Don't worry about Steamy," Saunders told us. "He'll be back if and when I want him back." I felt that that Steamy, undoubtedly a decent player at this level, had reaped what he had sown but I also thought it was worrying we didn't have another central defender in the club good enough to promote into the first team so we had to mess around with personnel, which was against Saunders' "philosophy". Then again it all meant I was back in the team so why should I care?

As it happened Chesterfield didn't put up much of a fight and the new central defensive pairing wasn't tested as we ran out comfortable 3-0 winners, courtesy of Moy (almost inevitably), Halliday on debut and a Tyler penalty.

It wasn't all plain sailing though as Tyler went off injured and was still in obvious discomfort after the match. There were also rumours that a couple of bigger clubs were showing an interest in Steve Bamford who, despite our struggles in the first half of the season, had shone between the sticks. The backup to Bamford was third-choice at his previous club and hadn't played a single minute for us. Which was another worry.

For the first time that season, we enjoyed back-to-back home games with Scunthorpe visiting four days after Chesterfield. They were a rugged lot, intent on stopping us playing at all costs. Three or four of them were booked. It should have been three or four more. My passing practise paid dividends when I pinged a long pass straight into the path of Winters (in for the injured Tyler) whose early cross was headed home by Halliday.

Consecutive wins for the first time this season. Consecutive clean sheets for the first time this season. If not *the* corner turned, then certainly *a* corner turned on a long, winding and at times rocky road.

We then went on the club's best run for several years winning six out of the next nine, losing just one. Goalless draws at Notts County and Southend, a 2-1 defeat at Peterborough and wins at home to Colchester (1-0), Oldham (2-0), Halifax (2-0) and Barrow (3-1) and away to Grimsby (1-0) and Northampton (3-

1). This meant we had picked up eighteen points from eleven games—or just over one-and-a-half points per match and we were seventh in the table only three points off a promotion place. Tyler had returned from injury after the Scunthorpe match and Windows had been recalled after the loss at Peterborough, which meant that Jackson was out leaving just me and Kevin Marr from the previous season in the first team.

Saunders was happy with the way things were going but wanted as much penetration on the left as on the right. Mark Bailey wasn't quick enough to play on the left flank as Saunders wanted someone who could mirror the skills and output of Tyler on the right, who had created numerous goals. But it wasn't happening on the left. Terry Green was tried there with Bailey dropping to left back and although he was quicker than Mark, he wasn't quite the real deal.

So Saunders brought in a left winger from the reserves. Lad by the name of Rob Davies, who had trained with the first team from time to time especially when the management team had wanted Tyler and Tom Butler to practise defending under a bit of pressure. Davies was quick, skilful, two-footed and had an eye for goal. He came in against Grimsby and immediately made a difference. It was tough on Bailey who had been moved around for the good of the team without complaint or comment and suddenly became our permanent substitute.

The jigsaw was taking shape and with nine games to go we were handily placed and for the first time some started to talk openly of promotion again.

Of those nine matches four were at home—against Swindon, Notts County, Aldershot and Grimsby—while the five away were at Bradford City, Scunthorpe, Stockport County, York City and Chesterfield. Over one thousand miles to travel but none of the trips were as far or as daunting as Barrow and they were all on Saturdays. But Bradford (runaway leaders), Stockport and York were all vying for promotion. Grimsby, who were in the mix at the turn of the year, had fallen away. Promotion, as they say, was in our hands.

As Bailey had moved down the pecking order so Dave Walters had progressed up it and had taken over the captaincy. He had a natural swagger about him and had undoubtedly improved us as a team. To me, he was the obvious choice as captain once Mark was left out. Steamy didn't agree and thought it should have been him given he was vociferous on (and off) the pitch. I thought mouthy was a better description. Kevin Marr was also disappointed given he was the club's longest servant but although he was a popular member of the squad, no one really gravitated towards him or sought him out for his advice or opinion.

It was Walters who pulled us together after training one day and suggested introducing a weekly players' dinner between now and the end of the season, regardless of results. It was true we didn't really socialise other than a drink and a chat in players' lounges up and down the country although Windows and Moy were good mates and spent a lot of time together, as did Tom Butler and Terry Green.

I was probably closest to Jack Winters and he and I and our partners would sometimes go out together. But Jack had become increasingly disillusioned as he rarely featured. He didn't think he had a future at the club and felt sorry for himself. Instead of trying to turn things round he simply went through the motions on the training ground. I pointed out to him that Andy Adams hadn't had a sniff of first team action all season, but he still trained hard. The hapless Steve Mower, who we all felt some sympathy for, kept a smile on his face. But Jack wanted people to feel sorry for him which I had no truck with and was one of the reasons I socialised with my old school mates and their partners rather than footballers.

No prima donnas there.

Windows, inevitably, was the first to cast a doubt on Walters' idea. "What's the point of these dinners and is the club going to pay? I see enough of you ugly buggers as it is."

Walters countered that with the end of the season in sight and promotion a possibility now would be a good time to meet once a week, away from the ground, to talk about recent games, discuss the next week or so and to air any grievances, concerns etc. Bailey, a true professional, backed Walters. "We need to be more together as a group. It's not that we aren't united, but this is the quietest group I've played with," he said.

"And it's everyone or no one," added Walters. "It's only for a couple of hours and it's not a piss-up."

I thought it was a good idea although I wasn't sure how it would be received at home given all five away games would include an overnight stay, and this would be one more night a week when I wouldn't be about.

The following night the first team squad met in a local Italian restaurant, hardly talked about football, laughed our heads off and got thoroughly pissed on Ruffino Classico, which came in rafia-covered bottles. Walters had mentioned to Roger Palmer what we were doing, and Palmer had arranged to pay the bill. Even the previously cynical Windows was impressed. It was a great night and was talked about for ages.

Training the next day may have been sluggish but Saunders and his team had known in advance of our activities and made allowances. We met every week for the rest of the season and although subsequent dinners were quieter and more sober affairs, I felt they really helped bring us together as a group at just the right time. They even helped to lift Jack.

The first of the nine matches which followed our initial night out was a home game against Swindon, solidly mid-table. There was no way they could get into the promotion race but there was also no chance they would roll over and make life easy for us. They even had the nerve to take the lead, following a rare error from Steve Bamford, and held onto it for the best part of an hour.

I scored our equaliser with a shot from the edge of the box and Halliday, proving an excellent signing, notched a late winner. There was bad news following the match when we learned Bamford's mistake was due to a finger injury and he would now miss a couple of matches and be replaced by the untried Rob Keen.

All of our remaining fixtures were at best tricky, beginning with a trip to Stockport, who seemed likely to go up with Bradford. Saunders had tried to get in another keeper without luck but had signed a new defender, Les Oldfield, from Derby. As Saunders was ringing round in his attempts to sign a keeper, he had been offered Oldfield for a nominal fee. He was another experienced player and a useful addition to our small squad as our promotion push gathered momentum.

Stockport were a good side, but we were full of confidence and went blow-for-blow with them and were unlucky not to take the lead on a couple of occasions before they grabbed a late winner. Hardly deserved. Keen didn't have much to do and looked fairly competent. We felt we should have come away with a point.

"If we want to go up, this is the sort of game we need to win. If we don't win, then we don't deserve to go up." This was Saunders' rallying cry before we went out to face Scunthorpe. They took an early lead. At least, that spurred us out of our stupor and into some action, and we played possibly our best football of the season. We had total control of midfield with Tyler and Davies running riot on the flanks. Moy scored twice and Davies bagged his first for the club. But a few minutes from time Moy pulled up lame. Given how hard he had worked throughout the campaign it was surprising it hadn't happened before. Calf strain. Not too serious, but he would miss at least a couple of games.

Les Oldfield made his debut at home to Notts County, in place of Kevin Marr. Saunders was concerned by the number of goals which had come through the middle of the defence and the lack of pace there. Marr wasn't happy but kept his own counsel. Again, the weekly players' dinner helped him. Oldfield and Windows immediately looked good together. Saunders pulled another surprise by replacing the injured Moy with Andy Andrews, who made his first appearance of the season after impressing in training, and he did well enough before he made way for Mower. Halliday netted the first and we were all delighted for Mower when he scored the second. It was to be his last goal for the club.

Two-nil. A straightforward win.

Bradford City were easily the best team we had played and were the runaway leaders, but we matched them blow for blow at Valley Parade. Walters put us ahead, we then fell behind conceding either side of half-time but equalised, through a Windows header, minutes from the end. Cue extravagant celebrations in front of our two thousand fans. Four games to go and we were up to fifth in the table, breathing down York's necks. We played them in a fortnight. Both Bamford and Moy were fit again.

Before yet another trip to Yorkshire—I can see why there used to be a Third Division North and a Third Division South—we were at home to Aldershot and were out to revenge the mauling we received from them at Christmas. But we were poor in the first half, trying too hard. It was Walters who pulled us together at half-time and he went on to score the only goal of the game. A great example of leading by example. We heard that York had only drawn at Colchester which meant we were level on points but ahead on goal average. Into the promotion places at last. The following week's game at Bootham Crescent was, as they liked to say, a four-pointer.

Our most important match in years. As our form had come together so York's had dropped off. Whether it was promotion jitters or a lack of experience of a promotion battle, but they had struggled recently. We viewed the match as a real chance to dent their promotion hopes once and for all while boosting our own. They saw it as an opportunity to get things back on track before the final couple of games, where their run-in looked slightly easier than ours. Close to two thousand of our supporters made the long journey to watch what turned out to be the dampest of squibs as both sides were seemingly paralysed by the fear of making a mistake. The goalless draw suited us more than it did them but we were all disappointed with how we played. Saunders was fuming as he thought they were there for the taking. Worryingly, Moy limped off and was in a foul mood after the match and sat on his own as we chugged our way home. Even Steamy didn't go near him.

Two games to go. If we won them both we would go up.

Our final home game was against Grimsby and for the second time that season there was a sell-out crowd. The main difference between today and Boxing Day which was also a sell-out, as far as I was concerned, was that I was playing. But Iain Moy was on the bench just as he was against Bradford on Boxing Day although obviously for different reasons. Saunders named AA in Moy's place, Mower's goose now well and truly cooked.

Grimsby spent the first half of the season in the promotion places and had high hopes of bouncing straight back to the Third Division after relegation the previous season. A bad post-Christmas run had seen them slump to mid-table obscurity. They had also sacked their manager and now had their third manager in less than a season. Some bloke called Frank Matthews. It was beyond me how he had got another job, but he was given a very warm reception when he walked to the dug-out.

Grimsby were poor. No cutting edge. No creative spark. Little desire. A very good goalkeeper, though, who kept us at bay virtually single-handedly (if a goalkeeper can only have one hand).

Call for Moy. Saunders threw caution to the wind and took off Oldfield, playing Moy just ahead of Halliday and AA in a triangle which further confused the visitors. Frank Matthews, not for the first time in his managerial career, had no answer. The move worked and Halliday scored. Moy thumped home a second. Tyler skied a penalty way over the bar. "That better not prove important," Steamy said to Tyler before adding, equally unnecessarily, "it was a fucking dreadful penalty." Tyler, a slightly delicate and sensitive flower, didn't speak to anyone and headed straight home.

We sat in the dressing room waiting to hear how York had got on at Swindon. There was a radio in the dressing room but Jack Winters was still dispatched to the players' lounge to watch Grandstand as the results clattered in on the teleprinter.

Swindon weren't a bad side and had a decent home record. Not an easy match for York. We sat and waited for the result to come in from the County Ground.

Finally. Swindon Town one, York City… please let it be nil… one. A mixture of delight and disappointment. We had a one-point advantage and a slightly better goal average to York going into the final weekend of the season. We were at Chesterfield, York were at home to, of all sides, Grimsby.

We wondered how Frank Matthews would feel if he managed to help pop our balloon.

The week leading up to the Chesterfield match was a strange one. We didn't have to train on Monday but I didn't want to hang around the flat for a variety of reasons and played golf with Winters, Bailey and Davies who, against all expectations, wasn't very good. Bailey more than made amends for his partner's shortcomings though and they took a couple of quid off me and Jack.

Winters was still downbeat. He knew he had no chance of making the team to play Chesterfield. "The only time the Boss has spoken to me in the last month was to tell me to go and watch fucking Grandstand," he moaned.

Training wasn't as intense as it should have been when we met up on Tuesday. Saunders stopped it at one stage to read the riot act—the coaching staff got it in the neck as well as the players. Maybe he was beginning to feel the heat as well. Moy, excused training but observing from the side-lines, enjoyed the moment immensely.

He was excused training all week in the hope he made the team on Saturday. Terry Green wished he had been excused training as well when he tweaked a hamstring which meant he wouldn't play. The smart money was on Bailey, who had only made a couple of substitute appearances in the last couple of months, taking his place. It was really tough on Green, but I would be happy for Mark if he played.

The players' dinner was subdued. Even Steamy was withdrawn. Not a drop of alcohol was drunk. It being a Thursday we shouldn't have indulged anyway, but we had had a couple of drinks in previous weeks which Saunders was aware of and hadn't commented on. A shame we didn't have a drink, though, as Roger Palmer again picked up the tab.

We were far from happy to see the directors and their wives climb on board the coach after training on Friday. We hadn't seen some of them all season, let alone spoken to them. They seemed to think they orbited in a superior universe.

"Hopefully, they will see we need an upgrade on this beaten-up coach," commented Bailey. At least Palmer walked down the coach and spoke to all of us at some stage as we made our way to Chesterfield. His fellow directors, we decided, were there on a jolly and the hope of basking in promotion glory.

Whether it was because the directors were with us or because of the importance of the match—or both—but we stayed in a plush four-star hotel on the outskirts of Chesterfield rather than a budget offering. Very nice, but footballers are superstitious beings and the budget hotels had become part and parcel of our preparations as we had gone on our good run.

There were a few mutterings. Others, including myself, were more than happy to stay in luxurious surroundings. We couldn't go mad with the food but it was a considerable improvement on the tasteless fare which had challenged us for almost nine months at every hotel we had stayed at.

Frank Matthews had been interviewed by The Observer. He may not have been a good manager but he was a decent bloke and harboured no ill feelings towards the club. "I was part of Northtown for a long time. Things didn't end well but I wish only the best for the club and hopefully we will do them a favour tomorrow," he said. This was part of a four-page promotion special. No "inside track" from Tom Border this time.

Saunders named the team before we left for Saltergate, which sits in the shadows of the parish church's crooked spire. As expected, Bailey came in at left-back. Moy hadn't quite made it and was named as sub. Saunders explained he would rather have the Scotsman coming off the bench than playing him and being forced to take him off given there was no way he would have made ninety minutes. Moy, understandably, was glum but for once understood. I wondered what would happen if Moy had to come on and then had to go off again.

Close to three thousand of our fans had made the journey. Three thousand sad bastards? I wondered where Border was today. I thought back to the last game of the previous season. There was simply no comparison. I also thought back to Boxing Day and New Year. Again, how things had changed.

Back in the dressing room Saunders reminded us how far we had come. "You deserve this. Since New Year you've been the best team in the division. Concentrate on the way you've been playing. If you play as you can, you will win and win promotion. And do it for the fans."

I remembered Frank Matthews had said something about our fans at Peterborough and some players taking the piss. Nothing like that this time. I looked around the dressing room and it struck me that I was the only one in the line-up who had played at Peterborough twelve months before. One other familiar face was in a corner, Roger Palmer. I caught his eye and he grinned. It was as if he knew what I was thinking.

We went onto the pitch for the final warm-up. I saw Saunders, Riley, O'Reagan, Moy and the injured Marr making their way to the dug-out. Almost comically Marr was carrying a transistor radio, aerial fully extended, tuned into the BBC Saturday sports programme in the hope of picking up details of the York v Grimsby match. No doubt there were several hundred similar radios among our supporters as well.

Chesterfield anticipated that Bailey would be in for Green and set out to make life as difficult as possible for him. Saunders had anticipated Chesterfield's thinking and had briefed Davies to track back more than usual even if that would dilute his attacking threat. As it was Bailey coped admirably and Davies was able to concentrate his efforts on creating problems for the home defence.

We began to unpick the Spireites. Tyler, as ever, was menacing on the right and a low driven cross found its way across the box to Bailey who, despite being instructed not to cross the halfway line, found himself in their area. He slammed the ball home. Bailey may have been the oldest player in the squad with very little recent match practise but there was no catching him as he wheeled away to celebrate. We dominated the rest of the half but didn't create any clear-cut chances.

At half-time, we heard York were also one-nil up at Grimsby. Frank was letting us down… Riley gave us both barrels. Did we want promotion or not? Why the fuck weren't we creating more? Walters and I were told in no uncertain terms we were being too timid. It wasn't what we were expecting.

Perhaps that was the point. Riley's tongue lashing galvanised us. Walters and I took it in turns to join the attack. A shot by Walters was only parried and Halliday bundled the ball home. Bailey's race was run, and Moy came on with Davies going to left back and Halliday dropping into midfield.

It was fitting that Moy scored the goal which sealed our promotion, following another goalkeeping error. I looked over to the bench and saw the radio flying through the air. A couple of minutes later and our supporters celebrated again. Grimsby had equalised at York. Thanks Frank! We were up, two points ahead of the Minstermen.

The Spireites and the Minstermen both playing a crucial role in my life on the same day. Perhaps I should start believing.

The dressing room was a sea of champagne and beer, naked men hugging each other and cavorting. Saunders was thrown into the showers; Moy was getting as much booze down his throat as possible. The directors wanted a piece of the action as well but were also worried about getting soaked in alcohol so decided to stay on the periphery. Roger Palmer wasn't bothered though and was in among us. As a long-standing mate of Saunders, he wanted to be with him. And he could afford plenty of new suits.

Our final record read played forty-six, won twenty-two, drawn ten, lost fourteen, goals for sixty-two, against forty-nine, points fifty-four. We would have finished sixth the previous season, so perhaps we were lucky to be promoted but our record since the turn of the year with fourteen wins out of twenty games and only two defeats and nine goals conceded was exceptional.

We averaged one-point-six points per match in that time and it was still only two points for a win back then. With the possible exception of Bradford City, we were the best team in the division over the second half of the season. Going up with us were Bradford, Stockport and Notts County.

It was later than usual when the coach left for the journey home. Much later. By the time we got back to the club, it was too late and I was too drunk to meet up with anyone else. The players' lounge was opened, some of the players' wives were there. I had no idea what time it was when I finally fell (almost literally) through the front door. I threw up. Fortunately, I made it to the toilet. I spent Sunday lying on the couch nursing a monumental hangover and fielding calls from equally hungover teammates and friends wishing me well.

None of this went down well at home.

My inertia allowed me to reflect on the season and it was obvious Saunders had done a tremendous job and having won two consecutive promotions with "unfashionable" clubs meant the national press would take an interest in him. Inevitably, his name would be linked with managerial vacancies at bigger clubs. And there tended to be a few vacancies at this time of year,

He had got off to a slowish start and had his critics, including myself, but it was important to remember he took over a club which had applied for re-election. It was a massive job, and I had a sneaking suspicion even he was surprised we had won promotion in his first season.

I was particularly impressed by his signings and the timing of them. On the face of it, some of them didn't seem that exciting. One or two were even underwhelming in my eye, but Saunders knew the type of player needed to get us out of Division Four. Iain Moy, as the leader of our attack, was an inspired signing. No one else had tried to get his signature and Saunders picked him up for a song. Don Tyler was excellent in midfield and Tom Butler and Terry Green were the best pair of fullbacks in the division by a distance, while Steve Bamford hardly put a foot—or hand—wrong in goal. Mark Bailey and Rod Windows also knew what they were doing and what was expected of them. Hardened pros the pair of them.

When we went through a bad run and needed a boost, he brought in Dave Walters and John Halliday, both of whom gave us real impetus in our brilliant run in the second half of the season. Introducing Rob Davies was a brave move. The signing of Les Oldfield was also a master stroke. I don't think any of us had considered we had a weakness in the middle of defence, but with Oldfield playing we were suddenly much more solid. Including the hardly-used reserve keeper, Rob Keen, Saunders had signed twelve players—and promoted Rob Davies—and only Steve Mower didn't work out. One failure out of twelve was pretty impressive.

He also made some good selection calls. Leaving out Moy against Bradford City fired him up for the rest of the season. Dropping me made me really think about my game and improve as a player. Rod Windows learned the hard way not to cross him. There was a message there for all of us.

We had some, maybe a lot, of luck as we had suffered very few injuries and suspensions were minimal. Saunders fined anyone booked for dissent and given our wages were hardly sky high that acted as a real deterrent. We were the only side in the division not to have a player sent off and in total, we used only seventeen players throughout the season. Champions Bradford City had called on twenty-four; the previous season we had used twenty-six. Undoubtedly, though, we would need to add depth to the squad during the summer if we were to make an impression in the Third Division.

It was going to be another interesting close season.

As things had come together on the pitch so they had started to unravel, for me, off it. My relationship with Hannah was, as they say in films, on the rocks. It had been going in the wrong direction for a while and sealing promotion just about sealed the end of us. One of the calls I had taken on Hangover Sunday was from the Club Secretary, David Bennett, who rang to say that the Mayor was holding a reception for the management and players and their wives and partners on Tuesday evening at the Town Hall.

Very nice too, although at the time I took the call the last thing I wanted to think about was more celebrating. There was, however, a problem in that Hannah, and I were due to go out for dinner that night with her parents. It wasn't an event I was hugely looking forward to despite there being a recent thawing in their attitude to us co-habiting. When I broke the news to her that I had to go to the reception instead, her reaction was less than understanding. And she flatly refused to accompany me. I was pretty sure her parents would understand and would be prepared to rearrange and I said I would phone them to explain. I was told in no uncertain terms not to.

We had met just over a year before at a party and there was an obvious mutual attraction. I also liked the fact she knew nothing about and had no interest in football. The early months were excellent, and we enjoyed Martini sex— anywhere, anytime, anyplace, anything goes. I had had a number of girlfriends before, but this had easily become the longest relationship. We had a great holiday in Corfu and suddenly talk turned to engagement. I hadn't expected that and wasn't quite sure how to react. Perhaps my suggesting she moved in to the flat I rented was an attempt to give myself some thinking time. As I've already said, I was good at shelving.

She was eager to move in, her parents didn't approve of the idea. We talked them round and instead of using the flat I lived in we rented something a bit bigger. It had an elevated kitchen going down to a spacious lounge/diner. There were two sizeable bedrooms, one ensuite, as well as a separate bathroom.

We ditched most of the furniture I had and enjoyed going out choosing new fixtures and fittings. Everything was fine for the first few months, or maybe it was only weeks. Perhaps things began to go downhill when I was dropped and concentrating on getting back into the side and had become more focussed on what I needed to do on the field. So maybe I didn't put as much effort into the relationship as I should have. It wasn't a conscious thing though. We had moved in together so everything must be fine and dandy, mustn't it? Probably a lack of maturity. I was still only nineteen. So was Hannah. But then I wasn't a "typical bloke" either. I didn't slob out when I was home. I've always taken care with my appearance, lived in clean and tidy surroundings rather than a man cave, enjoyed cooking. Done my bit.

As far as I could see Hannah was the only "WAG" never to attend a match. I didn't expect her to be a regular visitor but thought she could have watched the odd game. She didn't even try and discover our results but waited to be told.

Even her dad tried to persuade her to show a modicum of interest but to no avail. The trip to Skegness was frowned on even when I explained I was contracted to do these things. The overnight stops in budget hotels and arriving home very late was a problem. For me too, I said. Getting as pissed as I did the night we won promotion was unacceptable. I should have tried to contact her but I thought she would have been happy we were successful. Our friends were and didn't give a stuff I was AWOL.

We had also been talking about this year's summer holiday. This would, I'm sure we both hoped, help us clear the air. But when I explained it would have to be soon after the season ended and not in July or August when I would be pre-season training the lid came off. Why couldn't we be like other couples? She didn't agree to move in with me to spend Christmas Day on her own, to have me away for countless nights and not to go on holiday when everyone else did. I had even toyed with the idea of not attending the weekly players' dinners but didn't see why I should bail out of important bonding sessions so I could sit in front of the TV or argue.

By the time I left the flat for the civic reception on Tuesday afternoon, we were at crisis point. Hannah was still going to see her parents, although she didn't tell me whether they were going out for dinner or staying home. I determined not to get carried away at the reception and just have a couple of token drinks and to leave at the earliest chance.

The reception was good fun. The players were in club suits, the wives had all gone out and bought new outfits. We went onto the balcony of the Town Hall and received a great welcome from several thousand people who had gathered. The Mayor made a speech, Palmer was forced to say a few words, Saunders addressed the crowd. Champagne was sprayed around. The buffet food was very good. The booze was plentiful.

I kept to the promise I had made myself and had very little to drink. I was accosted by Windows and Moy, also on their own, and was encouraged to go on with them afterwards to a night club. I declined the offer. "Where's your missus anyway?" asked Moy. "I'm beginning to think you're queer. Hear you've got a bird, never seen her though."

Jack Winters and his girlfriend approached me. "Where's Hannah?" asked Sue. "I thought she would have loved this." I left a few minutes later and although I felt obliged to leave early, I didn't want to be at home either.

Nevertheless, I did the right thing and was home by 8.30pm. I heard the next day that everyone else continued until the small hours.

Hannah didn't come home. She phoned to say she was going to stay at her parents. When I said something about it would be nice if she did come back, I was told "you didn't let me know what was happening on Saturday night. At least, I'm letting you know."

Some sort of immature pay back I suppose.

If only we had mobile phones in those days, I would have contacted Jack and caught up with the rest of the squad.

"Fuck this for a game of soldiers," I shouted. Lucky we didn't have a cat. It would have been in for a hell of a kicking.

Before Winters and his girlfriend had spoken to me at the reception, David Bennett had cornered me. I had hardly spoken to the Club Secretary in two seasons and now two conversations in less than twenty-four hours. He asked to see me on Wednesday afternoon. Saunders would be there as well. This, I was sure, could mean only one thing—my contract. In fact, Saunders wasn't there (I expect he was hungover, and I hoped he was) and Roger Palmer took his place. Both he and Bennett were effusive in their praise for my efforts over the season and were particularly impressed by how I had reacted to being dropped. They emphasised that Saunders and the coaching staff felt the same.

They wanted me to sign a new contract which would keep me at the club for the next three years.

The terms were improved but I wouldn't say they were *much* improved. Like all employees, I felt I deserved more but I had no idea whether I was in a strong bargaining position or not and how much to ask for. At long last, I would be able to replace the now-definitely-clapped-out Datsun Cherry, but it wasn't going to do much more than that for me. I was also concerned that a new and improved contract just at a time when my relationship was spiralling out of control wasn't something I wanted in the public domain. I thanked them, assured them I was committed and wanted to stay at the club but, due to some issues away from the club, I needed time to think. And although the new contract was an improvement on my current terms, I felt it wasn't quite enough.

Bennett wasn't impressed. Players didn't question contract offers. They were supposed to say thank you very much, sign on the dotted line and back out of the room bowing and touching their forelocks. He wouldn't expect such a young member of the squad to ask for time to consider the club's offer, let alone suggest it wasn't attractive enough. "As far as we're concerned, these are the best terms we will be able to offer you, Ed," said Bennett. "I suppose we can give you a day or two to think things over, but we are planning for the season in a new division and need to know where we stand." I presumed he was only saying this because Palmer was in the room and he wanted to come across as a reasonable man.

We agreed we would meet again the following Monday. Part of me thought "sod it" I should just sign and get the matter dealt with, but I did think I was worth more than the offer. I knew that if my mates were offered a salary increase which they felt derisory they would argue the toss. Why shouldn't I? Football should be no different to the business world. Roger Palmer said nothing but shook my hand as I left the office.

I arrived home just as Hannah did. I told her I had been at the club to discuss stuff for the next season. I didn't tell her any details. I asked her how her parents were and what they talked about last night. She was evasive but conceded her father felt she should have attended the reception. Her mother took her daughter's side. I was neither surprised nor bothered by any of her news. "We do need to talk," she said. I agreed knowing full well the direction the conversation was going to take.

The phone rang. It was Roger Palmer.

"Ed, I wanted to catch up with you before I leave for Spain tomorrow. Are you free tonight?" Talk about terrible timing. I looked at Hannah. "Going out again? Typical. If you want to go, go. It's obviously more important to you than me." Had she said, "us" I may, just may, have stayed and talked.

A couple of hours later I was sitting in the restaurant of the only five-star hotel in Northtown. Tony Saunders, who was due to be at that afternoon's meeting but who hadn't attended, was also there. He didn't have a drink, so I reckoned he had been, and maybe still was, hungover. Good for him. I didn't know he would be there but given we were there to discuss my contract, it made sense.

Palmer began by saying he had discussed, with Saunders, what I had said and they both agreed I had a point. By the end of the meal, I had been offered improved terms from the afternoon's meeting and although we weren't talking masses, I was far happier.

I outlined my off-field problems to them and while they were sympathetic, they told me they were "obliged" to tell The Observer I had signed a "new and improved" contract. It was up to me whether I revealed the details to Hannah.

The improved deal meant I could not only replace my car but also afford to pay the rent on my own as I had decided Hannah and I would be going our separate ways. Palmer and Saunders explained they couldn't give me anymore because they had to offer improved terms to other players. And money had to be set aside for new signings. We agreed we would meet again at the end of the following season. If it had gone well and I had played my part, I could expect improved terms again.

Much of the next few weeks was spent sorting out my private life. Hannah moved back to her parents, much of the furniture going with her. She wanted some money as well and although at one time I was tempted to hand over the cash simply to draw a line under the whole affair, I pointed out I had paid considerably more of the rent and half of the furniture was mine. She backed off. It was all pretty squalid. We were both too young. I bought new furniture and a second-hand Rover to replace the loyal, if mis-firing, Datsun Cherry. I missed the car more than her.

I also managed a week's holiday in Portugal with a couple of friends where I recharged my batteries by lying on the beach and playing a couple of rounds of golf, as well as enjoying a dalliance with a girl from Blackpool. No strings attached. Windows and Moy had suggested I went away with them for a couple of weeks and although I was sorely tempted, I knew my fitness would suffer if I did. I also had to bear in mind Palmer and Saunders had gone out of their way to improve my salary—twice. Paying them back by returning from the close season overweight and unfit would have been wrong.

And I was certainly in better shape than Moy and Windows when we went back to Skegness for another week of pre-season hell.

Part II
Into the Promised Land

Chapter One
An Easter Rising

If getting out of Division Four proved tough, winning promotion from Division Three, at the first time of asking, was relatively straightforward. Much of this was—again—down to Saunders' planning and signings.

As soon as the previous season ended, he signed another central defender, his third in just a year. Having brought in Les Oldfield towards the end of the previous season to partner Steamy Windows, he obviously wanted a younger and more mobile centre half to either challenge the existing partnership or to replace one of them. Within a few days of the Civic Reception, Terry Bell a twenty-two-year-old reserve at Leicester City had joined us.

We had six midfielders—Walters, Tyler, Bailey, Davies, Winters and me—but Saunders was on the lookout to strengthen here as well. Ronnie Jackson was released and signed for Orient. Steve Mower had also left while Andy Adams decided he couldn't go any further and hung up his boots, leaving us short in attack. Back-up was desperately needed for Moy and Halliday and just a week or so after Bell's signing, Alan Deakin and Jimmy Seal signed. Deakin joined from Wolves while Seal, who could play anywhere across the front, joined from West Ham's reserves. All seemingly excellent acquisitions.

The main changes other than these arrivals and the departures of Jackson and Mower saw Ronnie O'Reagan go back to Oxford as assistant manager, with Andy Adams joining the coaching staff in his place. Rob Keen, our reserve keeper, had been agitating for a move so he could sample first team action but there had been no takers, while Jack Winters and Kevin Marr were both rumoured to be on the way out.

Last season when we went to Skegness there were just fourteen of us; this time round there were eighteen, including Pete Aitken who had been promoted from the reserves. That had a much better feel to it, even though the time spent there was again all about running, sprinting and stretching. Saunders was determined we would again be the fittest team in the division, the result being we didn't see a ball all week.

For the second successive season, we were due to start our season in Wales, this time against Wrexham. We were also due to visit the Principality to take on Cardiff City while there were a number of other very long journeys to endure including Hull City, Hartlepool and Torquay which were all 400-mile-plus round trips. The worst, and every professional's nightmare, was Carlisle United which is 290-miles each way. Luton, Oxford, Brentford and Portsmouth were among the less arduous journeys.

Saunders had put no pressure on us last season with public statements about winning promotion, but in his first column of the season for The Observer he stated that he was expecting us to be a Second Division side this time next year. He was happy with the squad, which had quality and depth, and as long as we steered clear of serious injuries and suspensions, we had a great chance of promotion. "Going up" was the headline, a little over the top in my opinion, especially as only three sides went up not four. However, the quality of the squad began to shine through in the pre-season friendlies against more exacting opposition than the previous year. We again played Charlton Athletic as well as Orient and West Ham, the latter a fixture connected to the signing of Jimmy Seal. We drew with Charlton, stuffed Orient and played well against the Hammers, losing narrowly.

The team to play Wrexham was Bamford; Butler, Windows, Oldfield, Green; Tyler, Walters, Roberts, Davies; Halliday, Moy. Other than Green, who missed the final match of last season through injury, it was the same team that had played at Chesterfield, while seven of us had played in last season's curtain-raiser. None of the new signings were included although Seal was on the bench. There was some surprise Bell hadn't been named—he had looked the real deal in training.

Saunders wanted us to continue playing as we had in the second half of last season—get the ball wide to Tyler or Davies as quickly as possible and they'd put it in the box leaving Moy and Halliday to do the hard work. The midfielders would charge forward like the Light Brigade but would hopefully enjoy a more successful outcome than the cavalry force experienced. This was fine and had proved successful, but would it work in the Third Division? I was also slightly concerned that I could be bypassed as the ball was pumped forward and when I did get it my instructions were not to play much but to get it wide or forward with a minimum of fuss. I thought there was a lot more to my game than that.

But there was no arguing that the tactic worked brilliantly, and we didn't taste defeat until the ninth game of the season. Saunders was even happier because we were conceding far fewer goals. And Moy and Halliday, who had looked good together last season, were scoring for fun.

By the time we travelled to Notts County in late September, we had won six of eight league games, drawing the other two. Moy had scored half of our twelve goals and we had only conceded five. We pulled into Meadow Lane as table-toppers with fourteen points but weren't quite "at it" and County, who had been promoted with us, looked a good side and deserved their 2-1 win. We had lost one other match, going out of the League Cup 2-1 on aggregate to fellow Third Division outfit Bristol Rovers. "We'll worry about the cups next season when we are in the Second Division," said Saunders afterwards.

The team didn't change until our sixth game, a 0-0 draw at Hull City, when Terry Bell made his debut in place of a very disgruntled Rod Windows. But Steamy hadn't been at his best in the last couple of games and Bell was never less than excellent in training. Deakin and Seal, the other summer signings, were chomping at the bit and alternated as sub. Both had scored as well. The next six games included trips to Hartlepool and Cardiff, but how we bounced back after Notts County was key. It was a home match against Brighton, and we scraped a 1-0 win, courtesy of a late Tyler penalty. We then drew 1-1 at Luton and won 1-0, again, at Hartlepool who were struggling but given the journey we were more than happy with the two points.

Saunders decided to replace Davies with Seal, playing three up front against Bury. We hit top form and scored five for the first time in over two years. Moy (2), Seal (2) and Oldfield scored. Rob Davies had done very well since he had come into the team late the previous season but had looked tired in recent games and was also carrying a couple of knocks. We then saw off Bristol Rovers easily enough, 3-0 at Wood Lane, and got a decent 1-1 midweek draw at Stockport.

Fifteen games gone, only one defeat, twenty-four points and top of the table.

Almost too good to be true. It was.

You can, of course, get an excellent curry in Bradford. You are also assured of a tough match. They had won the Fourth Division Championship the previous season and most of us expected them to be among the front-runners again, but when we met, they were only mid-table. The Bradford fans had taken against

Iain Moy last season and they were on his back from the start. It fired up Moy and he became our first player to be sent off for a couple of seasons when he took out their keeper. Not even a booking. Straight off. His only consolation was that he had a new bar of soap all to himself.

We were already behind when Moy walked down the tunnel and then imploded, losing 0-3. It could have been worse. A lot worse. Moy was left to stew in his own juice by Saunders but was given a private roasting during the week. No one would have been surprised if Moy had been sent off before given his combustible nature and that he didn't shirk confrontation.

I thought we would bounce back, at home to Lincoln, but struggled against their packed defence and drew 0-0. This was followed by two away games, Exeter and Bristol City. Exeter looked decent and beat us 2-1 while we were poor, lacking confidence and, without the suspended Moy, looking lightweight in attack. Bristol beat us 1-0 and suddenly we had failed to win in five, scoring just twice and conceding seven.

This was going to be another test of Saunders' managerial skills. All of a sudden, we had gone from comfortable leaders with opponents worried about playing us to a mediocre team almost ripe for the picking.

And no one knew why.

Moy's suspension hadn't helped, and Don Tyler wasn't the force of last season but after the superb performances against Bury and Bristol Rovers we had fallen off a cliff. My take on it was that Bamford was excellent in goal and the defence, with the addition of Bell, was even better than last season. We were still potent in attack, but things weren't going quite so well in midfield. Tyler's ankle injury had slowed him down, while Walters wasn't as influential as he had been. The dropping of Davies and occasional change in formation wasn't helping. For my part, the reservations I had about the tactic of getting the ball forward at the earliest opportunity was proving ill-founded as I seemed to have plenty of time in possession and I felt I was playing very well. My passing and ball retention had certainly improved.

I had also scored a couple of goals and was a regular seven and occasional eight in The Observer player ratings, a definite improvement on last season. Whether these marks count for much is highly debatable, but I'd still rather be rated seven or eight than five or six.

We now had three fixtures before the Christmas/New Year period. With another three over the holiday period, it meant we were facing six matches which would be instrumental to how our season would pan out. Saunders had never been one for wholesale changes and it was interesting watching him shuffle things around in training.

Who he would—or would not—pick for our next match, at home to Stockport, was anyone's guess. The axe fell on Don Tyler who was replaced by Pete Aitken, the youngster who had come to Skegness, while Davies was restored to the left. Alan Deakin made his full debut to partner Halliday with Seal dropping out. Moy was missing with a mystery illness. Neither Seal nor Tyler was impressed. Who would be a manager?

Stockport didn't know what hit them. With two fast and skilful wingers, a forward eager to impress and a reinvigorated Walters, who knew he was lucky to be playing, we were two up within twenty minutes. We could and should have buried them but had to be satisfied with two more second half goals, the latter being a late penalty which I took. With Tyler and Moy not playing, we needed another penalty-taker and my continued dead-ball practising had been noted. A couple of minutes from the end Saunders took off Aitken so he would receive a richly deserved ovation from the crowd. Tyler, whose place he had taken, didn't even acknowledge him as he entered the fray. Poor.

The performances of Deakin and Halliday left Saunders with a decision to make as Moy would be available for the next match, at Walsall. Saunders kept the same starting eleven for the next two games with Moy substitute. Surprisingly, Moy didn't kick-off. We won easily enough, 2-0, at Walsall but had to be satisfied with a 1-1 home draw against Hull in the last game before the Christmas programme.

We were back on track as Santa began to pack his sack.

Many people argue that you shouldn't change a winning team. I agree with former England cricket captain Mike Brealey who once said you change a winning side if you can strengthen it. That made me wonder how Tony Saunders felt given he had Iain Moy, our top scorer last season and this, sitting on the bench watching John Halliday and Alan Deakin playing very well. Again, I was glad I wasn't a manager. Last Boxing Day Moy had been dropped and went into a Vesuvius-like eruption but came back stronger as a result. This year he couldn't get in the team following suspension and his mystery illness and simply accepted the decision. This wasn't the Moy of one year ago or even a few months before.

Christmas hadn't been particularly kind to us in recent seasons, but this year saw an improvement as we drew at home to Luton, 2-2, and at Brentford, 1-1, both of whom were pushing for promotion places. We also won at Shrewsbury where Moy came off the bench to score the only goal. He was happy enough, but his celebrations were muted compared to previous occasions.

We had now played twenty-five matches winning fourteen of them, drawing seven and losing four. With thirty-seven goals scored and only seventeen conceded, we had thirty-five points and were four points ahead of Brentford.

Our autumn fall was well and truly behind us.

Transfer windows were still a thing of the future, but Saunders obviously liked to review things around New Year. Last season saw the arrival of Dave Walters and John Halliday in early January, and they had made a huge difference. As the cold weather of January 1981 took hold Rod Windows and Jack Winters left the club.

There was no great surprise when Winters left—he had hardly featured over the last couple of seasons and although he believed he should be in the team didn't force the issue either on or off the training ground. Many of us were surprised, though, when Windows was allowed to leave for Newport.

He had also made a big impact when he first joined and was a larger-than-life character, as well as a more-than-useful back-up. Sure, he wanted to play first team football, but I thought the end of the season would be the time for him to leave and I wondered if Saunders held a grudge against Windows for talking about him to The Observer. Everyone had noticed that Moy and Windows, once as thick as thieves, hardly spoke to each other when they returned from their holiday. "Good riddance," was Moy's reaction when he heard Steamy was leaving.

I wondered if Saunders thought that allowing Windows to leave would improve Moy. Dave Walters, however, reckoned Saunders was sure we were going up and was beginning to shape the squad accordingly. "Steamy isn't good enough for the Second Division," said Walters. Having not played at that rarefied level I had to take Dave's word for it.

After we lost at Bristol City shortly before the Christmas period, we went on a brilliant run going twelve matches unbeaten before losing, 2-1, at home to Bradford City, who were now on a fine run of their own. We lost at Oxford by the same score two games later, but then won seven and drew one of our next eight matches before losing our forty-third game of the season, 1-0 at Portsmouth.

We could be forgiven for our loss on the south coast as the previous two matches, home to both Cardiff and Walsall, were over the Easter period which we went into knowing that four points from the two games would guarantee us promotion. We had no problem seeing off Cardiff 3-1, with the goals coming from Walters, Moy and substitute Bailey. Easter Monday was a slightly different matter with Walsall proving resilient and ambitious in equal measure. Pat Stuart, signed on loan from Arsenal after some nervy performances from Rob Keen, was our hero with a penalty save and several other excellent stops. Not surprisingly, we were tentative for much of the game until Bell headed home from a free-kick. Which I took.

We celebrated long and hard on Monday night, didn't train on Tuesday and some of us met for a meal that night and found ourselves celebrating again on Wednesday and were somewhat jaded when we travelled to Portsmouth. After that, there were just three games left and we picked up maximum points against good opposition—Tranmere (1-0), Wrexham (3-0) and Brentford (2-1)—to ensure we would be flying the Champions' pennant at Wood Lane the following season.

We had gone from applying for re-election to the Second Division in just two seasons which meant we were still on target to achieve Roger Palmer's target of First Division football within five years.

Talking of Roger Palmer, he organised and paid for us all to go to Spain for a week to celebrate promotion. Wives/girlfriends/partners not invited which didn't go down well in some quarters. It was no problem for me as, apart from a fun but short-lived fling, I was still single. Saunders, Riley, Adams and Campbell all came, and we had a great time, if the size of the bar bills were anything to go by. And they are usually a reasonable gauge.

It wasn't all play though. Palmer and Saunders sat down with me—and several others throughout the course of the stay—to discuss my contract. I had been thinking about this for a while and considered myself to be in a position of some strength. I had had a very good season, playing in every game, was seen as our dead ball specialist and with Moy missing several matches and Bamford being sold (more of that later) I had been voted both the players' and fans' player of the season.

We had a long discussion over a relaxed tapas lunch and a "couple" of bottles of excellent wine, and spoke about the club in general, as well as my expectations and hopes. Interestingly, they asked for my opinion on a number of matters and buoyed by this and fortified by the wine I plucked up the courage to express my disappointment with how the club had handled the Steve Bamford "affair." I also volunteered my concerns about Iain Moy—more about him later as well.

"Let's just say we learned some harsh lessons as far as Bamford is concerned," said Saunders. Palmer, who I was beginning to realise had a huge capacity for wine but never seemed drunk, said: "I'm sure you've noticed that David Bennett isn't on this trip." I had but simply thought that bringing him would have been a waste of money—I couldn't imagine our Secretary in shorts, spending several hours propping up a bar and then indulging in what is loosely described as horseplay.

"He didn't cover himself in glory and he's not quite what I want for that position so I'm in the process of replacing him. He knows, and I've got someone else lined up. It's all under control," added Palmer. "And that's all off the record. Now, let's get another bottle of wine and cut to the chase."

I was beginning to worry that if we drank much more I would either forget or be incapable of saying what had been on my mind for several weeks. I started by saying I wanted a long-term contract, my wages doubled—and reviewed at the end of every season—a promotion bonus and bonus payments for various achievements.

Saunders almost choked on his chorizo. "Fuck off, Ed," he blurted. Palmer, more of a diplomat and politician, said: "That is pushing things a bit far, Ed."

"Your promotion bonus is this trip and everything you are putting down your throat while you're here. Doubling your wages simply isn't going to happen. We want to extend your contract and you will obviously get improved terms as a result of that. I know some clubs throw out bonus payments like confetti but I don't run my businesses like that. However, there is one area, we would like to talk through with you."

He handed over to Saunders who outlined his thoughts for the next season. They were far-reaching. He needed to overhaul the squad. A couple of keepers were needed, probably another central defender because Les Oldfield was unlikely to play every game, additional midfield strength was required as Don Tyler was going to be off-loaded, we needed to consider extra forwards as there were concerns about Moy, and although John Halliday had done well, he was also mindful he had struggled at the higher level before.

I was very surprised by some of his comments but then came the real bombshell. Dave Walters wasn't part of his plans, at least he didn't see him playing often. His trusted on field lieutenant, who had followed him from Doncaster, was apparently too old and too slow for the Second Division. This meant we needed a new skipper. That was going to be me. I thought Walters had been excellent for us and was really surprised by what Saunders was saying, but his judgement had been pretty damn good so far.

I was chuffed to be offered the captaincy which came with an extra few quid a week. Saunders said he would be talking to Walters when we got home. I also left the meeting with a thirty per cent wage rise, a three-year contract extension and a car allowance. "Our club captain shouldn't be seen driving around in a shitty old Rover," laughed Palmer. Other details for the whole squad would be announced once the new Club Secretary was in place and… the club coach was going to be upgraded.

We shook hands. Palmer ordered another bottle.

Half an hour later I wobbled my way back to my room, slept and showered and met the others in the bar. I had already had enough booze for one day, but I felt like celebrating. I wasn't very lively the next morning, but the hangover was worth it. I was very happy with my deal. So, I discovered later, were Palmer and Saunders.

Chapter Two
Stuck in Second and the Road to Goodison Park

Our new Club Secretary was Peter Christie who Roger Palmer had head-hunted. He was a lot younger than David Bennett and let's say seemed more in tune with the modern world and today's football environment. One of my first conversations with him was when he told me Dave Craig of The Observer wanted to interview me—something Saunders had already sanctioned.

I wasn't delighted—I had never really been a fan of Craig but then I had never really spoken to him either. I rang Craig, who explained he wanted to write a feature about the new captain and suggested we met for supper, a suggestion which meant he immediately went way up in my estimation.

He proved to be witty and more knowledgeable than I had expected, and I enjoyed his company. However, I hadn't given much thought to what he might ask or how I should answer and I hadn't been briefed by Saunders or Christie. Craig asked me what I thought our promotion prospects were. At this stage with players still due to come in and go out of the club, I thought they were non-existent but assumed there was a "party line" I needed to tow. I waffled for a while.

Craig then asked about projected signings, which I had no reason to know anything about. He dropped some names into the conversation saying he had heard rumours Saunders was interested in them. Christ, I thought, if any of them sign for us we are going places but he was obviously fishing. I told Craig of my admiration for Saunders and his excellent recruitment record and how approachable Palmer was (when he was in the country). I also spoke about how great it was to have three local youngsters—Davies, Aitken and yours truly—in the side and he wrote a decent feature based around all this.

Dave Walters, who I was replacing as captain, had wished me luck after Saunders had broken the news to him. "I don't agree with what he said about me as a player and I'm going to prove him wrong, but I wish you well. Feel free to come and talk if you feel the need." I liked Walters even more after this conversation and I genuinely hoped he did prove Saunders wrong. If he did, the manager would be the first to admit it.

Saunders also spoke to me about the captaincy. "I like the fact that you ask questions and express an opinion. Feel free to continue but just use your common sense about where and when you say things. I'm not looking for a squirrel in the nest, but you are a go-between between the players and me. If there are problems brewing, I want to know."

It wasn't an easy summer for Saunders. Rob Riley, who had been a very strong number two, had made no secret of the fact that he wanted to be a manager and when Mansfield came calling, he accepted their offer. Pat Stuart decided to go back to Arsenal and fight for the first team spot—fortunately, Rob Keen was still with us, but we needed a back-up. And finding additional midfield support proved difficult. Mark Bailey, who joined the coaching staff when Riley left, suggested going back to his old club Luton Town and signing his younger brother but Saunders didn't rate him highly enough.

We had just five midfielders which included the now unfancied Walters and Tyler whose form, confidence and fitness had nose-dived. We had expected him to leave but there were no interested parties. It seemed no time since he was one of our most prized assets. That was because it wasn't.

Finding a new central defender wasn't as hard as convincing the individual to join us. Finally, after weeks of chasing and talks, Mick Egan signed for us from Linfield, the part-timers from near Belfast. Saunders said he was quiet and unassuming. Egan made Moy seem like a shrinking violet and was all raw aggression and testosterone on and off the field. You could hear him a mile away which at least gave us the chance to escape from the room he was approaching. When we discovered he had prevaricated about joining because his mum was worried about him "leaving home" he copped a huge amount of stick, but it made no difference.

Nothing wrong-footed him. He wasn't easy to warm to but he either didn't care or was oblivious to the fact that he irritated everyone. His performances, however, were excellent and his partnership with Bell just as good, I don't remember Egan losing a header all season. How Saunders unearthed these rough diamonds I have no idea, but he deserves huge credit for doing so.

Promotion to the Second Division certainly had its benefits. No more Skegness—we went instead to nearby Bisham Abbey where England trained, and we trained with the ball on the pitches there as well as concentrating on our fitness. A modern coach as opposed to the near-vintage model transported us and we even travelled to some away games by train. There was also an upgrade on the hotels we stayed at—not five-star by any means but no longer doss houses either. Definitely a couple of rungs further up the hospitality ladder than we were used to.

On the field, though, we were treading water for the first time for three seasons. There were some excellent performances, one or two sobering defeats and although we finished a very respectable eighth, we were never in the running for promotion. But there was a feeling this season was simply a dress rehearsal for a full-on promotion campaign the next. Once again, the back four was excellent, Rob Keen who replaced Steve Bamford when he left for Huddersfield, did OK but made the occasional costly error—punching a corner into his own net when under no pressure against Rotherham is memorable for the wrong reasons—and reinforced the view, my view at least, we needed a new number one.

Rob Davies and Pete Aitken were creating headlines and interest with their skill, pace and goals and if we didn't go up soon, they wouldn't be with us much longer. The new forward partnership of Jimmy Seal and John Halliday, who certainly wasn't out of his depth at this level this time round, also worked well. Alan Deakin replaced Seal when the ex-Hammer was injured and did well enough. Iain Moy only featured rarely due to a combination of injury, palpable lack of fitness and off-field issues.

As soon as he realised he wasn't starting the season in the team, he hit the booze big time rather than trying to get his place back. The second central midfield position tended to alternate between Walters and Tyler, which made life difficult for me. When I mentioned to Saunders I felt he should stick with one or the other, I was put in my place in no uncertain terms. Given I didn't say this in front of anyone else I thought I had used my common sense as ordered.

The last couple of seasons had seen us treat both the League and FA Cups almost as afterthoughts. In fact, we had been knocked out of both before the leaves had thought about turning colour let alone falling from the trees. It was the same again this season in the League Cup when we again fell at the first hurdle to fellow Second Division outfit Bolton Wanderers.

Things went a bit better in the FA Cup.

Now we were in the Second Division, we were excluded until the Third Round (the Second Round in the League Cup) when we had a tricky away tie at Third Division Gillingham, scraping a 1-1 draw before winning the replay 2-0. Seal scored all three goals. Next up a home tie against our old friends from Yorkshire, Bradford City, who were less potent than the last time we met them. I opened the scoring while Green and Halliday also netted in a surprisingly easy 3-0 win.

Our Fifth Round opponents were First Division Coventry City, as usual fighting against relegation, and we felt home advantage could well give us the edge. But they were a step-up in class, and we struggled to get any sort of foothold in the game for the first thirty minutes with Gerry Daly, their Irish international midfielder, pulling all the strings. We couldn't get close to him, while Mick Ferguson who led the front line was also a real handful and obviously fancied his chances against Rob Keen as he shot on sight. At half-time, we were 2-0 down and had been thoroughly outplayed but then put in a great second half showing and Seal and Deakin, a half-time substitute for the unusually subdued Halliday, scored to give us a just-about deserved draw.

Going to Highfield Road for the replay was an eye-opener. Coventry's home ground may not have been the plushest in the division, but the facilities were so much better than those at Wood Lane, considered one of the best grounds in the second tier. If we were to go up, Roger Palmer would again have to splash the cash off the field as well as on it.

Rob Davies slalomed through the Coventry defence in the early minutes to put us ahead and that seemed to suck all the energy and confidence out of the home side until Ferguson bagged a lucky equaliser. Ten minutes from time a corner from Davies was headed home by Egan, who was suddenly the most popular member of the squad.

We were in the quarter-finals for the first time. In fact, we had never even been in the Fifth Round before let alone the last eight. Although we weren't due to go in for training the next morning, we all went to Wood Lane and crowded round a radio for the draw.

Everton. Away. In three weeks.

Goodison Park, Liverpool. Saturday, 8 March 1981. Everton v Northtown United. FA Cup quarter-final.

This is the biggest match in the club's history. It's also the biggest match any of us has played in. Even those a bit longer in the tooth and who have played for bigger clubs haven't played in an FA Cup quarter-final. And there are only a couple who have played at grounds as big and atmospheric as Goodison Park, which averages over 40,000 fans for every home match.

Roger Palmer, not surprisingly, has made it back from Spain. He and the Club Secretary, Peter Christie, have organised the trip, which includes all the directors. Funny how the glamour of Goodison appeals while the wilds of Hartlepool don't. We are travelling by train, direct from Northtown to Liverpool, and are doing so in style with a First Class carriage reserved for us.

The entire first team squad, with the exception of the listless Iain Moy is travelling. Saunders knows his side (he says), but he and Palmer think everyone, even if like Les Oldfield they have no chance of playing, should sample and savour the occasion. They have deserved it.

The train takes the strain for three hours. The directors enjoy the Full English breakfast, the price of which is included in the ticket. The players drink tea, coffee or water and munch on the complimentary biscuits. I stare out of the window and think about my upcoming duel with a First Division midfield. I wonder how Bell and Egan will cope with the international attack of Bob Latchford and Joe McBride. Will Seal and Halliday get any change out of the central defensive pairing of Kevin Ratcliffe and Mick Lyons, both of whom eat children for breakfast. Raw.

We book into a very comfortable hotel. It must be costing a pretty penny but then again this is our sixth game in the competition so we will have made a few bob. After checking-in and eating yet another light lunch—if I had a quid for every poached egg I ate during my career I would not need to write this book—I get a message from Saunders asking me to go to his room. Andy Adams and Mark Bailey are also there. "Tomorrow's team," says Saunders. I'm intrigued as I've never been involved in team selection discussions before. "I'm going for Tyler in central midfield rather than Walters and Seal and Deakin in attack. Walters or Halliday will be on the bench."

Saunders had told me to express my opinion and I presumed I could do so in front of AA and Mike, despite our recent spat. "Boss, I think Walters is a better player than Tyler and central midfield is his natural position. Walters and I play better together than me and Tyler. I also think Seal and Deakin are too similar." Bailey and Adams have differing opinions. Saunders is adamant Seal and Deakin will play. "Their mobility will be useful against Lyons." But I can see he's torn between Tyler and Walters. I've never known him indecisive like this. Nerves getting to him as well? "I'll sleep on it," he says.

We have a team meeting late afternoon where, as ever, we talk about our strengths and how we will play. Bailey and Adams spend a few minutes telling us about Everton. They don't talk too much about their strengths, probably they're worried we will be intimidated given their team is littered with internationals past and present.

"What's the team Boss?" asks Tommy Butler. "We'll talk after breakfast," says Saunders before making a quick exit. "What's happening, Ed? You were in the meeting with him. Who's playing?" There were a load of questions and I can't decide whether to stay with everyone or do a Saunders and beat a hasty retreat to my room which would be interpreted by everyone that I know the team. I stay with them and try and dead bat the questions.

The morning of the match brings bad news. Walters has been up for much of the night with a bug and is feeling so grim he doesn't even travel to the ground. So Tyler plays. Halliday is told, in private, he's on the bench. "I gave the Boss some shit, even though I know he's picking what he thinks is the best side for the match. But I reckon I could have done OK against their defenders. I can't say I'm happy. You knew didn't you?" There doesn't seem much point in lying. "I did John, but it's not my job to tell you. I did say I thought you should play." I don't think Halliday believes me.

We take to the Goodison Park pitch as the theme from Z-Cars greets the home team. The loudest PA system in the land announces today's visitors will be represented by Rob Keen, Tommy Butler, Mick Egan, Terry Bell, Terry Green, Pete Aitken, Don Tyler, Ed Roberts, Rob Davies, Jimmy Seal and Alan Deakin. Substitute, John Halliday. The Match of the Day cameras are here. It hadn't occurred to me that they would be.

Much as Coventry had done a few weeks earlier, Everton come at us from the off. They are having a middle-of-the-road season in the First Division but still have quality all over the pitch. I'm going toe-to-toe with Steve McMahon, a renowned tough tackler, who is being talked about as a potential England international. He's not the sort to take any prisoners and dumps me, unceremoniously, on my backside in the opening moments. A "don't-get-above-yourself" type of challenge. We spend the opening twenty minutes fire-fighting and struggle to get much possession but Everton don't create any noteworthy chances and we ride out the initial storm.

Then an Everton attack breaks down and Butler thumps the ball in the general direction of Aitken who turns on the retros and gets to it ahead of Lyons, skipping past his crude lunge. Having been pinned in our own half for so long there is no one in support, so Aitken puts his head down and carries the ball towards the Everton goal as Ratcliffe backs off him.

Almost resigned to the fact there is nothing else to do he lets fly from twenty-odd yards and the ball arrows into the top corner, leaving Martin Hodge clutching thin air. One hell of a goal and scored right in front of our supporters. We just about manage to catch Aitken before he is engulfed by the fans.

We are still 1-0 up at half-time. And after an hour. And after seventy-five minutes. We give as good as we get in the second half. Everton are getting tetchy with each other as well as us. McMahon leaves his foot in on me, and I trip him a few minutes later and have my name taken. Saunders decides to try and shut up shop. Deakin, who has run miles for the cause, comes off. Seal drops into midfield. Halliday is left to battle it out up front on his own but hardly touches the ball as Everton lay siege... and equalise.

Just five minutes from time Bob Latchford, a late substitute, slides the ball home after a scramble in the six-yard box. We claim a push on Keen but really it's our disappointment making the appeal. We almost lose when Bell attempts to head clear but sends the ball, at speed, towards his own goal. "Fuck," I think as the ball is destined for the top corner. Suddenly and from nowhere, a gloved hand appears and Keen, flying through the air, touches the ball over the bar. Brilliant stop.

We should have won. We could have lost. We'll take the draw.

We are all despondent on the train back to Northtown. Palmer brings wine, beer, champagne into the carriage and we have a few drinks. All except Dave Walters who looks as sick as a dog despite the care and attention of Laurie Campbell.

Whatever it is that has struck down, Walters is doing the rounds. By the time of Wednesday's replay, Bell and Deakin have both become regular visitors to the toilet and are spending lengthy periods in there. This calls for a considerable rethink on the part of Saunders and highlights the squad's lack of depth. Things get worse an hour before kick-off when Tyler makes a beeline for the toilets and is heard throwing up. Oldfield comes in for Bell, Seal drops into midfield, Halliday and Moy, who thought he would be a spectator, come into attack.

We play well but not quite well enough and Everton win with a goal in each half through Latchford and Asa Hartford. Our FA Cup journey is over. We slump in the dressing room. Heads down. Some reckon we would have won but for the mystery bug. I disagree. Everton had better players than us. We have certainly learned that if we do win promotion we will need far more quality and greater depth to the squad. Playing at the likes of Everton and Coventry, currently two of the lesser lights of the First Division, has whetted the appetite for the big time. I can't imagine what it would be like playing Manchester United or Liverpool, Spurs or Arsenal.

I'm hell bent on finding out.

Once we lost to Everton the season fizzled out. We had never been in contention for promotion and now we were out of the Cup we played with a new-found freedom for a while and won three games on the bounce before running out of steam which coincided with Iain Moy leaving the club. Spiky character though he could be his leaving created a sort of funereal atmosphere around Wood Lane and the training ground.

Saunders and his staff did their best to keep us focused but our final four games finished in two draws and two defeats and a final position of eighth with forty-three points from forty-two games. Respectable enough for our first season in Division Two, if a little underwhelming given the impetus we had gained over the last couple of seasons. But we were looking forward to the start of the 1981-82 season; it was as if we had subconsciously decided this was the campaign that would see us win promotion to the First Division.

Before the season ended, Saunders reached an agreement to sign Andy Hopkins, the Grimsby goalkeeper who had enjoyed a superb game against us a couple of seasons ago. The news of Hopkins' signing did little for Rob Keen's confidence and self-esteem and even less for his demeanour. Saunders maintained the two of them would fight it out for the number one jersey, but Keen was adamant it signalled the end of his time with the club. He didn't tell me as much, probably because I was skipper, but word of his disappointment got back to me. I have always believed that if you want to be successful you need a top-notch keeper and Rob, in my opinion, was very useful but not top-drawer.

If I was delighted by the signing of Hopkins, I was intrigued by the capture of Ross Davison from First Division Southampton, given he was a midfielder, which I learned about when I was on holiday. My new partner Tina (more of her later) read it first saying: "you've got a new playmate" and passed me the paper. The signing was good news for me, I hoped, as I had found it hard with Saunders chopping and changing between Tyler and Walters, two very different kinds of player, as my partner. Davison had a reputation as a tough competitor who wins the ball and gives it to a teammate leaving them to get on with it. I had no problems with that.

While I lay on my sun lounger doing the square root of absolutely sod all, I hoped Saunders was busy working on other signings with First Division experience. We had some good young players coming through, but we were still short of numbers and if we were going to make a realistic assault on promotion, we needed players who knew their way around the top two divisions. Up front we had only three forwards in Seal, Deakin and Halliday, while the back four was excellent but only had Les Oldfield as an experienced reserve, Kevin Marr deciding to retire and run a country pub, which is what a lot of retired footballers did back then.

With the signings of Hopkins and Davison, we had a first team squad of sixteen and that included a disaffected goalkeeper and the likelihood that one of Tyler or Walters, possibly both, could leave. Without more numbers we would be trying to fit round pegs into square holes when injuries and suspensions kicked in. And that, so Saunders had told us, was not his way.

Chapter Three
Own Goals

Things had been going well on the pitch and it appeared most of us were relatively happy campers off it as well. But you never can tell.

It's natural there will be a few who aren't happy with their lot, but these tend to be the players not seeing first team action. Then again, if you have a small squad, which we did, there are presumably going to be fewer dissenters. And contrary to popular belief footballers also suffer from personal issues just as everyone else does. During the course of the season, Iain Moy and Steve Bamford found themselves unhappy for different reasons—with Moy there had been numerous warning signs whereas Bamford was an established first team player one moment and signing for another club the next.

Iain Moy was a colourful character. Complex would also describe him. Some would say he was (with all due respect) a not untypical Scotsman… liked a drink, enjoyed a bet, thought he was God's gift to women, volatile at times, charming at others. Quite often felt the world was against him, didn't let too many people get close to him.

When he signed for us, there were rumours that the club had not only paid Clydebank for his services but had also settled a debt with a local bookie. None of us would have been surprised and if you can get someone else to settle your debts then you're canny as well. Not always easy to understand, apart from the F-word which featured large in his vocabulary. Quick with a joke and backchat. As I say, a not untypical Scotsman.

He was more than happy to move south of the border even if it initially meant only playing in the Fourth Division because—and again with all due respect— the Fourth Division represented a fair step-up from the mid-table obscurity of Scottish League II. Although he'd bagged quite a few goals for Cowdenbeath, none of us had heard of him and a few eyebrows were raised when news broke of his signing; it wasn't as if we were landing the next Denis Law.

It's also fair to say that Moy's first few days at the club weren't what he was expecting, he swopped a small coalfield town on the east coast of Scotland for a desolate, windy town on the east coast of England. And let's just say that although Moy knew he had to make a favourable impression with the powers-that-be, he was obviously more interested in running short distances, such as a couple of yards, rather than the long-distance loneliness we were subjected to at Skegness.

Fitness didn't appear to be something they were big on at Cowdenbeath and Moy certainly didn't take it upon himself to improve his condition. Although I never saw him eat a deep-fried Mars bar, he would take junk food over the healthy option every day of the week and admitted that his four days at Skegness was the longest he had been without an alcoholic drink since he was "wee." Although he was a willing participant at the players' weekly dinners introduced by Dave Walters, he considered pasta as "posh nosh." Having declared that wine was for "ponces" he quickly changed his mind and was as happy with a glass of red in his hand as he was with a pint of heavy. As long as it was a large glass.

Once we started training with a ball it was obvious he had something about him, and Tony Saunders deserves credit for signing him. Moy was slightly chunky but given he was also short it was hard work for defenders to get the ball off him. He was strong and surprisingly quick over the first few yards, good in the air for his size and loved scoring goals.

He found it hard to adapt to England in the early weeks and spent a lot of his spare time in the pub. He was earning far more money here than at Cowdenbeath but was keen to keep that quiet as he had a daughter—the result of a one-night stand—and didn't want her mother chasing him for more money. "I'm putting money aside for the bairn but her mother's not getting a penny," he kept telling us. That was the polite version.

Moy wasn't the worst trainer I've seen nor was he totally dedicated to it. He had good and bad days. The bad days would see him send teammates flying with fierce tackles and using his elbows as if he were playing in a match rather than training with his colleagues. He would also get in teammates' faces if he thought they had challenged him too hard. Some thought these days followed a night on the booze and he was working his way through a hangover.

The problem for Iain was that football was changing and even in the early 1980s he was becoming something of a throwback even if the game was full of fabulous footballers and flamboyant characters, often described as "mavericks." Alan Hudson, Tony Currie, Stan Bowles, Charlie George, Frank Worthington and a host of others were genuine entertainers on the pitch and went their own way off it. They were rarely trusted at international level and the fact that this famous five clocked up just over thirty caps between them is both testament to that and a crime against English football.

I'm not for one moment putting Iain Moy in the same league as those players—or anywhere near the Scottish mavericks like Jim Baxter, Jimmy Johnstone and Willie Henderson—but he was similar in that he didn't always play to instructions but got away with it because the end product was fruitful. There were times Saunders was pulling out his hair and probably thinking of hauling him off but then Moy would go past three defenders and stick the ball into the top corner.

Off the pitch Moy, like those mentioned above, did what he wanted. He was less colourful than the others and there were times when he was downright miserable and poor company but following rules wasn't part of his make-up. For example, where most of us followed Saunders' law regarding when to drink, Moy had made it known to most of us that he would have a drink "when I wanna fuckin' drink."

He could be contrary as well. Whereas figures of authority were usually scoffed at or completely ignored he wouldn't hear a word said against Saunders. "He's given me the chance to make a proper living outta the game. You wait, one day I'll score the winning goal against you bastard English at Wembley and I'll give my shirt to the Boss." He believed he would too.

But he was no fool and would have known the game was changing and was beginning to be "infiltrated" by individuals who thought more about their diet—solids and fluids—and fitness levels. Pasta and salad rather than pie and chips after a few pints of heavy was fast becoming the norm. Moy, I think, was bloody-minded enough to believe he could do what he wanted and that his natural striking instincts would see him through. He needed to change but there was as much chance of that happening as there was of Scotland winning the World Cup.

The one time we all really saw him lose it was when Saunders dropped him for the Boxing Day fixture against league leaders Bradford City a couple of years before. I thought it was an odd decision because although he hadn't been scoring, he had been receiving poor service and support. Still, as I was also dropped, I didn't dwell too much on the concerns of Iain Moy but whereas I kept my thoughts to myself, Iain let everyone know how unhappy he was. Interestingly, and again showing his loyalty to Saunders, when Dave Craig asked him for a quote on being dropped, he told the reporter to "get outta my fuckin' face."

Being put on the bench had the desired effect and once he was back on the pitch he was a different player for the rest of the season, and we would not have gone up without him. He was easily my player of the season that year. Although there were times when he withdrew and didn't welcome company, I found him a very interesting character and got on with him better than most but he never "let me in."

I was sorely tempted go on holiday with him and Steamy Windows at the end of our Fourth Division promotion season and if I hadn't had to sort out a number of personal issues I may well have found it impossible to resist. I'm glad I did have things to attend to—he and Steamy came back obviously out of condition and were put through hell at Skegness. It was when Iain returned from his holiday that people first noticed a change in him and not just a physical one. He had become even more surly and sarcastic and was sometimes downright unpleasant. There were rumours something unsavoury had gone on while they were away; Steamy claimed they had enjoyed themselves and over-indulged. Nothing more.

We began the season really well and Moy was looking sharp and scoring goals for fun until he was sent off at Bradford. Everyone was surprised that after serving his suspension he didn't bat an eyelid at being left on the subs' bench. "The other guys are doing good. I cannae just walk back into the team," he said. Twelve months previously he would have been knocking Saunders' office door off its hinges to tell him he should be playing, and neither was Moy the kind of character who thought he would get back in the team by being quiet and accepting. When I asked him if he was OK and whether he fancied a drink and a chat he simply said, "I'm fine Eddie, son. I don't need looking after."

I knew him well enough to know that meant the conversation was at an end. But I wish I had pushed Iain at this stage and regret I didn't. Everyone recognised he had changed for the worse in a matter of just a few weeks. As skipper, albeit a young one, perhaps I should have taken more responsibility. But his change was there for everyone to see and the manager or his staff could have spoken to him as well. These days a psychiatrist would be no doubt be consulted; back then the club, in general, failed him.

Steve Bamford had been an excellent buy. He came from Cardiff City where he commuted between the first team and the reserves but went straight into our first team as a replacement for the long-serving and fast-deteriorating Mike Williams. He had missed only a handful of games since, due to a finger injury, and had made even fewer mistakes.

He was, in my opinion, as important to us as Iain Moy. Quiet off the field he was a classic example of someone whose character changes as soon as they "step over the white line." Keepers need to communicate, and Steve did this in no uncertain terms, and everyone who played in or watched our matches heard his voice booming around the grounds. He was exactly the same in training. But once a match or training was over, he retreated back into his shell and spent as much time as possible with his young wife and baby daughter.

He also cared passionately about the game and would spend hours considering his performance, going over every goal he conceded analysing whether he could have done better, and having long and intense conversations with all his defenders. Everyone liked him and rated him very highly. Top-notch keepers don't grow on trees.

So it came as a huge surprise to hear he had been dropped in early February 1981, a decision which obviously wasn't performance-related. When he signed, Steve was only offered an eighteen-month contract which he turned down and was then offered a two-year deal. Such were his performances it seemed obvious the club should have tied him down to a long-term deal, but this hadn't happened.

He had also learned that he was paid less than the vast majority of the first team squad and had been to see Saunders about improved terms. Saunders had sent him to see the Club Secretary, David Bennett, who refused to consider increasing his salary until his contract renewal discussions at the end of the season. A fatal error.

Bamford, not surprisingly, was unimpressed with the whole situation including the fact he had to deal directly with Bennett and felt he didn't have the support of Saunders. He had obviously voiced his frustrations to old friends at Cardiff and word had got out leading to Second Division Huddersfield Town, managed by a former Cardiff player, putting in a bid for him.

The club turned it down, but Bamford knew what was going on and told Saunders after training one day that he wanted to sign for the Terriers. All this was going on without anyone else hearing about it, but the dirty linen was washed in public in The Observer, which told its readers that Bamford was in dispute with the club and was therefore dropped from the next day's home game against Portsmouth.

"I earn more here than at Cardiff but not a lot more and the standard of living is a hell of a lot higher. With a wife and kid, it's a struggle," he told a few of us. "For some reason, I'm earning less than everyone else and Huddersfield are offering really good money. But I still want to play for Northtown. If they can get close to matching Huddersfield, I will stay."

One way or another it was obvious that Rob Keen would be playing the next day and, quite possibly, for the foreseeable future. He had done well enough the previous season when he played but he wasn't in the same league as Bamford. There were further behind-the-scenes discussions between Bamford, Bennett and belatedly, Saunders, but the club's improved and best offer didn't get close to Huddersfield's. Within one week of the story appearing in The Observer Bamford had signed for the Yorkshire outfit leaving us with just one frontline keeper. How much the club received for Steve wasn't disclosed but it should have been a hell of a lot more than it paid for him.

The club, which had undoubtedly been negligent, deservedly got a lot of criticism from fans. This hadn't been an early case of player power or someone thinking he was bigger than the club and had Bennett agreed to give Bamford deserved parity with his teammates when they first met, he would have remained our player. I knew from experience that Bennett didn't like parting with the club's money or lowering himself to negotiating with footballers. Saunders should have been involved.

I thought back to when I had asked for time to think about the club's offer to me and that I emerged with a better deal but only after discussions with the owner and manager. It was hard to believe such an excellent keeper wasn't granted better terms and was allowed to leave. I also wondered what my end-of-season discussions would bring.

Keen did OK, but he didn't command the area the way Steve had and there were a couple of goals he conceded Bamford would have stopped. With keepers, it's sometimes about what you don't save rather than mistakes or saves made. Keen played the first dozen games following Bamford's departure but then made way for Arsenal's Pat Stuart who, having recovered from a long-term knee injury, needed playing time.

He excelled in the remaining nine matches and the hope was Saunders would be able to turn his move into a permanent one. Keen, meanwhile, continued to train hard but made it known he wanted away at the end of the season. I told him he should concentrate on being our number one next season and watch and learn as much as he could from Stuart. "I'm spending too much time here sitting on my arse," he said. One way or another we were going to need one if not two new keepers.

Chapter Four
Captain's Log

I had been delighted when I was made captain. Although I had been playing very well, I thought the appointment cemented my place in the team, gave me responsibility which I enjoyed and made me feel good about myself. I might have been one of the youngest members of the side but I believed my form had earned respect from my teammates.

With the captain's armband came some off-the-field responsibilities including representing the club at the occasional function. I was told I would have to attend "about four events" which I was relaxed about. In fact, they turned out to be hugely beneficial.

The first was at the local Honda dealer which had supplied me with my Prelude and had engineered a deal to ensure it was well within my budget. When they launched another new model, I was asked to attend the introductory event and "press the flesh" and although all I know about cars is if I like how they look or not and where to put the petrol, I was happy to do so and enjoyed the event as I met some interesting businesspeople and supporters I wouldn't have done had I been holed up in my flat. One of the former, who was also a long-time fan, was a financial consultant called Steve Russell. We got on very well and arranged to meet for a drink and dinner when our diaries allowed.

Driving home I reflected on how awkward I had found my first contract negotiation and although I had emerged with a much-enhanced deal I had occasionally wondered if I had sold myself short and not pushed Roger Palmer hard enough. I felt my stock within both the club and the game had risen since then and resolved to ask Russell for his advice when we met. I wanted to be well prepared when I sat down with Palmer again at the end of the season.

A couple of months after the Honda event I was asked to attend an open evening at The Observer and to talk about the relationship between the club and the newspaper. Tony Saunders had initially been approached but—fortunately, as it turned out—he told them to ask me. I was to do a double act with Dave Craig, and I entered The Observer offices looking forward to the session. Everything went well and I was more than happy to hang around for a couple of hours afterwards talking to readers, supporters and critics.

I couldn't help noticing a tall, slim, very attractive blonde girl about my age in one of the groups which had gathered. It transpired that Tina was a football fan, occasional visitor to Wood Lane and was one of The Observer's reporters. I arranged tickets for her and a friend for the coming Saturday's home match against Derby County. I also suggested going somewhere after the match. "We'll see," was the non-committal response. I hoped Tina's friend was female and that she would have to rush off as soon as the final whistle sounded. I was rather taken by Tina.

We beat Derby 2-1 in a scrappy match, and I did OK although I certainly didn't emerge as Northtown's super hero. Tina and her (female) friend were in the area reserved for players and their guests. "Six out of ten," said Tina as I went to say hello. "Just above average." Her friend laughed. I smiled. When her friend went to "powder her nose," I asked Tina if she was interested in going out that night. "Sorry sunshine, I don't go out with Mr-Just-Above-Average and I do have a previous engagement which I have to honour. Thanks for the tickets and just to let you know I'm working tomorrow." With that, she and her friend were gone but she had made sure I knew where she would be tomorrow.

When I rang The Observer the next day Tina was, of course, unavailable as she was out covering a story. I left a garbled message and phoned again the next day only to learn she was off for a few days. I decided to get my head down and refocus on the football, especially as we had another home match on the Wednesday night when we beat QPR and I had one of my better matches and set up the winning goal for Seal.

As I entered my flat at about 10.30pm the phone rang. "That's more like it. Seven out of ten tonight. Get to eight and we'll have that date." Followed by laughter. I would like to have known where she got my number from, but I didn't have time to ask before she hung up.

Saturday saw us playing at Cambridge United. I thought about asking Dave Craig to mark me as an eight if I had a half-decent match but then he had probably given Tina my number so may have had an inkling of what was going on. We had an excellent 1-0 win to continue our good run and I continued my good form.

In fact, I reckoned I was having my most consistent run of form since I came into the team three years earlier. I made my way into the players' lounge for a quick drink before the journey home and Craig came to talk to me as he did after most matches to get the "skipper's viewpoint." We chatted briefly before he passed me an envelope, with a knowing wink. I suggested he made himself scarce—or words to that effect.

The message in the envelope read: "At last, an eight. It's a date." Cambridge's ground was only fifty miles from Northtown and Tina, who lived with her parents in a village between the two towns, had come to watch.

The question was when would we meet? The answer came early on Sunday morning when she rang, and we agreed to meet for lunch in a country pub. We arranged to meet again later that week and within a few weeks Tina was spending a couple of nights a week at my flat before moving in. The only slight doubt we shared was a potential conflict of interests if a major story about the club broke. We decided that was a bridge we would cross if and when we had to, but we covered our backs to an extent by telling our respective bosses about our relationship.

Not long after we started dating, I was due to meet Steve Russell for dinner. I should point out that before I hung up my boots, I was vigilant about what I ate and on occasions such as this I would just eat a main course and was careful that I wasn't seen in public drinking alcohol. I knew that if I had one glass, I would want another, so I stuck to water. Steve was good company but a salesman by nature and wanted to know if I had spare cash I wanted to invest. If I did, he could help. Naturally.

I did have a few quid which I had been wondering what to do with but wasn't ready to commit it to anyone or anything just yet. From my point of view, I wanted to know if Steve could advise me on my end-of-season meetings with Roger Palmer. I didn't really want these to become an annual event and although I couldn't complain at my lot, I also wanted reassuring I wasn't being short-changed. At this time, players' agents/managers were a new but coming breed and although I wasn't looking for either agent or manager, I thought it was a prudent move to seek advice.

Steve agreed to help if he could and asked me numerous questions about my salary and benefits, but I wasn't happy to reveal these yet. "Jesus Ed, you're like an Italian midfielder playing every ball backwards or sideways." We agreed we would meet again in a few weeks after he had done some digging.

"If you want my honest opinion, they are taking the piss." Steve said when we next met. "I've done a lot of homework on this for you," he told me as I made coffee. I still didn't know him very well and wasn't sure if he made this statement so he could give me a bill, or whether it was to reassure me that he had done a thorough job. "I've found out salary details of a number of captains in the Second, Third and Fourth Divisions, which I think you will find very interesting."

He gave me a document which, without naming the club or player, outlined the salaries and bonuses some captains were earning. "How did you get this information?" I asked. "Ed, it's all legit. Let's just say I know a few people in the game. I don't want to say more than that." If the figures were accurate, I was indeed well down the list. In fact, I was close to the bottom of it. No wonder Roger Palmer and Tony Saunders seemed as pleased as me at the end of that boozy tapas lunch in Spain. We're not talking an Ashley Cole moment when he claimed he almost drove off the road because Arsenal were "only" offering him £55,000 a week but I needed them to know I wasn't a pushover.

I had to decide if the owner and manager had taken advantage of me because I was inexperienced in the art of negotiation or whether they genuinely thought that after only two seasons in the first team and aged twenty, they were paying a salary commensurate with my age and experience. I told Steve about the conversation in Spain. "Should have stuck to your guns and seen what happened," he said. I also had to bear in mind that regardless of these revelations I was well paid and comfortable, but Steve repeated he thought the club was taking advantage and I should let the powers-that-be know. Now.

"And if I do get parity with some of these guys, what will you want out of it?" I demanded. Steve looked at me and told me he would expect a percentage—to be decided—of any rise negotiated and for me to pay him an annual retainer—amount to be decided—which would enable me to call upon him for advice and his financial expertise at any time. What if I negotiated a rise but chose not to tell him about it? "I don't think you would do that but if you did you would lose out on a few sponsorships I could get you, which would be quite lucrative."

I said I wanted time to think. I've always been a passionate believer that people should be paid what they are worth, regardless of circumstances, and I needed to decide if that was the case with me or not. If Russell's figures were accurate, there were Fourth Division captains earning twenty per cent more than me. I also had to decide whether I was going to use Steve as an "agent" or my "representative" and if not, whether to give him anything if I did negotiate a rise. I wasn't prepared to follow Steve's advice and go to the club there and then for talks but I did know that this year's end-of-season conversation would be different to previous discussions.

As Steve went to leave, he produced a piece of folder paper from a pocket and said: "In case you're still wondering about those salaries I showed you, I know what you earn."

I unfolded the piece of paper which had a figure on it. He was spot on.

One night after we had gone to bed, the phone rang. I made my way sluggishly to answer it. "Skip, it's me. I'm in a bad way. I need some help." It took a second before I realised the slurrer on the other end of the line was Iain Moy. For someone who had been as withdrawn and private as him to make a call like that obviously meant he was in trouble. We got on well, but it was the only time he ever phoned me.

Iain said he was at Northtown Police Station after being arrested for drink-driving and I was the "one call he was allowed to make." Alarm bells rang loud and clear. Not only about Iain's state but was this the conflict-of-interest Tina and I had been worried about? Of course, it was.

I went back into the bedroom, told Tina what had happened and said I was leaving to see Moy and may even bring him back here. "No, Ed. Don't bring him back here. I don't want to be exposed to what he will say. It would put me in a really compromising position. And maybe you should let Peter Christie know what's happening." I paused as I dressed. "You're right, I shouldn't bring him back here. Sorry. But he phoned me and I'm going to see him. I'll ring Christie or Saunders in a while. Instinctively though, I knew she was right, and I should have handed this problem over to someone else.

I drove to the police station and met the duty solicitor who had advised Moy, who was more than twice over the legal limit. I didn't know that Moy could drive much less own or have access to a car. He would certainly lose his driving licence and cop a hefty fine.

Moy looked dreadful, a combination of being very drunk and moving into hangover mode, someone who knows he has screwed up big time, is embarrassed by what he's done but also knows there's not just music but a full-blown symphony orchestra yet to be faced. I drove Moy home and opened the fridge to find some food for him. All that lived in there was mould along with some just about drinkable milk, a bottle of tonic water and a shrivelled lemon. Which said it all.

I went to a nearby corner shop and stocked up on fry-up ingredients. I also called Christie from a phone box before letting myself back into Moy's place. He had, of course, crashed out by this time but woke when Christie arrived. They talked while I cooked an unhealthy breakfast for three, although all I could hear was the Secretary asking an occasional question and Moy mumbling a monosyllabic response, which was almost impossible to understand given it was broad Scottish still under the influence.

As we cleared up and Moy stared into space, Christie told me that if anything like this happened again I shouldn't "play the Good Samaritan" but let him know immediately. He would deal with it and would speak to me in good time. If necessary. I received his message loud and clear.

I stayed with Moy after Christie left. He told me the mother of his daughter was chasing him for a load of unpaid maintenance which he didn't have, that he was depressed because he couldn't see himself getting back in the team, he was probably an alcoholic and was in debt "up to my fucking eyeballs."

"I've just lost a load trying to win a load at the casino and even now I want a drink. I know I've got to do something about it, but I don't have a clue where to start." I gave him what I had left in my wallet and wanted to make him promise he wouldn't spend it on drink but thought it wiser not to. "Remember, Christie said he would be in touch so keep an ear open for the phone," I told him.

"No chance. Fucking thing's cut off." His laugh was one of those heaving, chesty coughs betraying a long-time heavy smoker.

Just before I left, I plucked up the courage to ask Moy what had gone on between him and Windows while they had been on holiday. "What do you mean?" he asked, squinting through the smoke of one of his countless cigarettes. "Nothing wrong with a fag, even Bobby Charlton smoked," he once announced when Saunders told him to stop smoking on the team coach. "When you score goals like Bobby Charlton did, you can smoke on the coach," was the Boss' quickfire response.

"You and Steamy used to be very close but you hardly acknowledge each other after your holiday," I said. Moy looked at me and took a long drag. "I've not told anyone else this so if it comes back to me, I'll know you blabbed."

He paused for a while, obviously unsure whether to continue or not. "Let's just say Windows didn't show any interest in chasing girls," he eventually said.

"If I pointed out a good-looking girl on the beach, he would pretend to show an interest but I knew he didn't care. He didn't once comment about a girl and the only time he talked to one was when I was trying to chat up her friend."

"What are you saying, Iain?"

"He's gay," sighed Moy. "I saw him looking at blokes as they paraded up and down the beach in their Speedos. He also went AWOL a few times late at night and told me he had been shagging a bird."

"Maybe he was?" I countered. I wasn't really sure what gay was like but I was pretty sure it wasn't like Steamy.

"Made me start to think," said Moy. "He's always first in the shower and last out. No one has ever seen him with a woman."

"That doesn't make him gay," I protested.

"I know he's fucking queer because I confronted him."

"And he admitted it?"

"Got all centre-half tough with me at first, then teared up and walked off. I didn't see him for over a day. At least, I had thirty-six hours when he wasn't cramping my style. Not that it made any difference. I had more chance of scoring for Scotland."

"You two were always out together," I pointed out. "Didn't you ever suspect?"

Moy sparked up another cigarette. "There were always other people around. Sure, we had a laugh together and got on well but we didn't live in each other's pockets."

I took a glug of tea. "Iain, that doesn't explain why you appear to hate each other, unless you hate homosexuals. He didn't try anything on with you?"

We sat in silence for a few minutes. "Being gay in any environment seems tough," I said. " It can't be easy being around a bunch of testosterone-fuelled athletes."

"He claims he's bisexual but he's gay as far as I'm concerned," retorted Moy. "He knew better than to try anything with me but one night when he was very pissed, he made it clear that if I wanted to experiment, he would be happy to oblige.

"I told him to fuck off and we've hardly spoken since, other than him pleading with me not to tell anyone. He's scared I'll say something and that will be the end of his career, especially with all the talk about Aids."

This was one of the longest conversations I had with Moy. It was also the last. I heard the club sorted out some of Moy's debts and paid up his contract in full. By the time he was banned from driving and fined—the story did appear in The Observer—he was back in Scotland, playing part-time for Clyde and knocking in a few goals for them. He was reunited with his daughter but there was no fairy tale ending as he continued to struggle with the demon drink and died at the age of forty-two.

Iain wasn't the main reason behind our climb up the leagues but he was certainly a significant catalyst for it. When I played in the first team during the 1977-78 season, by and large it comprised of has-beens, no-hopers and don't-carers. As the 1978-79 season dawned and the club was given a much more professional sheen by Roger Palmer and Tony Saunders, Moy was our first noteworthy signing even if he wasn't the healthiest or fittest of specimens.

The supporters had also been desperate for a "terrace hero" and Moy's pugnacious approach allied to his goal-scoring feats endeared him to the fans. Those goals kick-started our rise and he deserves a place in the Northtown Hall of Fame. It was a huge shame his stay with us ended the way it did.

I want to say that my attitude towards Steamy remained the same as it was before Moy divulged his secret and I think that by and large it did. But in the few weeks between Moy telling me and Steamy also leaving the club there were times when I did look at him and found it hard to believe he was gay. This was a man who was vociferous, aggressive (on the field), not afraid of confrontation and never shirked a tough physical challenge. I knew very little about homosexuality but his characteristics didn't seem to fit the general perception of a gay man. Of course, there is no typical stereotype of a gay man but there was back in the 1980s.

Steamy had always been a teammate rather than a mate and I continued to talk to him as I always had and I continued to share the same shower. I'm not being flippant and I'm not trying to prove that I'm an "inclusive" individual but there were plenty of "macho, Alpha-male" footballers who would have ostracised him purely because of his sexuality. And sadly that is still the case.

I always felt there was more to Steamy's departure than met the eye. A Northtown player one moment, a Newport player the next. Unexpected transfers which happened quickly were often the way but I didn't think the pieces quite fitted the puzzle. Dave Walters reckoned Steamy left because Saunders didn't think he was good enough for Second Division football; I have an inkling Steamy asked to leave so he could make a fresh start elsewhere. If that was the case, it was another damning indictment of society's attitudes towards homosexuality.

Steamy did "come out" once he had finished playing and he knows I am writing about him and what I am saying but preferred not to be interviewed. Homosexuality in sport, especially it seems in male sport, remains a stigma which I find surprising in today's supposedly open-minded and understanding society. Very few male footballers have publicly announced they are gay and of course why should they if they don't want to but presumably they don't say anything because they are afraid of the reaction.

Justin Fashanu was the first male footballer to admit he was gay in an interview with The Sun in late 1990 and it was a long time before he was offered a contract by another club. Almost a quarter of a century later Thomas Hitzlsperger, a German international who played in this country for Aston Villa, West Ham and Everton and who had a long-time girlfriend he was intending to marry, announced he was gay. This didn't signal the end his career, though, and he continued to play in Germany and became Head of Sport at VfB Stuttgart.

Did Thomas' announcement cause less of a shockwave due to the passing of time making it less shocking than Justin's revelations which were sensationalised by The Sun as only The Sun can do? Or perhaps Germany is more broad-minded?

It seems to me—and one has to be very careful in this super-sensitive world where everything you say is open to ridiculous misinterpretation and criticism by people who like to misconstrue things—that homosexuality is far more "acceptable" and less shocking in female sport. Is that because more women over the years have admitted their sexual preferences than men?

Megan Rapinhoe, who skippered the United States women's team to World Cup glory in 2019 is gay, while two of her teammates, Ashlyn Harris and Ali Krieger, were engaged and have since married. Across the whole of that tournament, there were over forty female players or coaches who were openly gay or bi-sexual.

At the time of writing, Blackpool's Jake Daniels has become the UK's first active male footballer to come out publicly as gay. Not surprisingly, he spoke about a weight being lifted from his shoulders but also said the subject in men's football is still taboo.

"It comes down to footballers wanting to be known for their masculinity. And people see being gay as being weak," he said. It will be fascinating to see how many others follow in Jake's footsteps.

In the men's 2018 World Cup tournament not a single player or coach admitted to being gay or bi-sexual, but… statistics tells us that one in ten men are gay.

An article headlined "Why are more female professional footballers openly gay or bisexual than male players?" which appeared on Itv.com in July 2019 put forward some interesting thoughts on the subject.

It is not that male football only attracts heterosexual males, or women's football a high ratio of lesbian or bisexual players, but largely due to the differing atmospheres surrounding the two games. "The women's game has a more open-atmosphere at matches, it's more family-orientated," explains Eric Najib, a former player and now manager for Stonewall FC, one of the world's premier LGBT+ football club.

While in men's football, he believes "there's still tribalism attached." Joe White, a co-founder of Three Lions Pride, an LGBT+ England supporters group, agrees, saying: "In the women's game, there's more diversity in the fans, less 'laddish banter'. It's more welcoming, more diverse and open, and this atmosphere is reflected on the pitch as well.

"Conversely, in the men's game there's more racism, sexism and homophobia," he adds.

Chapter Five
Blotts on the Landscape

Rob Davies was one hell of a player. He had come into the side as an eighteen-year-old and had been hugely influential in both our promotions. He was naturally left-footed, quick and skilful. He liked nothing more than to get the ball and run at pace, direct at defenders and in Divisions Three and Four there weren't many who could cope with that. He created at least a dozen goals a season, maybe more, and he weighed in with a fair few of his own.

It was a good job he was also brave because there were plenty of defenders in the lower divisions who simply kicked lumps out of him—quite often off the ball given they couldn't get near him when he had it. His shins and ankles were usually decorated with as many colours as a Dulux paint card and he was left out of the side on a couple of occasions simply to protect him from further damage. But Rob didn't complain about the treatment dished out to him nor did he moan when he was rested. Although you could tell, he was disappointed.

My feeling as soon as he became a first team regular was that sooner rather than later Rob would outgrow the club and one of the big boys would come calling for him and make an offer Roger Palmer couldn't refuse. So it came as no surprise when I read in The Observer and some of the nationals a couple of weeks before we were due to report back for training for the 1981-82 season, that First Division Manchester City had made an offer for him.

Whereas I had heard about us signing Davison while I was lying in the sun, news of the offer for Davies came when I was back home and kicking my heels before pre-season training kicked off. I phoned Dave Craig and asked him how serious City were about signing Rob. "You can believe everything I write, Ed," he chortled. " But as I understand it, they've put in a bid and the Board is discussing it. I know Rob's dad thinks it will be a good move. I think there's a good chance it will happen."

I wasn't sure it would be the right move for Rob. At the time, City were hardly a powerhouse, although they had enjoyed considerable success in the late Sixties and early Seventies. And as far as Northtown were concerned we needed midfield reinforcements rather than letting someone leave.

I rang Rob to ask if what I had read the papers was true. I told him I didn't think going to City was the right move. "Nah, I ain't going up norf but Spurs have made an offer for me. The gaffer says I should talk to them and me old man reckons it's the right move. Going to Spurs would suit me." I couldn't recall Rob ever speaking for so long. I told him I hoped he stayed for the coming season at least reminding him we were going all out for promotion this season and surely he would want to be part of a history-making team.

"And if we don't go up, someone will still come in for you. You'll be playing in the First Division one way or another next season." I kept private my view that I thought he would also play for England. And that he should negotiate an improvement on his current terms.

Rob did stay because Spurs wouldn't match the club's valuation and Rob didn't seem too upset, A couple of directors who thought we should have cashed-in weren't very happy though. Palmer said he thought Rob's value could well double within a couple of seasons and Saunders, although playing fair and allowing Rob to talk to Spurs, was more than happy he stayed.

One player who did, finally, leave was Don Tyler who moved to Portsmouth for a nominal fee. There was some interest in Dave Walters but he again stated his intention to stay and fight for his place, which I admired although I think some of the powers-that-be viewed him as a drain on the budget, especially as Davies—so Dave Craig told me—had taken the opportunity to negotiate considerably improved terms. Good for him. I wished someone had shown an interest in me.

Another phone call I received, this time about a week before the 1981-82 pre-season began, came from the club asking me—more telling me actually—to report at the ground the next morning for a meeting with Roger Palmer. It was, in my opinion, a conversation which was long overdue. I had tried to see Palmer towards the end of the season only to be told he was busy and would be abroad for several weeks. I was told to address any issues I had with Tony Saunders or Peter Christie and I went to see the latter.

That didn't work out very well.

Christie wasn't delighted to see me and was even less happy when I said I wanted to discuss my salary, having agreed with Palmer and Saunders this would happen at the end of each season. "The first I've heard about it. There's nothing in your contract, which still has a while to run by the way, to that effect. I'm not going to discuss the matter."

He played a dead bat to everything I said and although he didn't exactly kick me out of his office, he was hostile and the encounter meant our future dealings and conversations would be, at best, frosty. Maybe he thought this, on top on my going to the police station when Iain Moy was arrested, meant I was getting above myself.

The conversation had gone so badly so quickly I decided not to play my trump card—my knowledge about the salaries of other captains—thinking it would be better to hold back until I got in front of Palmer or Saunders. Preferably both.

When I finally did see Palmer some weeks later, he was as ever, courteous and friendly. "It's a shame we can't do this over a bottle of wine," he smiled. But he wasn't really in that sort of mood and was very direct. Before meeting Palmer, I rang Steve Russell but it being mid-summer he was on holiday—as a footballer you tend to have a different calendar to the rest of the world—and with mobile phones yet to dominate society I had to get on with things by myself.

"Ed, I know you met with Peter Christie a while ago and things didn't go well. I'm seeing you today to honour my promise but now we have a Secretary worthy of the name I want to put an end to these meetings. I'm always happy to talk but any negotiations should be with Peter and/or Tony and then the directors will make a decision based on any conversations you have. That's how it should work." He was polite but firm. "You don't look convinced."

"We agreed my salary would be reviewed at the end of every season." I said, "Peter was unaware of this and refused to discuss it. I obviously want to talk to you about it." Palmer said there was no money to spare. The manager, I was told, was making huge efforts to sign players who would help us secure promotion. They would be expensive and would command higher salaries than the club had paid in the past. The budget was finite.

"Roger, I know for a fact I earn less than any other captain in the Second Division and a fair few in Divisions Three and Four. Did you know that when we met in Spain? I want the club to address this disparity." Palmer didn't bat an eyelid when I played what I thought would be my trump card. I then started to talk about a promotion bonus for the squad if we made it into the First Division.

"Ed it's not your business to negotiate on behalf of the first team squad. I'm satisfied that what we pay you is a fair reflection of your experience and value."

"If that's all you think I'm worth you won't want a very high transfer fee for me." I couldn't resist lashing out. I liked Palmer and he had been good to me in the past and taken the club from near rock-bottom to having a realistic chance of competing with English football's big boys—unthinkable just a couple of years ago—but this conversation wasn't going the way I had hoped or expected.

"If the money isn't there, it isn't there. It's as simple as that. This maybe a football club but it's also a business and it will be run along business lines, my business principles, as long as I am here."

I thanked Palmer for his time and went to leave the room.

"I hope your last comment wasn't a threat but if it is then I don't deal with transfer requests," he said to my back as I was opening the door.

The contents of my stomach almost emptied themselves. That wasn't what I had meant but as with Christie in Moy's flat I been put well and truly in my place and started to believe that there was room for the likes of Steve Russell; I had certainly been out of my depth with Palmer, admittedly a highly successful and shrewd businessman, this time round and hadn't been able to steer the meeting in the direction I wanted.

And I certainly wasn't looking to leave. Not yet anyway.

The Observer's offices were close to Wood Lane, so I met Tina for a quick lunch. "Am I being greedy?" I asked her. "Palmer wouldn't entertain talking about a promotion bonus. If we go up income will grow massively, and we should be rewarded." I was beginning to sound like a TU rep. "And they will have to increase my salary to First Division captaincy levels. If that doesn't happen, I'll leave."

Tina calmed me down—a bit—but I opened a bottle of wine when I got home and not for the first time mused it was a good job we didn't own a cat. The more I thought about it the more pissed off I got and the more I thought about having a serious conversation with Steve Russell. I began to wonder what sort of deals the new signings were agreeing and why hadn't any of the old-stagers like Butler, Green, Oldfield and Halliday mentioned a promotion bonus? Maybe they had been talking about it but had excluded me as I was captain.

I thought and hoped this was unlikely but wondered if I should contact one of them and suggest having some sort of "representative," but I was uncomfortable about being the one to suggest it and make things difficult for the club. I didn't want to be seen as a stirrer, but I did want fairness and parity. The fact I was earning less than many others performing several rungs below me rankled. A lot.

Then again, we needed to start focusing on what we were going to do on the field in the coming season rather than being embroiled in tetchy negotiations with directors. An agent could be doing this while we concentrated on the football. If I weren't captain, maybe I would suggest the idea to my teammates. As it happened, I did have a drink and chat with Dave Walters a couple of days later.

Tina arrived home and told me I was probably over-thinking things but that I should talk with Steve. And until he was back in the country, I should forget it. The way I was feeling that was easier said than done.

We were introduced to new signings Andy Hopkins and Ross Davison just before we left for our five-day session at Bisham Abbey. On arriving at Bisham, there was a surprise in store for us in the considerable size and shape of Patrick Pieters, a six-feet seven-inches bull of a centre forward, signed that morning from Aston Villa for "a club record fee."

Patrick was a Jamaican international and to date his career had been a bit up and down, starting off at nearby Slough Town where he scored a hatful of goals and was quickly signed by Southampton. He made a big impression when he first arrived at The Dell but lost his place through injury and went out on loan to Crystal Palace where he scored a few and was then signed by Villa. He did OK there as well but another injury saw him drop down the pecking order and he was now looking to resurrect his career.

Pieters (pronounced Peters but he claimed the 'i' meant he had Dutch heritage and could play for The Netherlands and hence his nickname, Dutch) had a decent pedigree and was a proven goal scorer. A good signing for us. A statement of intent.

"There's the reason you can't get any more money," said Dave Walters as Dutch was being introduced to the squad. "He'll be on a fucking fortune." He was probably right, maybe I should shelve my conversation with Steve Russell or maybe this signing made it even more important that we met.

For once, the pre-season slog wasn't so mind-numbingly boring as Saunders and his assistants put us through our paces in the mornings while the afternoons saw us working on team shape and playing a series of gentle games against young FA professionals to put into practice the formation(s) we had been working on. It seemed obvious the strict 4-4-2 formation of the last three seasons wasn't necessarily going to be the way we would play in the coming campaign. Perhaps Saunders felt it was too formulaic for the higher divisions. I had, though, wondered when I heard about the signing of Davison if this signalled a possible change of approach.

We tried different formations in the pre-season friendlies. There was a welcome change to these as well as we travelled to the south coast and played Southampton, Bournemouth and Portsmouth, all of whom provided good tests. Saunders emphasised the need for performance and adapting to new ideas above results, which suddenly seemed almost immaterial. However, contrary to occasional thinking footballers do care and like to win so the 4-1 defeat at Southampton didn't sit well with us. We beat Bournemouth and Portsmouth with Pieters, so far much more subdued on the pitch than off it, opening his account at Fratton Park.

As the first game of the season (at home to Swansea) approached it seemed certain we would change from 4-4-2 to 4-1-4-1. As expected, Hopkins would play in goal; the back four would remain as Butler, Bell, Egan and Green. Davison would play just in front of them and the midfield four would see Davies and Aitken on the flanks with me and one other in the middle. Whether that would be Walters, Seal or Deakin, both of whom had played there in friendlies because of lack of numbers, wasn't clear. Pieters would be the lone frontman, which meant Halliday and quite both possibly both Deakin and Seal would be redundant.

So the dawn of the season where we had our minds set firmly on winning promotion, saw me feeling slightly unsettled. Quite apart from the conversation with Roger Palmer, which was still playing on my mind, and my feeling of being undervalued, I wasn't convinced by the switch in formation and was suspicious that Saunders was trying something different because of the arrival of Davison and Pieters rather than buying players who would fit naturally into the team.

Although I had no complaints about Pieters, I thought he should have a striking partner. For the second successive season, I didn't have an obvious midfield partner and the big clubs had begun to circle—with Rob Davies target numero uno.

There were also a couple of other things preying on my mind.

Ross Davison had spent all of his career in the top two divisions and was a very good player, had been close to international honours and was just the kind of signing we needed. Let me rephrase that. Ross Davison had been a half decent player, was maybe once the kind of signing we needed and according to him had been close to international recognition. But Ross Davison shouldn't have come to Wood Lane, he should have been dropped off at the nearest knackers' yard.

I had my first doubts about him during the early sessions at Bisham Abbey. He looked out of condition and slow. Out of condition? You are allowed that at the start of pre-season training. Slow? Well, possibly okay, as long as you are a very good reader of the game, especially if you are meant to be protecting the back four. By the time we played our friendlies, I wasn't convinced he was going to get fit or that he was a decent reader of the game. He had enhanced his reputation with Tony Saunders by having a "bit of a dodgy" back for the Southampton match, which we lost 4-1. Amazing how your reputation can improve when you don't play. Dodgy backs were the oldest trick in the book to pull—not always easy for the physio to detect but tended to self-heal pretty quickly if you took it easy. In other words, if you fancied a bit of time off you claimed a bad back.

It was also strange Davison was "injured" for the match against his former club. The former Saint did OK in the other friendlies, but it was noticeable he didn't snuff out many, if any, attacks in two fairly routine wins. What he did do was drop deep, take a short pass from one of the back four, pass it five yards to me or hump it long for Davies or Aitken to run onto and stay where he was. He didn't break sweat and it was obvious his legs had "gone." Saunders had achieved wonders in the transfer market but this time, as far as I could see, he had signed a dud.

Davison was after me. Not my place in the team but the captaincy. We had words early on at Bisham Abbey after I had been helping to organise the midfield shape in a training session. I wasn't trying to lay down the law but was simply interpretating something Saunders wanted us to work on and I hadn't criticised him. At the end of the session, as we walked to the dressing rooms, he caught up with me and told me "don't tell me what to do. I know what I'm doing and I'm not having a snot-rag of a kid telling me different. And I'll have that captain's armband off you before too long. Fuck knows why he's got a kid as captain." He then jogged off. Given he had got up close and personal to me the "exchange" didn't go unnoticed. "What was that about?" asked Tommy Butler. I told him. "Bloke's a tosser," was Tommy's take.

Davison was outspoken and continually referred to when he was playing in the First Division and loved to name-drop—people whose careers he had helped, tough opponents he had snuffed out of games. He also had the habit of wandering off the training ground mid-session, to talk to Saunders and his staff. He would nod his head ferociously and whirl his arms about as if he were conducting an orchestra. When we had lunch at the training ground, he made sure he sat with Saunders.

He wasn't winning friends or influencing people—at least, we hoped he wasn't influencing Saunders. Meanwhile, his performances on the field were neither here nor there—he wasn't making a major difference to us, and the point of bringing a new player into the team is that he should make a difference. He liked to think he was the manager on the field, directing players here, there and everywhere; I had a voice as well and although I accepted he had far greater experience I wasn't happy about his obvious attempts to usurp me.

Off the pitch, Davison had tried to win over some of the others and had taken the more senior pros like Walters, Butler, Halliday and Oldfield out for a drink, telling them he should be captain and that I was over-rated and wasn't even worth a place in the team. Walters told me about it the next day. "Watch out for him Ed. Washed up, over-rated and jealous. He's stirring things behind the scenes big time. He's a fraud, reckons he's on more money here than he was at Southampton." Which wasn't what I wanted to hear.

Butler and Oldfield agreed with Walters, Halliday was already fed up as he wasn't close to the starting line-up, so would have welcomed an ally but clearly disliked Davison who had also been in the ear of Rob Keen. The reserve keeper was deeply disappointed he wasn't playing but wanted nothing to do with him. Walters reckoned Davison would next go to work on Seal and Deakin, two others who were unsettled.

Fortunately results on the pitch weren't affected by Davison's shenanigans and we started off great guns winning five and drawing two of our first seven, the only loss being at West Ham, hot favourites to win the championship. Chelsea, down on their luck and making no impression in the Second Division, came to Wood Lane in late September and regardless of their shortcomings, we were excellent and could easily have won by far more than 3-0. Pieters grabbed a couple to move into double figures for the season and we went to Cardiff the following week full of confidence. The journey back, despite us picking up another two points, wasn't much fun for me, though.

This was my fifth season in the first team, and I hadn't missed a single match through injury. Sure, I had carried the occasional knock and bump into matches but nothing too serious or painful, especially compared to some of my teammates. Tommy Butler played a few games with a broken toe and given so much of his game was all about tackling, I have no idea how he managed. I think I have a reasonably high pain threshold, but I don't think I could have done that—painkillers or not.

Unfortunately, my injury-free record came to an end at Ninian Park just after half-time when I went to leather the ball clear from a goalmouth scramble. I must have taken my eye off it and somehow "stood" on top of the ball, which meant my foot turned. Whatever happened, there was a hell of a pain in my ankle and down I went. I've never been one for going down injured when I'm not and I have no time for those that do, teammates included.

The pain was the worst I had experienced; I knew I wouldn't be continuing and in the back of my mind I already knew this was going to take a bit of time to get over. Laurie Campbell helped me up and I left the pitch with considerable difficulty as I couldn't put any weight on my right foot. No stretcher or oxygen and air and believe me, I could have done with all three. Campbell and his assistant, Nev Dowd, half-carried, half-dragged me into the dressing room and onto the treatment table.

I took a deep breath as the boot and sock came off and they took a look at the already swollen ankle. "Sprained ligaments," announced Campbell. "You're not going to be kicking a ball for a while." I sat in the showers before struggling to change and lay on the table waiting for the painkillers to kick in and for the match—another straightforward 3-0 win for us—to finish. I was helped onto the coach and had the whole of the back seat to myself on the way home with Laurie sitting just in front of me telling me how to get comfortable and the best way to ease the intense aching.

We got back to Wood Lane just after 9pm and Laurie took me to the hospital right next to the ground (where my elder brother had come into the world) for an X-ray. I may have been captain of the local professional football club but there was no preferential treatment and going straight to the head of the queue—quite rightly. After a couple of hours, I was X-rayed and the results, which came back about one hour later, confirmed badly sprained ligaments. A nurse sprayed some "stuff" on my leg which would make taking off the sticky bandages, wrapped around my ankle and up to my shin, easier. These bandages were, she explained, to be part of me for at least the next two-to-three weeks.

Campbell helped me home—it was Sunday morning by the time I hobbled into the flat—and said he would arrange for my car to be driven home. The ankle throbbed like hell, so much so that the weight of just the duvet proved unbearable and I spent the night on the sofa with a blanket for company. Tina had heard about the injury and was sympathetic but there was nothing she could do. Worryingly, the pain killers were having little impact and all I could do was wait for morning—all-night TV and hundreds of Freeview channels to hop between were things of the future.

"Rest is the best cure," Laurie told me. "Keep that ankle elevated and don't do anything. The more you use it, the longer it will take to heal. I will ring you in a few days." And that was it, confined to quarters for the foreseeable. Under house arrest.

Being unable to play because of injury is a real bummer for a number of reasons. We spend a lot of time on the move, so inactivity is foreign to us, especially when you have to spend endless hours with your foot up. How serious is the injury and how long will you be out for? I wanted to miss as little as possible of a season where we were going all out for promotion to Division One. Crucially, would I get my place back in the team when I was fit? Of course you want the team to prosper but you're not exactly willing your replacement to be the star of the show. And who would replace me as captain? Would Saunders give it to Davison? God, I hoped not.

It took a while for the ankle to feel as if it was improving and I didn't put any weight on it for well over a week. I went into the club once so Laurie could cast his expert eye over things and although I was delighted to break the monotony of being at home the physio merely confirmed my fear that there was no treatment for the injury; it was simply a matter of time.

I approached Saunders and asked if I could head to the sun for a week as long as I continued the light exercises I had been given and looked after myself. He was happy for me to go so Tina and I had a week doing almost nothing somewhere in Spain. It may not have been mid-summer weather, but it was far better than sitting on my backside in wintery England moping about being injured and sweating on results I could not influence. And my place in the team.

The break did us both a power of good. Before we left, I took off the bandages, which I had been told would be easy to remove after soaking them in a bath. It proved to be anything but and every time I took off a piece of bandage it ripped the hairs from my leg. It was a long and agonising process and meant my right leg was bald for a while.

It was then another couple of weeks before I started light training and another couple of weeks before I worked with the first team squad. Even then, Saunders outlawed tackles on me. Privately I was concerned. The injury was dragging on for much longer than I thought it would and at the back of my mind was Don Tyler, who had suffered a similar knock and was never the same player when he returned. And although I had tried to remain positive, I was becoming grouchy and not great company.

I missed eight matches, including the trip to Newcastle, another "big club" going through difficult times, which I had really been looking forward to. We had won three, drawn three and lost two of those eight games, twelve out of twenty-four points this being the first season when a win was rewarded with three points, which was reasonable but not great for supposed promotion contenders.

There had been some interesting developments while I had been out. Ross Davison expected to be made captain, but Saunders elected to give the armband to Tommy Butler and also decided to do away with the idea of using a midfielder to screen the back four, reasoning it was a waste of a player. That meant Davison moved into the midfield four but only played the first couple of games as his lack of pace was obvious and opponents ran through him at will. Walters and Seal did a good enough job for the next six matches, but Saunders told me I would be back in the side once I had proved my fitness. I felt I had been playing well before the injury and that my influence was missed while I was side-lined but like all footballers, I was relatively insecure, and it was good to know that I was needed!

My comeback match was the home "derby" against Luton, who were also going great guns and in the promotion mix. Saunders told me I would be on the bench and although I was itching to play again, I knew he was right. I came on for the last ten minutes or so as we coasted to a surprisingly easy 2-0 win, and played a couple of nice passes, didn't have to make a tackle and was very happy that the ankle felt fine afterwards. There were eleven days before the next match, at home to Blackburn, and I was back in the side—as captain—for the 0-0 draw, although I came off after seventy minutes as I was running out of steam.

When we had another goalless draw at Sheffield United the following week, we were halfway through the season and well in the promotion mix. The only concern was that West Ham were runaway leaders which realistically left only two more promotion places. Swansea, Norwich, Luton and ourselves were the sides which would seemingly fight it out for those two places. Saunders told us in no uncertain terms we needed a stronger showing in the second half of the season if we were to go up but, without counting any chickens, out of the obvious promotion contenders we only had to play Norwich away and West Ham at home.

That left Davison out of the first-team picture after only half a season, but he was still as arrogant as ever around the place although he no longer broke off from training to talk to Saunders and the coaches. He told anyone who would listen that he had been carrying various niggles, that the break from first team action would do him good and he would be back "better and stronger" in a couple of weeks or so.

Apart from a couple of brief appearances as substitute he didn't play for us again and was jettisoned at the end of the season becoming player-coach at Fareham Town, close to his home in Southampton. Saunders later told me he realised he had made a mistake soon after signing him but continued to play him in the hope he would come good.

"It's ironic really, Ed. He was after you from Day One but it was your injury which really exposed him and ended his career. If I were you, I would take some sort of pleasure from that."

I did. A lot.

Chapter Six
Out of Second

Tony Saunders may not have admitted it but secretly he must have been delighted with our form and results in the second half of the season and with four games to go we were well placed in second—West Ham were way out in front and only needed a single point to become champions—but it was tight at the top with just five points separating us and Luton who were fifth. Two out of us, Norwich, Luton and Swansea would join the Hammers in the First Division.

	P	W	D	L	F	A	Pts
West Ham	38	24	8	6	74	29	80
Northtown	38	20	9	9	54	32	69
Norwich	38	19	8	11	49	28	65
Swansea	38	18	10	10	57	40	65
Luton	38	18	10	10	58	42	64

Our run-in, on paper at least, was favourable compared to those of our nearest rivals. We didn't have to play any of them, and neither were we up against any side battling to stay in the division. Charlton Athletic and Sheffield Wednesday away and Rotherham and Cambridge United at home. All solidly mid-table with, so they say, "nothing to play for." But that's a stupid phrase, as is "they are already on the beach."

Footballers, often quite rightly, are a much-maligned species but the vast majority possess—just as you see in other walks of life—professional pride. Of course there are shirkers, duckers and divers, individuals who go into hiding when the going gets tough but again, it's the same in any profession.

And at the fag end of a season if you're not in the race for promotion or the dog-fight to avoid relegation, the shackles quite often come off and a side which has been dour and boring all season starts to play expansive, free-flowing football making them tougher opponents. There are also players putting in even more effort as the season reaches its climax because they want to put themselves in the shop window given much of the transfer business was still done in the summer. Others are aware that a couple more goals or crucial saves could be the difference between being offered a new contract or having to find themselves a new club.

There are no easy games is one of the biggest clichés in football. It also happens to be true.

With all this in mind, we went to Bisham Abbey in the lead-up to our match at Charlton. We were all well aware of the importance of promotion and what it would mean to the club and us as individuals, but Saunders felt time away from the usual day-to-day activities would do us good. We still trained but at this stage of the season it was only light stuff, we spoke about our upcoming opponents but in no more detail than usual, we played some golf, watched films, swam, sat in saunas and gave individual talks about the ups and downs of our careers and our lives. Very amusing, and enlightening, but I'm afraid what is revealed at an Abbey stays within its four walls.

We had left for Bisham Abbey on the Tuesday and came back on Friday morning refreshed and relaxed and desperate to get at Charlton not because we wanted to get the game out of the way but because we were chomping at the bit. Those few days away were another Saunders masterstroke.

Charlton Athletic played at The Valley in London, halfway between Woolwich and East Greenwich. For much of its ninety-plus years, it had been one hell of a venue as well as being one of the capital's most iconic grounds. Seventy-five thousand spectators crammed in there to watch an FA Cup match between Charlton and Aston Villa in 1938. Unfortunately, when we played there on Saturday 17 April 1982, it's fair to say the ground wasn't in a great state. Huge, sweeping terraces ran along both sides but you could see from the pitch the concrete was crumbling and that flora and fauna had taken root in abundance.

They had some very good players in their squad, including the Wales international winger Leighton James, Terry Naylor and Don McCallister, who had played loads of games for Spurs and the legendary—as far as Charlton fans were concerned—Derek Hales who was their all-time leading goal scorer. And with Lennie Lawrence as manager many people, including myself, had expected them to be pushing for promotion but things hadn't quite clicked for them. They were capable of thrashing anyone and being thrashed by anyone.

Our team for the visit to the Valley was Hopkins; Butler, Bell, Egan, Green; Aitken, Walters, Roberts, Davies; Halliday, Pieters. The sub was Seal. By and large, this had been Saunders' first choice team when everyone was available to him and although Charlton had the advantage in terms of experience and household names they couldn't get close to us.

We won 2-1, a margin which flattered Charlton, who hardly threatened us until their injury-time goal scrambled home, inevitably, by Hales. Dutch, who was having a prolific season for us, bagged both of our goals but picked up a knock which saw him substituted. Norwich, Luton and Swansea all won as well so there was no change at the top.

Our final midweek game of the season was against Rotherham and the Wood Lane gates were locked well before kick-off with a record crowd of almost thirty-four thousand creating a brilliant atmosphere. Dutch was desperate to play but Laurie Campbell said he wasn't fit enough, not even for the bench. Saunders had to placate Dutch but it wasn't hard. "Son, if you play tonight and aggravate the knock you won't play again this season. Missing tonight is a small price to pay for playing here in the last game."

You could see the big Jamaican thinking ahead to scoring the goal that would seal promotion. Talking of seal, Jimmy Seal took Pieters' place and Alan Deakin, who hadn't seen much action for a while, was substitute.

Rotherham had done very well to stay in the division for a couple of seasons given they were a relatively small club with a small squad and reputedly the smallest budget in the second tier. They were game opponents and had a very tricky forward in Tony Carter who forced Hopkins into a couple of smart saves before we had got going.

Seal scored shortly before the break, Deakin, a half-time sub for Halliday, added a second soon after and we played some great stuff for the last half hour and were disappointed to win "only" 4-0. Pete Aitken bagged his first double for the club.

There was another huge roar from the crowd after the final whistle sounded—at least as big as those which greeted our goals. Luton had only drawn which meant that with sixty-eight points from forty games they couldn't catch our haul of seventy-five points from the same number of matches.

	P	W	D	L	F	A	Pts
West Ham	40	26	8	6	81	30	86
Northtown	40	22	9	9	60	33	75
Norwich	40	21	8	11	53	28	71
Swansea	40	20	11	9	64	43	71
Luton	40	19	11	10	61	44	68

Sheffield Wednesday away from home. It was almost three years to the day since we had set off for Chesterfield where we won promotion from the Fourth to the Third Division. Not surprisingly, quite a lot had changed since then and only four players were left from that game—me, Tommy Butler, Rob Davies and John Halliday. Terry Green, who was injured for that match, was another survivor from our Fourth Division days.

We travelled to Sheffield by train while we had journeyed to Chesterfield on our antiquated club coach and just as the journey to Goodison for our FA Cup game against Everton, there was a First Class carriage for players, staff and, of course, directors although there were far fewer caustic comments about them attending than on previous occasions. No doubt, though, we would see a lot more of them next season—as long as we went up. After all, who wouldn't want to be seen sitting in the directors' boxes at the likes of Old Trafford, Anfield, and Highbury?

Three years ago, there was a tense atmosphere in the lead-up to the Chesterfield match. This time everyone was hugely relaxed—Saunders' idea of a few days at Bisham Abbey had worked wonders as had our comprehensive wins over Charlton and Rotherham. We also knew that a win would see us promoted regardless of Swansea's and Norwich's results. They would need to win both their games and we would have to drop points for either or both of them to overhaul us. Not that we had any intention of failing to pick up the required three points, but you just can't help yourself working out the various permutations!

Like Charlton, Wednesday were among the early season favourites for promotion, played in an iconic stadium and had a handy squad. Again, like Charlton, things hadn't quite sparked for them this time round although they had demonstrated their potential with a couple of handy runs. Their squad included the tricky winger Terry Curran who, with his long dark locks and a drooping moustache, had a piratical look about him. He could win a game on his own but was also prone to go missing in action. Mel Sterland was an excellent full-back and went on to be capped by England, while Gary Megson was an "as-solid-as-they-come" midfielder. They were a bit lightweight in attack, relying heavily on John Pearson, who played for about eight clubs during his career, most of them based in Yorkshire.

Hillsborough was a hell of a stadium and you could see why it was a regular venue for an FA Cup semi-final but the stands were more than half-deserted apart, of course, from the away end which was rammed with thousands of our fans (Tom Border take note. Again.) In fact, I reckon Wednesday would need to be top of the First Division and in the semi-finals of the (then) European Cup to have any chance of filling the stadium.

We played very well but still ended up losing as we came up against a goalkeeper in inspired form. Bob Bolder was a mountain of a man and had one of those days when it didn't matter what came his way or where the ball was, he stopped it. Sure, we made it easy for him on a few occasions but this was one of our best performances—it wasn't a case of nerves getting the better of us and choking. Dutch Pieters still wasn't fit and whether he would have made a difference or not was irrelevant; he wasn't there. Jimmy Seal, playing in place of Dutch, had a really good game while John Halliday spurned a couple of gilt-edged chances.

Wednesday's winner came midway through the second half when they won their only corner of the match. Curran swung the ball towards the penalty spot and Pearson headed home—it was the first time I could remember that Mick Egan was directly responsible for a goal. He simply switched off allowing Pearson a free header.

We were angry with ourselves when the final whistle sounded. Not only had we failed to clinch promotion but we also felt we had short-changed the thousands of fans who had made the journey to celebrate and party and the news of wins for Norwich and Swansea dampened our collective spirits even further. Not even news of Luton only drawing which made it mathematically impossible for them to win promotion improved their mood—or ours. When we went to thank them, they were generous with their applause but were obviously deflated.

The language in the dressing room doesn't bear repeating. Not even a visit from Wednesday manager and England World Cup winner Jack Charlton telling us how well we had played and that we were bound to go up made us feel any better—and the train journey home was a quiet one. We were still in the driving seat but had to beat Cambridge in the last game of the season to go up. If we drew, we could be overhauled. If we lost...

Saunders worked his way round the carriage and spoke to all the players in groups of two or three and told us how well we had played and if we played half as well against Cambridge, we would be fine. Nevertheless, we still felt flat and wanted to get out on the pitch and atone for today. Saunders said unless we were injured, he didn't want to see any of us until Wednesday which meant kicking our heels for three days. I had done enough sitting around when I was injured. It was going to be a very long week.

Wood Lane Stadium, Northtown. Saturday, 5 May 1981. Northtown United v Cambridge United. League Division Two.

Cambridge United are relatively new to the party, having only been elected to the Football League a decade or so before and have done brilliantly under the canny management of the canny Scot, John Docherty. They had a great season last year winning promotion and although they were favourites to go straight back down they had held their own and were going to finish comfortably in mid-table.

With Cambridge you have to expect the unexpected. They have had seven goalless draws, five of them on their travels, and have only won twice away from their Abbey Stadium. One of those was 4-3 at Bolton, while they had lost by the odd goal in nine at Cardiff. Feast or famine as far as goals are concerned.

Saunders doesn't push us too hard in training and emphasises once again when we reported for duty on Wednesday that we had played exceptionally well the previous Saturday and if it hadn't been for the rock that was Bob Bolder, we would have won handsomely. He is sure Cambridge will shut up shop and try and catch us on the break so we spend a long time on the training pitch with the forwards and midfield attempting to pick their way through a massed defence which not only includes Butler, Bell, Egan and Green but Les Oldfield and a couple of reserves as well. At times, it is shambolic but it concentrates the mind and helps lift spirits.

We stay at a plush hotel in nearby St Albans on Friday night and although the gesture is appreciated, I think most of us would rather be at home, as usual. We set out for Wood Lane at noon, arriving about forty-five minutes later and the crowds are already gathering. Another

thirty-thousand-plus crowd is expected and the Golden Cod, opposite the ground, is doing good business with a long queue snaking down the road. I promise myself a large haddock and chips in the coming days—as long as we win today.

Despite my injury and Dutch's recent knock—he's now fit and raring to go—we have been relatively lucky with injuries again while the only suspensions served were by Dave Walters and Terry Bell for clocking up too many bookings. All this means Saunders has a full squad to choose from and he pulls a bit of a surprise by leaving out John Halliday and playing Jimmy Seal. Halliday, who is on the bench, isn't happy and thinks he's been singled out for missing a couple of chances at Sheffield. Saunders breaks the news to him in private but he's still sulking at the team meeting. "Jesus, John! I've told you it's a tactical decision. Jimmy's speed and mobility is better suited to breaking down a massed defence."

I have a quick word with Halliday after the meeting and he makes the point he was left out when we played Everton and now he's out again. "Two of the biggest games this club has played and he's made me sub for both." I think there's a good chance he will see some action but he wants time to brood and I want to start my own—and at times laborious—preparations.

Cambridge are hardly flush with household names but they do have the former West Ham striker Alan Taylor in their side. Taylor once sported a haircut which made him look like Brian Connolly, the singer in the glam rock band Sweet. Injury and age mean he has been in and out of the side but as we line up in the tunnel he looks fit and lean. Mick Egan spots Taylor. "Oi, old man. You're not getting a fucking kick today. More like you're going to get fucking kicked."

Taylor has been there, seen it, done it etc. He played in the 1975 FA Cup final against Fulham and scored both the Hammers' goals in their 2-0 win. He played in the following season's Cup Winners' Cup final. He may not be in the first flush of youth but what he lacks in pace he will make up for with nous and years of experience. Taylor grins and says nothing. But you know he's now even more determined to make our day harder.

"Mick, shut the fuck up and concentrate on your game," I tell Egan. "Just a little friendly banter, skip. Neanderthal man won't mind." Mark

Bailey walks past and reinforces the idea it would be good if Egan, for once, buttons it and concentrates on what he needs to do on the pitch.

It's a glorious spring day and Wood Lane is again packed to the rafters. Two recent full houses and thousands making the journey to Sheffield. What will it be like when (if?) we meet Liverpool, Manchester United and their like? I shake myself into the here and now—it's not going to be a cakewalk against Cambridge. I wander round during the warm-up and have a chat with a couple of my teammates. There isn't really any need as they are all pumped and don't need their concentration broken. It's probably me getting rid of some of my nerves.

As expected Cambridge play with everyone behind the ball bar Taylor which means that Davies and Aitken are going to be even more key to us than usual. We start well and win a few corners and I shoot from just inside the area but the keeper gets a touch on it and the ball comes back off a post. We don't need another keeper having a blinder. Dutch, who has shaken off his injury, is looking rusty and it takes him a good half hour to get anywhere near his stride, Jimmy Seal is looking dangerous and gets hacked down on the edge of the area. I decide to shoot from the free-kick but the ball disappears into the stand. Not very pretty. We are playing well but not as well as last week and there is a feeling of desperation about some of our play.

Cambridge don't have a single shot in the first half but Taylor looks sharp holding the ball up and twisting and turning while Egan is constantly in his ear about his age, how slow he is, how he should have kept his glam rock hair-do. All water off a duck's back as far as a seasoned pro like Taylor is concerned.

Saunders calms us down at the break. Tells us to give a bit more thought to what we're doing. Not to rush. Think about what we did during the week. No need to change anything. But... "Dutch, I need to know you're playing and that you're fit. You've done sod all." You can see Dutch bristle but Saunders is right, our leading goal scorer needs to show why he is our leading goal scorer.

We make our way out for the second half. Cambridge have made a change bringing on another veteran striker in George Reilly. Not instead of Taylor but to support him. Interesting. Maybe John Docherty thinks there's a weakness at the back they can exploit. Saunders calls across Dave Walters and tells him not to press so far forward for a while. Dave looks relieved. He also looks knackered. Father Time looks to be finally catching up with him.

Jimmy Seal, who is probably having his best game in our colours, is brought down in the box. Hardly a murmur of dissent from the Cambridge players when the ref points to the spot. Since I took over spot kick duties I've only taken a few and have scored them all and enjoy the challenge. Now, when I pick up the ball, I feel in desperate need of a toilet. I try to look calm and composed but promotion may rest on whether I score or not. This is the biggest moment of my career, possibly of my young life. I'm a bag of nerves and wish someone else had this gig.

The keeper makes himself as big as he can and starts to hop around but I don't ever look at the keeper when I take a penalty. I have a shortish run-up and look to put it to the right of the keeper, who dives that way. I open my body a fraction early and the ball comes off the wrong part of my foot and goes in the opposite side. If I didn't know where it was going, what chance the keeper! Wood Lane explodes, I'm enveloped by teammates. I trot back to the half-way line and look into the stand where Tina and a couple of mates are sitting. I receive one kiss and two thumbs' ups.

A few minutes later and Taylor goes on a run into our box and Egan trips him. As stonewall a penalty as ours. Egan talks himself into the book. "I thought you would keep up with a Neanderthal," smirks Taylor. Egan looks to move towards him. Terry Bell ushers him away. I'm starting to think that Egan needs to be substituted. He's on a suicide mission today. Taylor rams home the penalty. Twenty minutes left and promotion is back in the balance. We don't know how Norwich and Swansea are getting on. I have been so focused on this match the thought honestly hasn't occurred until then and Saunders didn't allow any questions about those games at half-time. Now it takes over.

I start to lose my concentration and I sense others are feeling the same way. Suddenly we are nervous, giving the ball away and failing to do the simple things. Cambridge are growing in confidence. Andy Hopkins has to make a couple of smart stops. Halliday is warming up—he must be coming on for Dutch. On a rare foray into the Cambridge half, we win a corner.

Pete Aitken swings it across and suddenly Dutch springs—literally—to life and rises high to head the ball home and promptly goes on a celebratory lap of honour, shirt off and being twirled high above his head. It's the quickest he's run all day. Quite possibly the most ground he's covered in a single run all season. The crowd are loving his antics, even the ref smiles. These days he would be booked or worse. Halliday returns to the bench.

Ten minutes to go. Taylor looks like a spent force but goes on another mazy run. He trips over his own feet and the ball goes out for a throw. Egan laughs and says something. As Taylor trots past him he pinches Egan's backside who reacts by kicking out. The ref has no option but to send him off for a second bookable offence. The crowd let the ref know what they think of him, some fans misguidedly cheer Egan as he makes his way slowly from the pitch and down the tunnel.

Saunders goes out of his way to ignore him. None of the players say a word to him. We are staggered at how he has behaved. Saunders takes off Dutch and Halliday goes to the middle of the back four. Cambridge resort to lumping the ball forward in the hope of catching Halliday out but he does well. Terry Bell, as ever, excels and Andy Hopkins commands the area and barks out orders to one and all. Cambridge don't threaten again.

The final whistle goes.

We are up. Again. Into the hallowed lands of the First Division.

Spectators rush onto the pitch ignoring the announcer's pleas not to. They want a part of the pitch and any part of any player they can get close to. I take my shirt off and keep a tight grip on it. No one is having that. We are finally ushered into the directors' box where the fizz is flowing. Roger Palmer is embracing all the players as they make their way into the box. He and Saunders spend ages in a man hug. First Division football in five years? It was Palmer's dream and Saunders had most definitely turned the water into divine wine.

Tommy Butler, Terry Green and I had been there every step of the way. It also meant everything to local lads Rob Davies and Pete Aitken, while Dave Walters and Mark Bailey had been long-term key components. I see Dave Craig who is joining in the celebrations. "Might be worth getting a quote from Border," I say.

I also see Mr Bushnell, our former Chairman and owner who is visibly moved. He comes across and shakes my hand. I thank him. "Can I ask you a question? What is your Christian name?" I'd been a supporter and player for about twenty years and I had no idea what his name was! "George," he says. Somehow I knew it would be. I go to congratulate Saunders. "Did you mean to put the penalty where you did?" he asks. It seems an age since I was on the verge of needing a toilet break. I raise an eyebrow. Saunders laughs.

We finally get to the dressing rooms. Mick Egan, who has been on the periphery of the celebrations thus far, sits on the bench clutching a can of Guinness, staring at the wall "I don't want to take the wind out of any sails (or words to that effect) but what were you up to out there, Mick?" demands Bailey. Egan can't bring himself to speak, which is a definite first. Pete Aitken, one of the quietest of the group, says what everyone else is thinking. "You were a complete wanker." Never a truer word and the comment breaks the ice. Celebrations continue and dealing with Egan will come later.

West Ham, surprisingly, lost their final game of the season, while Norwich and Swansea both won meaning Norwich edged out Swansea on goal difference, thankfully sparing us yet another visit to the Principality next season.

The final table:

	P	W	D	L	F	A	Pts
West Ham	42	27	8	7	84	32	89
Northtown	42	23	9	10	62	35	78
Norwich	42	23	8	11	56	29	77
Swansea	42	22	11	9	66	43	77
Luton	42	19	12	11	62	46	69

We drank away the night, although I don't remember many of the places we visited. At least this time I had a partner who was eager to join in our celebrations and did so, even though Tina doesn't drink. We met friends for lunch the next day. Lunchtime, became evening, became night.

There was another Civic Ceremony and, again, having a partner who wanted to share in my success made it a hugely enjoyable occasion and memorable for all the right reasons. Tina and I even found time to go to London to buy "outfits" for the occasion and as far as I am concerned, we were the original Posh and Becks.

Promotion achieved, celebrations in full swing, a holiday in the sun just around the corner (no problems that it was slightly earlier than high season) and the 1982 World Cup in Spain to look forward to. It was shaping up to be a summer to remember.

During the Civic Ceremony, Roger Palmer and Tony Saunders told me that the pair of them, plus Mark Bailey and Andy Adams, were having dinner in a couple of nights at the same hotel I had dined at with Palmer and Saunders two years ago. They were going to discuss the next season and Palmer said they hoped I could join them.

We met early, at 6.30pm, and Palmer had booked a private room. "We've got a lot to talk about and I don't want anyone trying to listen in," he explained. Saunders wanted to know everyone's thoughts on the first team squad and how it would fair in the First Division, or rather he asked Mark, Andy and myself for our views.

Not surprisingly they differed. I said we needed a more reliable back-up to Andy Hopkins rather than Rob Keen, that we needed greater strength and variety in midfield—even Dave Walters reckoned he was now running on empty—and that I wasn't totally convinced John Halliday could cut it at the highest level. Then again, I didn't know if I would.

When it came to Saunders, he said we would be saying goodbye to Rob Keen, Dave Walters, John Halliday and Alan Deakin. Les Oldfield would be released and he would also consider offers for Jimmy Seal who, despite a strong finish to the season, still hadn't cemented a regular place in the side after three seasons. Ditto Alan Deakin, who had signed for us on the same day as Jimmy but had made less than thirty starts. I always felt Seal deserved a longer run in the team but it hadn't happened. Saunders added he was in the market for a new left back. Terry Green had been tremendous but wasn't in the first flush of youth when he joined us four years ago from Nottingham Forest.

It was a shock to hear Saunders say this but making difficult and sometimes unpleasant decisions was part and parcel of his job. He added Green wasn't necessarily going to lose his place in the team but he needed strong back-up. He also had similar concerns about Tommy Butler at right back, even though he was a few years younger than Terry. We were covered here though, as Mike Sears, a young reserve, had been looking very good in training. Whether he was First Division material or not was for Saunders and the coaches to decide. Dave Walters, Tony said, was going to be invited to join the coaching staff—I liked the strategy of former players who knew the set-up joining the coaching team and I also had a lot of time for Walters.

"What about Mick Egan?" said Saunders. I looked blank. "OK, do you think he's a loose cannon?"

"He isn't the brightest spark in the box, Boss, and yes, I was shocked by his behaviour against Cambridge. But's he's been brilliant for us and he and Ding (Bell) are great together."

"We've had an offer for him, which we are seriously considering."

Palmer explained if we accepted the offer the club would make a tidy profit and given that we needed to make ground and training facility improvements, pay out a promotion bonus and activate promotion clauses in some of the contracts—not including mine!—it was going to be a very expensive time for the club. Apparently, we hadn't paid much "cash" for Egan but we furnished Linfield with balls, first team and training kits and a few other odds and sods. We had also agreed to play them in a friendly and now we were in the First Division they had already made contact asking us to honour the agreement.

"The cost of season tickets and admission will obviously go up and there will be increased sponsorship but we need to claw back some of the extra outlay." Saunders reckoned he could replace Egan for a relatively small amount. "I think it's almost certain he will go. I can't say where but it is another First Division club."

I was dead against the sale of Egan but I understood that even if it was a cold-blooded approach, it was a necessary one and that at some stage in less than a decade people would be sitting in a room talking about me like this.

"Roberts? Nah, don't fancy him, his legs have gone. Not good enough for this standard." I would do all I could to make sure that when my time was up, I would leave whoever I was playing for when I wanted and on my own terms.

"It sounds as if we need at least five or six players, maybe more if we are to have enough strength in depth to be competitive," I said. "You're saying there's a lot of expenditure as well as the cost of transfer fees, First Division salaries etc so, with respect, where's the money coming from? Apart from increased admission costs and sponsorship?"

Palmer explained the club had been planning for this for five years and had a robust financial plan in place. "What's our position if an offer comes in for Rob Davies?" asked Bailey.

"If the offer is high enough, we would give it serious thought. Now we are higher profile we will have to accept other clubs will make offers for our players. I know Ding and Pete Aitken have their admirers. Dutch only needs to score a couple of goals early next season and there will be even greater interest in him. First Division we may be but we will be viewed as small fry needing to sell. We do have to think seriously about all offers." This from Saunders the football man as opposed to Palmer the businessman. The football landscape was definitely changing and I didn't like the idea that we could become a selling team as soon as we had hit the heady heights of the First Division. If that was going to be the case, we wouldn't be in the top flight for long.

"Do you have any replacements lined up other than for Egan?" I asked. I also wanted to say that letting the Irishman go was a mistake but Saunders had signed nineteen players and only two—Steve Mower and Ross Davison—had misfired, so I stayed silent. And, of course, we were now talking "business" so I kept all my thoughts to myself.

"I know who I want but we haven't started any balls rolling. I want players with First Division experience but I also believe we have the basis of a squad which will do well so we shouldn't worry." I didn't think Saunders was the sort of man who would say things to try and impress or to fool people but I thought back to our matches against Everton and Coventry. Everton had threatened to run us into the Mersey for periods and we had held on by our fingernails for a while against Coventry. I didn't much fancy forty-two games like those.

But Saunders had a point—Hopkins, Butler, Bell, Green, Davies, Aitken, Pieters and yours truly was a decent base even though the number of First Division appearances among us didn't even number forty.

There was a quick chat about slightly changing our approach to how we would play although much would depend on the new signings and we began to break up. "Ed, will you join me for one for the road in the lounge?" asked Palmer. "Love to," I replied. I had a few things I wanted to discuss.

Saunders joined us.

I hadn't drunk much during the meal, mainly because I was aware of what I had ingested on Saturday, Sunday, Monday and Tuesday. In fact, it was noticeable that the five of us had "only" consumed four bottles of wine between us. Palmer would normally neck that amount himself. I ordered a small brandy to go with my coffee.

"How are you feeling about things, Ed?" A strange question to kick-off our discussion. "Exhilarated, excited, proud. It's also hard to believe that four years ago we had to apply for re-election." Maybe a bit thin and clichéd as an answer but I wasn't sure what the Boss wanted to hear.

"So you're totally committed?" continued Saunders.

"What do you mean by that? Until I sat down a couple of minutes ago, I was." I couldn't believe my commitment was being questioned. I gave everything every time I pulled on the shirt, even though, in my opinion, I wasn't being properly recompensed.

"What if I told you I've taken a call from another First Division manager asking if you're for sale?"

"Was the price right?" I snapped. "And when was the call made? And who made it?"

Palmer tried to pour oil on the troubled waters. "The call came a month or so ago and we didn't tell you because we needed to concentrate on the run-in. Until we know a bit more about your intentions, we won't say who showed the interest."

I didn't say anything.

"There have been one or two conversations about terms where neither you nor we have left the room very happy. What we need to know is whether you will look to leave if a club offering more money comes in for you. It's as simple as that."

"Roger, I don't want to leave. But what's all this about a promotion bonus and promotion clauses in contracts? What people negotiate is their business but you know I haven't been happy with my terms for a while. My question is do you want me to stay? Or does that depend solely on the amount offered? I think you should tell me and then we can move on or not from there."

I hadn't anticipated this conversation and the revelation that another club had shown an interest in me, also caught me off guard and I was struggling to think clearly. Was it all about money? No. For example, I wouldn't leave to go to a Second Division club, even if they offered me fifty per cent more.

Palmer deferred to Saunders.

"Ed, you're a very good player and you've done very well as skipper. The rest of the squad like and respect you. In many ways, you are Northtown because of your long-term and local association with the club. I don't want you to leave. But if you were unhappy, we'd give you permission to talk to the other club. I have felt for a while you're not happy, although I accept it hasn't impacted on your performances."

A waiter came across to tell me my taxi had arrived. Not great timing. I told Palmer and Saunders I wanted to stay but I also wanted to renegotiate my terms and that I wanted to include a third party in those discussions and that conversation needed a fruitful conclusion. Especially as Tina and I had been looking at the future. We both loved the flat we rented but were keen to buy, while Tina was keen to either try working on national newspapers or start a communications business in the area. We could afford to buy a house or start a business, but not both. And we were young and impatient and we wanted both. Yesterday. The promotion bonus was, I hoped, going to be a big help. If I were paid what I believed I was worth, it would mean we could seriously look at both options.

Palmer smiled and nodded his agreement to my representative accompanying me; Saunders didn't look too chuffed at this turn of events. "Got yourself an agent have you?" he almost spat. "We were only promoted on Saturday."

"By the way, Roger, can I ask what my promotion bonus is?" Palmer leaned forward and whispered the amount.

It was a going to be a big help. And Steve Russell was about to enter the fray. Not before time.

I had seen Steve after matches at Wood Lane from time to time but it had been quite a while since we had spoken and he seemed surprised when I phoned him to outline what had happened the previous night and that I wanted him to "represent" me.

Steve and I met the next day to iron out my needs and expectations before we met with, I presumed, Peter Christie and Saunders. I made it plain, again, I didn't want to be seen as greedy or difficult—although the fact I now had a representative would no doubt mean I would be seen in some quarters as both—merely that I wanted what I thought I was worth. Russell presented a "menu" of what he thought I should be asking for. This included an increased basic salary, extra for being captain which should be backdated because I had been underpaid for three seasons, appearance-related bonus, a loyalty bonus, goal-scoring bonus, extra money for finishing in the top six, top ten, avoiding relegation. I was surprised he didn't suggest a bonus for me turning up to training.

Russell was trying to squeeze every pip out of the lemon which made me uncomfortable. I told him it was too much and we would be laughed out of court and quite probably kicked out of Christie's office. "Aim high and see what we end up with," was his advice.

We then spent what seemed like an eternity with Steve's lawyer to draw up an agreement between us. I would have to employ (and pay) a solicitor to look at the draft agreement before I signed anything. Steve wanted the arrangement to be for three years; I had wanted a trial twelve-month "contract" before committing myself to anything long-term.

Inevitably, I suppose, we agreed on two years. I insisted, though, he would receive nothing if he didn't produce—I wasn't prepared to pay him for making a few phone calls and pressing the flesh occasionally. As Roger Palmer had once said to me, I wanted to reward tangible success. Clauses and changes to clauses were batted backwards and forwards and things became so complicated there were a couple of times when I regretted going down this route.

Steve was an interesting character, intent on making as much money as he possibly could as quickly as he could. He liked the fine things in life, wore expensive clothes, wined and dined in top restaurants, had a swagger about him and also possessed a very broad streak of arrogance, which he wore with pride. All very well if you can back-up appearances with results. I wasn't sure how Christie would react to him; I was sure Saunders would hate him.

The meeting with the club came before the contract had been finalised and although I was more wary of Steve than I had been when we first met, I had no choice but to go ahead. Christie was welcoming enough and knew of Steve via his dealings with Palmer. Saunders, thankfully, wasn't present having gone for a short break before spending the rest of the summer wheeling and dealing in the transfer market. Saunders had, said Christie, given his thoughts before jetting off to wherever he was.

It was, not surprisingly, a long and at times tense meeting during which I didn't say a great deal. Russell played an admirable game but Christie was a fine defender with an ability to turn defence into lightning quick counter attack. The outcome, however, was a good one as far as I was concerned. I hadn't become the club's highest earner although that had not been my aim but my salary reflected my status as the captain of a First Division side, my contribution and the length of time I had been at the club. Christie refused point blank to any back-dated payment as far as the captaincy was concerned but conceded a couple of minor points which made Steve feel good and cost the club nothing in the overall scheme of things.

"You agreeing to what we are offering you presumably means you don't want to talk to the club which was showing some interest in you?" asked Christie. For once, Steve allowed me to answer for myself. I confirmed that was very much the case and I just wanted the new season to start.

"Just one thing, Peter. Which club was it?"

Christie said silent for several seconds weighing up whether he should tell me or not and I didn't think he would tell me—after all, he was the ultimate control freak.

"London club. First Division. Play in white shirts. Now bugger off and I'll get all the paperwork drawn up for you to review and sign."

"Great," said Steve as we walked out of Wood Lane. "Let's celebrate with a good lunch." The smell of fish and chips wafted on the air from the Golden Cod. "How about haddock and chips?" I asked. "You must be fucking joking," he said. "I want some champagne. I'll even pay for it." The haddock and chips, although hugely tempting, could wait.

We glugged champagne and ate sea food—funnily enough, I seem to remember paying—did some impromptu business planning, spoke about holidays and made predictions for the upcoming 1982 World Cup, which I intended to totally immerse myself in.

"You know that if you move without requesting a transfer you get ten per cent of the fee don't you?" I did. "Well, when you do decide to leave let me know and I'll make sure that happens."

Happy days.

Part III
Dining at the Top Table

Chapter One
Failing to Reign in Spain

I had been looking forward to our pre-season tournament in Spain all summer. Not only did it extend my stay in the sun, but it was also a completely different experience and was the first time I had played football abroad since I played in a Boy Scouts' tournament in the Netherlands. Just to be clear, I joined the Scouts so I could play football; I wasn't interested in Scouting in any shape or form.

From a professional standpoint, it meant we would be playing with our new teammates in a competitive environment which made far more sense than playing against a few lower league English teams with the endless rounds of substitutions. And it was several rungs up the ladder from Bisham Abbey and on a completely different planet compared to Skegness.

There were two groups of four and the teams finishing top would contest the final. We were in the same group as tournament hosts Real Betis, based in Seville, Motherwell of the Scottish Premier League and Monaco from France Ligue 1. The second group comprised Nantes of France, Spanish outfit Celta Vigo, Augsburg from Germany's Bundesliga and Aberdeen, who had been invited on the strength of their Scottish Cup win. OK, maybe not the cream of the European football crop but some decent teams, nevertheless.

The attendances, despite being boosted by some interested tourists and a handful of travelling fans, were disappointing. I put this down to Spain's fairly inept showing in the World Cup just a few weeks previously despite their home advantage. Maybe there was also a case of football overload.

Spain had made it through to the Second Stage of the World Cup, despite losing 1-0 to Northern Ireland and drawing 1-1 with Honduras, thanks to a 2-1 win against Yugoslavia. The second stage saw them lose 2-1 to West Germany and draw 0-0 with England which wasn't enough for them to progress to the knockout stages. They had looked indifferent throughout the tournament, perhaps the expectation of the nation weighed too heavy on their shoulders, but in those days Spain tended to flatter to deceive.

England hadn't faired any better. They made a bright start beating France 3-1 and although they then beat Czechoslovakia 2-0 and Kuwait 1-0 those latter performances were turgid, unconvincing affairs. In the second stage, we drew 0-0 with both West Germany and Spain meaning we came home undefeated but hardly covered in glory. The general consensus was that the manager, Ron Greenwood, despite being an advocate of attacking football and having a couple of flair players, most notably Glenn Hoddle in his squad, had taken the advice of his coach, Don Howe, who had a reputation for a conservative approach.

How Graham Rix played and Hoddle hardly appeared remains beyond me; yet another example of England failing to trust a player with skill and panache who can win you a match. In fact, how Graham Rix played at all remains beyond me. My interest in the tournament waned and despite my intention to watch as many games as possible, I watched only a handful of matches and dipped in and out of the final between Italy and West Germany, thankfully won by Italy. Greenwood left the managerial chair and handed over to Bobby Robson and I wondered if I had any chance of being part of his squad for the next World Cup in four years.

Our performance in our slightly less glamorous tournament was somewhere between those of England and Spain. We started brightly thrashing Motherwell 5-1, then drew 0-0 with Monaco in a desperate affair which was awful to play in; God knows what it was like to watch. Having handed out a thumping to Motherwell we then got one back when we lost our third match against Real Betis 4-0. Not even an all-Spanish final stirred much interest and we returned home to continue our pre-season training. At one stage, there were plans for us to play Linfield which had been agreed as part of Mick Egan's transfer but the Northern Ireland "troubles" put paid to that. Instead, we paid a modest transfer fee—given how important he had become, it was more of a steal—and supplied them with more kit and balls.

With so much transfer business done during the summer pre-season was often a strange experience—probably it still is—not so much because of the new faces but more because of those which are missing. Come the end of the season a player is part of the furniture; the next time you walk into the club he's gone. And they tend to move to all ends of the country so the idea of catching up with an old teammate for a beer after work wasn't very realistic.

Saunders, as we knew he would, had been working overtime during the break with four players leaving and six coming in, a real revolving-door of a summer. Rob Riley, who was doing well as manager of Grimsby, had come calling (or maybe Saunders had tipped him the wink) and signed both Rob Keen and John Halliday. Dave Walters had thanked Saunders for the chance to join the coaching staff but decided he wasn't ready to hang up his boots just yet and went back to Doncaster, while Alan Deakin had signed for Sheffield United. One face I hadn't expected to see was Mick Egan's. He had been open to an offer from West Bromwich Albion but didn't much fancy the Birmingham area and couldn't agree terms. "Tight bastards," was his succinct summary.

I was delighted Egan was still with us and his importance was sharply illustrated when he didn't play against Real Betis and suddenly there were yawning chasms in our defence. Jimmy Seal hadn't been sold either but having spoken to him while we were in Spain, he was aware that the next couple of months would be make or break for him. "I know the Boss doesn't fancy me much. There are times I regret signing." I had some sympathy as I considered Seal to be a useful player who could operate up front or in midfield.

The new signings were goalkeeper John Webb (from Middlesbrough), Dave Stewart (Bolton) who could play anywhere across the back line, midfielder Bill Cooke (Swansea) and Nick Athey (Coventry) another midfielder. Forwards who arrived were Steve Baker, who was part of the deal which took Deakin to Bramall Lane and Manchester United reserve John Day on a season-long loan.

Of those, Athey, Baker and Cooke had First Division experience, while Cooke was a regular member of the Wales squad with over twenty caps to his name. Day might only have been with us on loan but his signing was quite a feather in the Northtown cap. Saunders announced all the signings as First Division quality but he may have had second thoughts after our experiences in Spain, even though it was very early days.

We had a squad of eighteen and although we also had some promising reserves to call on, I thought we were still light on numbers. A quick look at the Playfair Football Album showed that all our First Division opponents had in the region of thirty players listed. My biggest worry was that we didn't have a proven First Division goal scorer. Dutch had looked disinterested in Spain, Seal was trying too hard, Baker was finding his feet and Day had been signed too late in the day to make the plane.

Saunders and his coaching staff were so concerned about our performances against Monaco and Real Betis, they brought us in for extra training and arranged a couple of friendlies against local non-league outfit St Albans City. They felt we lacked energy while my midfield pairing with Billy Cooke hadn't clicked. Early days, I thought. But Dutch hadn't been at the races and his apparent disinterest did nothing to help the endeavours of those playing alongside him, especially Steve Baker, who was obviously bewildered by his strike partner's lack of effort. Although we had an easy day in the sun against Motherwell, they were very poor and we didn't get too carried away. Saunders was right about lacking in energy when we played Monaco; we were stuck in first gear for the entire ninety minutes and without Rob Davies, who had picked up a sore heel on the hard surfaces, had no real creativity especially with Aitken also going through early-season struggles.

We were as poor as I could ever remember against Real Betis, but to give it some perspective this was the first time we had been completely outplayed over the entire course of ninety minutes for at least three years. But no Davies, no Egan and a misfiring Pieters certainly made us look lightweight and I guess if I had been in Saunders' boots I would have been worried as well.

Saunders read the riot act to Dutch in front of all of us after the Real Betis game, making it quite clear that he needed to extract his digit from his back passage if he wanted to play First Division football with us. Pieters was the kind of player who responded to a kick up the backside but none of us had seen Saunders go on as loud and as long as he did that afternoon. Dutch, to his credit, took it despite not being happy about a couple of things that were said.

By the time our first-ever game in the First Division came round—at home to our old friends Everton—on 28 August 1982, he was back on track and bagged both goals in a highly satisfying 2-0 win. Bear in mind this was an Everton side which was on the cusp of becoming an excellent team. They won the FA Cup the following season, 1983-84, and the year after that they were crowned First Division champions and won the European Cup Winners' Cup for good measure.

It was an excellent start to our campaign and showed how quickly form can change. Three days after seeing off Howard Kendall's side we travelled to the south coast and stuffed Southampton 4-1 and our highly impressive start continued as we won four out of our first five games, which meant by late September we were looking down on the entire English football system. It was hard enough to believe how far we had come in such a short period but to think we were looking down on the rest of the country (and a little bit of Wales) was unbelievable.

A promoted team making an early, sometimes lasting impression, wasn't so unusual when I was kicking a ball about. Leicester City winning the 2015-2016 Premier League was undoubtedly a fairy tale come true and great for the game but really everyone knows now at the start of a new season Manchester City are likely to win the title, Liverpool will possibly run them close, Chelsea are likely to finish third and if Manchester United and Arsenal ever get their acts back together they will have a say, as will any team bought by a multi-billionaire Arab Sheikh who will spend as much as it takes to be successful. That's the way of the game now and although megabucks doesn't necessarily represent widespread success—Manchester City still haven't won the Champions League and given the amount of money they have thrown at it they should have—it can certainly buy you domestic success. But if I were a City fan, I would be getting a little bored with their domination of the League Cup and would swop some of those for a Champions League title.

I would also like to make the point that the Community Shield does not count as a major piece of silverware—you win the League or the FA Cup and consequently play a one-off match which raises the curtain on the next season. Pep and Jose may claim it as a major trophy, especially in the case of Jose when things aren't going so well for him and he feels the need to remind people of how many trophies he has won. But a major pot it is not.

I just can't see a newly-promoted side sitting pretty at the top of the table after five or so matches happening again. Nine years before we made our spectacular start just-promoted Carlisle United won their first three fixtures and topped the table, but their bubble burst quite dramatically and they ended up being relegated. The 1977-78 season saw Nottingham Forest, unbelievably, win the title in their first season back in the top flight having been promoted at the end of the previous season by the skin of their teeth.

The next season, also highly improbably, they lifted the European Cup. It's less hard to believe when you remember they were managed by Brian Clough, not forgetting his assistant Peter Taylor, whose influence is often over-looked. The same dynamic duo brought Derby County into the First Division in 1969 and they were crowned champions just three years later.

A little further back Ipswich Town won promotion from Division Two in the 1960-61 season and won the First Division the following season. Their manager was a certain Alf Ramsey, later to be knighted, of course, after he led England to victory in the 1966 World Cup.

While I didn't think it was very likely we would repeat the feats of Nottingham Forest and Ipswich Town I was equally certain we wouldn't follow in the footsteps of Carlisle United. I also knew that we were going to enjoy looking down on the rest of English (and Welsh) football for as long as it lasted, especially as many people in and around the First Division were looking down their noses at us.

Our seventh match was at home to Sunderland and we ran riot, winning 8-0, to record our highest-ever Football League win. It could easily have been double figures as we hit the woodwork four times and their keeper made a couple of excellent saves. Pieters netted four, Day and Davies two apiece. Sunderland looked like relegation candidates although they ultimately finished well clear of the drop; we played like champions and at the end of October Rob Davies, who was getting better and better and was giving First Division defenders as torrid a time as those in the lower leagues, was deservedly called into the England squad.

Like everyone else at the club, there were certain grounds I had really been looking forward to playing at. I couldn't wait to play Manchester United at Old Trafford but was disappointed in more ways than one. We conceded an early goal but equalised before half-time and were definitely a match for them in every aspect but conceded a second a few minutes from the end and lost the ball straight from the restart and United scored a third. The 3-1 scoreline indicates a relatively straightforward win for the home side but it was far from that. I also found the atmosphere—or lack of it—a real let down. I had expected the ground to be rocking, regardless of the opposition, but it was one of the quieter grounds we played at which was a real surprise given I watched United a few times in London with my mates and the travelling support was huge and equally loud.

It was pretty much the polar opposite at Anfield, where I had also been looking forward to playing. There was a hell of a din throughout the ninety minutes and I had been caught upfield and was looking directly at the Kop when the eventual champions scored one of their three goals. I don't know how many thousands were standing on the Kop but they all swayed as a single huge wave when the ball hit the back of the net. As at Old Trafford, we lost 3-1 but this time it was a more routine victory for the home side and we scored our goal in what was then known as injury time.

The Liverpool players went mad at each other when we scored our consolation with Ray Clemence blaming anyone who crossed his path for the goal. Liverpool were a tremendous side and also included Graeme Souness, Kenny Dalglish and Ian Rush. Anfield was undoubtedly my favourite away experience, regardless of the result.

As the season unfolded, we became more and more confident and showed resilience as well as skill and recorded some notable wins. We played particularly well against West Bromwich Albion at the Hawthorns, another ground I enjoyed because the pitch was tight to the terraces and the fans generated a great atmosphere. They weren't very happy that we won 3-0 but Albion simply weren't a match for us on the day and I think we played almost as well against them as we had when we trounced Sunderland at the start of the season.

I was also looking forward to visiting the City Ground to take on Nottingham Forest, mainly so I could see Brian Clough, even if it was unlikely I would be able to meet him. We managed an honourable draw, sharing two goals, but Cloughie wasn't firing on all cylinders that day. He sat on the bench in his usual scruffy green sweatshirt but didn't shout at his players or make any comments of note after the match. Saunders met him and described him as a "real gentleman—he wishes us well and said we should ignore any criticism of our playing style."

Inevitably, the season had a few downs including consecutive heavy away defeats to Aston Villa (4-0) and Stoke City (4-1). The former game was a nightmare for Dutch who was reminded throughout the ninety minutes by the Holt End he was a "Villa reject" and his day was made complete when he scuffed our only real chance of the game a few feet wide of the goal. Even a couple of us had a laugh at that but Dutch was in no mood for jokes when we got back in the dressing room.

Amazingly, we finished sixth. A team which had to fight hard to get out of the Second Division just twelve months earlier was now the country's sixth best side, and we hadn't made that many additions to the squad. Finishing sixth meant the 1983-84 season would see European football at Wood Lane for the first time as despite an end-of-season blip which saw us win just one of our last five games we qualified for the UEFA Cup. We finished with sixty-eight points and there were one-hundred-and-thirty goals in our forty-two games—guaranteed entertainment.

But while we were scoring goals almost for fun, we were also conceding them at a fairly alarming rate as well. We liked to play on the front foot, Saunders wouldn't countenance us approaching the game in any other way and was particularly scathing of any side which tried to catch its opponents offside or would constantly pass back to their keeper. We were also fortunate that Andy Hopkins had a stellar season between the posts, despite having to pick the ball out of the back of his net fifty-seven times, which meant we conceded more goals than any side in the top ten apart from West Ham who shipped sixty-four.

At the other end of the pitch Dutch, who had looked so sluggish and disinterested pre-season, was our top scorer bulldozing his way to twenty-eight goals and there were contributions from all over.

Of the newcomers, Dave Stewart did well at the back when he stood in for Mick Egan who missed games first through injury and then suspension. Some thought Egan was fortunate to regain his place but he was a class act. Mike Sears played a handful of games at left back in place of Terry Green as Saunders planned for the future and acquitted himself very well. Nick Athey didn't get much of a look-in but was a useful squad man. I liked the look of Steve Baker who scored a few goals but I don't think Saunders was sure of his best pairing up front. John Day was an enigma; brilliant on some occasions and totally anonymous on others and was the kind of player who, having left a string of defenders in his wake, then went back to beat the last one again and would fall over. It was a habit which annoyed the hell out of Dutch who, on a couple of occasions, was close to doing him physical harm. Day, though, was also adaptable and played left midfield when Rob Davies was injured. A livewire off the field as well as on it, Day was missed when he returned to Old Trafford.

Undoubtedly the new boy on the block who received the best end-of-season report was Bill Cooke and he was my player of the season by a mile. It was Dutch Pieters, however, who won the players' and fans' awards—with twenty-eight goals in the First Division it was hard to argue with those decisions, but people don't appreciate the hard graft us midfielders put into ninety minutes while forwards tend to cruise around and then bask in the glory when the ball deflects into the net off their backside!

Chapter Two
A Highbury High

Our promotion to the First Division was hardly greeted with universal approval as many "experts" branded us "long ball merchants" and there was often a barely disguised message that there was no room for our tactics in such a wonderful League.

If Glenn Hoddle played a long ball which led to goal, it would be considered a thing of beauty and would be analysed to death by Jimmy Hill on Match of the Day or Brian Moore on The Big Match. If one of us played a similar pass, it was considered to have been an aimless punt upfield which a forward managed to get on the end of. Alan Ball, one of my heroes, had predicted we would go straight back down and of course he is entitled to his opinion. When we won 4-1 at The Dell in our second game of the season, Tony Saunders was quick to remind Ball of his words and the World Cup winner took it very well and was gracious enough to buy all of us a drink in the players' lounge and wished us all the best.

Fans were guaranteed goals when they watched us. We were only involved, if memory serves me right, in one 0-0 draw all season, an admittedly dire match against Coventry who, as ever it seemed, were fighting against relegation and stuck ten men behind the ball for the entire ninety minutes. Goals equal entertainment and isn't it entertainment that people pay good money to watch?

We were still essentially a 4-4-2 team, although the midfield shape was changed slightly with Cooke lying deep and me playing a more advanced role than in previous seasons. Davies and Aitken, as ever, provided width, pace and skill on the flanks. This set-up made us more fluid but wasn't really commented on. When Terry Venable used a similar formation in Euro 96, it was described as a diamond or a Christmas tree and was seen as a tactical masterstroke.

Nevertheless, opponents looked down their noses at us and managers, pundits and press alike weren't effusive in their praise for our performances and results. Presumably we had been lucky to beat Sunderland 8-0 and every goal had come from a punt upfield? When we played Spurs at White Hart Lane, Glenn Hoddle thought he was ever so funny in the warm-up by continually kicking the ball as high in the air as he could mocking, in his opinion, the way we played. If clubs were going to look down their noses at us, we would do our damnedest to bloody them! The fact we won at White Hart Lane did nothing to improve Hoddle's mood or that of their fans who, as ever, were quick to get on their team's back when things weren't going well for them. We started to develop a siege mentality long before the phrase became widely used in football.

Arsenal. I've never been a fan. I'm a little surprised given I consider myself to be a "student" of the game and the history and heritage of a few of our leading clubs mean I have an interest in, and an affection for, some of them. Take Manchester United. When I first became interested in football, they had Best, Charlton, Law et al. They played attacking football and had a swagger about them. Then they won the 1968 European Cup, just ten years after the Munich Air disaster. I had a real liking for them.

I also admired the way Liverpool had come out of the Second Division to become a European power. I even admired what Leeds had achieved, although I was quiet about that. Both sides had brilliant players, Liverpool were blessed to have Shankly as manager, Leeds fans would say the same about Don Revie, but I wasn't keen on the rubbish he spoke about his lucky suit and having a gypsy lift a supposed curse on Elland Road.

Arsenal? I knew about their historic successes under Herbert Chapman and the marble halls of Highbury and the famous clock end, but they never did it for me. They famously won the Double in 1970-71 but did so without gripping or entertaining the nation and churned out a lot of 1-0 wins, despite having some outstanding players. And suddenly loads of schoolmates jumped on the Arsenal bandwagon and became lifelong Gunners. I was also rooting for Liverpool in the Cup Final when Arsenal achieved the Double.

In the lead-up to our game at Highbury, my dislike of them was intensified when their manager, Terry Neill, a former Arsenal player and Northern Ireland international, accused us of being "nothing more than long ball merchants." A few journalists had panned us and there had been some unattributed comments from people in the game but as far as I can remember Neill was the first manager to be openly critical. Perhaps he deserves some credit for saying it out loud rather than whispering it.

It got right under our skin though.

Saunders believed in attacking play. He liked the ball to be played out wide and crossed into the box. To say he was pissed off by Neill's comments would be a gross understatement and he made sure everyone at the club was aware of his comments by plastering copies of them on walls everywhere and kept reminding us during training what was coming out of Highbury—especially if anyone passed the ball more than fifteen yards forward. By the time, we were ready to enter the Highbury arena, nothing needed saying. Terry Neill had very kindly delivered the team talk and motivated us. Perhaps we needed the opposition manager to "dis" us before every match because we played out of our skins and won 3-1 in what was easily our best performance of the season. I would go so far as to say it was our best performance since I came into the team.

Highbury Stadium, London. Saturday, 27 November 1982. Arsenal v Northtown United. League Division One.

Arsenal may be "in transition," but they still reckon they are going to roll us over. Neill has obviously been at his players and they goad us for the first twenty minutes or so about us being "long-ball merchants" with no "class or skill." The Highbury crowd is on our backs as well and every time one of us gets the ball in our final third they chant "hoof, hoof, hoof." But the players soon shut up and their fans fall silent because they collectively realise they have a serious match on their hands.

Rob Davies has been brilliant this season and it is little wonder he's made his England debut. Today he is on fire and is running rings around the Arsenal defence which can't cope with either his pace or his trickery, while Pete Aitken on the right flank isn't far behind him and with Pieters bullying the central defenders the once almost-impenetrable Arsenal defence is showing signs of wear and tear. It is Rob who deservedly opens the scoring, picking up the ball just inside the Arsenal half and going on a mazy run before cutting in from the left and rocketing a right foot shot into the top corner. Even some Arsenal fans feel the need to greet this effort with half-hearted applause.

It's 1-0 to the good guys at half-time but Arsenal really haven't been in it as Saunders points out. "They are there for the taking. Keep giving the ball to Rob and Pete and they will do the rest but don't lose concentration and let them back into it."

One minute after the restart and it's 1-1. Despite Saunders' warnings we switch off and concede a corner straight from kick-off and Arsenal, presumably having received a half-time rocket from Neill, score from the resulting scramble. Saunders and the coaching staff are going berserk on the touchline while some of the Arsenal players—God knows why they hated us so much—are in our faces. We are all seriously pissed off and a rallying cry from the skipper isn't needed. Arsenal, the wind firmly in their sails, have a sustained period of pressure but Bell and Egan are superb and Hopkins is hardly tested. Gradually, the wind dies down and we get back on top. We win a free-kick on the edge of their box and I have a crack, but the ball hits the wall before spinning out to Aitken who sends in a low hard cross which skims across the six-yard box to Davies, standing completely unmarked at the far post, and he taps the ball home. Cue celebrations in front of the Arsenal "hard nuts" occupying the North Stand who don't appreciate our gestures. Who cares?

Neill throws on his substitute, tinkers with his formation and we score a third, fittingly, through Aitken, who has been even better this half than in the first forty-five minutes. I get the ball deep in our half, go forward as Arsenal back off and move it to Day, who has dropped into midfield. Day skips through one challenge, looks up and plays a pass over the heads of the centre backs and Aitken runs in, controls the ball and rounds their keeper before rolling the ball into the empty net.

Cue more celebrations in front of the Arsenal "hard nuts" occupying the North Stand. This time, they aren't swearing and snarling at us or threatening us with actual bodily harm, they are telling their team what they think of them and chants of "Neill out" ring loud round the stadium. Again, who cares?

We continue to have the best of the encounter—by far the best of the encounter. Perhaps we should have scored more but we were happy to keep possession and see out time. "It's just like watching Brazil" is the chant from our supporters. The North Bank responds with "We're shit and we know we are." My partnership with Cooke had been coming together nicely in recent weeks, here it reaches maturity and the Arsenal midfield can't get a look-in.

The final whistle sounds. Boos ring out. One or two Arsenal players offer congratulations, but they are half-hearted at best. I look over to the tunnel and there's a bit of argy-bargy going on. In fact, it's really kicking off between Saunders and Neill who have been at each other's' throats—figuratively if not quite literally—throughout the match. Stewards and officials charge in to calm things down but inevitably only add to the confusion and a few lazy punches are thrown by players on either side. "If only Iain Moy was playing," I think.

We celebrate long and loud in the changing room. When the results are read out on Sports Report we bellow the score, so the sound carries into the Arsenal changing room. We have a quick beer in the players' lounge and Dave Craig gains access. He tells us that when Neill met the press he still maintained we were a long-ball team and became very agitated when one reporter from a national newspaper suggested we had played Arsenal off the park.

This is one of the most satisfying wins I can remember. We not only beat Arsenal, but we were also better than them in every aspect of the match and whatever Terry Neill said before, during and after the game, we had shoved his words back down his throat.

The result and the performance are a major statement—we are more than worthy of our place at the top table of English football.

Chapter Three
Cup Fever

I have to admit to having a few concerns before the start of the 1982-83 season started, thinking a long, hard slog lay ahead. I should have had more faith.

After a few weeks, and not just because of our Usain Bolt-like start, I was in no doubt we would be more than fine and the early days of the season made it obvious there were a lot of teams not as fit and committed as we were and although our squad was small, which did continue to nag at me, we rose to the occasion most weeks. However, I would not have put money on us qualifying for a European competition through our final league placing.

At one stage, though, there was the distinct possibility we could have qualified for Europe through winning either the FA Cup or its sister competition, the League Cup—maybe even both! As I've already said we didn't have a great record in either competition and had lost our fair share of cup ties to teams we really should have beaten. The 1982-83 season saw our record improve as we reached the quarter-finals of the former, while the twin towers of Wembley were within our sights in the FA Cup. Confidence was coursing through our veins and after every game we couldn't wait for the next one—if we had to wait seven days it was too long, so I wasn't at all surprised that we did better in the cups this season than before.

The League Cup, known at this time for sponsorship purposes as the Milk Cup, has been much maligned down the years. It was introduced in the 1960-61 season and the first winners were Aston Villa, who won a two-legged final against Rotherham. Due to fixture congestion, it wasn't played until the start of the following season so was possibly seen as a distraction by some clubs, even though there was only the League and the FA Cup, plus European competitions for a much smaller number of teams than today, to contend with.

From 1968 onwards, the winners would earn a place in the Fairs Cup, the forerunner to the UEFA Cup/UEFA Europa League, so it had to be worth taking seriously. And it produced some memorable finals such as Third Division QPR beating First Division West Bromwich 3-2 in 1967 after being 2-0 down and another Third Division outfit, Swindon Town beating the mighty Arsenal 3-1 a couple of years later. Ridiculously the winners would only play in Europe if they were a First Division side—let's look down our noses at the outstanding success of a small team.

No doubt the powers-that-be felt they were proved right when Arsenal went on to win the Fairs Cup the following season. Swindon would not have done that but they could well have won their first round tie against Arsenal's opponents at that stage, Glentoran. And in all likelihood, they would have fared better than Dundalk, who played Liverpool in the first round and lost 14-0 on aggregate.

These days the importance of the Premier League and Europe means the League Cup is a distant fourth on the priority list of the "big" clubs, who field weakened teams in many of the rounds and then often bring back the A-list players if they make the final. Even average sides field weakened teams because they are so worried about playing too many games, running out of steam, and being relegated.

If I was a supporter of, for example, Wolves I would want to see them going all out to win one of the cups and get into Europe. Over the years, the League Cup has abandoned its two-legged first and second rounds and semi-finals and final, as well as replays, making it easier, perhaps I should say less hard, to win. And let's face it, teams like Wolves will never win the Premier League unless a seriously rich sugar daddy decides to chuck a few billion quid their way.

We began our campaign with second round 2-1 home and away wins against Bolton Wanderers of the Second Division. With a squad which included former Manchester City skipper Mike Doyle, who had also played a couple of games for England, John McGovern, the Scottish international who had played for Brian Clough at Derby, Leeds and Forest, Steve Whitworth, ex-Leicester and England, Ian Moores, ex-Stoke and England Under 23 and Peter Reid, soon to be transferred to Everton and become an England international, we expected a really difficult encounter but it was straightforward enough and Bolton ended up being relegated at the end of the season. With players like that, they should have been in the promotion picture.

The third round saw us closer to home and winning 2-1 again, at Crystal Palace. Next up was Barnsley, like Bolton and Palace from Division Two. They proved a tough nut to crack but Dutch, inevitably, headed us into the lead and Bill Cooke weighed in with a rare goal to make the tie safe.

There must have been something about Second Division sides whose name began with a B and were based in Lancashire in the 1982-83 season. We drew Burnley in the quarter-finals and like Bolton they had a really impressive squad—the cultured former England midfielder Martin Dobson, the much-less cultured but very effective Scottish defender Willie Donachie who went to the 1974 and 1978 World Cups, Brian Flynn with over sixty caps for Wales, Billy Hamilton, the feisty Northern Ireland striker with forty caps and who appeared in the 1982 World Cup, future England international Trevor Steven, Mike Phelan who went on to play for Manchester United and once for England. One hell of a squad for a Second Division outfit. Like Bolton they were relegated. Unlike Bolton, they beat us.

Not only did they beat us they ran us ragged at times and the 3-1 scoreline didn't flatter them. It certainly flattered us. Despite our mainly good form, there were a couple of occasions during the course of the season when we played as if we were in a daydream and this was one of those occasions. Some observers suggested we were over-confident and possibly we were but I don't remember having that feeling.

Burnley simply played as they should have played with the players they had at their disposal, we had an off night and were one down within five minutes and two down within twenty. Andy Hopkins limited the damage and we played better in the second half but we could have no complaints. Burnley drew Liverpool, the eventual winners, in the semi-finals so we missed the opportunity to play again at Anfield, which I would have loved.

The FA Cup, the world's oldest knockout tournament and so famous even natives living in the deepest Amazonian jungle have heard of it, has also become devalued as football has grown out of all proportion as a sport. TV companies have done their best to regenerate excitement which of course they would but while so many teams, and not just the "big boys," rest their players and treat the competition almost as second class the FA Cup will never have the glamour it used to have. It needs a Wigan to beat Manchester City or a Sunderland to beat Leeds in the final more regularly for it to recapture its former glory.

Another problem is that the bigger teams treat it with disdain in the early rounds but their squads are so strong they win regardless of the individuals they field and make it through to the latter stages. In the ten years since the Cup Final returned to Wembley, only eleven sides have contested it. Arsenal and Chelsea have appeared in it four times, the two Manchester clubs five times between them. I understand that clubs are terrified of being relegated if they take their eye off the ball and don't put survival first, but it would make a real difference to the lustre of the competition if some of the "middle-of-the-road" clubs put as much emphasis on the cups as the league.

Having said that, we had never done much in either competition, the 1980-81 season aside when we were beaten by Everton in a quarter-final replay. We certainly didn't dismiss these competitions, although Saunders did make the comment about concentrating on the cups when we were a Second Division side, but I don't think there were the same levels of intensity in training in the lead-up to a cup match or in the dressing room in the minutes before one. It was almost a "tomorrow is another day" attitude—if we don't do well this season there's always the next campaign to make our mark. It was strange how we then had excellent runs in both competitions in the same season.

Our name was the first out of the hat in the third round draw and the more superstitious among us—Dutch—felt this was a good omen. We were paired with Third Division Plymouth Argyle who we saw off easily enough, 2-0, on a bitterly cold January afternoon. The Fourth Round saw us drawn at home, again, to Second Division Derby County who gave us a shock by taking an early lead and holding on to it until very late on when Pete Aitken fired home from the edge of the box. Reminiscent of his goal against Everton at Goodison Park a couple of years before. The replay was on the following Wednesday at the Baseball Ground, notorious for being a mud-patch of a pitch from about November to April. Goals from Baker and Davies cancelled out Derby's early opener. They had run us close and could feel slightly aggrieved it wasn't their name going into the velvet bag for the fifth round draw.

I had always wanted to play at Elland Road and I was finally granted my wish when the draw for the fifth round was made. Leeds' glory days were, of course, well behind them but although they were in the Second Division we expected a stern test in a hostile environment. It wasn't to be and although Leeds had a number of seasoned professionals—code for they've seen better days—

several of whom were ex-internationals, we had little trouble as we ran out 4-1 winners.

The home crowd, noisy as hell in the opening exchanges, and quick to tell our supporters they were a bunch of "Southern poofters" had the wind taken out of their sails as we ran riot in the first half scoring three times in twenty minutes immediately before half-time. After that, they satisfied themselves by telling everyone "there is only one Yorkshire Ripper." Class.

Quarter-final day in the FA Cup used to be a special one in the football calendar. All four games kicking off at the same time on the same Saturday afternoon, generated interest and intrigue among soccer fans across the country. TV coverage now means one tie is held on a Friday night, another on Saturday, one on Sunday and the last one on Monday night. Another reason why the magic of the FA Cup has been diluted.

Aston Villa, away. There were a number of ways at looking at this draw. One is that there were few harder draws given that Villa had won the League two seasons ago, the European Cup the previous season, were going well in the competition again and were showing well in the League. With that recent record they had, as you would expect, some top-notch players including Gordon Cowans, Gary Shaw and Peter Withe. They also had Dennis Mortimer who I felt should have played for England and Tony Cowans who did play for England but should have played more games and should certainly have gone to the 1982 Spain World Cup. Again, all in my humble opinion.

They were strong all over the pitch, but much as in the previous round against Leeds, Villa didn't prove to be nearly as tough opposition as we expected. We certainly played very well again but Villa disappointed on the day. Dutch, much to his delight as he had been baited all afternoon by the home fans who were again quick to remind him of his unsuccessful spell at Villa Park, and Mick Egan scored the goals in a 2-0 win.

We celebrated long and loud in the Villa Park dressing room before a train took us back to Northtown, where we celebrated even more loudly and for much longer. On the following Monday, Saunders made it abundantly clear that once we knew who we would be playing in the last four, all talk of the semi-final would be banned until it became our next match. Understandable but impossible to enforce given the fervour among our fans and the local and national press.

We knew what Saunders meant—"don't lose focus on the bread and butter of the league. We've come a long way and done so well. Don't let the semi-final distract from what we are doing in the league." He added if he thought a player was distracted by what was coming up, he would drop him. He expected total effort and commitment.

The draw meant we would be going back to Villa Park for the semi-final as we would be playing Manchester United. The other tie, between Brighton and Sheffield Wednesday, would take place at Arsenal's Highbury Stadium. Same day, same time. Not anymore, of course. Another reason why the semi-finals aren't quite as special as they were is because they are now played at Wembley instead of a neutral ground. I know, I know. Money drives the game and Wembley is not only the home of English football but having cost such a ridiculous amount to build, means the FA has to recoup as much as it can.

I'm sure there are plenty of players and fans who think playing both ties at Wembley is a good idea—if they play at a neutral venue and lose, they may never get the chance to play or see their team at Wembley. I get that but for the semi-final winners they are back at Wembley, just a few weeks later. To me, that takes away from what a special and unique occasion the final should be. It also costs a lot of money so for fans who earn the average wage, two trips to Wembley with all the added extras in a just a few weeks is a stretch on their finances. That is if they are lucky enough to get a ticket given the number which go to corporate hospitality and sponsors. "The prawn sandwich" brigade as Roy Kean so famously and accurately once said.

Taking the field at a fabulous stadium such as Villa Park, Hillsborough, Old Trafford or Highbury with the ground full and virtually populated by fans from both sides, is a great occasion in its own right. If I were still playing, I'm pretty sure I would be happy with that arrangement. That doesn't make me a dinosaur by the way.

Villa Park, Birmingham. Saturday, 27 November 1982. Northtown United v Manchester United. FA Cup semi-final.

The lead-up to the semi-final is crazy. Everybody wants a piece of us. And not just from this country. Word has quickly got round that only six years ago we could have lost our place in the Football League and now we are just one match away from Wembley. There are demands for interviews, TV appearances, photoshoots, requests for tickets from people I haven't seen or heard from for ages. You name it we've been asked to do it. God knows what it will be like if we can get to the final.

Saunders is faced with a difficult conversation in the week before the game. John Day is on loan from Manchester United and although he hasn't played in any previous ties to avoid him being cup tied, he has been involved in training sessions and attended the games. Saunders talks to John and explains he doesn't want him training with the squad. Rather him than me but Day takes it in good heart and zips back to spend a few days with his mates in Manchester.

Birmingham is only an hour's train ride away so our journey on Friday is a leisurely one following a short training session, at the end of which Saunders announces he will play Pieters and Baker in attack, with Seal on the bench. We spend more time than usual looking at the opposition and analysing their strengths and weaknesses. Before we played at Everton we didn't talk too much about them for fear of worrying ourselves about their quality. It's different this time as we spend a few minutes looking at the likes of Bryan Robson, Ray Wilkins, Frank Stapleton, Remi Moses, Norman Whiteside, Gordon McQueen, Arthur Albiston, Gary Bailey. It's a Who's Who of famous—and bloody good—players, not that we need reminding of who we are up against.

We are overwhelmingly the underdogs but that doesn't worry us. We've been underdogs nearly all season and have pushed United hard in both League fixtures. But this is different. It's a one-off. Robson, Wilkins, Moses, Whiteside. That's a phenomenal midfield for myself, Cooke, Davies and Aitken to contend with. We know a difficult afternoon lies ahead but we wouldn't have it any other way. And United would be worried about the attacking abilities of Davies and Aitken in particular and would spend time working out how to keep them quiet.

We are told there will be an equal number of Northtown and United fans. You could have fooled me. When we walk out to have a look at the pitch and soak up the atmosphere, it seems seventy per cent of the ground is the red and white of United and they are making a hell of a din. More evidence that United get better support on the road than at Old Trafford.

They are managed by the flamboyant Ron Atkinson, Big Ron to the media, and he likes to play the sort of football which matches his character. They move the ball quickly and are good to watch.

Many semi-finals are cagey affairs and not great entertainment. This one, though, bucks that trend and both teams go for it from the start trading punches all over the pitch. Robson, just back from injury, is looking particularly hungry while the seventeen-year-old Whiteside—seventeen and he's already played in a World Cup—demonstrates his skill and aggression in equal measure. We are making some inroads as well and Pieters and Baker aren't phased by the size and physicality of Gordon McQueen and Kevin Moran.

United are probably just ahead on points when we take the lead. Saunders and his coaching team had highlighted that United's keeper Gary Bailey is a potential weakness. "He either flaps at crosses or drops them. Can be slow when he dives," Mark Bailey had told us about his namesake. Aitken gets into the box but loses the ball to Albiston who, in turn, can't clear it. Aitken stubs a weak shot at Bailey who pushes it away instead of making an easy catch and Baker pokes the loose ball home.

The United defenders stand with hands on their hips, some are shaking their heads. Whether that is in disbelief that we have taken the lead or because they have a goalkeeper who's dropped a sitter I can't say. It's a hot day and Cooke and I are feeling the heat at half-time. Keeping Robson and Whiteside at bay has been a full-time job but we have succeeded. That success doesn't last much longer and five minutes into the second half Egan, fatally, waits for the ball to come to him and Robson nips in front of him, chests the ball down and shoots, low and left-footed, into the far corner.

Twenty minutes later and Whiteside takes his turn. Albiston plays a long ball into the box and the Northern Ireland international doesn't break stride, sending a perfect volley past Andy Hopkins.

Two one down against a very good side and struggling to keep it at that, Saunders takes off Cooke and introduces Seal as we move to 4-3-3. It almost pays off as Baker sets up Seal but he scuffs his shot straight at Bailey, who this time holds on to the ball. It is our only real chance of the half and Seal, despite a lack of action in recent months, would take it nine times out of ten.

Pete Aitken has had very little change out of Arthur Albiston this afternoon but a couple of minutes from the end he collects a pass with his back to goal, turns quickly and sprints away from the Scottish international full-back. Albiston is no slouch and is almost level with Pete when he slides in to tackle and both players go to ground amid a flurry of limbs and dust from the pitch. Penalty! Our supporters, herded behind the goal Aitken was heading for, are in no doubt but then they wouldn't be.

Aitken usually placid, reserved and undemonstrative goes berserk when the ref waves play on, chasing him half the length of the pitch and picks up the one and only booking of his career. I have to move in before yellow becomes red. I couldn't see clearly from where I was but Aitken's reaction was telling. He wouldn't usually dispute anything. Our bench goes mad. Saunders is screaming at the ref and had he heard what the Boss thought of him he would surely have sent him to the stands. The idea of the fourth official hadn't yet been introduced which was probably just as well because he would have been in for one hell of an ear-bashing from Saunders, who is apoplectic.

By contrast, as I look to our bench I notice Atkinson with his hands in his pockets and staring at the ground. "Sheepish" doesn't do his look justice. He knows United have probably got away with one. United play keep-ball for the last few minutes and we can't get possession. The full-time whistle sounds and the ground explodes as United's fans celebrate. Atkinson lumbers on to the pitch to congratulate his players, a few of their fans also get onto the pitch—nothing new there these days!—while we sink to the ground, totally knackered. Two or three surround the ref, Saunders is waiting for him at the entrance to the tunnel but a combination of stewards and Mark Bailey manage to get him away before the official leaves the field and Saunders talks himself into a fine and a touchline ban. Or both.

One or two are in tears in the dressing room. That's not for me. I sit on the bench staring into the middle distance, reflecting on what's just happened and what it means. United were better than us on the day, much better and fully deserved their win. Although I know Bryan Robson is a hell of a player, I didn't realise just how good he is. He had been decent against us in the league match at Old Trafford without being special and was injured when we met at Wood Lane. Today, his performance for a huge match was at a different level.

I wanted more of these occasions and to be able to raise my game for them like Robson. I don't take defeat well but I am able to be realistic and I'm certainly not one to carry the baggage of a loss home with me and give people a bad time or sit moping for the rest of the weekend. Football maybe my life but life is too short for all of that.

The main point of discussion, inevitably, is the "trip" on Pete Aitken and the ref failing to award us a penalty. The debate goes on and on. I may give refs a bit of stick when I'm on the pitch but I see no reason to join in this pointless debate. Whatever we say and think it's gone and there is nothing anyone can do about it. If the ref cocked up he cocked up. If Jimmy Seal had taken his chance we may not even be talking about it.

Saunders and his staff finally try to lift spirits telling us how well we had played and how we had run United close but they know their words are falling on deaf ears and that time is the only healer. Roger Palmer enters the dressing room and congratulates us on what we have achieved and tells us how proud we should be. No one is really listening but we sort of appreciate his comments.

Someone suggests that if United win the Cup and we finish high enough in the table we could well play in Europe next season, which makes us feel a little better, but not a lot. We have a couple of drinks on the train back to Northtown and then go our separate ways—a very different ending to when we last played at Villa Park four weeks ago.

True to form, Saunders berated the ref in front of the TV cameras. Terrible decision. How could he get it wrong from where he was standing? Why isn't the standard of refereeing higher? The right call has to be made, especially in a semi-final. Also true to form, his opposite number, Big Ron, couldn't comment on the penalty incident because he was "too far away to see it." Inevitably. But "Arthur says he definitely got the ball and that's good enough for me because he's one of the most honest professionals around." The reality is that had it all been the other way round, Atkinson would have been ranting and raving and Saunders would have been unsighted. All very embarrassing and childlike. And I don't say that using the benefit of hindsight.

Things didn't improve when the headlines in Monday's Observer screamed about us being robbed of a place at Wembley by a bad refereeing decision. Saunders opined it was because the ref was "afraid to rule against the bigger club." Unedifying and Saunders did well to dodge a charge from the Football Association for bringing the game into disrepute.

We were beaten by a better team, although we gave them a decent run for their money, and the ref had a good game. Nobody will persuade me different.

Who would be a referee? Not me, that's for sure. You run around after twenty-two men and a ball for ninety minutes getting nothing but dog's abuse and at the end of those ninety minutes one of the teams will blame the man in black for their defeat. If the match is a draw, he could be even more unlucky with both sides blaming the fact they didn't win. Then, of course, the fans will make a call to the phone-ins to say how dreadful he was and, if it's a high-profile match, there will be a couple of pundits who will rubbish him on TV in front of the nation. No win, no win.

Of course, I have mellowed towards them since my playing days when I was never backward in giving a ref a bit of stick and I picked up a fair few bookings for dissent. Depending on my mood there were plenty of occasions when I was on the ref's back from the first whistle—I didn't start on him because I was frustrated by my or the team's—or his—performance but I would deliberately target a ref because I thought he was weak so I would hope to influence him. I'm glad to say I saw the error of my ways a long time before I stopped playing and take no pride from my behaviour. These days, I have huge sympathy for referees and quite frankly I find the endless criticism of them tedious in the extreme.

Surely fans don't want to see half-a-dozen managers come on Match of the Day or Sky Sports' Super Sunday and berate the ref for their team's shortcomings? The managers, along with their players, need to take some responsibility. Let's face it the average referee makes fewer mistakes in a match than players who will mis-control the ball, pass to or lose it to an opponent, miss an open goal, drop a simple cross, make the wrong judgement. We spend endless hours doing nothing but honing our skills and still make more mistakes during the course of ninety minutes than the ref.

It would be great to see a manager stand in front of the cameras and admit the reason his side lost wasn't because of a poor refereeing decision but because his forwards missed three open goals or his goalkeeper looked more like an amateur juggler. It happens but very rarely and when it does the pundits criticise the manager for criticising his players in public. Boring, boring, boring.

Albiston's tackle on Aitken was replayed again and again and I would say the ref probably made the wrong call and should have given a penalty but it took numerous replays for me to come to that conclusion, so what chance did he have in real time? He was up with play and had a decent angle but wasn't sure and if he wasn't sure he can't give it. Simple. Naturally there were a few accusations thrown around about the big team being favoured and getting the rub of the green, which I consider insulting. I thought he had a good game and contributed to an exciting semi-final.

The standard of refereeing has yo-yoed over the years. In the early 1980s, many of them weren't fit—several actually had pot bellies—and couldn't keep up with play and were making decisions from yards and yards away so were going to make mistakes. As players began to take their fitness and recovery more seriously so referees had to react accordingly and the standard of officialdom improved. They also seemed to understand the game better and I believe the standard of refereeing in England was higher than anywhere else, which wasn't widely recognised or acknowledged.

In recent seasons, however, the standard of refereeing has probably gone backwards and the culture of the game has an enormous amount to do with this. Players go out to win free-kicks by diving, laughingly called simulation, and the feigning of injury is shameful. But the game is quicker and the players very cute in their actions making it harder and harder for referees to make the right call. I would love to see players retrospectively booked for diving and if TV can hold referees to account why shouldn't players who cheat face the music?

VAR, which I'm generally in favour of, hasn't helped because if a referee is shown to have made a mistake it's human nature his confidence will take a knock and he will be less sure of his decision-making. And with the constant chopping and changing of things like the handball law, no one knows whether they are coming or going.

Where I do have sympathy for players and this is an area the authorities should have tightened up on years ago is the different interpretation of the laws in different countries. Referees in Britain allowed far more contact or, at least, that was the case when I was playing but elsewhere in the world you only needed to breathe near someone and the ref would blow up for a free-kick. Fabio Capello, the former England manager and another dreadful appointment by our dear friends at the FA, apparently stopped picking Peter Crouch for England because of the amount of free-kicks he conceded in international matches, whereas nine times out of ten he would not have been penalised for the same challenge on a Saturday afternoon.

There will be plenty of people who will say referees are paid to make the right decisions and if they can't get them right then former players should take the whistle because they "understand the game." Of course they have a better understanding than anyone who hasn't played the game at a high level but it's inevitable they would also make mistakes and get crucial decisions wrong, mainly because players cheat.

That's a strong word but it's true and I know they are encouraged to do so by their managers and teammates. Appoint former players as referees by all means but I guarantee you will hear managers and players telling the world "he should do better, he used to be a professional player." But perhaps it's worth thinking of having a former player involved in the VAR decision-making process at Stockley Park.

I wouldn't have become a ref for all the red wine in Burgundy!

Chapter Four
China Crisis

Northtown United FC training ground. Thursday, 5 May 1983

Training finishes and we trudge towards the sanctuary of the changing rooms and showers. "Ed, I need a word. Get showered and pop into my office." I'm not sure what Tony Saunders wants to see me about but I move a bit more quickly than usual. I know from experience the Boss doesn't like to be kept waiting.

There are two seats in front of Saunders' desk and I choose the one which is in slightly better repair. There's not much in it though. Palmer's fortune and the club's successes are yet to have a major impact on the training ground and its facilities despite us being a First Division club. Mind you, it would take a considerable amount of work and money to bring everything up to modern standards.

"Roger Palmer has arranged another tour for us," says Saunders.

"Great," I reply. "I really enjoyed Spain."

"This one isn't pre-season it's in a few weeks' time. As soon as the season is over. We are going to China."

I look at Saunders while trying to digest this information. China is, I think, about five thousand miles away. No club goes to China. Why the hell are *we* going? And at the end of a seemingly endless season. which started God knows how long ago with a week of pre-season running before a tournament in Spain. By my reckoning, our small and over-stretched squad will have played fifty-one competitive matches this season, many of us will have played in every one of them. Going to Chelsea would have been a step to far. But China? What is Palmer and his fellow big-wigs thinking of?

"Boss that doesn't make sense. We're knackered. Most of us have already booked holidays at the end of the season."

Saunders doesn't respond to that but explains we will be flying to Peking (now Beijing) four days after our last game of the season, in other words in just under two weeks. It will take a couple of days to get there. We will be there for just over one week playing three matches in Beijing and Shanghai, a three-hour return flight apart.

"What do you want me to say, Boss? If you've called me here for my opinion then I think it stinks and I can't see anyone liking it."

"It's not a case of anyone liking it. We are going. We have no choice. I'm telling you out of courtesy as skipper. We'll address the squad after training tomorrow," Saunders tells me. I don't think he sounds overly enthusiastic about going to China but he also points out it's a highly lucrative deal for the club.

"Hopefully you can get some better chairs then," I say. "But I think you should be prepared for a shit storm."

I walk down the corridor from Saunders' office to the changing rooms. Tommy Butler, Bill Cooke and Dutch are still hanging about obviously keen to know why I had been summoned. I'm not saying a word about China and brush aside their questions but I think they can see I'm not happy.

Friday, 6 May, 13.30 hours. Press Room, Northtown United. Stunned silence. Secretary Peter Christie has just outlined the club's plans for the end of the season. China. For about ten days. Lots of travel. Great for the club. Ground-breaking. We will be pioneers. Wonderful cultural experience for everyone.

"What if we don't want to go?" asks Nick Athey.

Not an option. Obliged to go. Failure to attend would be a breach of contract. Not a good idea to think along those lines.

"I'm supposed to be on holiday when we are due to be in China," says Terry Bell.

Rebook. Shouldn't have made arrangements without checking with the club first. Will consider reasonable reimbursement.

"Try telling all our wives and partners. You say we shouldn't book stuff but the club should give us fair warning," says Terry Green.

"Yeh, man. My Gloria ain't gonna like this," adds Dutch.

I talk about player welfare. Not just the long season but the endless hours of travel. Economy seats on a plane for the best part of two days there and two days back and then travel from one city to another. All this will put a strain on our well-honed bodies and put us at risk of injury. What about sanitation and food hygiene and accommodation?

All this has been considered apparently. The experience will be great for team bonding. We will be firing on all cylinders at the start of the next campaign. We have been assured of the best facilities.

The meeting ends. Although we have no option other than to go on the trip, there is a real anger among the squad with most of us worried about breaking the news to our families and having to rearrange our plans. I didn't tell Tina the night before because it will be yet another case of putting her in a difficult position— she will be professionally obliged to tell her editor, even write the story. The story won't break in The Observer until the beginning of next week as it doesn't publish at weekends. Tina isn't due to attend tomorrow's home match against Ipswich so unless she bumps into a player's wife or girlfriend she won't know until I tell her. Sunday, I think I will tell her on Sunday. There's a lot for me to consider.

Saturday, 7 May, 12.00 to 17.00 hours. Wood Lane Stadium, Northtown. Ipswich are a decent side who will give us a run for our money. The dressing room is quiet as we prepare. A few whispered comments, some head-shaking. Let's just say morale isn't good and that's obvious as we put in our worst performance of the season, losing 4-1. Ipswich can't believe how easy it is for them. I can't believe we managed to score a goal.

We go out in the evening with friends, almost inevitably to a Chinese restaurant. One of our number comments on how distracted I am. I'm hugely tempted to drink an ocean of wine but manage to confine my input to a small lake. A couple of fans in the restaurant talk very loudly about how crap we were today and isn't it great to see the captain out enjoying himself after a stuffing. I'm tempted to bite back but resist that temptation as well. Wankers. "What's wrong with you?" asks Tina as we make our way home. "I'm just knackered, I need the season to end." She knows there's more to it than that but doesn't push.

Sunday, 8 May, 19.00 hours. A bar near our flat. The phone rings. Tina hauls herself off the sofa to answer it. "Oh, hello Tom. Yes, he's here."

My turn to haul myself off the sofa and meander across the room. I get on very well with Tommy Butler and we have socialised with him and his wife on many occasions but I don't remember him calling before.

"Watcha, Tommy. How goes it?"

"Yeh, not bad. Sorry to disturb you at home Ed. Any chance we could have a chat? I mean meeting up. This evening would be good."

He obviously needs to strike while whatever iron he is holding is still hot. I assume it's got "made in China" stamped on it.

"No problem but you'll have to come here, Tom. I've had a couple of glasses of wine."

We agree to meet in a bar a few minutes' walk from the flat. I don't want to invite him to the flat because if he uses the C-word, and I'm certain he will, that will create problems as I haven't yet spoken to Tina about China. I'm still processing everything.

I walk into the bar and Tommy's sitting in a corner with a bottle of white wine in a cooler. He pours me a glass.

"Not driving are you, Tommy?"

"Nah, Jean gave me a lift. She's gone to see a couple of friends who live near here."

"What's on your mind?"

"It's China, Ed. No one is keen. As in no one wants to go. Absolutely dead set against it."

"How do you know?"

"We had a quick chat. The lads are really pissed about it."

This means "the lads" have spoken about China without involving me. Where and when? More to the point—why? Tommy must have seen my expression.

"Don't take it personally, Ed. There are a couple of the guys who were nervous about you being there given you have access to Palmer. And obviously because of your relationship with Tina and her working for The Observer."

"Bollocks, Tommy. I haven't seen or spoken to Palmer for ages. And I've already told Saunders I think it's a bad idea. China, for fuck's sake. I don't want to go to China. And I haven't spoken to Tina yet."

Tommy took a sip of wine and topped up our glasses.

"What are you saying, Tom? I'm not invited to a squad meeting, you tell me no one wants to go to China and now you want me to relay that to Palmer, Christie and Saunders on behalf of everyone?"

"Well, the thinking is that you are the skipper, and the message should come from you."

"Really? Anyone got the balls to accompany me given you didn't have the balls to invite me to your little chat? You know as well as I do, I've had my fair share of disagreements with those three." I'm not just angry, I'm really pissed off as well.

"Ed, I'm not here to fall out with you. If it counts for anything, I said you should be invited."

I'm tempted to add some theatre to the situation and storm out of the bar but there's little point adding drama to a crisis—and we need to agree some sort of strategy. It's at times like these I count my blessings my true friends are not involved in the game.

Tommy breaks the silence. "I'm surprised you haven't told Tina."

"I will do when I get back. It won't be an easy conversation but if she feels obliged to break the story that's fine with me. The story isn't so much that we're going all the way to China but that the players don't want to go."

We sit and chat for a while longer but I'm not in the mood for small talk.

"I will go and see Saunders after training tomorrow and you can come with me. We can then tell Palmer and Christie how everyone feels. Or Saunders can."

Tommy doesn't look thrilled with my suggestion but agrees. He realises that having become the players' spokesman he can hardly refuse.

Sunday, 8 May, 20.30 hours. Our flat. "I've got a story for you," I tell Tina deciding a light-hearted approach may help.

I spend a few minutes telling her about the tour to China and the players' reaction. I explain I hadn't told her because if the tour went ahead, it would ruin our plans for early summer and I wanted to resolve that. Tina points out it was a good job Dave Craig hadn't got wind of the story and spoken to her. She would have looked a fool.

I add the last thing I want is to put her in another difficult position—she has been given a tough time over a few things she has been privy to but not shared, such as Iain Moy's failed breathalyser and exit from the club—and I tell her about my chat with Tommy and our intentions.

"If you write the story, feel free to quote me and to hell with any consequences. Going to China is all about money. There's no thought given to player welfare. And this conflict of interest is beginning to happen too often for my liking even though we knew it would occur from time to time. I'm not going to let it drive a wedge between us."

Monday, 9 May, 12.00 hours. Northtown FC training ground. Training consists of just a few jogs and practising a new dead ball move Mark Bailey conjured up. I get to the changing rooms before anyone else and stand by the door, which I close after the last man enters. I call for silence and usher out a couple of the backroom staff who are hanging around for the sake of it.

"I have something to say and want you to just listen. You know that Tommy came to talk to me yesterday and you need to know that I'm really pissed off you had a squad meeting without me.

"This isn't about hurt feelings; this is about you creating an 'us and them' mentality within the squad. One of our strengths is that we work together, play together, support each other.

"I'm not pro-management anti-team or pro-team anti-management. I try and look at things realistically and act accordingly. I would have made useful contributions to your meeting and you would have learned I'd already spoken to the Boss and told him China was a crap idea. You don't know me very well if you think I'd have gone running to Palmer to tell him you weren't happy."

"Tommy and I are about go and see the Boss. Anyone care to join us?"

Silence. No surprise,

"Is the feeling still against going to China?" A few murmured assents.

"Is everyone against going? I'm not putting my head on the block for a minority."

"Yes, Ed, it's unanimous," says Tommy.

"None of you have anything to say but you're happy for others to do your dirty work. I'm even less impressed than I was yesterday." I couldn't resist having a dig.

Egan looks as if he has something to say but I catch his eye and for once his brain works before his tongue starts wagging and his mouth remains shut.

I turn my back on everyone and don't even bother to shower. "Hurry up Tommy, I don't want to be here for any longer than I have to be."

Monday, 9 May, 12.30 hours. Tony Saunders' office. Saunders, who I had asked to see after training when I arrived a couple of hours earlier, has heavy-duty reinforcement in the shape of Peter Christie. Saunders registers Tommy's presence but doesn't comment.

"What's this about?"

"Given that you've asked Peter here you know we want to talk about the tour to China," I say.

Saunders sighs. "I know what you think. We are going. End of."

"Boss, not a single squad member wants to go."

Christie wants to know "who's been stirring things up."

Tommy chimes in. "Just so you know, Ed wasn't aware about how we all feel until I spoke to him yesterday. There's a real groundswell against the idea. Everyone is dead against it."

The conversation goes back and forth, getting progressively more and more heated. The number of matches we have played this season is dismissed. The fact we are going to China as soon as the season is over, being there for ten days, coming back for a couple of weeks rest, back for pre-season training and then into our next First Division campaign isn't seen as a problem.

Phrases such as money ruling the Board's decisions and no thought being given to players' welfare are met with disdain by the suited and booted Christie, who at least is going to endure the hardships of China with us. The track-suited Saunders, who can see both the football and business sides of the argument, is looking tired and is less voluble than Christie.

"Boss, how can you be happy with us doing all that travelling and playing before the next season?" I ask.

"We'll be fucked by Christmas," warns Tommy.

"I imagine there will be something about all this in tonight's Observer?" says Christie looking at me.

"I imagine so," I say. "I'm not going to put my relationship in jeopardy by keeping my mouth shut. We all have jobs to do and professional standards to maintain. Some do them better than others."

Christie doesn't bat an eyelid. "You need to confirm to your teammates we are going to China," he says. "You've taken it upon yourself to represent them, you can talk to them again."

"This is getting fucking petty," storms Saunders. "I'm arranging a meeting for the first team squad tomorrow after training and I want you there, Peter. Roger is in the country and I'll ask him to come. After that, I want a line drawn under this whole thing. We're supposedly a football club and I've got a match to prepare for on Saturday."

The meeting is over, although Christie remains behind. I walk back to the changing rooms with Tommy. "Ed, I'm really sorry. You've been caught in the middle through no fault of your own."

As we get to the changing rooms, we hear raised voices coming from Saunders' office. Neither Tommy nor I are convinced that Saunders is completely sold on the trip to China.

Monday, 9 May, 18.00 hours. Our flat. I make my way home although I'm in no rush to get there. I stop off and buy some bits and pieces for our evening meal, although I'm sorely tempted to suggest we go out for dinner. But I also want a drink and won't have one in public on a week night. Not even this late in the season.

Tina comes home. I look at her. "Shit day," she says. "I've written the story but still have to talk to Christie and maybe Saunders and Palmer. It will be tomorrow's front page lead but it's about the club's vision and going on a ground-breaking tour." "Fine," I sigh. "I don't really care." We've both had a crap day, neither of is very hungry nor have any inclination to cook. We decide to relax by going to bed. Great therapy—even the wine can wait.

Tuesday, 10 May, 11.30 hours. Northtown FC training ground. We are told Roger Palmer will see us after training. We don't have to attend. I do so not because I want to but because I feel obliged to. Only a few others bother to turn up. Palmer, normally affable and approachable, is matter-of-fact and sharp. We are going to China. The club are your employers and the club you represent is going on a hugely important official visit. You should be proud to be part of it. I leave as soon as I can and go straight home, buying a copy of today's Observer on the way. The story tells its readers about the ground-breaking trip. Saunders and Palmer are quoted, denying any player disquiet.

Wednesday 18 May. Flight from Heathrow to Peking. The flight is surprisingly busy with our party of twenty-five players, manager, coaching and medical staff and Club Secretary taking up the first five or six rows of the Economy Class. As a slightly nervous flyer and someone who doesn't like to sit still for too long, I'm not looking forward to the long hours which lie ahead.

An hour or so into the flight I walk to the front of the cabin and ask Tony Saunders if I can have a word with him. Mark Bailey, sitting next to him, moves to my seat. I tell Saunders that having given considerable thought to the matter I wanted to resign the captaincy. I tell him I have been hugely proud to captain the team and would always be grateful to him for naming me skipper. I have no idea how Saunders will react but he remains calm, orders a couple of beers, and we spend an hour or so discussing my decision and what reason we will give for my stepping down. "Personal circumstances" is vague enough.

Saunders understands that being captain and therefore privy to more information about the club than my teammates, puts pressure on my relationship with Tina. He doesn't try to change my mind which, although it would have made no difference, would have at least stroked my ego. I feel strangely disappointed. He asks me, for the sake of simplicity, to remain as captain for the tour. I agree. He asks me if I have any thoughts on who my successor should be. I suggest Butler, Bell or Cooke. He notes my thoughts but doesn't comment.

"How's life with you, Boss?" I ask. He smiles and takes me into his confidence. "I think we're doing the right thing by coming here but it has been badly handled and it meant I had a falling out with Palmer, which I didn't want, and Christie, which I don't care about. Other than that, I have a few decisions to make. We need a three-year plan while a couple of clubs have made tentative enquiries about my availability." He sees my surprise. "I've been here for five years and I'm not sure if I can take the club much further without huge injections of cash. And I'm not sure where that will come from."

"Maybe you need an agent," I say with my tongue partly in my cheek.

"I have one. The game's changing Ed and Steve Russell is doing a good job for me." We laugh and have another beer before I swap seats with Bailey again.

Saturday, 20 May, to Monday, 29 May. China. The trip could be a lot worse; it could be better. Everyone is highly delighted we are here and are very friendly. We are "escorted" everywhere we go and there are severe restrictions on where we can go and what we can take pictures of. We have to attend three official functions which are hideously boring and where the food isn't exactly suited to our Western palates.

No spare ribs, sweet and sour chicken balls, special fried rice or chicken Chow Mein. On one occasion, we are served hens' feet which are inedible. Pang, our guide, tells us if we don't eat them, we will cause severe offence. Mick Egan, who else, tells him we are more than happy to offend. There is also talk of one of the dishes being monkey brains.

The hotels, like the training facilities, are basic with electricity and running water occasional optional extras. The beds, unsurprisingly, aren't nearly big enough. But the stadiums are excellent and over sixty thousand turn up to see us play the national team in the Peking Workers' Stadium and we are encouraged to go on a lap of honour after beating them 4-2.

We fly to Shanghai and play a Shanghai XI in the Jiangwan Stadium, win 2-0 and fly back to Peking to play the National Side again in the Workers' Stadium. The flight from the two cities may be "only" three hours but no one had mentioned the endless hours we have to wait around the airports. Let's just say the facilities are as basic as they come.

The facilities on the planes are not much better and by the time we play our last match, we are running out of steam and lose 3-1 and it could have been a lot more but for Andy Hopkins. This time, we are encouraged to go on a lap of honour with the victorious national team.

We are treated to a feast on the last night and the local "wine," which could double-up as rocket fuel, flows fast and furious and much of the food is left untouched. There are some extremely tired and hungover professional footballers on the flight back to London and the toilets at the front of the cabin are in constant demand by us. The other passengers hardly get a look-in and have to use the toilets at the back of the plane or cross their legs.

We arrive home in the early hours of Wednesday morning, jet-lagged and completely knackered. But… we are told the tour has stirred great interest and ticket season sales for the 1983-84 season have gone through the roof. Grudgingly, I accept the tour was more of a success than I thought it would be. I wasn't impressed that none of the directors chose to accompany us. Palmer had business commitments all over Europe but one or two others could have shown willing. In fact, I would have thought the Chinese would have taken offence but Peter Christie was a brilliant ambassador for the club and worked his socks off. If he was going on holiday once we got home, he thoroughly deserved it. I didn't warm to him as an individual—in fact, I actively disliked him and didn't trust him, either—but I respected the way he worked.

Did we over-react to the China crisis and make it into a problem that wasn't really there? I don't think we did and not many of us were happy while we were in Peking and Shanghai, although there were some undoubted highlights. The club made money from the tour and it stimulated increased sales so the directors, conspicuous by their absence, would have been happy and in that regard it was a success, which we all contributed to but there is no doubting it was poorly handled by the club.

Again, I don't think this was a case of footballers being pretentious and having overinflated opinions of themselves. Had we been told months in advance I don't think there would have been any problems. Some of the scars ran deep and I don't think the club learned any lessons.

Chapter Five
Taking Stock

As the 1982-83 season drew to a close, I took time out to reflect. We had done far better than anyone could possibly have imagined in our initial campaign in the First Division. Everyone had played their part and I knew I had just enjoyed my best-ever season, despite my initial worries about the pace of the game at this level being too fast for us. I had also thoroughly enjoyed my slightly advanced position, which had led to my best goal tally to date with nine, four of them penalties. And playing with Bill Cooke had been great. I had enjoyed playing with Mark Bailey and Dave Walters as we progressed up the League, but Cooke was a standout player and I learned a lot from him.

There had even been talk of a possible international call-up for me. If I'm honest, I was disappointed I wasn't named in the England squad which went to Australia for three matches, although I had no idea if I was international class. I was often left bemused by some of the (midfield) selections and couldn't fathom how the likes of Graham Rix, Brian Talbot, David Armstrong and John Gregory pulled on the white, sometimes red, shirt of England. I don't remember my thought process being "I should be playing instead of them"—and possibly it should have been—I simply didn't consider them to be international footballers.

As the season progressed there were more and more favourable reports of my performances in the national papers and I began to think being called up to the national squad was a realistic ambition. I was twenty-four-years-old which, according to those in the know, meant I wasn't far off reaching the peak of my powers but my best years still lay ahead. In short, I was very marketable. I also knew that some of my performances had been particularly good and had been mentioned on TV as well as in the papers. Was I good enough to play for England? No one would know unless it happened, which is possibly why those mentioned above, plus countless more like them, had been capped.

Steve Russell was quick to jump on these favourable reports and suggested I had a better chance of making the national team if I played for a more high-profile club. I didn't necessarily go along with his way of thinking—Northtown had done brilliantly and were getting plenty of publicity, as was I. And Rob Davies was now an England international, having made a couple of appearances as substitute before being named in the squad to tour Australia at the same time we went to China. Steve had asked me whether I was interested in moving clubs in early 1983 and although I appreciated he was looking to feather both my nest as well as his own, of course, I told him I would let him know if and when I decided to leave.

Then came the China crisis. I was deflated by the way the club had handled this and I had been annoyed by my teammates not trusting me. I put this into the mix along with some other incidents including the mishandling of Steve Bamford and Iain Moy and drew the conclusion that the club didn't really act in the best interests of its players, despite the seeming affability of Roger Palmer and Tony Saunders.

Football was becoming bigger and bigger every year which meant clubs had to come up with new and different ways to make money just to maintain the status quo. In turn, this meant players were being used as pawns and as far as I was concerned, we had to fight back and if that meant being mercenary so be it.

I was becoming high profile and valued. If I was going to move now was the time to take advantage. I was also aware a move of club would mean not putting Tina in a difficult position so often unless she moved to a national newspaper. I had been at Northtown for over six years and had played under Tony Saunders for all but one season and much as I rated and had learned from Tony, having a new teacher with a different voice and different ideas also appealed.

It seemed to me all the planets had aligned and it was time to seek pastures new. We were due to head to Italy for a two-and-a-half-week holiday just a couple of days after arriving back from China so I arranged to see Steve Russell the day before flying to Peking.

He assured me he had the right sort of contacts at other clubs and I told him I wanted London clubs to be alerted that I was interested in moving. "I'm assuming that my terms will improve quite dramatically. If I get ten per cent of the fee, I'll give you five per cent of that and you will benefit from my improved terms. And I want this done quietly and not plastered all over the papers."

Transfer fees were beginning to inflate and we thought a conservative estimate of my value was £300,000 and as the money was getting bigger so agents started to rear there, quite often, ugly heads. So if Steve wasn't interested in my proposed terms, I was confident I could find someone else. OK, he wasn't going to earn anywhere near the same percentage that Mino Raiola, Paul Pogba's agent, reputedly coined when Pogba moved from Juventus to Manchester United in 2016 for £89 million—rumours are that Raiola pocketed a staggering £41 million, or nearly fifty per cent of the fee but five per cent of £30,000 plus a cut of my increased salary was a decent pay day in the mid-1980s, especially for making just a few phone calls and attending a couple of meetings.

It's reasonable to say that Steve wasn't hugely impressed with how I thought things should pan out between us and insisted on talking again on my return from China, although he agreed to "put out some feelers" while I was away. This played into my hands as I learned he was representing Saunders and hadn't mentioned it to me so I asked him why he hadn't given me a "discount" for the work he was doing on his behalf.

"You didn't introduce him to me, he contacted me direct," said Steve.

"He wouldn't have known of your existence if it hadn't been for me," I countered. It was a relatively light-hearted exchange but we were definitely sparring and we agreed to disagree.

Steve had spoken to, or left messages, for contacts at Arsenal, Spurs and West Ham but as people were on holiday there had been, as expected, no movement. "Difficult to gauge the responses I got," he told me. "Given Spurs had shown interest last summer I thought they would sound enthusiastic but either the guy I spoke to is a good poker player or he genuinely didn't know anything about their previous interest. Are you sure you're not interested in the Midlands or South coast? That would give us Forest, Villa, West Brom, Birmingham and Southampton. Maybe even Coventry. What about QPR seeing as they've just been promoted to the First Division?"

I told him I had no intention of going to Coventry, West Brom or Birmingham, or QPR for that matter, but I would talk it all over with Tina and gave him the name and number of the hotel we were staying at in Italy for the next two-and-a-half weeks. But for the first week or so of our break I didn't want to think about or talk football unless there was genuine interest from a major London club. I intended to relax, swim, see some sights, eat great food and drink great wine and somehow keep off the pounds.

But one thought insisted on invading my thought process no matter how hard I tried to switch off. Spurs, the team which had shown interest in me twelve months ago, had one hell of a midfield with Glenn Hoddle, Ossie Ardiles, Mick Hazard and Ardiles' Argentinian international teammate Ricky Villa. But Villa had just left to join Fort Lauderdale Strikers in the USA—so Spurs must surely be in the market for a midfielder soon to reach the peak of his powers and I quite fancied playing alongside Mr Hoddle.

Part IV
Going InterContinental

Chapter One
Split End Our European Dream

There was no contact from Spurs. Nor from West Ham. Or Arsenal. And I had no interest in moving to the Midlands. Southampton was a possibility but having bought a house only a year before neither of us were keen to up sticks. And Southampton had finished six places below us the previous season so going there would hardly be a step up, although I was an admirer of their Manager Lawrie McMenemy.

Steve Russell assured me he was doing all he could to help engineer a move but he was annoyed with me for being so choosy. "You need to broaden your outlook," he told me. "That's what my old man said to me when I told him I wanted to play football for a living," I replied. I was a little bewildered there had been no interest even if I wasn't casting my net very wide and, yes, my ego was a little bruised as well.

Still, there was a lot to look forward to at Northtown. We would be going all out to improve on our sixth position, a major challenge in itself, and I couldn't wait for our European experience to begin. That was new to all of us, with the exception of Bill Cooke who had played abroad with Wales a few times, and I was sure that playing in a European competition could only stand me in good stead if the international call did come.

The UEFA Cup had been introduced in 1971 and teams which finished high up their domestic leagues were eligible for qualification. The number of teams that qualified from each country differed and depended on a complicated rankings and seedings system, which administrators struggled to get their heads round let alone a humble midfield player. The 1983-84 season saw Spurs, Forest and Villa competing on the strength of where they finished in the league in the '82-'83 season, while we crept in because Manchester United, who finished second behind champions Liverpool, won the FA Cup so were competing in the

Cup Winners' Cup. If United hadn't triumphed at Wembley, we wouldn't have been involved.

Playing in Europe wasn't only going to be a new experience it was going to be a completely different one as well. That may seem an obvious statement, but by and large the teams we played against week in week out were similar in approach. Of course, some were defence-minded others put the emphasis on attack and formations may have varied slightly—I think we are obsessed with formations in this country and slavishly follow the latest "fashion." At this stage, 4-4-2 was still in vogue, 4-5-1 wasn't far off, 4-2-3-1 (why the need to have so many defensive players?) was, thankfully, to come well after I walked down the tunnel for the last time.

Europe would provide very different challenges. Opponents would be cagey and play possession-based football with loads of short passes being made as players waited to spot an opening. At times, it could be slower than chess and at least as boring so we would have to learn to be patient and to cope with the lightning-quick counter-attacks most foreign teams appeared capable of launching and most English teams seemed highly vulnerable to. The players were more technically gifted and although I think we have improved over the years this still tends to be the case today. I'm not completely sure why.

They also constantly played for free-kicks, would roll around in mock agony before recovering from the brink of expiry to full recovery in seconds, and were not averse to off-the-ball kicking, spitting, pushing and punching. Should the referee happen to look in their direction they would fall to the ground clutching their face. Ok, so this a generalisation but not a very big one—just ask Trevor Cherry, who was sent off playing for England in a "friendly" against Argentina for the heinous crime of having a couple of front teeth knocked out. At least on that occasion, the aggressor was sent off as well.

The 1966 World Cup, which spawned my interest in the game, was full of diving and feigning injury with the South Americans and West Germany particularly notable for the number of rolls they made on the ground despite apparently having lost a couple of limbs. This is all now too widespread throughout the game and nobody is doing anything to stamp it out which, thinking about it, probably isn't the best phrase to use. Those same players who would go down injured if you so much as breathed near them were also the ones who would kick, punch and spit at you away from the action.

European referees were also a different breed to our men in black, who were possibly too lenient. Across the Channel, they allowed very little, if any, contact and would blow for a foul as soon as a player hit the deck. Being aware of all this and adapting to it though were entirely different matters.

If we played a team behind the Iron Curtain—the Berlin Wall would stay standing for another six years after our European debut—we would have to be prepared for not only long, arduous journeys but also a different way of life, albeit if only for a day or two. There were many stories of hotels which numbered cockroaches among their regular guests, where the beds were built for dwarves and the food was inedible and you shouldn't use the water even to clean your teeth. And your every move off the pitch was monitored by shady-looking men wearing trilby hats and trench coats. Perhaps going to China hadn't been such a bad idea after all.

Nevertheless, we couldn't wait for our European journey to get underway.

We were drawn against Kaiserslautern in the first round. Some of us knew it was in Germany although I doubt if anyone knew where exactly (the southwest) or anything about the club. Playing a German team meant two things—the facilities we would encounter would be fine but, more importantly, it would be a tough match. English sides rarely had it easy against German teams. We may have beaten them in the 1966 World Cup final but since then all I could remember was losing the 1970 World Cup quarter-final in Mexico 3-2 after being 2-0 up—anyone who watched on that dreadful Sunday afternoon/evening won't forget it—and being completely outplayed at Wembley in the first leg of the 1972 European championship.

My dad managed to get a couple of tickets for that game and the thrill and excitement of going was outweighed by the bitter disappointment of seeing Germany win 3-1 and England's performance. Even as a young lad I could see the Germans were light years ahead of us in every aspect of the match. On the club front, English teams had also suffered their fair share of defeats at the hands of German opponents and Bayern Munich were one of the European club superpowers. So it was with a fair amount of trepidation that we took on Kaiserslautern on 14 September 1983, especially as our league form had hardly set the world alight with just one win from our opening five fixtures.

We had good cause to be worried and like England back in 1972, we were thoroughly outplayed and also lost 3-1 leaving us with a huge task if our European adventure wasn't to end before it had really begun. We flew home and thumped Stoke 4-0 at the Victoria Ground before losing narrowly to Spurs at Wood Lane the following Saturday.

Four days later Kaiserslautern came to town and left wishing they hadn't.

Within quarter of an hour, we were 2-0 up which meant we were level on aggregate and ahead on away goals. The Germans were unusually generous and gifted us an own goal to set us on our way before Steve Baker tapped home the second after the keeper dropped a cross. Whether the Germans were over-confident—even arrogant!—I can't say. Our crowd certainly helped us, although strangely Wood Lane was far from full. We played well and certainly with more urgency than we were showing in the League and Terry Bell's header, which put us ahead on aggregate, was the icing on the cake. It was a great win and at that time one of the best in the club's history.

Meanwhile, our League form left a lot to be desired and after seeing off Kaiserslautern we promptly lost three successive games to West Bromwich and Norwich in the League and Second Division Huddersfield Town in the League Cup—we drew the second leg and lost 4-3 on aggregate. By the time Levski Sofia turned up we had played twelve games winning just three and losing seven.

It was impossible to identify what had changed so dramatically in a matter of months. Tommy Butler, who had taken over the captaincy, reckoned the tour of China was catching up on us. There is also a theory that promoted clubs which do very well in their first season are found out by their opponents in their second and suffer from what the press called second season syndrome. It's a theory I only semi-subscribe to—after all, if the managers and coaches are worth their salt shouldn't they work out how an opponent plays during the course of their first season in a division? I think it's more likely that a team which exceeds expectations one season finds it hard to maintain that form the next.

One or two thought it was fixture overload, which I wasn't convinced by. After all, the previous season Liverpool won the League and the League Cup, reached the fifth round of the FA Cup and the quarter-final of the European Cup (Champions League) playing a total of sixty games and using just sixteen players, three of whom played only fourteen games between them.

We suffered from having a small squad and there was no doubt some tiredness after arriving home on a Thursday following a European away tie and then playing a League game on Saturday. Saunders simply didn't have enough players to shuffle his pack. The core of the team—Butler, Bell, Green, Aitken, Davies and myself—had played a lot of games over the last few years while

Cooke, Pieters, Baker and Hopkins had obviously been playing games at other clubs albeit not at such intensity.

Saunders hadn't bought anyone during the summer. He was fond of talking about "promoting from within" as he believed we had some genuine talent in the reserves. I felt we should have bought, in particular a forward, and while there were a couple of reserves who certainly had a bit about them there wasn't another Davies or Aitken—or Roberts for that matter—that I could see. Our domestic form was a cause for concern and needed to be addressed.

Surprisingly we had no problems with diving, now laughingly called simulation, feigning injury or petty officiating against Kaiserslautern. We had plenty to contend with in the next two rounds, though.

First up was the Bulgarian outfit Levski Sofia, who left Wood Lane with a 1-1 draw after one of their players threw himself to the ground and the referee, unbelievably, awarded a penalty. He also handed out several yellow cards as we surrounded him to protest and did it in such a way no one had a clue who he had and hadn't booked.

We also encountered off-the-ball antics such as kicking and shoving and after committing a foul the player responsible would suddenly become your best mate with handshakes, pats on the back and smiles before putting their hand behind their backs and bowing to the referee as he gave them a finger-wagging admonishment. These Basil Fawlty-type fawning apologies did the trick though as none of them were yellow-carded. Ridiculous.

The draw wasn't a great result but we knew we were the better team and that if the referee allowed the game to flow instead of constantly blowing his whistle, we had a good chance of progressing. But after just four minutes the third round became a distant speck on the horizon as the Sofia centre forward scored with a bullet header, meaning we needed to score three times to ensure our name was in the hat for the third round draw. Which is exactly what we did in the second half through Steve Baker, Pete Aitken and Dutch Pieters.

This did not go down well with the home crowd, which had been in the stadium since well before kick-off and made the place rock. Literally. When we emerged for the kick-off, it was almost impossible to see through the pungent smoke caused by hundreds of flares and the noise the crowd was generating was almost deafening. Bulgaria and England were enemies in both World Wars and throughout the ongoing Cold War and maybe as a result of these conflicts, the crowd hated us with a real passion.

Some teams, faced with such a hostile crowd and falling behind so early would have wilted, but we were full of strong characters and played our best forty-five minutes of the season, despite the Bulgarians provoking us with an assortment of tricks which wouldn't have been out of place in a circus ring.

When Dutch scored our third goal which put the tie beyond Sofia, bottles rained down onto the pitch. The referee, who strangely had been much better than at Wood Lane, stopped play but couldn't take the teams off for fear of us being hit by missiles as we made our way to the dressing rooms. Both teams gathered in the centre circle for about ten minutes until the crowd had nothing left to throw or had lost the enthusiasm to launch their missiles.

There was time for a Bulgarian defender to see red for an horrendous challenge on Steve Baker, which left him with an ugly gash just above the shin pad and ruled him out for a month. Saunders hailed this as the best win of his managerial career, albeit tempered by the injury to Steve, and we made our way back to our hotel which, like the referee, was much better than we had expected.

We stayed up until the early hours having a moderate drink to celebrate. I decided to try Bulgarian white wine and really wished I hadn't; I could feel it burning as it made its way down my throat and into the pit of my stomach and had no doubt it would have been an excellent paint stripper. I love Greece and although I've had some very ropey wine there over the years, nothing compares to this which remains the worst tasting experience of my life. When we heard we had been drawn against Hajduk Split in the next round I swore to myself, I would not imbibe in Yugoslav (now Croatian) wine.

Split is a very attractive city and is hugely popular with holidaymakers but there was nothing attractive about either of our matches with them. We thought the play-acting and off-the-ball antics of Levski Sofia were bad but we hadn't seen anything. And then there was the matter of the referee who came across as a Hajduk Split fan with a whistle, although we didn't help our cause by having a player sent off in both legs.

One of those was me.

It was the only time in my career I saw red and although there were mitigating factors, I can't pretend to be proud of my actions.

There had been numerous reports of alleged bribery with referees succumbing to having their hands crossed with silver and quite a few English teams had supposedly fallen foul of corrupt men in black, although it usually happened in the away legs or at a neutral ground. Derby County lost 3-1 to

Juventus in the first leg of the 1973-74 European Cup quarter-final and the German referee booked both Archie Gemmill and Roy McFarland who, it just so happened, were the only Derby players already on a yellow card meaning they missed the return leg. Gemmill was booked for a trip having just been elbowed in the face—no action was taken against the perpetrator. McFarland was booked when he and an Italian forward clashed heads in what was an obvious accidental coming-together.

The referee generally ruled against Derby and also welcomed a Juventus player into his room both before and during half-time. That Juventus player was a fellow countryman of the referee, one Helmut Haller. Haller was one of the biggest "roll models" of the 1966 World Cup and his actions are well worth looking at. If you are having a bad day, look him up on YouTube—it will help lighten your mood.

In another European Cup semi-final involving English and Italian sides, this time in 1965, Liverpool took a 3-1 lead to the San Siro Stadium, where the referee awarded Inter Milan two highly contentious goals, disallowed what most observers considered a perfectly good goal for Liverpool, and apparently didn't give the men from Anfield "a decision all night."

The 1975 European Cup Final in Paris saw Leeds lose 2-0 to Bayern Munich after they had what appeared two stonewall penalties denied them and a perfectly good goal from Peter Lorimer disallowed for offside. Of course, you tend to only hear the English point of view but in the ensuing years a couple of the Bayern players have admitted Leeds were robbed by those contentious decisions. Please note, that is German players expressing sympathy for an English team. The French ref, despite receiving very low marks from FIFA officials, had no action taken against him.

In the season we played in the UEFA Cup, Nottingham Forest—managed by Brian Clough with Peter Taylor as his assistant just as at Derby when they played Juventus—found themselves on the wrong end of some controversial decisions when they played the Belgian outfit Anderlecht. Forest took a 2-0 lead with them from the first leg at the City Ground but ended up losing 3-0 in the return. Some years later enough evidence was unearthed to prove Anderlecht had paid the referee to ensure they won, but because it took over ten years for the facts to come to light, Anderlecht were only banned from European competition for one year.

Pathetic. And by the time all had been revealed the Spanish referee had been killed in a car accident so avoided prosecution.

At least, Spurs beat Anderlecht in the final, although it was close with the two-legged final being decided by a penalty shoot-out. Presumably had Anderlecht won they would have been stripped of the title. But with football authorities there is absolutely no guarantee.

Wood Lane Stadium, Northtown. Wednesday, 23 November 1983 and Stari Plac stadium, Split. Wednesday, 7 December 1983. Northtown United v Hajduk Split. UEFA Cup third round.

We know the Yugoslavs are going to provide difficult opposition. Tony Saunders has managed to watch them a couple of times and tells us, for the umpteenth time before we go out, they are skilful and quick and we must watch out for their counter-attacks. Like us, they play with two quick wide men but only one out-and-out forward who has licence to roam, two good feet and will shoot at the slightest opportunity.

The first half is helter-skelter. We start well and take the lead through Pieters. They come back at us and score two quick goals, the second of which goes under Andy Hopkins' somewhat cumbersome dive—more of a fall than a dive. Pieters, who has been having a few verbals with one of their defenders and is ticking, equalises in injury time.

As we go down the tunnel something is said by one of the Split players. Dutch goes flying after him, but as he gets to him he's pulled back by Mick Egan, of all people. Nearly everyone piles in. A few fists are thrown. Unlike at Highbury the previous season a few telling blows are landed, Terry Green is kneed in the thigh which results in a dead leg. It takes the authority of Saunders and the bulk of a couple of stewards to usher Dutch into our changing room. "He said 'monkey get in your tree'. I don't take that shit from anyone," shouts Dutch. "I'm going to fucking kill him." He only begins to calm down when Saunders threatens to sub him. Green can't continue and Sears replaces him.

The first half hasn't been too bad as far as play-acting is concerned. The second half is like facing a different side. Split bring all the tricks of the trade and then some to the party and the referee, despite seeing many of them, ignores what's happening but waves his yellow card at a couple of us for dissent. Bell picks up his second yellow of the competition and will miss the next leg.

Pieters goes on a run and is hacked down by his abuser; the big Jamaican goes to confront him. A load of Split players surround Dutch, we pile in as well. All very tribal. The Split defender is on the ground writhing in agony, hands covering his face, more rolls than a bakery. Dutch didn't touch him; he couldn't have given the number of opponents surrounding him. The referee decides he threw a punch and sends him off. Ridiculous decision. Now we are without both Bell and Pieters for the second leg.

Things get worse.

I send in a free-kick from the right—yes, the ref did give us the odd decision—Bell heads home as the keeper flaps in a typically Continental way. The ref disallows it. Bell wasn't offside—there was no flag from the linesman—and if the keeper came into contact with anyone it was with one of his own. Our heads go down. I have to pacify Egan who wants blood, revenge, retribution. You name it, the Irishman was after it. Then we concede a third. Sears is bundled off the ball by their tricky forward who although it pains me to admit it, is a tremendous player. I reckon nine out of ten European refs would have given us a free-kick because of the contact but Sears was dicking about so reaped what he had sewn.

As soon as he wins the ball, the forward looks up and lobs Hopkins from well outside the box. Again, it pains me to admit it but it was a hell of a goal from a hell of a player. Maybe Hopkins is too far off his line but let's give credit, however grudgingly, where and when it's due.

Our defeat to Split at Wood Lane was the third in a run of four straight defeats but we fly to Yugoslavia in a slightly improved mood having won 5-0 at Wolves the previous Saturday. Wolves, bottom of the table, are abject but we are more than happy to take advantage of any pick-me-up which comes our way. Baker, recovered from the injury he picked up in Bulgaria takes the place of Pieters, Stewart is in for the suspended Bell. Both are ring rusty. Saunders pulls a surprise by leaving out Aitken and bringing in Athey for a rare appearance in an effort to strengthen midfield. He too is ring rusty.

We are aggrieved about what happened in the first leg. Saunders tells us to put it behind us, and that we still have a chance. "The odds are against us so think what a win it will be," he says. "We've been underdogs in nearly every match we've played for the last two years and it hasn't stopped us." None of us were impressed with their keeper's performance at Wood Lane and reckon we should put him under as much pressure as we can.

Our first half showing is decent although it is a very cagey affair and can't be great to watch. If we can nick a goal... instead Split score with a deflected effort which sucks all our energy. We are now 4-2 behind on aggregate and will need three second half goals and not concede. Which is exactly what happened in Bulgaria, but today's opponents are far superior to them. In fact, they are the team which scores three second-half goals without conceding.

After they go 2-0 up I have a petty run-in with one of their wingers who walks away but not before he spits in my face. I'm sure the ref must have seen it but does nothing. I'm not having that. As I ponder how I'm going to get my revenge I lose concentration and let the winger go past me and score. Saunders is going mad at me. Fair enough.

Up until this point I have never gone out to intentionally hurt anyone, although I admit I've often gone out to "assert my authority" and if that leaves someone in a crumpled heap so be it. It works both ways. I decide to track this tricky little sod rather than patrol my usual area. Completely unprofessional.

I think about thumping him off the ball but I want him to be in full flight when I take him out to ensure I inflict maximum pain. He receives the ball wide on our left, pretty much foreign territory for me given my left leg is, as they say, only good for standing on. I let him go past me and then I dive in two-footed and make hugely satisfying contact with the back of his calf and his ankle.

It is undoubtedly a red card offence but the "challenge" is embossed by the winger's scream and number of rolls. He deserves points for artistic merit. To use an old English expression he's pole-axed. The ref, for the first time I can remember, moves out of a trot and sprints towards me. The Split players surround me and the ref to whom they brandish imaginary red cards. The ref produces the real thing and there is some pushing and shoving before I can make the long, lonely walk off the pitch.

For good measure I tell the ref what I think of his performance. He doesn't speak very good English but there at least a couple of words I use which he will understand. I avoid eye contact with Saunders but the manager lets me know what he thinks of my performance and behaviour and makes sure that my teammates hear. Fair enough. But no one had spat in his face.

Looking back, I'm not proud but the red mist descended when the guy spat in my face. The most worrying aspect was that I took satisfaction from taking my revenge. I have to say I am a little ashamed of my actions but then I wonder how I would react if someone spat in my face today. I don't think I would hold back. I also did what I did because I knew we were going out of the competition and decided I had nothing to lose. I like to think that if it had been a close tie I wouldn't have behaved as I did.

The flight back to Luton from Split is subdued as we are all immersed in our own thoughts and analysis. We had been eliminated 7-2 on aggregate and although Split were good they weren't five goals better than us. We made the fatal error of losing our concentration and getting dragged into confrontation. Split were quicker, more skilful and far more streetwise than us, but we have to look at ourselves first.

Would a stronger referee have made a difference? Undoubtedly. I'm not saying our referee had been "got at" he was just fairly typical of Continental referees at the time—fussy, pedantic, swayed by the loudest voice, quite likely to turn against the side which gave him most face-to-face grief, certainly more likely to take decisive action against dissenters than aggressors. We were led to, and fell into, several traps set by Hajduk Split, who had a huge amount of European experience. Nevertheless, we should have been better prepared—we knew simply by watching British sides on TV in European competitions how Continental referees acted and reacted.

On the Friday morning when we reported to the ground for light training and discussions about the next day's home match against Nottingham Forest, Saunders held me back when the others left. "Wednesday was your poorest performance for this club. In fact, I don't think you've been playing very well for a while but then no one has. I thought long and hard about dropping you tomorrow," he says. I begin to protest, but he cuts me off. "I'm not going to. But if you had been spat at and it had been 0-0, would you still have hacked him? Would you have done it had you still been skipper?"

I told Saunders that it was because we were going out that I acted as I did. "I know the provocation was high but next time you are playing for a club which qualifies for a European competition you will miss three matches. That might not be for a couple of years. You'll regret your actions when that time comes."

As was usually the case Saunders was right but I was still pleased I took that winger out. What worried me was that I enjoyed it so much I might just do it again.

I was also told, by my close friend and confidant Peter Christie, that our sponsors had taken a dim view of my actions. Quite frankly, I didn't give a damn what our sponsors thought. They were hardly going to withdraw their support for the club because I had clobbered a nasty little so-and-so who had spat in my face and I made this point quite forcibly to our Club Secretary who, it seemed to me, wanted to cross swords with me every time we spoke. His response was that sponsors were becoming increasingly important in the game and although I agreed with that statement, I still didn't care what they thought about my behaviour in Split.

Average league attendances had been declining for years. From the late 1970s, they had dropped every year until an increase in 1985. After that, they declined again until the end of the decade. Football wasn't alone in this, there had been a dramatic decline in the number of people who went to watch cricket, as well as other sports.

As far as football was concerned there were a number of factors, quite apart from the economy, which as is so often the case, was not in a great state. The national team was hardly pulling up any trees and generating interest. After losing to West Germany in the 1970 World Cup quarter-final, we didn't even qualify for the 1974 and 1978 tournaments. Our performance in 1982, where we made the second stage but drew both games 0-0, didn't exactly get the country on the edge of its seat. We always talked a good game but we weren't—and still aren't—world-beaters.

Hooliganism hadn't been stamped out (again, probably not the most apt phrase) and suddenly there were more matches being shown on live TV. League games were being broadcast on BBC and ITV, as well as the FA Cup final and major internationals. So it was tempting to sit in the armchair, pop open a can, put the feet up… and fall asleep. Maybe not fall asleep but staying at home was an attractive alternative to watching your team when the weather was rubbish or the journey was a long and expensive one.

TV has a lot to answer for as football is scheduled around the broadcaster's demands and although this can be infuriating, it was the advent of regular live matches on TV which did much to rekindle the game's popularity. People who weren't prepared to spend all day travelling to and from a match could afford the time to tune in for a couple of hours. Players became personalities through TV, there was analysis from former professional players so making the game more understandable. Admittedly, this wasn't new but it was now at a different level. Programmes were fronted by the likes of the debonair and hugely amusing Des Lynam and many turned on just to watch Des!

And with the new popularity came an injection of money into the game, beginning with the TV revenue, even if it was only a very small fraction of today's vast and, quite frankly, ridiculous sums. It was as if the marketeers could sense a sea-change was coming and more and more companies started to advertise at grounds and the way the ads were displayed became eye-catching. Instead of remaining static the ads changed, one moment extolling the virtues of Coca-Cola, the next reminding us of the excellence of McDonald's products. When the perimeter ads change, your eye is inevitably drawn towards this action.

The next step was shirt sponsorship. There were some early problems around this because it was seen as free advertising and a handful of clubs were even fined for wearing shirts with sponsors names on them. Although Coventry City had a shirt sponsor in the mid-1970s, the idea didn't take off for a few years but by the early to mid-1990s every team in the Football League were wearing shirts with sponsors names, even if in the lower divisions some of the sponsors were local companies supporters had previously been totally unaware of.

Our first sponsors, in the 1983-84 season, were a national haulage company. The amount of money they pumped into the club wasn't disclosed but I imagine it was substantial by the standards of the early eighties. I don't think any of us had a problem with the name of a sponsor emblazoned across our chests, it was all part of the changing face of football. However, the way the kit *per se* was being vandalised didn't sit comfortably with me as our shorts changed from the traditional and well-suited black to red as did the socks while the gold shirts suddenly had a red collar.

I have a real bee in my bonnet about shirts. I know it's all about generating money and has become part and parcel of the game but I hate the fact that kits change every season with the expectation that fans will shell out ludicrous amounts of money for a new replica shirt every twelve months. But I don't dislike that as much as clubs wearing "change" shirts for away matches. If an away side usually wears red and the home side wears white, it's ridiculous the away side changes to blue. There is no colour clash which used to be the reason a side would change its strip. And why do clubs change their traditional away strip colours to something kaleidoscopic?

Liverpool used to wear white shirts and black shorts and socks and very smart it looked. Since then, they have explored all grey, all yellow, green and white, green and blue, black and grey, all black and all blue. Manchester United, for a while had a very similar white and black look when they changed kit but have sported all black and have gone through a myriad of colour combinations. I even saw them play at Bournemouth a couple of years ago when they wore something akin to "crushed peach." Personally, I would have thought all blue, the colours they wore when they won the European Cup for the first time in 1968, should be their change colours. If I was a fan, I would feel ripped off.

Anyway, with sponsorship came changes to the ground and what was expected of the players. Rooms were named after the sponsors and there was a lounge, which carried the name of our biggest sponsor. Their guests would have lunch and a few drinks before the match and then watch the game before another couple of drinks after the final whistle and we were expected to do the rounds once we were showered and changed. Not everyone was comfortable with "pressing the flesh" and making small talk. Mick Egan, for example, found it hard to get through a sentence without a liberal sprinkling of the F-word so was a rare visitor but on one occasion when he ventured in, he met his future wife. Every cloud.

I was usually fine with popping in for a while and it was always good to meet and talk to fans. The other side of the coin was that you would inevitably discuss the match, which you've spent all week preparing for and just discussed with the coaching staff. Win, lose or draw there comes a time when you need to leave it behind. And although we were aware our sponsors were spending money, which ultimately should benefit the club, there were times when too much was expected of us.

The haulage company's marketing director seemed to think the players were his personal property after matches and wouldn't listen to anyone who said they would prefer to remain in the players' lounge. On one occasion, he cornered me saying there was "someone I had to meet" and put his hand on my shoulder to guide me from one room to another. For some reason that afternoon, I simply didn't want to mix with his guests and told him so in no uncertain terms. "Well, it's not exactly a hardship," he told me. "And we do an awful amount for your club."

Fortunately, Dutch came to my rescue and went into the sponsor's lounge in my place. We played well over twenty home games that season and I reckon I did my after-match duties for the sponsors about fifteen times so they got their pound of flesh out of me. I also attended a couple of Q&A sessions they arranged which were attended by fans and corporate guests and hosted by the aforementioned marketing director who certainly enjoyed being the centre of attention. sitting on a stool with a microphone.

Those events were enjoyable, although they were held at a time when our league form was dreadful so there were a few searching questions from the audience.

While we could be relatively pleased with our exploits in the UEFA Cup, our domestic form continued to be dreadful and by November we were in the bottom three and a return to the Second Division was a distinct possibility. A tough fight to preserve our precious status lay ahead.

We all knew things had to change but none of us knew what they were. Even Saunders appeared lost for ideas. We had a long chat on the coach home after our 3-0 defeat at Sunderland—believe me, there's plenty of time for analysis when you are on a four-hour coach journey. Saunders listened, saying little, asking the odd question. There were a few suggestions, a little bit of finger-pointing but no full-on arguing. Saunders followed up by making some changes to the way we trained, we all gave up alcohol for a couple of weeks—easier than I thought it would be, by the way—ensured we were definitely eating the right things, concentrated on how we "recovered" after matches. To coin a phrase, we were going back to basics but none of it made a jot of difference and when we lost at home to Split it was our fourth defeat in five games.

Saunders' input to training had been the same since he joined the club. He would watch most sessions from the side-lines leaving the hands-on, detailed coaching to, in the early days, Rob Riley and Ronnie O'Reagan and latterly Andy Adams and Mark Bailey. He would only interrupt sessions if he didn't like what he was seeing or wanted to tweak things. There were days when we didn't see him but we knew he input to all sessions and when he did get involved with individual players, he was excellent.

The more our League form nose-dived the more Saunders involved himself so side-lining both Adams and Bailey and there were days when they were little more than ball boys and cone collectors. We could see that Adams, a more volatile character than Bailey, was far from happy.

Having picked up a much-needed win before we flew to Split (5-0 at relegation-bound Wolves) we compounded those three points with a 3-2 win against Forest three days after being knocked out of the UEFA Cup.

Had we turned the corner? Saunders obviously didn't think so. On the Monday after beating Forest, the manager took the training with no input from Adams or Bailey. Which was because they had left the club. There was, however, the familiar face of Dave Walters, patrolling the side-lines. It was a quick session after which Saunders called us together to explain he had to make changes and freshen things up. I was delighted to see Walters but was disappointed for Bailey, while Andy was a loyal servant although I had little direct contact with him as he tended to work with the forwards.

Walters had re-joined as assistant manager and Saunders told us there would be more additions to the coaching staff in the coming days.

Morale had been low, confidence lower, our form on the floor so something had to give, he explained while outlining he had been looking to make changes for a few weeks and well before we beat Wolves and Forest. There were a few who thought Saunders had been unnecessarily ruthless and that Adams and Bailey were being made scapegoats for the manager's failings.

"He had to do something or we'll be back in the Second Division next season," was how Bill Cooke summed things up. "He will live or die by that decision."

I stood by my assertion that we should have strengthened during the summer. Maybe some budget restrictions had been imposed on Saunders but it was obvious we needed players. I still didn't see any real gems sparkling in the reserves and once there were injuries, suspensions or lack of form—and there was plenty of that—we were in trouble. And this season we were suffering from all three. It was all very well making changes to the coaching staff but it was on the pitch where the games were won or lost.

Looking at the individuals, Andy Hopkins was letting in efforts he would have easily stopped last season; as Saunders had predicted time was beginning to catch up with Terry Green; Dutch Pieters, never less than a large unit, had gained weight which meant it took him even further to get into his stride; Pete Aitken appeared to be more interested in off-field interests. That meant the other seven, none of whom were playing as well as last season, were carrying four passengers which was clearly untenable.

No one had heard of Steve Reid. Saunders recruited him from St Albans City, where he was a coach. Reid was one of the many in the game whose playing career had been cut short by injury and had rebuilt his career as a coach. St Albans was just down the road and it was where I lived and I had been to a couple of their games but didn't recognise Reid. Saunders also attended their games when time allowed and had presumably got to know him as a result. But from non-league to First Division in a single step? This bloke was going to have go some to win us over.

He was like a breath of fresh air. Young, full of energy, new ideas, everything done at top speed, no hanging around, lots of laughter, players taken out of their comfort zones. He energised the place as if he were shaking it from the core of its foundations and you could see enthusiasm and confidence returning. We played a number of short, sharp practice matches but, apart from the keepers, not in our usual positions.

I found myself playing at full back (no thanks), sweeper (no Franz Beckenbauer but I really liked it) and as a No10 (I enjoyed it but wasn't much cop). Reid wanted everyone to have an understanding of different positions so we could switch formations and positions without problems during a match. It was very different and after initial scepticism from one or two, it became a regular part of our training.

We may have lost two of the first three games after Walters returned and Reid joined but we could all see improvements and knew we were going to turn a corner. It just needed to be sooner rather than later.

After we beat Forest, Johnny Webb replaced the shell-shocked Andy Hopkins in goal, Mike Sears came in as first choice left back, Nick Athey went into midfield and Pete Aitken was the new strike partner for Dutch. We lost 3-1 at Arsenal, where the home fans gave me some fearful stick because of an interview I gave after our win at Highbury the previous season. Ironically they had sacked Terry Neill, who had been so outspoken about our playing style, the previous day and replaced him with Don Howe.

We then won 3-2 at home to Villa and lost 1-0 at Southampton but should have at least had a share of the spoils. Things were coming together and we then embarked on our best run of the season, taking twenty-two points from our next nine matches which included a run of four straight wins.

We also received a late Christmas present. Saunders had again gone north of the border and plucked another striker, Gerry Byrd, from St Mirren. Gerry went straight into the team making his debut at Coventry where he scored in a 2-1 win. He stayed in the side for the rest of the season playing alongside first Dutch then Steve Baker, which meant that Pete Aitken was left out. When he made the mistake of moaning in public about being dropped, Saunders told him he needed "to make up his mind whether he wanted to be a footballer or a fucking beatnik"—a reference to Pete's interest in all things fashion. Probably not the right word to use but we knew what he meant. Credit to Aitken, at least he had a serious interest away from the beautiful game.

Byrd gave us a new dimension in attack in so much as he was fast, good in the air, skilful, strong and brave. In previous seasons, we had players who boasted some of those attributes but no one had them all in a single package. He began by playing alongside Dutch and within a couple of games he looked to be the senior partner, with Dutch unable to shift the weight he had put on which severely restricted his mobility. He swore he wasn't over-eating and that Gloria was under strict instructions not to cook intricate Caribbean dishes for him. He was never a big drinker but continued to pile on the pounds regardless and was left out in favour of Steve Baker after we lost at home to Liverpool.

The Baker-Byrd axis was an immediate hit with one instinctively knowing where the other was or what he was about to do with the ball. It would be wrong to say we stayed up because of Byrd but he certainly made a significant impact netting ten of the thirty goals we scored after he joined and setting up a few as well. Reid and Byrd, two Saints who no one had heard of and who had made a real difference. Saunders had done it again.

We suffered a couple of heavy defeats towards the end of the season but ended up a respectable eleventh. The two sides who had been promoted with us had also done well in their two seasons in the top flight with West Ham finishing eighth and ninth and Norwich fourteenth in both seasons, which also helped to disprove the second season syndrome.

Saunders knew he would be busy again in the summer as it was announced Rob Davies would be leaving for Liverpool at the end of the season for the little matter of £900,000. I was very pleased for him but at the same time couldn't help feeling envious. The speculation surrounding me last season and talk of a possible international call-up had completely died out. And as far as I knew there had been no interest in me from other clubs. This time round the ego was definitely bruised and the confidence dented.

I had to be honest with myself though. My form hadn't been as good or as consistent and I had been much less influential than in our promotion year and initial season in Division One. As Saunders indicated, perhaps I had been lucky to keep my place in the team, although things picked up after he spoke to me following my act of revenge in Split. Not being captain had been strange; I certainly wasn't as involved as I had been but I knew that would be the case when I decided to step down and it had meant there was no tension brought into our home. That had been a relief for both of us.

Chapter Two
Saunders' Bombshell

Summer was always a strange time of year. On the one hand, I looked forward to getting away from football, spending some precious time with Tina, lapping up the sea, sun and sights and indulging in a few guilty pleasures either denied to me or by me during the course of a season. On the other hand, I would dread the thought of pre-season training—and the older I got the more I despised the thought of run, run, run followed by boring friendlies unless, of course, they took the form of a pre-season tournament in Spain. Even though the club had rung the changes over the years in terms of where we went to endure this torment, there were still elements which were repetitive and monotonous in the extreme. Thank God, it was only once a year.

Although I could leave the day-to-day rituals behind, I could never completely switch off. I wanted to know what was going on at the club and what the future held for me. This wasn't insecurity or paranoia it was simply a need to know and an ambition to do the best I could with my career. Who, if anyone, were we signing? Who have we let go? Is my place under threat?

The summer following the 1983-84 season wasn't my most relaxing as I spent a lot of time looking back while at the same time trying to pan to the future. I had just completed my seventh season as a first team player and had not far off three-hundred appearances under my belt. I had sampled three promotions, exciting FA Cup and League Cup runs and the taste of European competition. And yet.

I worried about the coming season, my main concern being who was Saunders going to replace Rob Davies with and how we would fill the very large hole he had left. How much of the £900,000 the club received for Rob would be made available to Saunders to reinvest in the squad? Roger Palmer had hardly been seen over the last twelve months and although Saunders continued to pull the occasional rabbit out of the hat—Byrd, Baker, Reid—there was always a feeling he was restricted in terms of how many players he could bring in at any one time.

I had the distinct impression we were treading water and it all felt a bit directionless. The days of "First Division football in five years" were a thing of the past and although Saunders had spoken to me as we flew to China about a "three-year plan," there was scant evidence one existed. Were we content simply to retain our First Division status? If that was the case it would mean we would head in only one direction and it wouldn't be in the right one. Would we target the FA and/or League Cups? The chances of us winning the League were non-existent so to my mind we should target these competitions. Had I been captain I would have been able to corner Saunders and tell him of my worries.

I still had hopes of playing for England although my chances were far more distant than twelve months before, but I still saw players being capped who I felt I was better than. And although my stock had fallen—at least, that was my interpretation—I still wanted to play for a club with ambition, with the desire to improve season after season. I didn't want to be held back because the club was happy with the status quo.

People who work for organisations away from football for a period of time look to move on. New challenges, a different culture, fresh ideas, different voices and ideas and a desire to learn and improve. Many feel the need to move on because they think they've achieved all they can where they are. Footballers are just the same and shouldn't be criticised for it.

I decided to contact Saunders and ask him to outline his thoughts. On the strength of what he said, perhaps I would have to abandon my hopes that a bigger club would come calling so affording me a lucrative pay day, and that I would have to request a transfer. I also decided to dispense with the services of Steve Russell. After all, he was my agent and had failed to find me a new club. I didn't want to fall out with him but if that was what it was going to take, I was ready for it. He was getting money from me for doing close to nothing. I decided that for the foreseeable future I would negotiate everything myself.

If I had any chance of rekindling my international prospects and regenerating interest from clubs I fancied moving to, I would need to start the new season in tip-top shape, fully motivated and firing on all cylinders. I went to the hotel "gym" every day, swam endless lengths of the pool, never had a three-course meal and kept a strict eye on my alcoholic intake.

I also rang the club to arrange to speak to or meet with Saunders. Peter Christie in his usual pompous, arrogant and controlling way tried to put a block on that but when I pointed out I wanted to talk about my future and that I was certain that Saunders would want to talk to his longest-serving player with the most appearances of any squad member and now that Davies had left, probably his most valuable asset, he relented. Christie wasn't the only one who could be pompous and arrogant.

Christie, in his far more effective mode as an administrator and organiser, arranged for me to ring Saunders from my hotel room—today's equivalent of sending emails from by the pool—and I gave him an overview of my feelings and asked him if he was prepared to think about them and meet when I was back in the country.

Ten days later Saunders and I met in his office at Wood Lane.

"Has anyone ever told you you're a pain in the arse, Ed?" I didn't consider myself to be that but certainly, as the years passed, I had become a more confident individual and therefore comfortable to speak my mind as well as asking searching questions and not being fobbed off with shallow answers. I had come to realise that was my right. Saunders seemed pleased enough to see me, though, and I wondered if my presence was an antidote to the tedium he endured at this time of year with few people in and around the club, countless telephone calls not being returned and no immediate matches to plan for.

I repeated what I had said to him when we spoke on the phone a few days earlier and told him I thought the club had become stuck in a rut and lacked ambition. I asked him to convince me otherwise. I explained I would have to seriously consider my future if he couldn't. I was confident I could have this conversation without raising his heckles because I had an inkling Saunders felt the same about himself. He had intimated as much when we spoke on the flight to China and there had been a few other tell-tale signs in recent months, that although he remained committed to the cause, he wasn't quite as enthusiastic as he had been. The difference between us was that if he put out the word he was thinking of leaving he would have plenty of suitors.

Saunders listened to what I had to say, sipping on one of his endless mugs of tea. Knowing his idea of tea was most peoples' idea of tar I had brought water and politely declined his offer of a mug of rosy.

He was candid in his response. He had no replacement for Rob Davies lined up and we may have to consider using Nick Athey as a stopgap on the left, which would mean a far less attack-minded approach. That didn't sound good. He didn't know how much of the £900,000 he would be given to reinvest in the squad. Surely he should have been fully aware by now! He was currently drawing up a list of players to present to the Board and would know more after the directors met in a couple of days. A bit late in the day, I thought, as pre-season training began in a week.

I had read that Brian Clough, especially when he was manager of Derby County, had been in the habit of going out and signing players without the Chairman's knowledge or approval and was that something he had thought of doing? Saunders grinned. "Maybe if I had won the title I would but even though Roger and I are mates I don't think that would go down very well."

Saunders added we went out to win every game regardless of the competition and he was surprised I didn't recognise that. He wouldn't prioritise the FA and League Cups over the League as this would send the wrong message. He completely disagreed with my assertion that we were simply content with First Division survival and that the aim every season was to finish as high as we could and hopefully qualify for Europe. I told him that if we didn't invest in the squad—and soon—we would struggle in the coming season. He disagreed. But then he would, wouldn't he?

When I left his office after a couple of hours, I didn't feel any more confident about the club's ambitions or my future. I wish I had known it was the last conversation I was going to have with Saunders as manager of Northtown United FC as I would have pushed him harder.

Two days later I was playing golf with Bill Cooke, Tommy Butler and Dave Stewart when a somewhat dishevelled and obviously stressed Dave Craig, accompanied by a photographer, pulled up in a buggy to bring an abrupt end to our round. "Have you heard? What are your thoughts?" asked Craig as he struggled to get out of the buggy. Given he had hunted us down on the golf course and the state he was in it was obvious something serious was afoot. My first thought was that Palmer had sold the club. "Dave, it would be a great help if you could tell us what the hell you're talking about," I said.

"Saunders has gone. I don't know if he was sacked or resigned but apparently last night's Board meeting only lasted about half an hour. Can I get a couple of quotes and can we take a quick pic? I don't have long to deadline." It was difficult to know what to say. Saunders had given no indication when we met, he was on the cusp of quitting. Naturally I couldn't say anything about our meeting, even the guys I was playing golf with weren't aware of it.

We gave Dave our thoughts. A complete shock. No idea what was behind it. Did a fantastic job for the club. Had made some tremendous signings. Was responsible for improving a lot of players. No idea if Dave Walters will take over. Don't think there's any significance in Dave returning and Saunders leaving. Craig and the photographer returned to the Observer offices, the four of us went back to the clubhouse, found a table in a corner, digested some food and drinks as well as the news and discussed.

Looking back it was obvious not everything was rosy in the Saunders garden. He had looked tired and drawn despite having had his first two-week break in years, his usual sparkle was missing, and although he spoke well enough it wasn't with his usual passion. There was a time when he would have lost it with me over one or two of the things I said. I had simply thought he was in the doldrums due to the time of year and lack of activity. Again, looking back, he didn't ask me whether I was staying or going to move. There was a time when he would have demanded to know.

Perhaps he knew the forthcoming Board meeting would signal his swansong.

A handful of golfers, some of whom we knew some of whom seemed to think that we knew them, had heard the news on the radio—being a First Division outfit it was announced on national as well as local radio—to ask us what we knew and how we felt. There's always at least one know-it-all. Ours claimed he hadn't missed a match home or away, including the UEFA Cup for ten years, told us he had seen it coming and that it was obvious we needed a change because "Saunders had lost his way." "Mate, just piss off." This from Tommy Butler, who encapsulated all our thoughts.

I was genuinely sad. I was the only one left at the club from the day Saunders arrived amid a huge fanfare and high expectations. He had taken us from the arse end of the Fourth Division to the First Division and established the club on the English football map. Some of his signings had been inspired, he never wavered from playing attacking football. He had never shied away from making tough, sometimes brutal, decisions.

We had been lucky to have played for him and I owed him a great deal. On the other hand, if I wasn't going anywhere maybe I needed someone new to come to me. From a purely selfish point of view, this might not be such a disaster. I excused myself for a few minutes and phoned Tina. "I've just been talking about you with Dave," she said. "He was hoping to meet you tonight and interview the club's longest-serving player."

"I was going to suggest meeting him to see if he's learned anything during the day. I think Tommy should come as well," I told her. Butler wondered whether we should get Peter Christie's approval or try and let Roger Palmer know of our intentions. "Sod Christie, he will probably tell us not to meet and I've no idea how to get hold of Palmer. Let's just do it," I said.

Dave Craig wasn't in the best frame of mind when we met. He had been blissfully unaware of any behind-the-scenes tensions which resulted in his being hauled over the coals by his editor and had then spent the rest of the day chasing people who wouldn't take his call or failed to phone him back. Peter Christie refused point blank to see him and wouldn't even talk to him after the next morning's press conference.

Consequently, all he had managed to get were the "we're dumbfounded" quotes from us on the golf course, along with his own thoughts. He would need to write up his interview with us overnight, attend the press conference and write a story from that as well.

"It will be interesting to hear what comes out of the press conference because we know only as much as you," Tommy told him. "I couldn't get hold of Christie. A few players have rung me but all I can do is speculate. We honestly didn't see it coming and as yet the club hasn't arranged to brief us."

The press conference appeared as part of the local news and was the dampest of damp squibs. Christie chaired it and read out a statement from the absent Palmer, which paid tribute to Saunders' achievements and said he would always be welcome at Wood Lane etc., etc. Predictably, we were told the parting of the ways was a mutual decision which is the blandest of explanations and can, and usually does, cover a multitude of reasons.

Sitting next to Christie was Dave Walters, who had been appointed caretaker manager and said all the right things about Saunders, how he wanted the job, how he knew the club inside out. More puff, especially as I thought it was highly unlikely Dave would want the job full-time and would probably only oversee the pre-season training and friendlies. It was clear from the way the club reacted—or failed to react—Saunders' exit had caught it on the hop. It was completely unprepared. Normally there are rumours or you get an inkling something is about to happen. We concluded there had been a major fall-out at the Board meeting and Saunders had walked out. Even the normally unflappable Peter Christie was looking a tad stressed.

Tony Saunders was always going to be a tough, almost impossible, act to follow regardless of who took his place but Sam Carmichael was the polar opposite in character, so whoever was responsible for appointing him had not done the necessary due diligence.

Saunders wasn't just the man who masterminded our journey up the divisions leaving an indelible stamp on the club—and he was only there for six seasons, so it's hardly surprising Manchester United are still coming to terms with Fergie's retirement given he was there for twenty-seven years! Saunders may not have been with Northtown long enough to have created a dynasty but he wasn't far off doing so.

He was brilliant in many areas but where I think he really excelled was in the transfer market bringing in countless players who may not have been household names but who fitted our style of play and made us a better side. I admit I had reservations about some of them at the time but nearly all of them came up trumps. Iain Moy, Mick Egan, Terry Bell and Gerry Byrd hadn't even been heard of but were tremendous.

Fans would have been aware of others like Tom Butler, Terry Green, Les Oldfield and John Halliday but their signatures wouldn't have been the first thing spoken about over the breakfast table. They all did a great job. And Saunders wasn't afraid to blood youngsters with Rob Davies, Pete Aitken and Mike Sears all thriving under him.

From a personal point of view, Tony gave my confidence the boost it needed during his first pre-season and I became a regular under him. He dropped me at the right stage although I was unaware and unappreciative of that at the time but it improved me as a player; he made me captain of "my" team and was understanding when I resigned; some spirit went out of the door with him and I wasn't the only one left with an empty feeling.

We had our ups and downs but neither of us were the kind to hold grudges so our relationship was a strong, albeit distant one—he knew he couldn't get too close to his players and although he would have a drink and a laugh with us those occasions were rare. The players trusted him and showed him the respect he deserved and when he did mingle with us no one was daft enough to "talk shop."

To this day I don't think I have the full story behind his leaving. I've asked him many times but whether he is stone-cold sober or had a couple of glasses of his beloved French red wine his answer has always been the same: "Forget it, Ed. What happened, happened." I do know, though, that he and Roger Palmer aren't as close as they were. Palmer remains steadfastly loyal and only speaks of Saunders in the highest terms, as he should. But when I've quizzed Palmer about events, he's always told me to "ask Tony." Peter Christie, it will come as no surprise, plays a dead bat and refuses to shed any light on events at the same time as making it clear it's none of my business—without actually saying it.

My guess is that Saunders wanted to buy some fresh blood and funds weren't made available. Perhaps he had taken the club as far he could, I wish he had stayed for another season or two.

There was another parting of the ways to come and although this one was planned, I hadn't worked out when it would come and how calm it would be. I had phoned Steve Russell to see if he could shed any light on why Saunders had left but he said he was unable to contact him. When I told him I wanted to review our arrangement, there was a deep intake of breath.

"OK, Ed. Listen I've loads of clients now and I get a very small amount of income from you. If you want to call it quits, that's fine by me but still feel free to call me." I got the feeling he was as happy to be shot of me as I was of him and I could now look at things through a different lens.

I liked Steve and we had initially got on like a house of fire, but as he took on more clients our friendship became more of a business relationship. I had liked the way he introduced himself to me and our first few conversations were really enjoyable, almost exciting, and reinforced my view that I was being undervalued by the club. He had helped me get improved terms but I felt I had already laid much of the groundwork for him and he benefitted from the relationship as well as me.

He hadn't helped me get a move though. Far from an easy task but Steve hadn't even generated any interest. He would say I was too choosy; my response is that he should come up with an alternative solution and I don't mean, with all due respect to them, suggesting QPR or Coventry as alternative destinations. And Steve only tended to make contact when my good performances increased my profile. I was his first "client" and although that shouldn't necessarily afford me special treatment, there were times when I think he neglected me as he concentrated on adding to his "portfolio." One of the golden rules of business is that you don't just concentrate on new business, you have to keep your existing client base happy to retain it. I think Steve lost sight of that,

We still bump into each other occasionally and get along fine recognising our relationship was in the early days of players and agents, that we were both young and that mistakes were made on both sides. More on his than on mine, of course!

Chapter Three
Player Power

When Steve Reid joined the club, I described him as a breath of fresh air. When Sam Carmichael was appointed manager, it was like someone with particularly bad halitosis stepping into the room.

Carmichael's managerial CV had a couple of promotions and a couple of relegations on it, hardly setting him aside from the crowd. All the right noises were made about him being the ideal man for the job; a cynic would say that could only mean no one else was interviewed. A former old-school take-no-prisoners centre half he was bold and brash and seemed intent on ruling by fear. He didn't have the intelligence to realise that different people are different characters and need to be treated and managed as individuals. A different way of looking at this is that he simply didn't give a damn about that sort of thing. He was certainly a "my way or the high way" type of manager and his appointment was a complete mystery to one and all.

It was immediately obvious to the players he was not the man to take the club up to the next level but certainly appeared capable of undoing all the great work of the previous six years. He was scathing about our style of play but then changed nothing. He was less than complimentary about the quality of the squad but didn't sign anyone. Was this because the financial shackles were on? Even if that was the case a new manager could freshen things up with a couple of loan signings. He wasn't a great one for the training ground, although he did coach Terry Bell and Mick Egan, the latter being more receptive as he and Carmichael were from the same mould. It's fair to say that the more sophisticated Bell and the new manager were never on the same wavelength.

Jimmy Seal and Terry Green, still at the club but hardly likely to feature—especially in the case of Jimmy—were ignored and didn't even train with us. Jimmy was so disaffected there were a couple of occasions when he simply didn't turn up and his absence wasn't even commented on, although it must have been noted.

Carmichael also made it clear we should only call him "gaffer," a term I have always hated although I can't explain why so I tried to avoid calling him anything—at least to his face. He did have some early meetings with some of us and I was one of the chosen few but it was a one-way discussion which was also short and of no use to me other than confirming what I already knew about the man. I wondered if he just wanted to size me up. When I told him, I harboured ambitions of playing for my country he was dismissive. He looked at me for a long time and said: "If it was going to happen, son, it would have happened by now." Thanks for that, and why do football managers insist on calling players "son"?

Crap communicator, rubbish motivator, showed a lack of respect. It could have been that club and manager were well suited because one was caught on the hop with no plan of succession when Saunders left and the other was desperate to get back into the game and happy to take any job regardless of possible financial restrictions. Why he was appointed instead of keeping Dave Walters in charge until an obviously suitable candidate became available remains one of the mysteries of my life. The club had made some decisions I didn't agree with in the past but this appointment was plainly ludicrous and regardless of how the relationship had been formed, most of us predicted a stormy and short-lived marriage.

The 1984-85 season began promisingly enough with a well-merited 1-1 draw away to Manchester United on 25 August but that was a false dawn. We didn't win a match until late September when we beat Second Division Cardiff City in the League Cup. By this stage, we had played seven League matches drawing four and losing three. We lost our next two games, including the second leg against Cardiff, before recording our first win of the season, 3-2 at Chelsea. We then drew or lost our next four matches.

Carmichael's reaction to a loss was generally to blame the players for not following his game plan—or not being capable of following his game plan. There was the occasional criticism of the officials and a general "what am I supposed to do with this squad" approach. Some players had become a shadow of their former selves. Pete Aitken, having returned for pre-season with renewed enthusiasm and commitment, was an easy target for Carmichael. Still young, he was quiet and relied more than most on confidence and an arm round the shoulder. He spent forty-five minutes of every match on the touchline near the dug-outs from where he received dog's abuse, regardless of how he played. His confidence nose-dived and he then became a target for the fans. During one half-time outburst, Dutch stuck up for Pete. "Leave the kid alone. You give him shit for no reason. Give it to someone bigger and older." Carmichael wasn't intimidated by anyone and was straight in Dutch's face and ten minutes into the second half hauled him off. Dutch stormed straight down the tunnel and was nowhere to be seen at the end of the match.

We picked up a couple of wins but by late November we were still in the bottom three and had consecutive home games against Southampton, who were sailing along in the calm waters of mid-table obscurity and recently-promoted Newcastle, closer to the bottom than mid-table but in no real danger and supposedly no great shakes.

We saw both of these as not only can-win but also must-win games but we were wretched against Southampton who returned to the South Coast with the easiest 3-0 win they would pick up having dominated from start to finish. We managed just one shot on target. It was a performance which clearly demonstrated that not only were we in serious trouble of going down but also all was not well behind the scenes. The fans, understandably, were highly unimpressed.

For the first time since a couple of early season games, Roger Palmer was at Wood Lane. The last time he and I had spoken at any length was just before we flew to China and although our relationship had become a little strained, I still liked him and had huge respect for what he had achieved both at Northtown and outside of football. Other than appointing Sam Carmichael that is. He was of course a highly intelligent man and would know things weren't going well at his club. I thought he needed to know just how bad things were behind the scenes and told Tommy Butler what I was thinking.

"Isn't that a bit OTT, Ed?" he asked. "Sorry mate, but you are on your own. I don't want to be part of it." I asked him if he thought the manager was doing a good job. "Of course I don't but I'm sure Palmer and the other directors will make any decision they need to. I don't like the bloke but I'm not prepared to shaft him."

"It's not a case of shafting him, for fuck's sake Tommy." It was rare Butler and I disagreed but this was definitely one of those occasions. "This is for the good of the club."

I grappled with the idea of approaching Palmer over the rest of the weekend. I was fairly certain I knew where he would be staying but once he left the country in a few days I wouldn't be able to contact him. The Vice-Chairman, Arthur Knowles, seemed nice enough but I had never had a long conversation with him, and there was no point involving Peter Christie. I wondered about asking Dave Walters for his thoughts but didn't want to put him in a difficult position. I thought about talking to some of the other players but remembered how annoyed I had been when they met behind my back to discuss the China tour.

Maybe I was getting above myself and possibly the directors needed to work things out for themselves. But I had some loyalty towards Palmer and none towards Carmichael and time was becoming short if we were to turn the season round. I decided to see how things went against Newcastle on Wednesday night.

Training on the Monday wasn't great. Carmichael read the riot act again and went over each goal we conceded against Southampton in minute detail, apportioning blame hither and thither. There are ways of doing things but he had no idea how to go about criticising a player without shattering his confidence.

Mistakes should be pointed out so you learn from them. The way Carmichael went on players became petrified they would screw up again. "Man management" was a completely alien concept to him. He was a one-size-fits-all manager with no empathy for his players and staff. He couldn't spell subtle let alone define its meaning. There was an air of despondency as we showered and changed. The only positive aspect as far as I could see was that my own form was very good and I believed I was playing better than I ever had.

If Monday wasn't great, Tuesday was a disaster. The usually effervescent Reid, who had gained the nickname Tigger for his non-stop action, wasn't very happy at being told to "fucking step on it" by Carmichael as he went to retrieve a loose ball.

Then, at the end of training Carmichael announced the team for the following night. Andy Hopkins, out. Tommy Butler, out. Terry Bell, out. Dutch Pieters, out. He told the four players he was dropping the exact reasons why he was doing so. In front of the rest of us. His reasons included being lazy, dozy, slow, cack-handed, lacking discipline and his old favourite, not sticking to the game plan. He should have spoken to the four individually but yet again alienated the entire squad with his approach. You simply don't out players in public like that.

He had needed to do something but waiting until this stage of the season and then making wholesale changes instead of gradual evolution smacked of a man losing direction—if he ever had one—and panicking. Dave Stewart was to come in for Butler at right back and there was a debut for Garry Harris, who had been doing well in the reserves, at centre back. Steve Baker was in for Dutch and Johnny Webb, who had ended the previous season as first choice and, much to his bemusement, had begun this one as second choice, would take over in goal. Our new skipper was to be Mick Egan.

The four who had been dropped were seething; Walters and Reid were none too happy either as they had been expecting to discuss the line-up with "the gaffer" after training and knew nothing of his plans. Back in the changing room our new skipper was talking loudly and telling everyone he was the "on-pitch gaffer" and that we needed to stay on his right side. "If you don't listen to me on the pitch, you won't play the next game."

"You fucking thick Mick," shouted Bill Cooke. "You're just like the Boss. Who's going to listen to you? You've never said anything sensible in your life."

There had been a few coming-togethers in training over the years but never a fully-fledged punch-up. That was about to change.

It was almost comical to see the six feet four inch Egan and the five feet eight inch Cooke lock horns in the first Northern Ireland v Wales knockout international for many years. Despite Egan's height and weight advantage Cooke more than held his own in the opening exchanges, but then found himself outgunned.

Remarkably, the man who broke it up was Dutch, not known for his United Nations peace-keeping qualities. The fight only lasted a few seconds but it was long enough for Cooke to sustain a badly cut lip and for Egan to receive a bloodied nose. Carmichael, Walters and Reid must have heard the commotion from the manager's office but chose not to put in an appearance.

"This isn't the club I joined less than a year ago," said Gerry Byrd as the dust began to settle. "If things don't change, we'll be relegated by New Year." I walked to the car park with Tommy Butler. "I know what you're going to say, Ed. Let's focus on tomorrow night first."

Newcastle had been having their own off-field problems and had allowed their Manager Arthur Cox to leave replacing him with Jack Charlton. They were an up and down side recording some notable wins but also had a tendency to leak goals. Kevin Keegan was no longer in their playing ranks but they did have Chris Waddle and Peter Beardsley, both of whom would be selected for the Mexico

World Cup in 1986, while Paul Gascoigne would make his debut towards the end of the season.

We had all been embarrassed by our capitulation against Southampton and started brightly against Newcastle, even taking the lead through the restored Steve Baker. Waddle then went to work and had a field day on both flanks against Mike Sears and Dave Stewart, scoring one and putting the others on a plate for Beardsley. As soon as we conceded the equaliser our confidence evaporated and it was inevitable the Geordies would score again and they finished comfortable winners. It wasn't so much losing to Newcastle that brought things to a head it was the events of the previous weeks and if the directors weren't going to confront the issues, we needed to force them to do so or at least make them see how we felt.

"When are you going to do something about Carmichael?" This from Nick Athey, who was showering beside me. "You may not be skipper but you are Northtown more than anyone else, and you also have Palmer's ear"

The events of the last few days had brought things to a head and Athey wasn't the only one with an opinion. Pieters had made his known by not turning up for the Newcastle match and would, quite rightly, be fined. If you are a member of the first team squad, you attend home matches. Others had been grumbling for a while and were seriously concerned we would be relegated. I wanted to have a word with Tom Butler but by the time I arrived in the players' lounge he had left. I tried phoning him later that night but as I half-expected there was no answer. I knew there were enough disaffected players to justify us approaching Palmer but I felt strongly Butler, as skipper, should be one of them and was disappointed he was avoiding me.

If he wasn't going to get involved, I decided I should be accompanied by at least one other senior figure and asked Terry Bell but Ding said his presence could be construed as sour grapes at being dropped. I thought about contacting Pete Aitken who was still young but had a lot of appearances to his name. And what about Walters and Reid? Let them know what was happening or leave them out of it? I decided to contact Walters and he could decide whether to tell Reid or not.

I told Tina trouble was brewing and I would reveal all if she wanted to know the inside track now or, if she preferred, wait until events unfolded and I would furnish Dave Craig with all the details as long as nothing was attributed to me. She decided, on this occasion, ignorance was bliss.

We didn't have to go to the ground the next day unless we had picked up a knock against Newcastle. I hadn't but decided to drive to Wood Lane to see if anyone else was about. I bumped into Laurie Campbell, who was disappointed I wasn't a "customer." "Why are you here then?" he asked. "You look like a man on a mission."

I made a hasty exit and found an empty office and tried phoning Butler. Again, there was no answer but I left a message on his new-fangled answerphone so at least he knew what was happening. I was irritated Tom had gone AWOL.

I guessed right where Palmer was staying and asked him if I could see him on urgent club business. He didn't sound delighted at the prospect but agreed, probably reasoning that our past conversations, even if occasionally strained, had never been trivial. Time to gather some troops and I got hold of Bill Cooke who, with a split lip and Welsh accent, wasn't easy to understand but he was up for it. I decided against calling Pete Aitken because we didn't want too many voices. I did, though, phone Dave Walters. I outlined what was happening and invited him along but he politely declined. "Good luck, I don't envy you," he said. "Call me later if you can."

There was plenty we felt Palmer needed to know—how to begin the conversation was what worried me. He hadn't been expecting to see Bill, while I hadn't anticipated seeing Peter Christie. After Palmer poured glasses of water, I took a deep breath and began.

We had the best interests of the club at heart. He and Christie may not like all they were going to hear. No personal agendas. The vast majority, if not all, the first team squad felt the same. We outlined Carmichael's complete lack of man management skills, how his behaviour was undermining the performance of individuals and the team as a whole. We didn't see much of him and he didn't contribute anything of substance. We seriously feared for our First Division status and that we had no confidence in him. In short, if he stayed, we would go down.

Palmer and Christie took the occasional note and waited until we had finished before they asked questions. "Why isn't Tom Butler here?" asked Christie. I explained the conversations Tom and I had had. "Who else knows you are here?" asked the Chairman. The two of us, plus Bell, I told him leaving Walters' name out of it.

"Don't the players have anything to answer for?" said Palmer. "I was embarrassed by how we played against Southampton and we capitulated against Newcastle. Is the manager responsible for that?"

"Those performances were symptoms of what's been happening since he arrived," I said.

Bill Cooke played a defence-splitting pass. "I've been here before Mr Palmer and went through a similar experience at Swansea a few years ago."

"And did you go to the Chairman on that occasion?" asked Christie. "The manager was sacked before it got to that," responded Cooke. Nice one, Bill.

"And is that what you think should happen? We should sack Sam Carmichael?" snapped Christie.

"We're not saying that Peter," I said. "Those sorts of decisions have nothing to do with us but we want you to know what's going on. It's a multi-million-pound business after all."

"But won't be if we get relegated," observed Palmer.

"Can I ask if the Board has imposed a transfer embargo? It's hard to believe we haven't replaced Davies and the squad is too small and lacks quality in depth." Sod it, I thought, I might as well put my head on the chopping block but I couldn't quite pluck up the courage to ask why Saunders had left.

"The manager can put forward the names of players he wants to sign and if the Board feels the club can afford it and the deal represents good value, we'll make the signing," said Christie. Which didn't quite answer my question and I was miffed Christie had answered and not Palmer. There were times when he behaved like an adviser to an under-fire politician.

There was a lot for Palmer and Christie to absorb. I think they were surprised players had gone to see them indicating the manager wasn't up to the job and they were definitely shocked by some of the details. Players not turning up, punch-ups in the changing rooms and public dressing-downs appeared to worry them almost as much as the results.

"Peter and I need to talk," said Palmer. "I'm sure it wasn't easy coming to see us so we appreciate you doing so. None of this should go any further. We'll be in touch."

Cooke and I went our separate ways and when I got home, I tried calling Walters but his phone was constantly engaged, I presumed Palmer was talking to him.

The following morning's training session had been going for half an hour when Palmer turned up out of the blue. Even after he first bought the club, he was hardly ever seen at the training ground. Carmichael told Walters and Reid to "keep things going" and wandered over to talk to his Chairman. Most of us had one eye on what we were supposed to be doing and the other on the body language between the two men, who were out of earshot.

It all seemed amicable enough and at the end of the session Carmichael called us together to name the team for the next day's match at Queen's Park Rangers. Before he started, Palmer asked where Dutch Pieters was. "Absent without leave, Mr Palmer," replied Carmichael. Palmer nodded slowly, wished us good luck for the following afternoon and went on his way.

That night's Observer made very interesting reading with the main front page story about how Carmichael had "lost the dressing room," how Dutch had disappeared and the fact there had been a fight between two unnamed players. Dave Craig had written a comment piece about how Carmichael would be out of a job unless he turned things round very quickly. I had no doubt I would be blamed for the leak and although I was on tenterhooks all night waiting for the phone to ring it stayed silent. Tina had been off that day and had no idea the story was going to run or who the source was. She said she would try and find out who had briefed Craig but he wouldn't reveal anything.

The atmosphere at Wood Land as we climbed aboard the coach ahead of the short journey to Loftus Road wasn't pleasant. There was hardly any conversation and even Mick Egan had picked up on it and kept himself to himself. I made sure I sat next to Tom Butler, back in the team after the mauling Dave Stewart had taken at the hands of Chris Waddle although not reinstated as captain, but he didn't say much. "Did you get my message?" I asked. "Yep. Thanks. Who spoke to The Observer?" I assured him it wasn't me.

As we prepared for the match Carmichael said: "Obviously, someone has it in for me. I reckon I know who it is but can't prove it. It's just a shame no one had the balls to tell me what a shit manager you think I am. If you don't want to play for me today, play for yourselves." It was a bit lame but he wasn't a fool and the fact the Chairman had visited training on Friday for the first time in six-and-a-half years and The Observer reported on behind-the-scenes events would have sent a very clear message to him.

Like us, QPR were struggling and we played out an extremely average 1-1 draw in front of a small crowd. Those that did attend must have wished they had spent their money more wisely. I scored for us from the penalty spot. Had the same decision been given against us we would have been disgusted. It was probably the most sterile game of the season but it was a point away from home and ended our run of defeats.

Palmer had obviously extended his stay in the country and he was among the spectators along with Christie and Knowles. They did watch away games but it was rare all three were in attendance at the same one which was another clear message to the manager. Like the players and coaching staff, they would have been glad of the point even if they didn't think much of the performance, but when times are desperate you take what you can get. I wondered if they had come with the intention of sacking Carmichael after the match but thought they would have a touch more class than that and if the deed was going to be done it would take place at Wood Lane or the training ground.

We headed back to Wood Lane and Tina and I had the usual Saturday night out with friends, arriving home after midnight. Like Tom Butler, we had invested in one those new-fangled answerphones and for the first time the light which indicated we had a message was flashing. It was quite exciting to discover who had left the very first message—it was Peter Christie asking me to meet him and Roger Palmer on Sunday morning at Palmer's hotel.

Tommy Butler had also been summoned, as had Bill Cooke. Arthur Knowles and Christie completed the line-up. Palmer started by asking Butler for his opinion. Given he had been summoned to the meeting by the club, Tom was happy to give his point of view, which mirrored mine and Bill's.

"Anyone think different after yesterday's result?" asked Palmer. No one did. Palmer took a deep breath. "I maintain some of the responsibility has to lie with the players. If we do decide to make a change, I damn well hope I see some improved performances from the dross I've been subjected to over the last week or so." It was rare for Palmer to comment on how we were playing. He thanked us for attending and virtually ushered us out of the door.

"What he should be thinking," ventured Bill, "is that we would be playing a lot better if he hadn't appointed that idiot. I thought Palmer was meant to be a clever bloke."

"Shall we have a drink while we are here?" asked Tommy. I didn't feel inclined to sit down with him after his refusal to take a couple of my calls and made an excuse about going out for lunch. Bill said he had things to do. Tommy shrugged his shoulders and we went our separate ways.

When I got home, I suggested to Tina that she let Dave Craig know Carmichael was on the brink of losing his job. She got off the phone to him and told me that someone had already briefed him—my money was on Christie. At least, Craig would avoid another verbal kicking from his editor for missing the story.

As I drove to training the following morning there was no mention of Carmichael losing his job on the local radio but when we arrived Palmer and Christie were there and gathered us together in the dressing room to announce that Carmichael had been dismissed an hour ago. Dave Walters had agreed to be caretaker manager until the end of the season with Steve Reid assisting him. The Board would then take stock and make a permanent appointment. Dutch Pieters, who had been contacted by Christie on Friday afternoon after he and Palmer had visited the training ground telling him to be at QPR or face having his contract cancelled, summed things up as we made our way to the training round. "Good riddance but they took too long to make the decision."

That night's Observer, naturally, went to town. The front-page headline told the world—or it's thirty thousand readers—"Carmichael Sacked." Underneath there was a sub-headline: "Player Power brings about Manager's downfall." I wasn't happy to see that but neither was I going to lose sleep over it.

Without belittling anything Dave Walters and Steve Reid achieved there really was only one direction we could go in. Carmichael's sacking immediately lifted a pall covering the club and Walters had everyone's respect and knew the club inside out, while Reid's enthusiasm was infectious and they worked together very well.

One of Walters' first actions was to tell Mick Egan he was giving the captaincy back to Tom Butler and then told Dutch he was fined a fortnight's wages and that he was palpably unfit and wouldn't play for the first team until he was back in shape. Nothing was said in public, obviously, but Walters was aware the news would get back to the squad. It was important that he wasn't seen as a pushover. He also fined Jimmy Seal but restored him to the first team squad and told him he would play if he proved his worth.

The major concerns were our left flank where Nick Athey had struggled manfully in an alien position and behind him Mike Sears was a "modern" fullback—better going forward than defending. Dave reasoned, quite rationally, that if you are a defender you need to be able to defend so recalled Terry Green to the starting eleven and took a punt at playing Sears on the left of midfield.

Bell returned in place of Harris and Webb was retained in goal. The biggest change was playing a fifth midfielder, Athey, instead of two up fronts although Nick would play high enough up the pitch to support Steve Baker, while Gerry Byrd had recovered from a long-term knee injury.

That was pretty much the starting eleven for the rest of the season—although Dutch made a couple of appearances towards the end of it and Dave Stewart deputised for Egan when he served his annual suspension. Slowly but surely we hauled ourselves clear of the relegation zone—Stoke, Sunderland and Norwich, who won the League Cup, went down—and we ended up fifteenth, which looked safe enough, especially as for the first half of the season we looked odds-on to go down. Carmichael being sacked helped save us but I think everyone knew the team needed a complete rebuild.

We looked OK in goal where Webb did well but Butler and Green, stalwarts and still good players were beginning to be found out and there were no ready replacements at the club. Pete Aitken's focus had again shifted towards the fashion world, Sears worked his socks off but wasn't a natural midfielder, while Dutch's health and fitness wasn't going to see him through another season in the top flight and Jimmy Sears wanted away.

Dave Walters had done a good job but he didn't see himself as a number one so the Board had to recruit another manager, which would inevitably be a long-winded process unless they had someone already lined up. I didn't think that was likely. It was going to be another nerve-wracking summer and I wasn't going to help things because I wanted a fresh challenge and was going to request a transfer.

The Observer had used the phrase "Player Power" in a headline and it was an early example of that. Were our actions disingenuous? I know there were some people who thought they were but we did what we did for the club. I felt the bigger problem was the appointment in the first place, compounded by the Board's failure to recognise it had created a major predicament for the playing and coaching staff. Whatever anyone at Board level may have said about the players' performance, that was very poor business That disappointed me.

I was proud of the part I played in helping secure our First Division status but was also aware that I had been at the heart of the players' reaction to two challenging and sensitive issues in two years (although the club didn't handle the trip to China very well there was certainly an element of over-reaction from the playing staff) and didn't want to get involved in any other differences of opinion.

In any case, I doubted the club would have welcomed more "interference" from yours truly and there was the little matter of my transfer request to be negotiated.

Chapter Four
Going Dutch

Everybody loved Patrick "Dutch" Pieters. A big man with a big personality to match. You could be a teammate, a member of the coaching or office staff, a fan or even a journalist—he treated everyone the same and was unfailingly polite. The phrase "gentle giant" could have been invented for him. Well, for most of the time. His wife, Gloria, was an equally larger-than-life and popular figure and was forever pregnant. When Dutch joined the club, she was pregnant with their third child; by the time I left five years later they had five.

When he joined Northtown, Dutch was close to drinking in the Last Chance Saloon, despite his record price tag, as injuries and inconsistency had counted against him but he was a more than decent player and not just because he was the size of a brick outhouse. He had a good touch, an explosive shot and once he managed to get going, he was quick.

His close control when he was running with the ball was something to behold because he often had no idea where he was going or what he was going to do with the ball. As a result, he would occasionally become confused and fall over himself or the ball or both and he would go to ground in a flurry of legs as he crashed down like a Grand National runner coming to grief at Becher's Brook. He didn't tend to see the funny side but supporters of both sides would find it highly amusing, we tried to not laugh but usually failed. It all added to his popularity.

Because he was such a big man, things occasionally went "pop," much like a fast bowler. Pulled muscles, torn hamstrings and a suspect calf had seen managers at his previous clubs run out of patience, but Saunders signed him for a club record fee in the knowledge it was a bit of a gamble. He and his staff worked hard to keep Dutch fit and he would often sit out training sessions. "He can score goals at this level," Mark Bailey told me when we were having a round of golf. "The Boss reckons if he stays fit, he will get a load for us if Aitken and Davies can provide the ammunition. The problem is that he's missed over thirty per cent of matches throughout his career."

Dutch joined us as part of our promotion push to the First Division and certainly contributed to that, although I wouldn't say his impact was spectacular and few would have predicted he would end the following season as the First Division's top scorer with an enormously impressive twenty-eight goals. The more he played and steered clear of injuries the more his confidence grew and First Division defenders seemed more intimidated by him than their Second Division counterparts.

He led the line brilliantly and there were many highlights to his first season in Division One. He didn't get on the scoresheet at Highbury but his performance was one of the main reasons others did. He played as well as anyone that day. He scored four against Sunderland and although they were unbelievably poor, Dutch was irresistible. A towering header, a right-foot rocket from outside the box, a left-foot tap-in and another right-foot finish made it a night to remember for him.

He also walked off with the match ball at Wood Lane after another "perfect" hat-trick—left foot, right foot, header—against Stoke, but it wasn't just at home where he was deadly, he netted twelve times at away grounds.

Like many gentle giants, though, when Dutch lost his rag, he lost it in quite explosive fashion and it took a little while for the switch to return to the off position. When he lost it, the best thing to do was to beat a hasty retreat and evacuate the room, leaving him to calm down. Even the bigger members of the squad, like Bell and Egan, weren't interested in trying to pacify him when he erupted.

We didn't so much see him when he lost his temper for the first time but we certainly heard it. Saunders had summoned Dutch to his office after training one morning to tell him he didn't want him to go on international duty. Dutch is fiercely proud of his Jamaican heritage—when the West Indies cricketers tour here he instantly switches his allegiance from England—and he was hell-bent on going. The Regga Boyz, as the national team is known, were no great shakes back then and didn't even try to qualify for the World Cup because the national association couldn't afford it.

Saunders was dead against Dutch going on a long-haul flight to a training camp and then playing in a friendly against Trinidad and Tobago and taking another long-haul flight home, which wouldn't land until Friday afternoon, meaning Dutch would probably be in no fit state to play for us the following day.

"This club paid a fortune for you, it pays your wages, it's doing its best to keep you fit and make you a better player. I don't want you going," shouted Saunders as the volume increased.

"No one tells Dutch—he had a habit of talking in the first person—he can't play for his country. You try and stop Dutch and he is outta this club."

Saunders, of course, couldn't stop him from going, he could only "advise" him but I think he was banking on Dutch not knowing this when he shouted: "You're not fucking going and if you do go, I'll kick you out of the club." Dutch stormed out of Saunders' office not just slamming the door behind him but SLAMMING it, thundered into the dressing room and proceeded to knock seven bells out of his locker, Muhammed Ali in his pomp would have been proud of a few of those punches. Dutch didn't say anything and no one dared to say anything to him. He didn't shower, he didn't even change and left his "civvies" hanging on pegs. His car could be heard screeching out of the car park as he made his way home to his beloved Gloria and brood of children.

This was a tough call for Saunders. The pull of playing for your country is huge and you don't want to miss a match, even a friendly on the other side of the world. Everyone knows it's very different today and players will supposedly pick up an injury which rules them out of a match but they are then one hundred per cent fit to play when the following Saturday comes. Ryan Giggs famously once missed eighteen consecutive friendlies for Wales and it's obvious he didn't pick up eighteen niggles—Fergie didn't want him risking his fitness.

This was Saunders' point. The club was wrapping Dutch in cotton wool and so far he hadn't so much as reported a twinge and was firing on all cylinders. It surely wasn't worth his while risking all this to fly to the Caribbean for a friendly on (probably) a poor pitch and certainly not receive the standard of care he was enjoying at Northtown. Saunders wanted some payback from Dutch and I was definitely with him on this one.

Dutch turned up the next day and it was as if nothing had happened twenty-four hours earlier. He trained as normal and mingled with the rest of us exactly as he did every day. All that was left to remind us there had been a bust-up was a mangled locker in the corner of the dressing room, which lay there for several weeks as Saunders thought it would serve as a reminder to the big Jamaican. Dutch didn't go to the Caribbean for the match against Trinidad and Tobago and

I heard a few years later that as a trade-off he didn't have to pay for the replacement locker.

It would be an exaggeration to say that trouble followed Dutch around. But only a slight one.

Riley's was a nightclub in the centre of Northtown, which Tina and I went to semi-regularly with friends. It was a huge place, set on two levels with numerous bars and a couple of dance floors. You could either stand around or book tables and most weekends there were live performances—we had seen Tavares, the Chi-Lites and the Detroit Spinners, as well as splitting our sides at the legendary comic Tommy Cooper. All of which shows my age. But believe me, they were all very good.

Terry Green suggested we visited Riley's during the international break Dutch was banned from and Saunders was OK with the idea. Terry booked a couple of tables as wives/girlfriends/partners were coming as well, although numbers dwindled as the night drew closer but for good reason as Rob Davies, Pete Aitken and Mick Egan were called up for international duty—Rob to the full England squad, Pete to the Under 21s and Mick for the senior Northern Ireland squad. By the end of the night, we were wishing Dutch had played for Jamaica after all.

The evening started well enough with players and partners meeting in a wine bar, owned by a mate of Terry's, a few minutes' walk from Riley's. The girls all looked glamorous in their finery, the players all trying to out-do each other in the latest fashion stakes. Looking back, it's not unreasonable to say that the fashion trends in the mid-1980s weren't great!

We had a few drinks and wandered to Riley's going straight to the front of the VIP queue, which we had to pay for. Inevitably this sparked a few comments from other punters. "Fucking footballers think they're so important"; "Look at those tossers"—that sort of thing. Inflammatory if you allowed it to be but we ignored it all, went into the club and to our tables. We had a few more drinks and a meal of something-in-the-basket and chips. Once the meal was finished there was half an hour or so before that night's entertainment, The Three Degrees, took to the stage.

Some of us went to the bar, most people ignoring us or engaging in friendly conversation. A couple of lads hurled relatively harmless insults at us and then pissed themselves laughing thinking they were drop-dead funny.

Dutch was leaning on the bar ordering a round of drinks and flirting with the barmaid. The guy next to him moved closer and whispered something in his ear. The next moment Dutch had one of his massive hands around the man's throat and looked as if he was going to inflict some serious damage. A couple of bouncers appeared from nowhere and pulled Dutch away. Given what the guy had said to Dutch he should have been bounced down the stairs and onto Northtown High Street.

"What the hell happened Dutch?" asked Tommy Butler. As I've said, Dutch is mostly a laid-back individual but he was revving up to losing it. "He told me to keep my black cock in my pants and not to hassle white women." Gloria gave him the kind of look that would turn most men into pillars of salt. "Dahlin', I was just talkin' to the girl while she poured the drinks."

When Tommy suggested he stayed away from the bar, Dutch gave him one of Gloria's looks. "Dutch will do what Dutch wants to do. And he's gonna be shakin' his fat ass on that dance floor soon. Ain't no one gonna stop him."

It looked like the rest of the night would pass without incident. The Three Degrees came and went—too much saccharin for my taste—and Tina and I sidled off to the dance floor and then to the bar from where we heard the sound of crashing glass and a girl's piercing scream.

We looked across to where the disturbance had come from and saw one guy lying on his back, spreadeagled across a table while another two were punching and kicking Dutch. Steve Baker and Jimmy Seal were trying to defend him while Gloria was hitting a fourth guy on his head with the sole of a shoe she had quickly taken off and was using very effectively as a weapon. The thought that it was a good job it was a flat sole and not a stiletto passed through my mind. "She's done that before," said Tina.

By the time I arrived at the scene, Dutch was being held back—just—by a couple of bouncers, another of his attackers was bent double after being kicked by Seal and the other two had backed off. The bloke who had been spreadeagled across the table was the same individual who Dutch had grabbed by the throat earlier. He was now sporting a nose which was a completely different shape to the one he had been born with and was ranting about calling the police and prosecuting Dutch. He should think himself lucky he wasn't a metal locker.

Dutch was escorted from the club and in a show of solidarity the rest of us went with him, a string of bouncers didn't let anyone else out until we were well clear. We went back to the wine bar and Terry's pal rang a fleet of taxis to take us all home.

"Those guys were surrounding me and Gloria on the dance floor. I hit that guy because he put his hand on Gloria and asked me how I liked white men moving in on a black woman," said Dutch. "The man's lucky he went down after just one punch."

The incident was going to create problems for us and would obviously make the papers. Once again, there was a conflict of interest for Tina—she was there, she knew what had happened and she couldn't be expected to ignore it. We talked about it in the cab home. "I have to ring the editor. I'll try and persuade him that I'm interviewed rather than write a reporter-on-the-spot piece."

I also had an awkward call to make as Saunders needed to hear what had happened from one of his players rather than from the local radio station in the morning. And as I was still captain when this happened it was my call to make. Tina's editor told her to get in early with a detailed account of what happened while I phoned Tony Saunders three or four times but there was no answer, leaving me with no choice other than to call Peter Christie. Great.

"Who's calling?" were his first words. I explained what had happened as succinctly as I could. "OK, all the players who were there need to come to the ground at 11am tomorrow. I'll organise that. I imagine this will make the papers?"

"Yes Peter, it will." I didn't warm to Peter Christie, but he was efficient and did things with a minimum of fuss.

The following morning we trailed into Wood Lane like errant schoolboys about to go into the headmaster's study for a caning. Saunders was there but it was Christie who addressed the troops. He simply repeated what I had told him. "It was obviously an unsavoury incident but it's happened and there is nothing we can do about it. Like it or not, as First Division footballers this sort of thing comes with the territory."

"Will it definitely appear in the papers?" asked Dutch.

"It will appear in The Observer and would have done regardless of whether Tina was there or not," I replied. "She also said we should be prepared to see stories in the nationals because someone at The Observer is bound to sell it on."

As the meeting broke up Saunders told me, Pieters, Baker, Seal and Butler to hang back. "Boss, none of us were pissed. Those guys were spoiling for a fight and were racist. They had it coming. If someone touched your missus, what would you do?" This came from Steve Baker, one of the quieter and possibly more sensible members of the squad. "OK, let's move on," said Saunders.

Sure enough a story appeared in some of the next day's nationals, but the forthcoming international programme took up most of the space on the sports pages and the incident, fortunately, only warranted a couple of column inches on an inside news page. Had mobile phones and cameras been around it would have been very different… a picture of a bloke spreadeagled over a table having been put there by a First Division footballer would have made an excellent story. Coverage in The Observer, not surprisingly, was different to that of the nationals with the story being the front-page lead and turning to an early news page.

We were all, including Tina, upset there was no reference to it being a racist incident and the story gave the reader the impression that there was an alcohol-induced punch-up which involved several footballers and members of the public. Christie wrote a letter to The Observer setting out the facts but it wasn't published. "The editor said if the club couldn't be bothered to speak to us then why should we publish their letter." The letter appeared in the next home programme but by then it was old news and people would have made up their minds about what happened.

Things could have been worse, though. They certainly would have been if Mick Egan had been there. He had spent the night sitting on the subs' bench at a wet and windy Windsor Park as Northern Ireland played out a goalless draw against an obscure opponent. "I'd have knocked the shit out of the bloke," he said when he heard what had happened on his return from Belfast. The fact he still hadn't made his international debut had done nothing to lighten his mood.

This wasn't the only racist incident Dutch had to endure and he was sent off against Hajduk Split in the UEFA Cup after one of their lots made a monkey reference. There were grounds where he suffered abuse and it hurt him but he knew the abusers were worthless and I think the fact everyone at the club was so pro him helped as well. It's staggering that all these years later racism still hasn't been stamped out. FIFA fine clubs whose fans are racist piddling amounts instead of throwing them out of competitions or docking them points and fining them more than loose change while social media, another odious invention of modern society, allows cowards to hide behind their comments. I simply do not believe they would say these things in public.

Then Dutch fell ill. Looking back this was a slow-burning illness. When we were in Spain before the start of the 1982-83 season which saw our debut in the

First Division, Dutch was listless in the games and was particularly poor against Real Betis who thrashed us 4-0 and received a major rollicking from Saunders. I thought Saunders was risking his health with a couple of things he said but Dutch, surprisingly, simply sat on a bench with his head down and said very little.

"It's nothing to do with not trying or caring," said Dutch when a few of us were having a leisurely beer back at the hotel. "I feel like a car trying to move but the handbrake is on. Nothing is happening, I just can't get going." "Have you spoken to anyone?" I asked. "Mention it to Laurie Campbell."

"Maybe I will," said Dutch trying to hide his lack of enthusiasm with the advice. "And I keep putting on weight, man. Nothing to do with over-eating. Gloria and I are eating exactly the same stuff but while she sits on her ass she's losing weight. I run around and put it on." He was again advised to speak to Campbell. "He may be our physio but he is a qualified doctor as well," said Butler. Dutch looked a little more convinced.

By the time we played Everton a couple of weeks later in our first match of the season, Dutch had come out of his lethargy but was still carrying a bit of excess poundage and as he bagged almost thirty goals that season no one gave any further thought to his health, although he did say on a couple of occasions how knackered he felt. The amateur doctors among us put this down to an unusually big man exerting himself. It was surely bound to have some sort of toll.

Shortly before Tony Saunders left the club it was noticeable that Dutch started to pile on even more pounds. He kept his place in the team for a while playing in partnership with first Pete Aitken, then Steve Baker and Gerry Byrd until he was finally left out and Baker and Byrd began to form an excellent relationship. It was becoming obvious there was no way Dutch could continue to perform at the top level but more concerning was the fact that he just wasn't the man who had joined the club almost three years ago.

There were a couple of days when he didn't come in because he felt so unwell and the club started to arrange tests but we then heard he had been rushed into hospital because he was suffering from an underactive thyroid. I'm not a medicine man but I did know this wasn't particularly uncommon and I was sort of aware that it was treated by taking hormone tablets.

What I wasn't aware of was that someone who has had an underactive and undiagnosed thyroid for a period of time is susceptible to heart disease and a condition called myxoedema coma where the symptoms include confusion and drowsiness. In extreme cases, it can be life-threatening and Dutch did receive emergency treatment, staying in hospital for a few days where fluid around his lungs and heart was discovered which meant he would be a long-term absentee. Even though he had his health problems and missed a number of games towards the end of the season, Dutch still had a decent fourth season taking his total of goals for us to just over fifty.

But he wasn't to score many more because of his illness which saw him miss the entire 1985-86 season and restrict him to just a couple of starts and a handful of substitute appearances the following campaign but it was obvious his time was up. He had half a season at Brentford but as he had said a few years before the handbrake was on and his body just wouldn't respond to the messages from his brain.

It was a desperately sad end to a stop-start career but it was great to play in the same side as him when he enjoyed his best years and had he not fallen ill I am sure he would have scored the thick end of one hundred goals for us. In the modern era, I have no doubt his illness would have been picked up very early, he would have missed a few games and would have been back firing on all cylinders in no time.

Dutch being Dutch he doesn't look back in anger or with regret and returned to his beloved Jamaica, where he worked for their association for a few years. I have an open invite to visit him and one day I will take up that offer.

Chapter Five
Duty Calls and Chopped by Souey

Despite the shenanigans both on and off the field at Northtown, I began the 1984-85 season in fantastic form. Concentrating hard on my fitness while I was on holiday, plus working harder than usual during the dreaded pre-season, meant I was in excellent shape when the season started and I felt I was playing the best football if not of my career, then certainly for a long time.

I can't really describe the difference between this and previous seasons and what was making me a better player, especially as the team was struggling towards the bottom of the table and we had a new manager I had scant respect for. It would have been easy to have played indifferently and blame the manager for my poor form. Perhaps it was because Carmichael spent little time telling me what he expected of me so I just went out there and "did my thing." Maybe there was a positive psychological impact of not being captain.

Whatever the reason, I was finding the art of playing First Division football a lot easier—the obvious result of that being that I was enjoying playing more than ever, not that being a professional footballer had ever been a hardship for me. Rather than being dragged down by our travails I rose to the challenge. I'm not blowing my own trumpet too loud when I say I was our stand out performer and although the team was struggling, I think it would have been in even deeper trouble without me.

My thoughts began to turn back towards the international scene and hopes of an England call-up. Rumours were that I hadn't been far off recognition a couple of seasons ago and although the last twelve months had seen my chances recede for various reasons and my new manager told me I was too old (I was at the advanced age of twenty-five when he told me this which, admittedly, isn't the first flush of youth in football terms) I allowed myself a sneak peek at the international fixture list.

We, as in England, had a dozen fixtures, five of them World Cup qualifiers, during the course of the season. I knew the first game, against East Germany in mid-September, would come too soon and I thought it unlikely Bobby Robson would gamble with an uncapped player in the World Cup qualifiers against Finland, Turkey and Northern Ireland, the latter of which was in February. The match after that, in March, was a friendly against the Republic of Ireland and I targeted that game, meaning I would have to retain my new-found excellent form for six months and more which was some ask.

I was, of course, also mindful of the excellence of the midfield players who were current England regulars. Of those who occupied the central midfield berths, there was simply no replacing Bryan Robson, who was one hell of a player. God knows how much he would be worth in today's transfer market. Nevertheless, he did miss quite a few games through injury and despite his undoubted brilliance I thought there was sometimes an almost over-reliance on him and the manager spoke about him in such reverential terms, especially when he missed a game, it was almost as if we would struggle against anyone without him.

His usual partner was Ray Wilkins, who was one of those players not always appreciated by fans but everyone in the game knew how good he was. You don't play for Chelsea, Manchester United, AC Milan, Paris Saint Germain (not quite the power then as they are today) and Rangers without having a bit about you. He and Robson had played together at United as well as England, knew each other's games inside out and complemented one another perfectly. I was under no illusions that ousting either of them wasn't going to happen unless there was a long-term injury to one of them.

There were plenty of other excellent midfielders with Steve Williams and Trevor Steven among them, players I respected but I thought I could give them a run for their money. And then there was Glenn Hoddle who was a very different kind of player. If he and I were ever to compete for one place, I knew my chances would be close to zero. At best.

Another barrier to possible international recognition was our form. In the first four internationals of the season, we beat East Germany 1-0, Finland 5-0, Turkey 8-0 and Northern Ireland 1-0. Fifteen goals scored, none conceded and maximum points from the three World Cup qualifiers. I had to keep playing well and hope my chance came. Which it did.

The squad for the friendly against the Republic of Ireland on 26 March 1985 at Wembley was due to be announced and to be honest I had no expectations of being part of it such was the form of the national side. During training a week or so before the match was due, I saw Walters in conversation with a young lad from the stadium office. Walters called us together at the end of the session and went through its highs and lows, which he did every day. "One last thing," he said. "Ed, you're to report to Bisham Abbey on Saturday, you're in the England squad."

I was a bag of nerves when I arrived. Bryan Robson made a point of coming across and introducing himself; Bobby Robson, who had a reputation for getting names muddled up, got mine right first time which was encouraging.

I found Monday's training difficult. Chris Waddle, who had run rings round us the previous season, looked an even better player now, it was almost impossible to get the ball past Peter Shilton, Gary Lineker looked completely disinterested in proceedings until the ball went into the box when he suddenly came alive and made beating Shilton seem fairly easy. I found myself in awe of these players although there was no reason why I should have. After all, I had played against most of them and had won my fair share of battles while admittedly losing at least as many.

Playing against them in a match you miss some of the details of their skills and the intricacies of their play; training with them and it was very apparent why they played regularly at an elite level. When I had played against Spurs and Glenn Hoddle, I had often admired some of his close skills and passing ability but I was too busy doing other things to think much about it. Here, you would watch him hit a "fuck me" pass and do it time after time. And if he felt like it, he would put backspin on the ball for good measure. And he wasn't even a regular in the side.

I might have been having a stellar season but there was still a long way to go until I got to their level. Let's just say I didn't feel like I belonged in this illustrious company and that was disheartening to say the least.

"How are you finding it, son?" asked Bobby Robson. "Great, thanks Boss," I lied.

"When I've seen you play, you impose yourself on the game, I want to see more of that from you." I took this as an early warning that I wasn't coming up to expectations and I needed to do something about it. Unfortunately, in my eagerness to impose myself and make an impression, I sent Bryan Robson flying with a slightly late challenge. That provoked laughter from most of the squad, a worried look from coaches given Robson's injury record and a stuttering apology from me.

"Don't fucking apologise," England's captain told me. "But you better watch your back." It was said with a smile on his face. I think.

When it came to briefing us before the match, the manager and his staff went into the kind of detail that I didn't know existed. It was hugely impressive and once again demonstrated the massive gulf between domestic and international football. Tony Saunders and Dave Walters put a lot of importance on detail and subsequently invested considerable time in it, ensuring we were thoroughly briefed, but their undoubted hard work and knowledge paled into insignificance compared to this.

I didn't expect to be picked and in that regard I wasn't disappointed. However, I was pleasantly surprised to be named as a substitute while I was also surprised and disappointed that less than thirty-five thousand turned up to watch. It might only have been a friendly but England were on a good run and deserved better support. My next surprise was more pleasant as I made my international debut. This time Bobby Robson did get my name wrong as I heard him tell Don Howe to "tell Redwards to get ready."

I came on for Bryan Robson when we were 1-0 ahead and had a hand in the second goal, scored by Gary Lineker, after seventy-five minutes. Well, the ball was passed to me and I knocked it about five yards to Waddle who did the rest other than scoring; Lineker going from disinterested spectator to goal scorer extraordinaire in the blink of an eye. Liam Brady pulled a goal back in the dying minutes but it was an easy enough 2-1 win.

For me, it was a mixed experience. I was, naturally, hugely proud to have represented my country, delighted to have had almost half an hour on the hallowed turf of Wembley and contributed to a win. These feelings were tempered by the enormous gulf in quality I had experienced and which I was totally unprepared for and stunned by. At times, I had felt like a first-year schoolboy attending a university lecture and it took me a little while to process the experience and fully come to terms with it.

How did Bobby Robson think I'd faired? I had no idea. We showered, changed, listened to what Robson and his staff thought of the team's performance and disappeared into the night. I thought I had done OK; the newspaper reports were reasonably encouraging and Dave Walters, Tommy Butler, Terry Green and Pete Aitken, who had come along to support me, said I had done well. I wasn't convinced that Bobby Robson was convinced by me but I would have to wait until May to find out when England had two World Cup qualifiers, against Romania and Finland, and a friendly against Scotland.

I didn't make the squad for those games or for a mini-tournament in Mexico which saw us lose to both Italy 2-1, and the hosts, 1-0, and thump West Germany 3-0, as well as winning 5-0 in the USA on the way home. England had played twelve games that season, winning seven, drawing two and losing three and were in a great position to qualify for the 1986 World Cup. Since I had made my debut Everton's Peter Reid, who I really liked as a player, had forced his way into the side and it was becoming more and more likely that I was going to be one of the countless One Cap Wonders. But as we've already said football can be a funny game and things can change quickly. And did.

At the start of the 1985-86 season, my good form continued. In fact, I realised it was no longer a case of good form, I had become a much-improved player and I suddenly became a regular member of the squad when we played Romania, Turkey and Northern Ireland in World Cup qualifiers—drawing 1-1, winning 5-0 and drawing 0-0 respectively—friendlies against Egypt, Israel, USSR and the Rous Cup match against Scotland.

I got a few minutes as a sub against Turkey and played the whole ninety minutes in the 4-0 win against Egypt and did, according to one and all, pretty well. I came on as a sub against both Israel, won 2-1, and USSR, won 1-0, which took me up to five caps. Gordon Cowans of Aston Villa, another supremely talented player, had forced his way into the squad and had started a couple of games making the competition for the World Cup squad even tougher.

Our win against Turkey saw the midfield of Robson, Hoddle, Waddle and Wilkins perform superbly, even accepting Turkey weren't as good then as they are now. I reckon if I had been Bobby Robson I would have decided there and then they would be my midfield four for the World Cup and indeed they did start the first two games, against Portugal and Morocco, but injury to Robson and suspension to Wilkins put an end to that quartet. Reid and Steven replaced them and played the next three games against Poland, Paraguay and Argentina.

I was disappointed to travel all the way to Tbilisi and only get a few minutes as a late sub against USSR and had no idea where I stood in the pecking order other than if I did go to Mexico as part of the squad, I had little chance of making the starting eleven.

When I was told I was playing against Scotland in the last match before the squad departed, I knew I needed to have a storming match to book a seat on the plane.

If there was an international to stir the blood and get the pulse racing, it was England against the Jocks, the Sweaties (Sweaty Socks = Jocks) or from their point of view Scotland v the Auld Enemy, the much-hated Sassenachs. The oldest international in football history.

As a kid, about the only live football shown on the TV, apart from the FA Cup Final and the World Cup, was the annual British Home Championship battle between us and the Scots. We also played Wales and Northern Ireland in this (usually) end-of-season tournament between the four home nations but as far as I can remember those were relegated to a late-night highlight show.

England v Scotland was the real deal. And the Scots—among many other nations it has to be said—hated us with a passion. In all sports, there is *a* fixture which is *the* fixture. In cricket, we have to beat the Aussies, in rugby union losing to Wales is a criminal offence. And back then, we just had to beat the Scots (with more-than-honourable mentions to Argentina, Germany and Italy) at football. And still do.

Scotland, it just had to be them, were the first team to beat England after we won the World Cup in 1966 and as far as they were concerned that made them the unofficial world champions. I love the story that their former striker, the wonderful Denis Law, couldn't bring himself to watch the final and had an entire golf course to himself that afternoon. Just in case anyone from Scotland reads this, the date was 30 July 1966. Throughout my childhood there were interviews with Scottish footballers who went on about feeling ten feet tall when they pulled on the blue jersey before doing battle with us. Didn't those Jocks think England footballers felt the same?

I also love the story of Alf Ramsey, pre-knighthood, taking the England squad to Scotland for a Home International in the mid-1960s. "Welcome to Scotland Alf," a Scottish journalist said. "You must be fucking joking," was Alf's alleged response which really says it all about England v Scotland.

There had been some epic battles between the two countries down the years and there was always a brilliant atmosphere whether the game was played at Wembley or Hampden Park, where there were crowds well in excess of one hundred thousand for the fixture and England suffered its fair share of defeats home and away, but also enjoyed some famous victories. I particularly enjoyed us winning a very scrappy match 1-0 at Hampden Park in May 1978 with a goal from Steve Coppell.

We had failed to qualify for the 1978 World Cup in Argentina, the Scots had made it through and didn't they let us know about. The poor, misguided fools seriously believed they were actually going to win the tournament. Our victory, just before they departed for South America, took the wind right out of their bagpipes and just as I hoped they went on and to have a miserable World Cup, losing to Peru and drawing with Iran before beating the Netherlands 3-2. No medals for brave losers, I'm afraid.

My favourite memory of these games, as a spectator, came at Wembley on 24 May 1975 when we thrashed them 5-1. My dad had somehow managed to get me a ticket for the game and we drove to Wembley, and while dad wandered around the London suburb, I had the time of my football life. The combination of Alan Ball, Gerry Francis and Colin Bell in England's midfield and the ineptitude of Stewart Kennedy in Scotland's goal made for hugely entertaining viewing. I was staggered at the number of Scots fans in the stadium—but when Bell put us 3-0 up after forty minutes there was the biggest inter-clan fight since Glencoe, followed by the exodus of thousands of kilt-clad clansmen trailing out of the stadium, no doubt in search of a nearby hostelry where they would drown their sorrows. Dad said seeing them leave was probably like the Scottish retreat from Culloden—another small battle where the English were decisive winners.

This performance was undoubtedly the highlight of Don Revie's reign as England manager but amazingly he never picked Alan Ball, who had a brilliant match, again. But then in my opinion Don Revie was one of England's worst managers. Which is some statement.

Wembley Stadium, London. Wednesday, 23 April 1986. England v Scotland. The Rous Cup.

Eleven years after we slaughtered the Scots at Wembley I am lining up against them. So dreams do come true. This wasn't a British Home Championship match, though, as that had been dropped at the end of the 1983-84 season with the authorities citing a perceived lack of interest, increased hooliganism and the crowded international fixture list.

The Rous Cup, between England and Scotland, was introduced in 1985 meaning a lack of crucial income for the Northern Ireland and Wales governing bodies. The competition was soon extended to three nations

with a South American team invited—Brazil, Colombia and Chile all participated once. So much for the crowded international fixture list.

Both us and Scotland had qualified for the summer's World Cup to be held in Mexico and this was a "warm-up" for the tournament but given the animosity between the nations it was a dangerous match to be held just a few weeks before the start of the most prestigious sporting event the world has to offer. No one wanted to miss out on a place in their final World Cup squad but neither would any quarter be given. Scotland have had some wonderful players over the years, far too many to mention, but one of these and a player I much admired—despite his being born north of the border—was Graeme Souness.

In my opinion he was a thoroughbred of a player, a leader on and off the pitch and was about to play in his third World Cup. Everything he says and does has a streak of arrogance about it but he is a proven winner with Liverpool, where he had picked up silverware every season and had earned the right to be high and mighty. These days he's a TV pundit—and one of the very best—and used to write a highly informative column in the Sunday Times. Souness could also be nasty. Very nasty. He would let you know he was around and was just as happy to use foul means as fair and some of his challenges over the years were definitely X-rated. One of the most competitive men I've ever come across.

And I was up against him. I was desperate to get into the final squad of twenty-two but was well aware I was on the periphery so this was a do-or-die occasion for me, representing my last chance to force my way into the squad and I would need to emerge as the winner from a head-to-head battle against a genuine world class player in an otherwise fairly ordinary team. This was going to be some test for me, even though I was playing alongside the hugely experienced Ray Wilkins and the greatly talented but still mistrusted Glenn Hoddle. I'm glad to say that Hoddle, having been criminally underused four years earlier in Spain, went on to play in all five of England's matches in Mexico.

As a child if I had been asked to choose which single fixture I wanted to play in it would have been this one. I was thrilled walking out of the tunnel, lining up for the national anthems and being introduced to various dignitaries. I was again surprised and disappointed by the attendance with Wembley just over half full but the adrenaline still flowed. My orders were very simple—"stop Souness playing. He's the one who makes them tick. Get the ball and give it to Glenn." Straightforward instructions and much easier said than implemented.

Souness, who was now playing for Fiorentina in Italy, didn't disappoint in putting himself about—he really hated the English, was Scotland's self-appointed assassin-in-chief and it wasn't long before his studs came into contact with my ankle a split second after I had passed the ball to Ray Wilkins. I wasn't impressed and told him so. I still remember the look he gave me. It was a who-the-fuck-are-you-you-unproven-nobody sort of look. He clattered me again later in the first half and this time I needed some treatment. As the trainer made his way onto the pitch Souness hovered over me pretending to apologise and see if I was OK. It won't come as a surprise to hear he was telling me that the next time he caught me I wouldn't be getting up. And that he would definitely catch me again. There were a few Anglo-Saxon expletives thrown in for good measure. Just putting me in my place.

I had no problem with the abuse but wasn't happy that he didn't give a shit if he ended any chances I had of going to the World Cup. Wilkins came across as I struggled to my feet. "Don't worry, Ed. He clattered you because you're doing a good job on him." Souness was also steaming because Terry Butcher had put us ahead a few minutes earlier and was looking to nobble anyone in a white shirt. He should have been booked but the French referee was another one of those officials who liked to preen for the cameras and although he waved his arms about took no action. A schoolteacher who can't control his class.

Hoddle put us 2-0 up before half-time and we were in complete control until Scotland won a penalty early in the second half when Butcher brought down Charlie Nicholas—from where I was it looked outside the box—and none other than Mr Souness converted, which gave him obvious great pleasure.

I had been having a decent game and even won the ball from Souness on a couple of occasions and gave it to Hoddle, as per my pre-match instructions but the ankle Souness had thumped into, which happened to be the one I had injured three years earlier at Cardiff, was causing me problems. Not only was it cut and grazed but it was also swollen and fifteen minutes from the end I was substituted and sat on the bench with an ice pack on the ankle. "Well played son, well played," said the ever-enthusiastic Bobby Robson.

Had I done enough to get into the squad? I wouldn't know for a couple of weeks but I imagined there would be some tell-tale signs and a few stories in the national newspapers which would give me an indication of whether I would be spending my summer in Mexico or Marbella. I felt I was at least a match for some of the players who were also in the running but also knew others were higher up the pecking order.

I didn't make the squad. In fact, I was nowhere near making it.

I had tumbled a long way down the list as I wasn't even named as a standby. Robson, Wilkins, Hoddle, Reid, Hodge, Stevens and Steven were the midfielders chosen. Stewart Watson and Paul Bracewell were the standbys. Of those who went, Robson was injured early on, Wilkins was sent off in the second match and didn't appear again, Steven, Reid and Hodge all did well enough. I was desperately disappointed not to go but made it my mission in life to be part of the 1990 tournament, in Italy, and while some footballers who don't get selected in the squad of twenty-two find it "too painful" to watch the tournament I absorbed as much of it as I could.

England, of course, started slowly losing to Portugal and drawing with Morocco before beating Poland and Paraguay and bowing out to Argentina in the quarter-finals through the Hand of God and Goal of the Century strikes by Maradona. Gary Lineker, meanwhile, went to the 1986 World Cup a relative unknown to the general football world—maybe not even every England supporter's choice as a starter—but returned as the tournament's top scorer which helped secure him a move from Everton to Barcelona and completely changed his life.

It was never really made apparent to me why I hadn't been selected. Later that summer as I reflected on the what-ifs, I recalled my first training session with the England squad and Bobby Robson telling me to impose myself. Perhaps I hadn't been aggressive enough for him. And I guess Souness emerged from our encounter as a winner on points. I still wonder if things would have worked out differently if I had exacted some revenge on him. Was Robson looking for someone who put "put it about a bit?" I could do that but rarely did.

Although I had targeted a place in the 1990 World Cup squad, I never got another sniff of an England cap. A disappointment but perhaps I wasn't quite good enough to bridge that unexpected gap. But I won six caps, played at Wembley and took on Scotland. Things could have worked out a lot worse.

Chapter Six
A Brit Abroad

I had invested considerable thinking time about my future over the years and had discussed it in detail with many people close to me and by the end of the 1985-86 season I had decided the time was right to leave Northtown. Not making the World Cup squad was also an influential factor in my decision. I wasn't at all sure of the protocol, and thinking back there hadn't been that many players who had asked to leave so I didn't have a point of reference. I assumed I would inform Dave Walters but he had enough to contend with. Peter Christie? I didn't see that it was any of his concern, which was probably being slightly bloody-minded of me.

I had thought of giving notice to whoever I needed to speak to before the end of the season that I would be seeking a transfer but felt that would make me appear self-important so shelved the idea. We were reluctant to up sticks—talk about wanting your cake and eating it—which meant my choice of clubs would again be very limited. London would obviously be ideal, although with the road networks improving considerably since I had last seriously thought of leaving the Midlands had become far more accessible. But the only clubs which appealed from that area were Villa and Forest. Choosy? Me!

We decided to have a holiday and I would hand in my request when we returned. But for a variety of reasons, we could only go for just one week which is never long enough for me; just as you are settled and beginning to relax it's time to head for the airport again. So I had another week golfing in Portugal—and at that time of year the Algarve was a Who's Who of famous, not-so-famous and I-recognise-that-face-but-can't-quite-place-it footballers from across Europe, even though a World Cup was being held. One face I instantly recognised was that of Tony Saunders, just installed as manager of Real Oviedo in Spain's Second, or Segunda, Division.

I saw him as he walked off the course we were playing and hoped he would still be in the clubhouse when we finished our round. Given I had spotted him from the elevated thirteenth tee we wouldn't finish for at least an hour depending on whether we hit straight, didn't spend time looking for lost balls and weren't held up by the fourball in front of us which appeared to be practising for a major event.

Saunders was exiting the bar as we walked in and I managed to catch him before he disappeared. I hadn't seen him since he left Northtown a couple of years before following the mysterious Board meeting where no one knew what happened. Since then, he had managed in Asia and had spent time visiting some of the biggest clubs in Europe to see how they functioned from top to bottom and to watch world-renowned coaches in action. We agreed to meet that night for a drink and a meal—our respective golfing buddies would have no problem coping without us for one evening.

"You may not believe me," said Saunders as he attempted to spear a piece of sardine with his fork, "I was waiting to be told my budget before I contacted you but seeing as we are here… I've got to get Oviedo into La Liga within two years and I could do with someone with your drive and experience. Interested? Potentially?"

I think, hand on heart, I knew I was kidding myself if I thought I would play for England again. And the best and biggest clubs in the country didn't seem to have need of someone with my skillset. Which meant, as Steve Russell had told me, I needed to broaden my horizons and although I recognised this, playing abroad hadn't even registered on my radar.

"Very interested Tony," I said trying not to sound desperate and not caring I would be going from England's top division to Spain's second tier. After all, if someone is interested in your services…

"Great culture, great climate, great challenge. Great everything as far as I can see. I'm sure you would love it."

Saunders went on to explain how he had been appointed and what his approach would be. "I'm a better manager and coach than when I was at Nothtown." There wasn't a hint of arrogance, he was merely stating a fact. We chatted for several hours and the more we spoke, the more I fancied the idea of plying my trade in Spain.

I finally plucked up the courage to ask him why he had left Northtown. He was evasive saying something about it being time for him to move on.

So after a chance meeting in Portugal, an excellent seafood meal and a couple of bottles of very decent white wine I agreed, in principle, to join Real Oviedo in northern Spain. Saunders said he would be in touch in a few days to confirm if the deal could proceed and to agree terms. "You'll do very well out of it," he told me. "If you think Palmer has money, you should see this owner."

I managed to phone Tina. It was late and I was slightly merry but it was good to hear her voice and she didn't seem too upset I had called. "How do you fancy living in Spain for a couple of years?" I asked, convinced she would love the lifestyle.

But Tina wasn't quite so enthusiastic about moving to Spain as I was, which she made plain when I got home. We had seriously considered starting a communications business and had agreed to discuss this in detail on my return from Portugal. We had even started work on a business plan and made some tentative contact with a lawyer. The idea was Tina would run the company and when I hung up my boots, I would become more involved.

She was very keen to advance our plans and let's just say wasn't best pleased I had virtually agreed a move to Spain while I was on a golf holiday in Portugal. Without her. She knew how I felt about wanting and needing a new challenge and that things weren't happening for me as I had hoped in England.

Tina and I had been together for over four years and her support for me had never been anything less than total and that wasn't something I could ignore. But I felt moving to Spain afforded us the opportunity of a lifetime with a fabulous lifestyle in a far better climate and considerably more money, much of which we could save and so have far more to invest in a business in two or three years.

"There's nothing to stop us making trips back to England to get the business moving," I said. We had a long and frank conversation and at one stage we even considered me playing in Spain while she stayed in England and we would visit each other as time allowed. We realised this would be a recipe for disaster but I understood Tina's argument that waiting another three years was too long and we agreed that I would sign for two years—if they actually made contact and the offer was as lucrative as Saunders had suggested—and we would then review our situation after eighteen months. Tina admitted she actually quite liked the idea of living in the sun it was just that the timing wasn't great.

Saunders, or someone from Oviedo, made contact with Northtown and Peter Christie rang me at home to ask me to attend a meeting with him, Saunders and a couple of representatives from Oviedo and "presumably your agent." Christie, in his most pompous mode, said: "you are no doubt aware they want to sign you. They've offered £300,000 which, given you get ten per cent, isn't enough. They say they won't offer a peseta more. Should be an interesting meeting." There were times when I really wished I could go in for a 50-50 ball with Christie or even 60-40 in his favour. He wouldn't have known what hit him.

Roger Palmer was also at Wood Lane when I arrived, nervously pacing the room and smoking a particularly strong-smelling Spanish cigarillo. He wasn't nervous about this meeting, he was spinning a lot of plates and working out how to make sure he didn't drop any. But he was cold towards me, making it obvious he wasn't happy I was on the verge of leaving. I wondered if he was like that to all his employees who chose to try and better themselves.

I had expected a difficult meeting and that is exactly what I got with Northtown hanging out for more money and the Oviedo officials refusing point blank to go any higher. The meeting was going nowhere and all the participants were getting scratchy. Christie was being particularly officious and even Palmer, who had remained quiet throughout, looked embarrassed on a couple of occasions.

After an hour or so of toing and froing and no progress, I snapped. "Right. I need a new challenge and you know that. I want to go to Oviedo. If you insist, I stay, you will have to match their terms and you can damn well throw in a loyalty bonus for fucking up my ambitions." I was almost in Christie's face and was aware I sounded like a truculent schoolboy but I'd had enough of him and was fed up with being told I "was under contract." I was acutely aware of that. "And the way you've conducted this meeting," I was pointing at Christie, "it's no wonder the rest of Europe think we're arseholes." Even the normally unflappable Christie started to redden.

Palmer called an end to proceedings for a while to allow things to calm down and speaking fluent Spanish went into a conversation with the delegation from Oviedo, although pointedly not with Saunders. I didn't get it. I was a good player just shy of being top drawer, a realistic fee had been offered for me and there was no counter offer to me from Northtown. It should be straightforward. I sat with Saunders for a few minutes sipping on a cup of tepid coffee feeling pissed off and wondering how I would react towards Christie if the deal fell through. "Don't worry, son, I'm sure things will work out." I wasn't so sure but then again the last time Saunders had told me not to worry things had come good.

Half an hour later everything was finalised. Palmer had negotiated a further £25,000, as well as a couple of clauses where Northtown would receive money depending on the number of appearances I made. So simple, so straightforward, so why the need for all the debate?

Tina and I had met Saunders and his colleagues the previous evening and the personal terms had been ironed out in no time. I was to receive a bonus for signing for them, my salary was almost doubled, we had a sponsored car and were to be housed in a beautiful apartment, owned by the club. There would also be a significant bonus if we won promotion and the club would pay for a Spanish teacher—we both felt it was imperative we learned the language.

Saunders wanted me in Oviedo the next day to sign all the official documents, attend a press conference, tour the stadium and to have a look at where we would live. Tina had to scramble for a couple of days holiday and also decided to hand in her notice at The Observer before we flew to Spain, which set alarm bells ringing at the offices but only for a few minutes as Christie phoned Dave Craig to announce my transfer. Craig contacted me asking for an interview but I was too busy flying about, although I promised him a face-to-face interview when I returned.

Quite a lot was made of my signing and there were at least a dozen journalists at the press conference. They wanted pictures of me on the pitch of the impressive Estadio Carlos Tartiere which had been rebuilt for the 1982 World Cup, juggling a ball—as this sort of thing was never really my bag it took quite a while to complete. I was introduced to the club's President Senor Henriques, who was perfectly pleasant but made it clear—or as clear as he could through my translator, Ramon—that a lot was expected of me. He may have told Saunders he wanted to win promotion within two years but he wanted it to happen in the coming season. "El President changes his mind about promotion every time I see him," said Saunders. "Still, we won four promotions in five years in England, we should manage one in two years here."

We returned home two days later completely shattered and in desperate need to draw breath but certain we had made the right decision—all the facilities were fantastic and our apartment, which came with a private pool, was "magnifico." We had one week together before I had to return to Spain for pre-season training while Tina would stay in England for a few weeks to help tie up any loose ends before joining me.

It's hard to describe how delighted I was with the move. Close as Northtown was to my heart it was time to move on and to sign for an ambitious club in Spain was beyond my wildest expectations. And Oviedo did everything to make all aspects of our move as easy as possible. What I wasn't aware of was that I had signed on the eve of the busiest and most complicated season in Spanish football.

The eighteen teams played each other home and away and then the top twelve teams qualified for promotion groups. Teams finishing in odd and even places went into separate groups while the bottom six played in the relegation group (Group B).

In the second phase, teams carried their record from the first phase record. Three teams were promoted to La Liga and three were due to be relegated but during the season the authorities decided to expand the Segunda and there were no relegations. It seems it doesn't matter where you go, football authorities share the ability to over-complicate matters.

I couldn't claim to be a trailblazer even though very few English players had plied their trade in Spain. Gary Lineker, of course, signed for Barcelona just a few weeks before I went to Oviedo and went on to make a huge impression, far more than yours truly. Mark Hughes signed for Barcelona at the same time as Lineker, while Steve Archibald had also signed for them from Spurs in 1984 and had reasonable success with a couple of dozen goals in fifty-five appearances. Gerry Armstrong, who had scored the winning goal for Northern Ireland against Spain in the 1982 World Cup, had a couple of seasons playing for Real Mallorca and his stay was most memorable for the abuse he received from opposition fans, who weren't prepared to forgive and forget.

There had, however, been plenty of Brits who had played in Italy over the years who had met with varying degrees of success. John Charles signed for Juventus from Leeds as long ago as 1957 for £65,000 a fortune in those days. He became one of the sport's first superstars as he scored over ninety goals in one-hundred-and-fifty-five games, an incredible record in the defence-obsessed Italian league and one that had him rubbing shoulders with Hollywood stars— did they know what "socca" was back then? Two other great British goal scorers, Jimmy Greaves and Denis Law, signed for AC Milan and Torino respectively in the 1960s for large sums but things didn't work out for them and they were soon back in this country despite doing well in terms of putting the ball in the back of the net. Greaves came home to play for Spurs and Law for Manchester United.

We felt that learning the language (as best we could) and immersing ourselves in Spanish culture would stand us in very good stead. Oviedo was a lovely city with a stunning cathedral, a medieval old town, a fine arts museum and excellent restaurants. And if we got bored with the pool, we were only twenty miles from the coast. If I could then perform well on the pitch, and I saw no reason why I shouldn't, we were confident our time in Spain would be highly enjoyable.

What I hadn't anticipated was the huge expectation of both myself and the team. I was, in modern parlance, a Galactico signing. Don't get me wrong, I didn't for one moment see myself as a Galactico or whatever the mid-1980s equivalent term was but I was the highest profile member of the squad, which I wasn't expecting. Saunders had been looking to sign some Spanish players but hadn't succeeded in tempting any big names to climb on board his latest project. Was that because he was English or because the Spaniards had an inside track and knew a few things Saunders and I were blissfully unaware of?

As much as the facilities in both my professional and private lives were brilliant, the standard of the squad was equally poor. "If you win promotion with this lot, they should give you the England job," I said to Saunders one night when he came to our apartment for supper. Although he was throwing himself into the job with typical gusto, he was also at a loose end as he was recently divorced, an episode which had hit him hard. "I don't blame her I was never at home," he said about his wife leaving him for someone else.

There was also huge expectation—I refuse to use the word pressure—piled on Saunders by the President who wanted promotion in double-quick time. Although Roger Palmer had spoken about First Division football within five years, it was an ambition and one he never spoke about in public. And he would never have gone on local TV stating the club had a squad capable of winning promotion. If Saunders had ever been in doubt about the enormity of the job, he wasn't after that.

Saunders' tour of many of Europe's leading clubs to understand how they operated and observe how players were coached had obviously borne fruit in terms of his approach and thoughts. Despite some differences, I had always thought highly of him as an English "manager." Now he had become a modern Continental coach with plenty of fresh ideas for training sessions and more adaptable tactics—and the ability to adapt his tactics to an indifferent group of players. He still refused—and rightly in my opinion—to try and fit square pegs into round holes.

For example, if the right back was injured someone who had played before in that position would be drafted in. In the worst-case scenario, a right-footed player would play. He refused to upset the balance of the team and put players in a foreign position and leaving them to cope.

You could see how his coaching improved players—and quickly—and it was this as much as anything which accounted for our start to the season, which was far better than I had expected. We had a young Argentine centre forward, Gabriello, who was an excellent all-round player and an instinctive finisher and his goals were instrumental in us being top six after a dozen games. Unfortunately, Gabriello didn't like me because I was English and although I attempted to speak to him, he didn't want to know. When I went to congratulate him after he scored, he blanked me, when I scored my two goals, he trotted straight back to the halfway line without saying anything. I put it down to the Falklands War. He listened to Saunders though.

It wasn't beyond the realms of possibility that had Gabriello continued to score as freely for the rest of the season we would have been involved in the promotion race but, unfortunately, his season was ended in November when he had his ankle broken and dislocated at Cartagena by a lump of a centre half intent on kicking him out of the match and did so by diving in with both feet on Gabriello's standing leg.

The lump saw red and received a three-match ban while Gabriello missed the rest of the season and a chunk of the following one. Not what I call justice. Although I've touched on European referees being fussy and pedantic, a hallmark of Spanish football when I played was the number of vicious challenges. They happened every week and some referees let them go—but would book you for complaining about their leniency—which meant the overall standard of refereeing, especially in our division, was really poor.

We were also doing better than I expected because the standard of play wasn't very high across the division and we were a long way from being the worst team. This meant I was one of the standout players and I quickly became very popular with the fans, a couple of hundred of whom turned up to watch us train every day. At the end of training, some of us would have to spend up to a couple of hours signing autographs and having our pictures taken and although I have always been keen to accommodate fans as best I could, a couple of hours every day four days a week soon became a tad trying.

We had some other interesting players including a goalkeeper called Lucas Morales, who could have been responsible for the phrase about having to be mad to be a goalkeeper. His lowest setting was "excitable" and that was off the pitch. He could pull off quite extraordinary saves that the greats of the game would have been proud of but he was just as likely to let a tame shot squeeze through his legs while he was so woeful dealing with crosses, Saunders banned him from going out of his six-yard box because he created complete mayhem.

After a mistake too many Saunders dropped him for a seventeen-year-old reserve who made neither incredible saves nor ridiculous mistakes. Morales reacted to being told he was dropped by screaming at the coach, pleading with him to change his mind and then breaking down in tears, sobbing inconsolably for ages before heading to church, presumably to prey for some sort of divine intervention. With a squad like that we were never going to win enough games to go up, but the overall standard was so low we were almost guaranteed mid-table obscurity.

I waited with great interest to see how our President would react to another season in the second tier. Here was another character. Before every home game, he would wrap his club scarf round his neck and embark on a lap of honour around the stadium, accompanied by a couple of minders. He lapped up the applause of his so-called adoring fans, applauded them, waved to the terraces—even the empty spaces—and blew kisses, while sporting a smile as wide as the Mediterranean. It reminded me of Mohamed Al-Fayed when he owned Fulham. I was once at Craven Cottage to watch Fulham play Liverpool and as the owner made his way through the lounge I was in, people put down their cups and saucers and applauded him—which, of course, he loved. I found it cringeworthy.

As Saunders often said, the day our fans stopped applauding our President and started booing him would signal the beginning of the end for him. Strangely, he didn't seem too bothered by the thought.

Off the field we were loving our lifestyle. The food, the weather, the people—with the possible exception of Gabriello—everything was wonderful. We swam nearly every day and enjoyed the downtime to make plans for the future, we visited galleries and dined out without having to worry about the number of calories ingested. And yet. Life wouldn't be life without an "and yet."

Much as we were loving life it wasn't perfect because I was very aware that the team I had joined was no great shakes, the standard of football was poor—I reckoned the second tier of the Spanish League was no better than the English Third Division—and although I was seen as the star of the local show, I felt I had taken a step back in time and certainly wasn't improving as a footballer.

It would have been very easy to soak up the lifestyle and the money and sit in my comfort zone but I've never been comfortable sitting in my comfort zone. I need challenges or need to know that one is just around the corner. Some observers may have thought that trying to play a key role in Real Oviedo winning promotion to La Liga was a challenge but I had been in the game long enough to know the chances of that happening were zero unless there was a massive change to the playing staff.

I felt I had signed under false pretences and wondered if I had been conned. There were games where I wasn't in the least motivated but no one knew because I could freewheel through this standard of football. Bottom line? I wasn't sure I wanted to stay at Oviedo.

I didn't look forward to explaining this to Tina who, although she was loving life, had come here and postponed her business aspirations because I wanted us to move to Spain. I also wondered if Saunders had any words of wisdom to impart. He and I spoke much more freely and frequently than when we were at Northtown, partly because we were the only Brits there but also because there was no tension between us.

In other words, I wasn't asking for more money, demanding he explain why he had dropped me, moaning about a tour to China, telling him he was picking the wrong midfield partner for me, criticising the club—and by implication, him—for letting Steve Bamford leave. Christ, I had been a pain in his backside. I almost felt guilty.

It was the Conservative politician Rab Butler who made the comment that a week is a long time in politics. Well, an awful lot can happen in a short period of time in football as well. It's also amazing what a 4-1 home defeat to the team which is propping up the rest of the division does for facing up to the truth. We were truly dreadful against Xerez who recorded one of just four wins against us. After we took an early lead, it was us who were stuffed and were rightly booed off at half-time, full-time and when we came out of the ground to make our way home.

Saunders was strangely calm about the performance and the result. It was close to midnight when I arrived home—Saturday matches kicked off at 8pm, which I struggled to come to terms with initially—and I sat by the pool nursing a beer which although cold, wasn't quite as cold as the night air.

Tina had heard me stomping through the apartment and came out to see why I hadn't gone to bed. "I think I've made a mistake," I said. "We were shite tonight and have been all season and will continue to be shite. We have no chance of promotion and I'm playing in the worst standard of football I've played in for years. I came here to improve not to go backwards. We have to have a rethink. I'm going to invite Saunders here for lunch tomorrow and have it out with him. I want you to be part of that."

"Are you really thinking of giving all this up?" asked Tina indicating the apartment, the pool, the flash car.

"I'm only twenty-seven and I feel as if I'm on the scrapheap and that I've been sold a pup. The trappings are great but I'm not sure there's a point if the football is rubbish. And Saunders can help chase the money they owe us."

My mood hadn't been helped when the day before the 4-1 defeat I had taken a call from our accountant telling me that the deadline for my signing-on bonus had passed and there was no evidence of the money in our account. I had no reason to be concerned that I would have to wait for the money, Saunders had a similar agreement when he was appointed manager and his money arrived a couple of days early.

On top of that, the ankle I had injured against Cardiff and which had been hurt again when I played against Scotland, was giving me problems. It wasn't as if I was in any pain but there was something which didn't feel right in the Lateral Malleolus—in plain English that's the "knuckle" on the outside of the ankle—I could feel some crunching and there was swelling from time to time. I probably needed to rest it but I also wanted to keep playing despite my concerns about the club.

Tina and I spoke for a long time, going inside after I finished my beer because of the cold, grabbed a couple of hours sleep and got up early so she could call Saunders—she would hold more sway than me in getting him to agree to come for lunch. He was hesitant at first because he was due to play golf but Tina thought he may have had a "visitor." When she told him we were cooking Iberico pig, he was quick to accept the invite and roared into the drive shortly after 3pm.

"You could have invited her you know," smiled Tina. Saunders shrugged his shoulders. "I assumed I would be here to talk football?"

"That's the big problem, Tony," I said. "I don't think what we play can be described as football."

I went on to tell him what he already knew—we had a head case in goal, me in midfield, hardly any defenders worthy of the name and now that Gabriello was out for the foreseeable no one who could put the ball in the net. In short, we were a complete mess. "On top of that, the President seems to think he's Napoleon and that we will win promotion. Please don't tell me you knew it was going to be like this."

I told Saunders I felt I had three options. To engineer a move back to England, to somehow get a transfer to another Spanish club, but in La Liga, or go elsewhere in Europe. Staying at Oviedo wasn't going to happen.

"Ed, you've only been here for half a season and you're wanting away. What's wrong with you?"

"I'll stay for the season. If I don't, I have to pay back my signing-on bonus which I haven't yet received by the way. Now, let's see your cards."

Saunders was quiet for so long I wasn't sure if he was going to reply at all. Finally, he poured himself a glass of wine. "I don't know what to say other than I feel conned as no doubt you do and I'm waiting for them to sack me. That may not do much for my reputation but I'll bounce back. The problem is I don't think they can afford to sack me. I didn't know you were owed money and I'll see if I can do something about that, but I imagine you haven't been paid because they don't have the money.

"I was sold a dream and got carried away by that. I did some due diligence but obviously not enough. I'm sorry for what's happened. Did you conduct any research?"

"You were my due diligence, Tony." I was seething. "I won't be at training tomorrow. I will have to make some calls and right now playing for Real Oviedo is way down my priority list. Who will you speak to about my bonus and when? If it doesn't turn up, I'll take legal action. Feel free to tell them and I don't care if they don't like threats." Saunders left soon after and for the second consecutive night I found myself sitting by the pool with a bottle of beer for company.

Whatever it was that Saunders said about my bonus worked because a couple of days later, the money entered my account and I received a telegram—emails were a long time in the future—from the club apologising profusely for an "administration error." By this stage, I hadn't attended training for three days and had little appetite to do so. Saunders told me to take the week off and to ensure everything appeared above board he told me he would leave me out of the team for Saturday's match, which suited me just fine.

This was all put down to food poisoning and the protocols were so slack the club doctor didn't even visit me and no one said anything about me not having lost any weight when I finally returned to training.

We enjoyed a slight upturn in form as we went four games without losing, although three of those games were draws but the writing was on the wall and when it did appear it appeared in capital letters. Saunders was sacked just before Christmas. It was the second time I had played for him and the second time he had left. On the first occasion, he simply disappeared and none of the players had a chance to wish him the best. This time, he phoned to let me know what had happened and took us out to dinner.

He didn't seem to be too down; he had been compensated and was confident he would dust himself down and looked forward to working in England again. Even in the mid-1980s managers had a habit of being sacked and getting another decent job in fairly quick order. He would probably be seen as a failure at Oviedo but few people were aware of the inside story and what he achieved there with the players he had was quite remarkable. Ferguson, Clough, Pep. They would all have struggled to do any better.

While Saunders was relatively upbeat about being out of a job, I was about to encounter a few problems while still in one. Tony's replacement was a former manager who had been sacked a couple of years previously and hadn't worked since. He didn't like foreign players, didn't speak English and certainly wasn't going to learn just for my sake. Fair enough.

My Spanish might have been improving but it wasn't nearly good enough to understand what he was saying when we first met, which meant that Ramon re-entered my life for a meeting where I was told I was playing poorly (I was playing as well as I could, given the circumstances), that I was out of the team (it could only be worse without me playing) and that I could leave (if that's the way he wanted it all the club had to do was pay what was owed me and I'd be leaving on a jet plane).

I hadn't been dropped since Boxing Day 1978, almost ten years ago. "Ramon, feel free to tell the coach that he hasn't got a clue what he's talking about and that if he wants me out, I will be happy to leave at the end of the season and not before." I wasn't going to forfeit my bonus because some insignificant coach didn't like foreign players. "And Ramon, I want you to tell the President of this conversation and I would like you to tell me when you have spoken to him."

I walked out of the room. Little did I know that I would never set foot in the impressive Estadio Carlos Tartiere again.

Later that afternoon a car pulled into our drive. If the car which the club provided us with was flash, this was uber flash. Ramon, the trusty translator, emerged from the passenger side with no little difficulty, while the driver who was about the same age as Ramon but considerably more beautifully "manicured" and a lot slimmer, alighted without any problems. He turned out to be Pablo Henriques, the son of "Napoleon Bonaparte," who I had seen occasionally but had never spoken to and until that moment had no idea who he was. It turned out he spoke excellent English but wanted Ramon with him so nothing was lost in translation. He was also as polite as he was well-groomed. And smelt as if he had bathed in after shave.

Pablo explained that his father was unwell but didn't elaborate on the seriousness of the illness and that he would be taking over the running of the club and that he had already been looking at what he had to do to save money and keep the club afloat. An ominous beginning.

"My family is very rich and we have invested a lot of money in the club. Too much in my opinion," said the new President who went on to say that Ramon had briefed him on our conversation with the new manager that morning and that this matter needed to be cleared up.

"I am not going to interfere in team matters and if the coach doesn't pick you then you have to use your football skills to make him change his mind. But I have to make changes within the club." Pablo wanted me to understand that the club didn't want me to return the bonus I had only recently received! "But we cannot afford to keep paying your salary and we want to find a way which both parties agree to."

In other words, they wanted me to leave but could not afford to pay me the rest of my contract. I was also told I was welcome to stay in the apartment, owned by the club, and keep the car until the end of the season. But once the season was over, they would require both back immediately. "I hope you understand and that you will be willing to discuss all this with us? We need to have this talk urgently."

Quite frankly, the way things had been going I wasn't too upset at the prospect of leaving. "Tina and I will need to talk this through and I want to speak to our accountants. I would like your reassurance that any financial agreement we come to is paid to us in advance."

The atmosphere changed from business-like and warm to frosty. Ramon almost fell off his seat while Pablo pursed his lips. Obviously, one should not indicate a lack of trust. "I don't want to cause offence," I said, "but it took months for my other payment to reach me." And if I wasn't in the country, I imagined it would be a lot harder to chase down money I was owed. As soon as our guests left, I contacted our accountant and he agreed to fly out the next day to help with the negotiations.

Pablo Henriques, not quite as friendly as he had been when we first met, was joined by a couple of other very smartly turned out club executives, one of whom was loud and verbose, the other much more reserved. The former spoke no English, the latter was fluent. My Spanish wasn't nearly good enough to understand what was being said but Ramon, the trusty translator, was on hand to... translate. Ramon decoded what the non-English speaker said. My accountant and I would then discuss. Ramon would translate our response. The executives would digest and respond. It was like a rally on a clay tennis court—endless. And the six of us sat in a small and hot office and tempers sometimes matched the temperature.

The way this should work, I thought, was that the club would say they couldn't afford to pay me a bean. I would say I wanted full payment. Then we would meet in the middle and all go home happy. Not a bit of it. The club was trying to save money at every turn and the meeting became a tortuous process to put it mildly.

"My time at your club has been challenging and that isn't down to me. Now you want me out because the club has been mis-managed. I accept you can't pay me in full but I'm not going for free either." I had had enough of Spanish business meeting protocol.

"You talk among yourselves and then tell me what you will pay me. If it's not reasonable, I'll see out the remainder of my contract, which also allows me to keep the apartment and the car." I had no intention of playing for Oviedo again but neither was I going to roll over for them. "I'm going back to the apartment; you can reach me there." I walked out of the office, accountant in tow, and found somewhere to have lunch.

Pablo and Ramon arrived at the apartment at about 8.30pm. Nice enough men and they were there for an important meeting but I was becoming tired of seeing them. And I was worn down by what seemed to be constant contract negotiations, it was only a few months since I had lost my temper with Peter Christie when we were talking about my transfer. Our visitors, it appeared, felt the same declining my offer of water. And wine. And coffee. They obviously wanted to get out as quickly as they could.

The new President told me they could only offer me one-third of what was due to me. Mark, that was the accountant, sighed loudly. "That's a paltry offer Senor President," he said. "If that's all you can do, then the money has to be paid before the end of the season. If it isn't, Senor Roberts and Senorita Howard (that's Tina) will remain in this apartment and retain use of the car as their contract allows." I think Pablo and Ramon were expecting this. Certainly they didn't react with the same affront as they had done when I had suggested it last time they had visited.

Pablo nodded slowly. "We agree," was all he said. He sounded weary and resigned and he hadn't even been President for a week. I wondered about asking them to cover Mark's air fare and services but I reckoned that might be pushing things.

All I had to do now was to find another club. I didn't have an agent and I couldn't see me having another chance meeting with someone who coincidentally wanted to sign me. Where did I go with this?

Steve Russell? He might be interested in taking me on as a new client as long as I wasn't too choosy. Roger Palmer? He didn't owe me any favours and was less high profile in football circles than he had been. Go direct to clubs? Only as a last resort. And then it hit me. I had last spoken to Dave Craig as I was preparing to leave Northtown and had given him the interview I had promised. He had also moved on and was now working for one of the nationals.

Former England international who had been part of Northtown's dramatic climb up the leagues being forced out by over-ambitious Spanish (second tier) club. They may not hold the front page or stop the presses, but I assumed this would make decent copy. Tina thought so too. Get the story out there. Wait for the phone to ring. Simple.

There was a fly in the ointment, though. My ankle had gone from feeling not quite right to constantly aching. There was also swelling and tenderness. I hadn't knowingly injured it so why had the problem suddenly flared up? The fact I was genuinely unfit made me feel slightly better that I wasn't playing but then who wants to sign an injured player?

As I was no longer playing for Oviedo, I wasn't allowed to use their physio, although from what I had seen of him that wasn't necessarily a bad thing, so I made an appointment to see a physio in the city. He spent a lot of time massaging the ankle, shaking his head and tutting. He managed to achieve all this without disturbing the ever-present cigarette which tangled from his lips. Little wonder his greying moustache also had a large nicotine-coloured patch right in the centre. "It's not good, senor, you will need to see a specialist." At least, that was the gist of what he said.

Things then moved even more quickly which meant seeing a specialist went on hold for a while. The money was paid into our account, we had no desire to stay in Spain and the club was so desperate to see the back of us, or me at least, that they helped move us back to England with even more efficiency than they had moved us out to Spain. And we were able to move back into our house, which we had rented out, almost immediately.

From being a player for Oviedo to being back in England in less than a week. The Spanish can move quickly when they need to.

Chapter Seven
Back Home

Dave Craig's paper had run an interview with me. It wasn't quite a "woe is me" story and I would have been unimpressed if it had been, but it painted the picture of a very good footballer who had been sold a dream which turned into a nightmare being ready, available and eager and open to sensible and attractive offers. But the phone didn't ring off the hook. In fact, it didn't ring once. Things weren't as straightforward as I had hoped.

It was early 1987 when we returned. The weather in Oviedo might not be tropical at that time of year but it was a shock to step off the plane in England to a considerable drop in temperature and to be greeted with driving rain. That was a sobering moment.

I hate the phrase "the grass isn't always greener." It's nearly always a smart arse who comes up with it using, of course, the benefit of hindsight. No one was dumb enough to say this to my face when we returned to Blighty after our sojourn to Spain although I felt one or two came very close to doing so.

Do I regret going to Spain? In some ways yes, in others no. I admit I was quickly and probably too easily seduced by the idea of playing abroad having previously given it no thought but we both loved the lifestyle and benefitted from some very useful "life experiences." I was also lured by the thought of going to the sun and Saunders' vision of success. I wasn't bothered, initially, by the idea of playing in Spain's second tier because I thought we would quickly win promotion and I would be playing in La Liga, which would have been a wonderful experience. It quickly became apparent there was absolutely no chance of that happening but financially we did very well and although neither of us were thirty by the time we returned home, we were very comfortable.

And there lies the irony to my venture (misadventure) to Spain. I had been well paid at Northtown but I felt I never quite received my just desserts as a First

Division footballer who had represented his country half a dozen times. When I finally got paid what I considered my worth—and a fair bit more besides—the standard of football I was playing in was woeful.

Despite the positives, there was undoubtedly a feeling of returning home with my tail, if not between my legs, then dragging close to the ground.

Would I do it all again? Let's just say I wouldn't play in the Spanish second tier again. And it's fair to say that if anyone compiled a league table of the success of Brits abroad, I would probably be propping up that list!

So, there I was. Back home. No contract. No club. No agent to help me find a club. A free agent if not quite a free spirit. This was no time for "shelving" and I needed a proper plan to get me back into the game. I still couldn't believe the phone hadn't rung—just one call would have made me feel wanted, loved, needed and would have confirmed I was a decent player.

The most important thing was to maintain my fitness levels, which is much easier done in Spain at this time of year than England. I would have taken to pounding the streets but I was still bothered by my ankle. Strangely enough, it was less painful in the cold and wet of England than it was in the relative warmth of Spain, but deep down I knew I would struggle to play a match without treatment. In an effort not to make the ankle worse, I religiously went through what I considered to be a punishing schedule of exercises I "invented" for myself.

Sit ups, tummy tucks, toe-touches and a couple of others—one hundred of each, twice a day. It seemed to me the only thing I wasn't indulging in was self-flagellation as I pushed myself hard to stay in shape. Whether my regime tallied with what the modern athlete does I have no idea but it damn well felt as if I was preparing for the Olympics. I did this for a week or so and I impressed myself with my dedication, which was married to a diet as close as possible to the one we had enjoyed in Spain. Mind you, could you find a Pimento pepper in England in 1987? Could you hell! I also eschewed alcohol not even allowing myself a single cold beer.

It was obvious a club wasn't going to call me even though it was less than a year since I had last played for my country, so I would have to pick up the phone. My obvious starting point was, of course, Northtown. I didn't expect to be greeted with open arms but if I could train with them that would be something. It would also mean, I hoped, I could get some regular treatment on my ankle. I could ring Dave Walters, who had stayed as assistant to John Brennan, appointed as manager shortly after I left, and who was "enjoying" a far from easy first season in charge. But I thought I should be up front and go through the proper channels, so I took a deep breath and rang Peter Christie.

"Yes, I heard things hadn't worked out for you in Spain," said Christie after I had explained my situation. There was, undoubtedly, a tone of "and I'm delighted to hear that's the case" and if I had been in his shoes, given what I said at our last meeting, I imagine my attitude would have been exactly the same. "Well, it would be the manager's decision but I do know there is no budget left for new players, especially players who expect to be paid a small fortune."

Despite our differences over the years, and there were more than I have documented, I respected Christie and knew that by and large he did a fine job for the club and that he had the trust of Roger Palmer. But I was damned if I would cow-tow to this smarmy so-and-so. "Peter, all I'm asking is if I can train with the club. If you can't help me, I'll find another way to contact the manager." Christie agreed to let Brennan know I had called—he had had his moment of fun at my expense but it was never going to be a case of letting sleeping dogs lie between the two of us.

"Are you interested in playing for us again or are you just using the club to stay fit?" This was the first thing John Brennan said to me. Talk about cutting to the chase. "I don't care that you played here before, that's all history. If you train with us, you train as if you are part of the first team squad. If I think you're not pulling your weight, you will be straight out. That's how it will be." I had stayed in touch with Tommy Butler and Bill Cooke while I had been in Spain and they had told me that Brennan was straight-talking and didn't suffer fools. He wasn't like Sam Carmichael, though, and listened to what his players had to say, worked closely with them and was popular enough with the squad.

"I want to stay fit and if you think I'm good enough I'd love to play here again. I'm not looking for a free ride, I won't take the piss." That was how I felt and I'm sure that was what Brennan wanted to hear as well. "Good," he said. "Be at training at 8.30 tomorrow morning and we'll have a look at you before the main session."

That was exactly what I wanted to hear. It was good news all round because off the pitch Tina and I were going through a strain in our relationship. I was at home all day either exercising or trying to find something to occupy my time— and I don't mean gardening or DIY, both of which I understand the need for but can't abide—and she was at home all day working as a freelance writer or resurrecting her business ideas.

And although she appreciated I should be involved in the latter, our ideas didn't always tally and as she was the one who would front the business, she felt she should have the final say. And I was probably feeling sorry for myself. You get the picture; it happens everywhere and just because you are a footballer who has done reasonably well you are not immune to this sort of stuff. We even had a major row and we had never rowed before so after almost five years together this took some coming to terms with.

I got through my trial training session without any problems and I think Brennan, Walters and a couple of other members of the backroom team were surprised at how well I did. My fitness levels had improved without measure since I first came into contact with the sand dunes of Skegness. "OK, be back for training tomorrow at 9.30," said Brennan. Walters winked at me as I trotted past him to the changing rooms.

After a week's training, I was back in the swing of things and had even had some treatment on my dodgy ankle which was giving me more pain at the end of a session than I was admitting to. After training on Friday and before the team left for its match at Newcastle, Brennan called me into his office. "How do you fancy a short-term contract? You can still play and we need more numbers."

Damn right I fancied it! This was my ticket back to the top flight. "There's no signing-on money and your salary will be less than it was when you left and there's no negotiation because there's no budget. At the end of the season, if things have worked, out we can look at addressing all of that." I wasn't bothered. I would have given my drinking arm just to play a decent standard of football again.

"How's the ankle?" This from Dave Walters who had been asked to join us. "I may need painkillers from time to time," I admitted. This wasn't a route I wanted to go down but it was a small price to pay.

"We'll get the ankle properly looked at next week," declared Brennan. "You need to go and see Peter Christie to sort out the contractual details. I know the two of you are close!"

Christie, just as I thought he would, took obvious pleasure from outlining the details of my contract. We both knew I wasn't in a position to refuse the offer or to try and negotiate better terms but at least I had a contract which Christie had said wouldn't happen so he didn't get everything his own way. And John Brennan was spot on when he said the squad needed greater depth because it had a tired look and feel to it and the team was again struggling near the bottom of the division and was haunted by the spectre of relegation.

Brennan hadn't been appointed until July and hadn't had much time to wheel and deal before the season kicked off. Andy Hopkins and Johnny Webb were still battling it out for the number one spot; Mick Egan had left for Wolves, which meant Garry Harris partnered Terry Bell in the centre of defence, Mike Sears was at left back and Dave Stewart, a central defender, was at right back.

Pete Aitken's contract had been cancelled while I was in Spain and he had dropped out of the game to concentrate on his first love, fashion, which meant the midfield comprised of Bill Cooke, Nick Athey and Rod Hunter, signed from Northampton. Jimmy Seal was still at the club and he was the fourth midfielder, all of which meant the defence and midfield had a Heath Robinson look about it—square pegs and round holes again—while the forwards were Gerry Byrd and Steve Baker, who were struggling to score because not many chances were being created. Tommy Butler was also still at the club and made the occasional appearance.

The old chestnut of not having enough players was again seriously jeopardising the club's chances of staying in the division and there was a desperate need for fresh blood. Which wasn't something I could claim to be.

The combination of age, lack of quality and lack of numbers added up to a difficult season and Butler told me there had already been some press speculation about Brennan's future but the players, said Tommy, were firmly behind him. And although I had had very few dealings with him, he had come across as a real professional who knew his stuff on the training ground. He simply didn't have many tools at his disposal and if he managed to keep us in Division One this season, he would need a serious injection of cash to bring in new players or the following season would surely see us go down.

Our current problems were there for all to see at Newcastle where we lost 3-0 and the limited highlights I saw made us look dreadful. Chaotic at the back, no creativity in midfield and toothless in attack.

I spent Monday having some treatment on my ankle followed by numerous scans at a private clinic. Things may have been standing still on the pitch but at least off it the club was moving with the times. The club physio Bob King, who had replaced Laurie Campbell at the end of the previous season, accompanied me and spent a long time consulting with the specialist. When the scans came back, the pair of them hovered over my bed like a couple of worried aunts, fidgeting and avoiding eye contact. That could only mean bad news.

"You have an arthritic ankle which is degenerative and will only get worse. This stems from the ligament injury you sustained and the lack of appropriate treatment available then, as well as other knocks it's taken plus the wear and tear of playing professional football." It was only three years since I had travelled back from Cardiff in agony on the back seat of the coach. Had treatment for such an injury advanced that far in such a short time?

"What does all this mean?" I asked.

"If I were you, I would stop playing. If you get another bad injury to the ankle, it will have an impact of your mobility." I wasn't expecting this, I had anticipated if not a miracle cure, then at least some advice and treatment which would ease the pain. I looked at Bob King. "Can Ed play if we give him painkilling injections?" he asked.

The specialist took a deep breath. "I would never recommend that course of action," he said. "You both must understand another injury to the ankle will compromise Ed's mobility. I'm not saying he would need a wheelchair but walking would be harder and would mean a quicker deterioration. You have to make your own decision; I can only recommend."

I hadn't even made my comeback appearance for Northtown and here I was being told I wouldn't be coming back at all. There was a pub over the road from the clinic. "Do you mind if we go for a drink, Bob? I need to try and think things through before I go home." We sat in the pub for an hour where I demolished three large glasses of wine while Bob nursed a small soft drink of some kind. "I will play with pain-killing injections," I told him.

"I think that's something the Boss will need to think about. I'm not sure it's as straightforward as that," said King.

Brennan, Walters, King and myself agreed that I would have pain killers before each training session and see what impact they had on me, good or bad. This meant I would have to watch the next home match, a midweek fixture against Norwich, from the stands. There were a couple of "welcome backs" as I made my way to my seat and there were also a few people I had spoken to in the past who ignored me. I could live with that. I found it harder to live with the standard of football in a tame 1-1 draw between two sides short of confidence and who would probably have taken a draw had it been offered to them before kick-off. The truth was that had either side demonstrated any ambition they would surely have won and both sides needed the three points.

I went to the dressing room at half-time and when the final whistle sounded and it was a strange atmosphere. Brennan analysed the match quickly and succinctly, while Dave Walters and Steve Reid both input. Everything they all said made sense but I was surprised by the lack of response from the players. "Anything to add, Ed?" This from Brennan, which I wasn't expecting and didn't welcome. I had only trained a handful of times with the first team squad and I had the distinct impression not all of them were delighted I had returned. They certainly wouldn't want to hear my thoughts on their performance as I waited in the wings to hopefully take the place of one of them. Neither did I want to be seen to be sucking up to my new Boss.

However, I was saved by the Bell—literally. "A point's no use. We were set up to be too negative. If we keep playing like this, we'll be relegated." A stormy debate followed which I stayed out of but I caught up with Tommy Butler later. "I thought you said everyone was behind Brennan?"

"Ed, they are just letting off steam. They're frustrated because they know the team's not good enough."

I kept my head down on the training ground and worked hard without offering any opinions or advice. I did what I was told and enjoyed it. The painkilling tablets I was ingesting worked on my ankle but caused a few problems with my insides. But I was pretty sure I could complete ninety minutes and was desperate to play. And I knew I would make a positive difference to an ailing side. By a quirk of the fixture list, our next four matches were all against London sides—away to West Ham and Charlton and then at home to QPR and Chelsea. All four were in the bottom half of the table and Charlton and QPR, in particular, were, like us, looking nervously over their shoulders. All four games were winnable.

I was named sub for the match at Upton Park and came on for the last twenty minutes in the 1-0 loss. Clubs were now allowed to use two subs and I was mystified by Brennan's decision to introduce me and not an attacker. We then lost 4-3 in a crazy match at Charlton and were thumped 3-0 by QPR so three of the four winnable games hadn't rendered even a single point. I was left on the bench against Charlton and came on at home to QPR when they scored their third with orders to "steady the ship."

A bit late in the day I thought as I trotted on to make my first appearance at Wood Lane for nine months not, I have to admit to whole-hearted enthusiasm. There were a few shouts of encouragement, some boos and one loud voice calling me a "fucking traitor" as I took to the fray. After the QPR result and performance, it was obvious something had to give and we heard that Brennan, Walters and Reid spent much of Saturday night and most of Sunday working out what to do before the visit of Chelsea on Tuesday.

The problem for Brennan was that like Saunders before him, he didn't have many players at his disposal and he had to shuffle his existing pack, which was older and slower than it had been under Saunders.

Out went Webb who had looked hesitant at Charlton and even worse against QPR. He was replaced by Andy Hopkins. Garry Harris was out of central defence with Dave Stewart moving across from right back and Tommy Butler coming in. I finally had a starting place with Jimmy Seal moving from midfield to attack and Gerry Byrd dropping to the bench.

Gerry Byrd was a very different sort of Scot to Iain Moy in that off the pitch he was quiet and reserved, wasn't much of a drinker and wasn't burdened by a chip on each shoulder. At least, that was my opinion of him until he heard he had been dropped when logic disappeared. He cornered me after training and called me all the names under the sun.

Apparently my reappearance had upset the morale of the squad, if it wasn't for me, he would still be in the side, why should a forward lose his place in the team because a midfielder has arrived, what made me so special that I could "fuck off to Spain and come back when I felt like it?" The club should hang its head in shame at re-signing me and no doubt I was earning more than anyone else even though I wasn't fit. There was a lot more as well.

I was completely unprepared for this tirade and even though I'm thick skinned I was stunned. I was also taken aback that no one tried to intervene, even the likes of Butler and Cooke who I considered friends and who had stayed in contact while I was abroad, didn't say a word. Every time I opened my mouth to respond he became louder and louder so I decided to ride the storm. Byrd for his part hadn't scored for weeks and didn't look the player he had been before his knee injury. Maybe he saw this as the writing on the wall for him.

I rang Cooke that evening. "There is some resentment among some of the squad," he admitted. "You shot off to Spain, earned a load of money and when it didn't work out come back here. Gerry was way over the top but you're a big boy and can look after yourself." Hardly a great comfort and I had no idea where people got their information about how much money I made; it's not as though I flaunted it. I was disappointed by what Bill said, but at least his comments had a positive impact because I was still boiling when I went out for the Chelsea game, played as well as I ever had and even slammed one into the top corner from outside the box. Real Roy of the Rovers stuff which made a bit of a change from the previous few months.

"Got anything to say then Gerry?" I asked as we sat in the dressing room. "Just so you are aware I haven't just walked back in here. The club offered me the chance to play and I had to prove myself to get a short-term contract." Although this was aimed at Byrd, I wanted the rest to know the background to my resigning. And if they didn't like it, they knew what they could do.

A win like the one against Chelsea does wonders for the confidence and you can almost feel it being injected into your veins and see people grow in front of you. We then won our next three matches at Manchester City, home to Luton and at Leicester, which put an end to our relegation worries. We played City and Leicester at a good time as they were both struggling and were relegated at the end of the season. I played well in those matches as well but my ankle was either painful or bloody painful and I went from tablets to injections and from training to hardly training and by the end of the season with our safety just about assured, I was playing for an hour and coming off or coming on as a sub for twenty minutes or so.

I knew my number was up and had known since I had seen the specialist shortly after re-joining this was going to be my last season. Nevertheless, it's a hard thing to come to terms with and I had been thinking about what I would do once I had stopped kicking a ball about ever since we returned to the country. The truth was I didn't know what I would do. I would be involved in our business but I wasn't sure that would be fulfilling enough and it was really Tina's brainchild. For once, I wasn't "shelving" but I was struggling to work out what I would do.

Our last game of the season was at home to Spurs. I started and managed to last the whole game, which was a fairly typical end-of-season affair and did OK as we won 1-0 to ensure a just-under-mid-table finish. We had to be satisfied with that given the difficulties we had endured in terms of form, confidence and lack of depth to the squad.

The final whistle sounded at (approximately) 4.45pm on Saturday 9 May 1997 and that was that. The curtains shut. After ten years as a professional footballer, not far off four hundred matches for two clubs, six England caps and far more ups than downs I was out of a job.

There was no send-off. No John Terry-like leaving the pitch after twenty-six minutes because twenty-six was his squad number (I would only have been on the pitch for four minutes had that been the case!), no guard of honour, no presentation of something silver. I turned up, played, showered and changed, had a bottle of beer in the players' lounge, went home and then went out with Tina and friends.

Absolutely no pomp. Distinct lack of ceremony.

Epilogue

Tuesday, 24 January 1989

Shortly before noon, the sound of the phone ringing shook me out of my stupor. It had been a slow start to the year and the biggest decision I had that morning was which wine bar I would pop into for lunch and whether I would opt for red or white.

"Hello Ed. It's Roger Palmer. A belated Happy New Year and I hope you are well?"

Even though I was a season ticket holder at Northtown United's Wood Lane ground, it was a long time since we had spoken and I had a very clear recollection of our last conversation. It was when I had given notice, less than two years ago, I intended to leave Northtown and he hadn't been best pleased.

Palmer, Chairman and owner, was peeved I wanted away and I was peeved he was antsy with me for wanting to better myself. I had pointed out the club was getting a fairly fat transfer fee for me, while in previous years they had let Iain Moy leave for nothing and Steve Bamford slip through its fingers for a fraction of his worth. I had given years of service and they were getting good money for me. Everyone should have been happy. But Palmer had hinted I was letting down everyone connected with the club.

Given I had played for the club for eight seasons and had been part of its history-making climb from near the bottom of the Fourth Division to the First in just four seasons that didn't sit very well with me.

"I'm good thanks Roger," I replied wondering what the hell he was calling me for. "How can I help?"

"You will have seen things aren't going very well."

He wasn't joking. The concerns of recent seasons had come home to roost and the club was struggling again. This time it looked as if things could be fatal, even though manager John Brennan had been given some cash to splash and had brought in a few new faces. In recent years, the club had specialised in free-wheeling; this season it looked as if it was free-falling towards the First Division relegation trap door. They had turned in an apparently abject performance the previous Saturday when they lost 4-0 at Nottingham Forest which left them occupying the last of the three relegation places.

"Would you be interested in returning as manager?" asked Palmer. I almost fell off my very expensive, shiny, leather executive chair which was situated in my plush executive office. The communications agency my partner Tina and I had launched nine months previously had been doing well and given some of the clients we had attracted we needed a smart "face" to it, so we had moved into appropriate offices with similarly appropriate fixtures and fittings on the outskirts of Northtown. Not too expensive that clients thought we were over-charging them but easily accessible for us and our employees and modern enough for us to be considered serious players.

"I thought you had a manager?" I said.

"Not for much longer." Palmer sounded weary.

I wasn't sure I was comfortable discussing a job when someone else was still in the role and possibly had no idea he was about to lose it. But then again, this had become the name of the game. From what I had seen from the stands, Brennan had lost his way, the new faces either weren't good enough or hadn't had the expected impact and there were no obvious tactics or style to the way we played. The team was chopped and changed every week and there were some tell-tale signs that Brennan had "lost the dressing room."

Personally, I thought they should take a punt and appoint the young and dynamic First Team coach Steven Reid but I was intrigued that Palmer had called and I wasn't going to reveal my thoughts. The work I was doing—client services director—was sort of OK. It was filling my time but was a long way from fulfilling me. Although there were deadlines to meet and full creative pitches to prospective clients, it didn't come close to the cut and thrust of football. And when Saturday came... as any ex-pro will tell you, watching football is a hopeless substitute for playing the game.

We enjoyed a very healthy income and lifestyle and would also benefit from dividends. I had a swanky car which the business paid for and I was enjoying talking to potential investors. But office life was never going to measure up against football. Not in a million years. Tina, who was the face of the agency, was aware of my restlessness and my future had been the subject of some, occasionally heated, debate between us.

I wasn't sure what I wanted to do long-term but rather like playing abroad, which I had done for a few months in 1986, the idea of football management really hadn't occurred to me until I "got the call." If anything, I had some embryonic thoughts of becoming an agent.

"I need some time to think about that, Roger, and will obviously need to talk to Tina."

"I will phone you at the same time tomorrow. We need to move quickly and I will need an answer one way or the other then."

The line went dead.